BETRAYAL

GRACE HARRISON AND NICK BASSANO

C K ADAIR

ISBN: 148278047X

ISBN 13: 9781482780475

Library of Congress Control Number: 2013905406
CreateSpace Independent Publishing Platform
North Charleston, South Carolina

Grace Harrison has spent her entire adult life ensuring that her world is safe, stable, and routine. All of that changes in the parking lot of the Athens-Clarke County Police Department when Detective Nick Bassano assists her with a dead battery in her car. She's immediately attracted to him, but wants to stay away. She finds him to be sarcastic, and sees that he dates many different women around Athens. When the wealthiest couple in Clarke County are murdered in their home, Grace and Nick are thrust together professionally and personally. He turns her world upside down in many ways, and more than one person will end up dead.

Book Dedication

For Mark
On May 9, 1997, you made a promise to me, and kept it.

Cover Acknowledgements

Cover Design by:
Ginger Luke Andrews

Cover model:
Mary Ann Smith

Acknowledgements

I couldn't have written Betrayal and brought Nick and Grace to life if I hadn't stopped using drugs. I wouldn't have been able to get out of active addiction without an all loving, all mighty God, the fellowship of NA, and the love, devotion, and support of my family and friends. The three combined, along with my sheer determination for a better life, keep me clean. For the addict who's still sick and suffering, hope and healing do exist. I found it within the walls of my local NA meeting room.

I have a cheerleading squad of many, many wonderful people who keep me going, believe in what I'm doing, and love me on days when I don't want to keep this up. I've spent six months writing three books, hoping to keep Nick and Grace alive because they continue to live in my head.

To my husband, Mark, my rock, my friend, my lover, the father of our beautiful children, my sounding board, my first reader and head cheerleader. You've sacrificed much over the years for me. You live in my craziness and just go with it. When I'd walk in the room and yell that I needed to pull you up to six foot five, you'd roll with me even if you were rolling your eyes. Thank you for loving me when I couldn't love myself. You'd listen to me patiently on days when I was deep in self-doubt and trepidation over these three books. You've stuck by me on many things for twenty years. You celebrate every day that's another clean day for me. I love you.

To my mother, Billie, who invented the whole idea of a cheerleading squad and got on the team in the very beginning. When I gave you a piece of Betrayal to read, you said, "We need to get you published." You knew early on that the end result would be publication of this book. You support me in everything that I do. It doesn't matter what it is. Your unconditional love for me is never ending and never failing. You're proud of me and aren't afraid to tell me. You're the best mother, and I'm so happy that God gave me to you. I think Daddy would be pretty darn proud of me. I think he's watching, and likes what he's seeing. I love you.

To my BFF, Kirsten, my closest and deepest confidant, the sister I always wanted, my other therapist. You've stood by me, seen me at my absolute lowest, and loved me harder. You didn't abandon me those years that I abandoned you, life, everything. You get my craziness, laugh at it, and laugh at me. You've pulled me back to reality on more than one occasion. You've cried with me, laughed with me, and propped me up on all kinds of crazy things. You've listened to me exhaust the same things over and over again, over the course of the last decade. I'm blowin' a kiss your way girl. Thank you for you. I love you.

To Kellie, my voice of reason, such a sweet friend, whom I've had such great laughs with, and plan to keep the laughter going and going for many years to come. I love my time with you. You decided to pick up Betrayal, still rough, unpolished, full of typos, and got into it. You love Nick and Grace almost like I do, and you've decided to keep it going and read Revenge that again, is still rough, unpolished, and full of typos. You've made me sit back and take a look at some of the pages, and helped me realize some changes needed to be made. You've validated me as a writer over and over again. Your hunger for more of this couple makes me want to keep writing about them. I may live to be a hundred, but will never forget a conversation over Nick Bassano, and we were talking like that man is real! Double Date 2014! Thank you for your support, your friendship, and celebrating my clean time. I love you.

To Robin, my wonderful, dear friend, my editor, the only person who I want to see Nickelback with. I love when we trip around the restaurants in Athens because I know it's always going to be a fun date. I know there will be much laughter, it will be loud, and we don't care. Thank you and bless you for taking on the role of editing Betrayal and wanting to be a part of this crazy process. Don't put your feet up yet, you've got two other books to edit, and most likely the fourth. Right now, all I can give you is my friendship, my love and my thanks. We'll see what happens, and maybe I can give you a trip or something. Whatever you want for doing this for me. Did I hear you say another Nickelback concert? When they roll back into Atlanta, girl, we're there! I love you.

To Ginger and Billy, I've got to gush about Ginger first. When we first talked about you doing the cover of the book, it felt like joking because in my head, I never thought we'd get to the point of publication. Then it got real. I'm blown away at your talent. I pulled out that bank envelope after church, scribbled down what I wanted, probably spoke too fast, and you instantly had it. I was speechless at the first version of the cover. It's beautiful and way better than what I had in my mind. The Wednesday night that you and Kellie stood there, smiling, excited, and gave me that first print out of the cover, I think that's when I realized this is happening. This is going to happen. Thank you isn't enough for what you've done. I'm hoping to give you more than my thanks. I can't wait to see what the cover for Revenge and Resolved look like. Billy, you walked up to me one night during a dinner at church, and I'll never forget what you said to me. "I heard you were a world famous author." I was beginning to share that I was writing, and for you to say that to me, it meant a lot. I love y'all.

To Mary Ann, you're beautiful on the inside and out. When Ginger mentioned you "Gracing" the cover of the book, I was in total agreement. I was excited when Mark came home and told me that you were on board with the whole idea, and how excited you were. Thank you, sweet lady, for agreeing to it. I can't imagine having anyone else on the cover. Stop thinking that your part in this is small. It isn't. The cover wouldn't be what it is without you. I love you.

To Cindy, you provide me a safe haven for me to process life, love, and all that comes with it. You force me to look at things, analyze things, and encourage me. You talk big things for me, and I'm trying to think big things for me now. You have this belief in me and my writing in such a way that I'm starting to believe it too. You make me stop, breathe and slow down when I start talking too fast. You took on Betrayal in its original form and have loved it, and I think I saw you salivating as I was handing Revenge off to you. Yes, hear me say it again, I want it all. My time with you means more to me than you know.

To Steve, my sweet friend, the man whom I consider to be a second dad and watched me grow up. I couldn't believe that you wanted to read a book that's geared toward women, but I love that you wanted it. I love our Facebook time, talking all things Nick and Grace, and anything else that we come up with. You made the decision to take a look at Betrayal, decided to stick around for Revenge, and you swallowed Resolved whole. I couldn't type fast enough for you. You make me laugh with your silliness. I love tripping down memory lane, talking about the neighborhood, and all of us kids growing up together. I love you, man.

To Kim, my dear friend who is the second reader of Betrayal. I pretty much typed the last word and sent it to you. You have the original rewriting of it. Your text made me laugh the morning after you finished it, when you said you blamed me for a sleepless night because you had to finish. Your voicemail later in the day made me cry when you gushed over how good you thought it was, and saw a New York Times Bestseller in the making. I don't know about that, but I love that you've loved it. Thank you for your continued support, your excitement and love. I love you.

To Lori, the sweetest woman that I know. Your kind heart, friendship and devotion to Mark, the kids and me, just goes to the kind of woman that you are. You love me, pray for me and are just happy that I'm clean. When I decided to share that I'm writing, you were the first person that I shared that with. I was unsure about what I was doing, and you've supported me from the beginning, sent me sweet pictures and messages on Facebook, and completely believe in what I'm doing. Thank you for your words, your love, and for believing in me. I love you.

To Allison, my sweet friend, who knows I'll be dragging my laptop with me every Wednesday night, typically scattered in twenty different directions, talking too fast most of the time, and I'm probably too loud. I enjoy all of my time with you. Your friendship is dear to me as you are. I wouldn't want to do Wednesday nights with anyone other than you. Yes, Mark and I really do talk about you, and it's always good because we love you and your family very, very much. I love you.

To Chrissy and Chris. Y'all are wonderful and special to my family and me. I enjoy my Wednesday evenings with you, Chrissy. I've always enjoyed your friendship, and being around both you and Chris. Chris, thank you, thank you, thank you for helping me with some of the Law Enforcement details that are found in Betrayal. Thank you for answering my crazy texts and calls and putting up with some of the questions that may have seemed ridiculous. I appreciate at the end of the day that both you and Chrissy would still admit to knowing me and keeping me in your phones. Thank you for supporting me and loving me. I love y'all.

To Amy and Tim. Y'all really are the salt of the earth. I don't know of a sweeter couple who I enjoy being around more than you two. Amy, I love our laughter that we share, and have just rejoiced in being reconnected with you. Our crazy texting back and forth sometimes results in tears and a sore stomach later because I'm laughing that hard. Tim, thank you for answering random Law Enforcement questions when I know that you're busy, and have had the patience of Job with me during some of the times that I've rambled on and on. Thank you both for supporting me and believing in me. I love y'all.

To Chad, I have to give credit where it's due. The Smith & Wesson Bodyguard .380 was a beautiful idea, and it worked. The informant idea was brilliant, and it worked too. Thank you for answering texts and calls and bouncing ideas around with me. You know I'm crazy, and have just gone along with it. Thank you for agreeing, really at the last minute, to take a look at one of the scenes, and giving me your opinion on it. I appreciate you helping me out with some of the Law Enforcement aspects of it.

To the men and women who serve in our military, you sacrifice your lives and time with your family, and because of your service to The United States of America, I have the freedom to write and put it out there for people to enjoy. Thank you and God bless you.

To the men and women who took an oath to uphold the law, and risk your lives every day serving and protecting all of us, thank you. You answer calls, go to places, and deal with those the rest of us don't want to have to think of. God bless you.

To all those in Social Services who run from the north end of your county, to the south end, and then east to west, I remember it well. It seems like it was yesterday that I was putting all those miles on my vehicle, hoping to keep one child safe for one more day. God bless you.

-C K

Trademark Acknowledgements

Betrayal is an independent publication and has not been authorized, sponsored, or otherwise by the following trademarks:

Toyota® is a registered trademark of Toyota Motor Corporation.

Ford® is a registered trademark of the Ford Motor Company.

iPhone® is a registered trademark of Apple.

OtterBox® is a registered trademark of Otter Products LLC.

Jack Daniel's® is a registered trademark of the Stilton Cheese Makers' Association.

MANOLO BLAHNIK® is a registered trademark of Manolo Blahnik.

GLOCK® is a registered trademark of Glock, Inc.

SMITH & WESSON® is a registered trademark of the Smith & Wesson Corporation.

CRISTAL CHAMPAGNE® is a registered trademark of Champagne Louis Roederer.

Stella McCartney® is a registered trademark of Stella McCartney Limited.

McDonald's® is a registered trademark of McDonald's.

TYLENOL® is a registered trademark of McNeil Consumer & Specialty Pharmaceuticals, a Division of McNeil-PPC, Inc.

BMW® is registered trademark of the BMW Corporation.

Baskin-Robbins® is a registered trademark of BR IP Holder LLC.

Prologue

She tries to focus her eyes, but the drugs are so powerful. She's flat on her back, looking up at the ceiling. The lights are dim, and it's hard to see. She's completely naked and should be cold, but instead, she's numb. She isn't sure if she's numb from the drugs or what's being done to her. She's lost all track of time. Has she been here two days? Two weeks? Two months? She feels the needle go into her arm again. She moans but makes no movement. She rolls her head over to the right and sees the woman pull the needle out. She's such a horrible woman, pumping her so full of drugs. Sometimes she craves the next hit but not wanting it. But when those horrible men do things to her, she's almost grateful to the woman for making her high, *almost*.

There are two women. The one that pumps her full of drugs and the other that uses her just as horribly as the three men. Both women are just as sadistic as the men. They are just as abusive. The mask that the woman wears is scary as hell, just as scary as the woman is herself. She takes so many pictures of those men doing so many disgusting things to her. The woman suddenly slaps her in the face.

"Wake up, you whore. They're coming."

She tries to focus her eyes again. Oh, God, no. Not again. She's lost count- today or is it tonight? She doesn't know. She just knows they have used her again and again for so long. The masks that the men wear are scary too. She can see their mouths and eyes, and that makes it worse. She knows the evil is there because she sees it in their eyes and their smiles. It scares her. It's all scary. It's like being in hell and being alive. She wishes that her thoughts were more disjointed than what they are. She finds that even though she's always doped up, she can think too clearly. She thinks that's out of fear more than anything. Her fear is powerful.

One of the men approaches her with a sick and twisted grin on his face. He yanks on her hair, and she screams. He likes it when she does that. She swore to herself, every time, that she would not let him hear her scream again, but he's so mean. He backhands her across the face again even harder this time. The ring he wears cuts her cheek, and she can feel her warm blood dripping down her cheek. *Oh, her blood is warm.* She really is alive. If she could kill herself, she would.

"On your knees, whore," he says, in her face.

She cannot control her body. It feels incredibly heavy. She feels like they have strapped cinder blocks to her. She looks down at her arms and legs to see if that's the case. No, there's nothing there. He hits her again, and she starts crying. She had promised herself that she wouldn't cry anymore, either. But the tears come, and that seems to excite him even more. The other two men have come into the room. They look at her like lions, and she's the lamb about to be slaughtered.

Chapter One

One Year Later

April 2, 2012

The alarm clock's buzzing. It's the most annoying sound in the whole universe. My head's buried under my pillow, and the covers are wrapped around me like a cocoon. I fight to get out of the covers and hit the alarm much harder than necessary. The day is coming when I throw the son of a bitch straight out my window.

It's Monday, and I hate Mondays. I hate them more than anything else in life, and I do try not to hate anything. I'm not always successful in not hating, but hey, I'm not perfect. Mondays just suck. It's getting bright outside, and I can tell it's going to be a sunny day. That's something. There's nothing worse than a Monday and rain. I get out of my bed and shuffle downstairs into the kitchen. Jake Echols is in the kitchen at the coffee maker. He's my roommate's boyfriend. Jess Rider also happens to be my best friend.

"Good morning, Jake," I say, smiling at him and at least making an attempt at being in a good mood. No one likes a morning grump.

Jake has his own apartment, but he spends most of his time here with Jess. If he's not here with her, then she's at his apartment with him. They're serious.

"Mornin', Grace. Coffee?"

"Please, the stronger the better. Is Jess up?"

"She should be. Your hair looks crazy."

My hand flies to my hair. It feels crazy.

"I must've slept well last night," I say. "Do you want me to fix you breakfast?"

"No, thanks. I'm going to drink some coffee, get ready and head to the law library."

Jake is a third-year law student at the University of Georgia. We all live in Athens-Clarke County, Georgia. Jess is a school teacher at Rocky Branch Elementary School in Oconee County. Oconee is west of us. She's also getting her Ph.D. in Education.

"Okay," is all I say. I take some cereal out of the cabinet and pour a bowl, and when I look in the fridge, I realize I forgot to buy milk last night. "Shit," I mutter and slam the door.

Did I mention I hate Mondays? I hate dry cereal, too. I eat it anyway and mentally cuss myself further for forgetting milk. I hope Jess doesn't want cereal for breakfast. She'll probably get something on her way to school. That's what she usually does. I'm drinking my coffee and talking with Jake about all things law school when Jess makes her appearance.

"Hey, you two. Good morning," Jess says, all cheery.

"Good morning," I say, not so cheery. I'm all pissed about the milk now.

"Oh, we always know when it's Monday, because Grace Harrison is a grouch," Jess says, way too chipper for my liking. I stick my tongue out at her, and she responds, "That's so mature."

I want to give her the middle finger as well, but she would only respond with the same remark. She kisses Jake loudly on the lips. Holy Heaven, those two are a mess. They make the best looking couple. Jess is tall and slender with an athletic build. She has thick blond hair that's straight as a rod and she's constantly changing style and length. She may go with a short bob for a while and then let it grow out and cut it into layers. She's keeping it short at the moment. The one constant is she keeps it lowlighted with coppers and browns. Her eyes are the same shade as emeralds. They're big and beautiful. Her eyes pop out at you. I think she's one of the most beautiful people in the world on the outside and inside. I love her dearly and couldn't ask for a better best friend. I think her face looks like an angel's face. She's as sweet as one, too.

Jake isn't much taller than Jess. He has short brown hair that he always keeps neat and brown eyes. He's slender and athletic-looking, just like Jess. He has boyish good looks and sweet Southern charm. He's crazy about Jess, and I keep waiting for him to ask her to marry him. It's coming. I know she's ready.

I dump my dishes in the sink and say to Jess, "I forgot milk."

"That's okay. I'll get something on the way to school."

"I'm going to get ready for a great day," I say sarcastically, walking from the room.

"See you tonight. Remember you promised Jake and me that you'd go out with us and meet his friend William," Jess calls to me.

"Shit!" I yell, walking back upstairs to my bedroom. I really had forgotten that. Their response to my expletive is laughter. "Okay!" I yell, acquiescing.

There's no point in arguing, since I did agree and agreed about a week ago. I'm trying to get back into the dating game. My ex-boyfriend, Cooper, and I broke up a year ago. We'd been together for over two years, and I thought he was the *one*. I loved him like I had never loved any other guy. He loved me too, until he met someone else. Then, he loved her more.

I've given myself a year. I've dated here and there over the last year, but nothing serious. I've had a few one-night stands over the last year, with a couple being drunken one-night stands. Those, I'll live to regret for the rest of my life. I decided a few months back- no more sex until I find someone I really want to have sex with. I miss it. I miss the companionship of a good guy even more.

Cooper was a good guy. He was safe. When it comes down to it, that's what I loved most about him was how safe he is and how smart he is. I've always been attracted to guys I consider safe. Jess has often asked me if I'm trading feeling safe for a certain level of passion in my life. She's such a romantic. I'm not a hopeless romantic, but I would like to fall in love, get married and maybe have kids.

I haven't decided on the whole kid thing, yet. I love kids. I just don't know if I want to be a mother to one or more. Even if I do decide one day to have any, I'm not sure that I can. My periods are irregular and crazy. I may have a period or I may not. I asked the doctor about it one time during an appointment, and he said I may not be ovulating, and I should track it. *Why?* He said it would become important later if I wanted to get pregnant. I told him that I would inform him when later rolls around. My thirtieth birthday is less than a month away. I've not lived my life thinking I *have* to be married by a certain age, but in the back of my mind, I've thought I'd be married by now. I have to believe that there's somebody out there for me, *surely right?*

I stand in front of the mirror and pose like I always do. I don't know why I do this. I pucker my lips, put my hands on my hips and twist my hips from one side to the other. I look at myself and give the sexiest look that I can manage. It ends up resulting in hysterical laughter because I look so ridiculous.

I take a body inventory as well. My hair really is crazy. I have naturally dark brown hair. It's curly, and at the moment, completely unruly. I keep it so it falls past my shoulders settling at my shoulder blades. Some people hate their curly hair. I love mine. I take care of it the best that I can and am rewarded with shiny curls. I do think that my face is too round, and my eyes are too big for my face. My eyes are dark brown, and I sometimes think I see gold flecks in them.

When it comes down to it, I wouldn't change anything. We're given what we're given for a reason, and I like what I've been given. I like to think I have a certain sex appeal about me. That's what I think at least. I've never been told that I'm sexy. I'd love a guy to tell me that. Well, not just any guy. Some guys could say, *"Hey baby, you're sexy,"* and it might come out sounding stupid. I think I probably would've died with laughter if Cooper ever told me I was sexy.

I'm curvy. At least, that's what I've been told by my girlfriends, and I tend to agree. I have to admit, I can rock a pair of blue jeans with the hips that I have. Jess always tells me that she'd pay good money to have the same breasts that I have. And I didn't have to pay a dime for them. I love that my skin is olive complected. That's most likely due to my father being a Latino. Well, I think he's my father. He was with my mother when I was a child, and I don't know of any other father.

Frankly, my childhood was complex, confusing and sad. I don't dwell on it. I don't use his last name. I use my mother's maiden name.

I don't have any association with the man I called Daddy for the first five years of my life. I don't think about that, either.

I get ready quickly and choose from my wardrobe. It's not a hard choice, since I don't have that many clothes. Brown dress slacks with a brown top that has creams and burnt orange patterns in it. Low-heeled brown sling black shoes that have seen better days, but I wear what I have. Both Jess and Jake have left by the time I get back downstairs. My handbag is slung over my shoulder, and I leave for the day.

My car has to be the crappiest car in our condo complex. Jess's parents bought her a condo for a graduation present a few years back. I pay next to nothing to live here, which is a good thing because I make next to nothing. I get in my Toyota Corolla that I bought used seven years ago. It has served me well, but it's been acting up more and more lately. I say a silent prayer and turn the ignition. It starts, finally. I put an old Lifehouse CD in, turn it up and pull onto Timothy Road heading to the bypass. From there, I make my way to North Avenue and the Clarke County Department and Family Children Services building. I'm a case worker there.

A few years back, our official title changed from Social Services Case Manager to Social Services Protect and Placement Specialist. What a mouthful. I'm not sure who had the bright idea to change it. I never use that title. When people ask what I do, I say I'm a *Case Worker* or *Case Manager*. I've been in Social Services since I got out of college several years ago. I managed to get my Master's in Social Work three months ago. It took me forever to get through grad school, since I had to do it all online, but I made it. I work in Foster Care, and I love what I do. I pull in the parking lot, seeing a familiar face lurking around the employee entrance. I sigh. I'm not up for this today. I walk toward the door.

"Hey," I say. "What're you doing here?"

"I went to the police department yesterday to ask about Naomi. Nobody would see me."

"Did you go high?" I ask.

"What does it matter?"

"You're lucky you didn't get arrested," I sigh again. I don't want to do this. "Have you used today?"

"No."

He's lying to me.

"Are you going to?"

"I didn't come here to talk about usin' drugs. Will you go today and see if someone will talk to you? I know you got connections over there. I know you got connections here," he says pointing to the building.

"My day's pretty busy, Matt."

"Are you too fuckin' busy to find out about our sister? Damn, Grace, have you put all of us in a box and on a shelf? If you don't think of us, then we don't exist, right?" My brother is biting his nails. He looks terrible.

"Where're you staying?" I ask him.

"Salvation Army right now."

"Is that where you're really staying, or are you telling me what you think I want to hear?" He doesn't answer me. *That's what I thought.* "How'd you get over here?"

"I bummed a ride."

"How do you plan to get back?"

"I'll figure somethin' out," he mumbles.

"Do you have money?"

"No."

"Have you seen or talked to mom?"

"Not in the last few days." He's still chewing on a nail.

"Where is she?"

"Tent City, I think. Have you seen or talked to her?"

"Not in the last few months," I admit.

"I guess you just been too damn busy. You probably not even tried to find her, have you?"

I ignore his remark.

"I'll go to the police department today and ask around," I say.

"Okay."

"Why don't you go to an NA meeting today?"

I always throw it out to him. He never goes, but one day, I hope that I'll plant the seed with him, and he'll go. Even if he goes high, even if he goes and sits in the back, *reservation row* is what the addicts call it who are living and working the program. If I could just get him in the door and then get him to keep going; I've even offered to go with him.

I really want to get him to detox and then a recovery house, but the few times I've brought that up, he's freaked out on me so badly that I decided to stick with trying to get him to an NA meeting. I'd do anything to get him off the streets and help get him clean. The only thing I won't do is take him home with me and allow him to live with me. I can't live in his chaos. I've lived in that chaos, and I don't want to go back there. It would be too much for me. I have to stay in a healthy place in my life. If Matt were to get clean and stay clean, I'd live with him in a heartbeat.

"I'll think about it." He bends down and kisses my cheek.

I can smell that he hasn't bathed in probably several days. His hair needs cutting. He needs a shave. He needs so much, yet he has so little. I pull a few dollars out of my bag and give them to him. It's not enough to buy drugs, but if he puts it with money that I don't know about, he *will* buy drugs. I hate to enable him, but he's so skinny. I worry about him. I feel like the big sister instead of the younger sister.

"It looks like you could use a new backpack," I say, pointing to the backpack that he has with him at all times. He shrugs his shoulders at my statement. I've asked him what he has in it, and all he'll tell me is that it's his whole life. "Do you have any food in there?"

"I got stuff," he says.

I nod my head at him. He won't tell me what he has or doesn't have. It's always been that way. Matt's guarded even with me. I think it's more the drugs than it is Matt. He wasn't this guarded with me when we were kids.

"Is there anything I can get for you?"

"No."

He's not going to tell me what he needs.

"Matt, please get something to eat, and take care of yourself. I love you. You know that, right?"

"Yeah…You're the only one. I love you, too."

I watch him walk away. Matt's my half-brother. He's older by nearly ten years. He has no idea who his father is. To look at us, no one would believe that we're related. While I have dark hair, dark eyes and olive skin, Matt is as white as white can be. His hair looks like the color of straw, and his eyes are light blue.

We have a younger sister who is fourteen. I don't know much about her. I didn't even know I had a younger sister until about two years ago, when Naomi came into Foster Care. I thought the world had fallen out from underneath me when I found out about her and learned who her mother was- *my mother*. Obviously, I couldn't involve myself in that case.

The only other person here at DFCS that knows she's my sister is my supervisor. I made her swear not to tell anyone else. When she asked me why the secrecy, I couldn't answer her. I simply told her that I didn't want anyone to know.

I met with Naomi a few times, and we were able to get her out of Foster Care and with someone the department thought would be stable and a suitable placement. It wasn't the greatest, but anything was better than her living with my mom, and it got Naomi out of the system. Now, I think maybe she should've stayed in Foster Care. She started running away and then would reappear. That went on for months, until she up and disappeared about a year ago, and she never showed back up. I have no idea where she is, and I don't think my mother does, either. And my mother sure doesn't give a shit.

Matt's convinced that Naomi's been kidnapped, but he has nothing to back that up, and I don't think he's gotten much assistance from the police department. I don't blame anyone there for not jumping on what Matt's told them.

I love my brother dearly for what he's done for me over the course of my life. By the time I turned ten, he was essentially stuck raising me. We would stay any place we could find. He did the best that he could, but he was a full-blown addict by the time he was sixteen. He protected me to the best of his ability and actually did more for me than our mom ever did. My mother would drift in our lives and then right back out. There would be months, sometimes even a year, before I would see her.

The worst years ever with her occurred from the time I was thirteen until I was fifteen. Those two years of living with her were a nightmare in so many ways. My contact with her has been sporadic since then.

Matt has stayed on and off with my mother over the years. They function perfectly together. Function is a poor choice of words. They do drugs well together. Matt's addicted to every substance known to man and possibly a few that he's made up. My mother's severely addicted to crack. She's been that way as far back as I can remember. I'm sure she's using meth these days as well. It looks that way the times I've seen her. Again, I don't dwell on it.

I go in the office and to my desk. None of the caseworkers have offices. We have very nice cubicles that are spacious, but we lack privacy. I pull some files out of top portion of my desk. I have kids to see. I have parents to see. I have court dates coming up. I have a mound of paperwork to do. The paperwork is a constant. I hate it. It's the part of my job that I hate. Everything else I can live with. Not just live with it, but love it, because I love what I do. I'm in and out of the office all morning. I put out the fires that need putting out.

I meet briefly with my supervisor, Valerie Locke. I adore her. I want to be her. She knows everything there is to know about policy and case plans and court and how to woo foster parents. She's my go-to person at all times. I feel like she's molding me into something more than a Case Manager.

Valerie moved from Chicago to Georgia fifteen years ago after meeting her husband. She recently turned forty but looks younger than I do. Her skin is the prettiest chocolate brown, and I've not seen any lines on her face. She has curly hair like mine that she keeps short, and it gets crazy-looking at times, same as mine.

At lunch time, I head over to the Athens-Clarke County Police Department on Lexington Road. I walk in the building and see the lady behind the glass that is the keeper of the door. You don't get beyond the front door without talking to Juliana Carson. She's not the most personable lady, but I would imagine when you hear what she hears all day long, you have to have a tough exterior.

"Hi, Ms. Carson," I say, politely. I'm sure she doesn't remember me. She never does. "I'm Grace Harrison."

"What can I help you with?"

The question is nice enough, but there's no smile.

"Could I speak with either Detective Rice or Detective Hall about my sister? Her name's Naomi Harding."

"Are they expecting you?"

"No, ma'am."

"The detectives aren't here. They're both out."

How does she know that without even looking? The detectives don't leave out of the front door. There's a back entrance that the detectives and other officers go in and out of. I know this because I have spent considerable time at this place.

The ACCPD and DFCS are notorious for not having a good relationship with one another, but I try to have a good relationship with certain officers. Some of them have helped me tremendously on more than one occasion. I'm not as familiar with the detectives other than one certain detective that works in Sex Crimes, but I think he either retired or is getting ready to retire.

"Could I leave my card with you, and you give it to one of them?" I ask, smiling at her.

"Sure. I would advise calling before coming next time, so you don't make a wasted trip."

I pull one out of my bag and place it in the tray and slide it to her.

"Okay. I'll do that next time. Thank you so much. Have a wonderful day." I give her my most dazzling smile.

"Thank you," she says, not smiling back.

I walk out into the bright sunshine putting my sunglasses on. It's a nice spring day. We're actually having a spring for the first time in years. It usually jumps from fall to summer. We had our first hard winter in years this past winter. I stand for a minute and let the breeze blow through my hair. I turn my face to the sun and feel its warmth. I look at my watch. I've just about blown through my lunch hour.

I go to my car and turn the ignition. It doesn't start. I try again. It still doesn't start. I get out and go to raise my hood. I don't know what I'm looking for. It just seems like the thing to do. Your car doesn't start, and you go raise the hood.

Holy Heaven, what to do? Any time I have problems with my car, I take it to Jess's dad. He's been great about helping out and letting me know what he thinks the problem is and sending me to places where I'm not going to be robbed blind. They wouldn't get much. You can't bleed blood from a turnip.

Jess's dad is a doctor here in town. I can't call him. He's busy. I could call one of my co-workers. I get along with all of them. The problem is that I have other people to see today. I have to have my car. It's my lifeline and totally connected with my career. Without it, I can't work at all.

I hear a car pull up beside me. I look up and see a guy get out of the car. He walks over to me, and I look up, up, up at him. I pull my sunglasses off and slide them in my hair.

"Do you need help?" he asks.

He's in a nice button up, long-sleeved white shirt with a nice tie and stylish black pants. I see a badge attached to his belt and a gun attached to his right hip. He's a detective or higher ranking, I would imagine, but I have no idea who he is. I look a little closer at his badge and make out the word *Detective*.

I focus my attention back on him. He's tall. He's incredibly tall. I'm not short at almost five foot nine, but I have to bend my head back to look up at him. He's got dark black hair that's cut neatly and close. It's not a buzz cut, but it's very short, forming into a subtle widow's peak in the front. *I could probably run my fingers through his hair*. Where in the *hell* did that thought come from?

He's thick, broad and incredibly muscular. His shoulders are broad, as well as his chest, waist, hips and legs. He has to work out, but he doesn't have the look of a body builder. It looks natural and athletic, like that's how he's been his whole life.

He takes off his sunglasses and, *whoa*, he has the prettiest blue eyes I've ever seen. They're dark blue. They're so penetrating, it feels like he can see right through me. I take a closer look, and he's attractive. He's a little too attractive. He's clean shaven, but I see where he'll have a trace of stubble by late this afternoon. He has full lips and a straight nose that fits his face perfectly. He looks like he would tan just as easily as I do.

"My car won't start," I say.

He walks and stands beside me. I catch a scent that's coming off of him. He smells good, too.

"What does it do when you turn the ignition?"

"Nothing," I say.

He looks at me and, wow, his eyes are *very* penetrating. I don't think I've ever seen anyone with eyes that color of blue.

"Get in, and let me see what's going on." He's got a smooth, deep voice, and his accent isn't Southern. I don't think he's from here. I do what he says and get in my car. I turn the ignition, and nothing happens. "Your battery's dead," he says. *Shit*. Perfect. I get out and look at my watch. Dammit, this puts me way behind schedule. "Have you got some place you need to be?" he asks me.

I look up at him, and he's smiling. *Holy Heaven*, he has dimples on both sides of his cheeks. I feel my heart starting to beat faster.

"Um, I was on my lunch break," I say. I didn't really answer his question.

"I could take you and get a battery if you'd like. I'm Nick Bassano, by the way," he says, holding out his hand.

Holy Heaven, his hand's big. I shake it, and his hand completely engulfs mine. The way his skin feels against mine, it's like he's shocked me. *Good God*, my heart's beating fast. I realize he's waiting for me to tell him my name.

"Grace Harrison," I say, finding my voice. "That would be great, if you aren't too busy."

"No problem. I was heading out to lunch. A detour isn't going to make much difference. Where would you like to go?" He's still smiling, and I keep looking at his dimples.

I shrug. "Wherever I can find the cheapest battery," I say.

"There's an Advance Auto store up the road. How about that?"

"Sure," I say. Nick Bassano drops the hood of my car. I pull my handbag out and get in his car. It's nice and neat. We're pulling out of the parking lot when my phone rings. It's Valerie. "Hey."

"Hey," she says. "There's a problem. The Dawsons want Cameron Moore moved."

"What?" I yell. I see Nick Bassano glancing over at me. "Shit. He just got there Saturday morning. How in the hell do they know they want him moved today? What's he done in less than three days?"

"They said he's tearing up their stuff. Can you go there and smooth things out? We're looking at some other possibilities, but we need him there for at least another two days."

"Holy Heaven," I exclaim. "Yes, I'll get over there as quickly as I can." I hang up my phone and cuss like a sailor in my head.

"Holy Heaven?" Nick Bassano asks.

"What?" I respond, confused.

"What you just said. *Holy Heaven*. I've never heard anyone say that before." He glances at me and then back to the road. I said that? I wasn't even aware of it. I shrug my shoulders, but he's not looking at me. "Problem?" he asks.

I'm still confused. "With what I said?" I need some clarification here.

He chuckles, "No, with your phone call."

"Oh. I'm a case worker for DFCS. One of my foster parents wants a kid moved *right now*."

"A social worker? I guess you're all touchy feely, huh?"

Is he making fun of me? Is he being sarcastic? It kind of feels like he's doing both.

"I guess if you call caring about kids and their welfare touchy feely, then yes, I'm touchy feely." It comes out sounding almost defensive, and I don't want to sound defensive about what I do. I love what I do, and I'm proud of it. I can see that he's laughing.

"Can you do anything else but talk on that phone?"

Huh? I'm lost. I look at my phone and look at him. "I'm not following you."

"Your phone looks like a reject from the late nineties."

I keep my eyes on him. "Do you make it a habit to insult everyone that you've just met, or is it just me?"

"Am I insulting you?"

"It kind of feels like it, yes."

"My apologies," he smirks. He's not sorry at all.

I turn back and look at the road. "My phone's cheap, and it does what I need for it to do." Why am I explaining myself to this man?

His only response is, "Okay."

We drive in silence the rest of the way. Fortunately, it's a short distance between the police department and the auto parts store. We walk in, and Nick Bassano leads the way to the batteries. I look at them, and I'm lost. I have no idea what I'm supposed to get.

"Um, would you mind helping me out?" *Oh, I hate asking him.*

He looks down at me and smiles. *Whoa*, his teeth are dazzling white, and those dimples. Shit. He's really attractive.

"You don't know much about cars, do you?" He's still smiling, but it's a smile that says, *You aren't very bright, are you?* Bastard. He's making fun of me again.

"No," I admit, but I'm blushing about it.

"Your boyfriend or your dad doesn't help you out?"

"No." I don't elaborate that I have neither. It's none of his business.

"No, that they don't help you? Or no, that there's no boyfriend or dad?"

I sigh, and it comes across as frustration, which is exactly how I want it to come across, because that's what I'm feeling, very frustrated.

"My best friend's father helps me when it comes to car trouble." Again, why am I explaining things?

"Hmm." He looks back up and points to a battery. "That one's good. It'll work. It's a little pricey."

I think quickly as to how much is in my bank account. All of my bills are paid; however, I don't want to go broke. I'd like to get out and do something this weekend.

"Maybe something a little cheaper?" I ask, looking up at him.

"How about this. You tell me your price range, and I'll pick it out; that way, we won't stand here all day." He sounds quite snappy.

Well, just take out your gun and shoot me. "Excuse the hell out of me," I say under my breath. Damn. He didn't have to stop and help me. My face is burning at this point.

I want this done and over, and let me get on with my day, and he can get on with his. Of course, I have to ask him about prices, which he regards me with a look that I then want to stick my tongue out at him for. I make my decision, pay for it and thankfully make it back to the police department. He puts the battery in and ends up getting some grease on his shirt. Dammit. He's probably going to make a big deal out of that. He says nothing.

"Okay, get in and start it up." I do what he says. It turns on immediately, and my music blares from my speakers. "Are you deaf?" he yells. *No, just embarrassed.* I turn it down. "You do realize there's a noise ordinance in Athens, right?" He's smiling as he says it, but dammit, he's one sarcastic son of a bitch.

I just want out of here and away from him. I get out of my car and move to take the old battery from him. He says he can drop it at the police department shop. They recycle.

"Thank you for helping me. I'm sorry about your shirt," I say, pointing to the small grease stain.

"I'll send you my dry cleaning bill. See ya." He's smiling as he says it, but I feel like he's not joking about it.

He leaves driving away too fast out of the parking lot, I think. I realize that I've been holding my breath, and my heart's still beating far faster than it should.

Chapter Two

I make it to the Dawsons' house and spend an hour convincing them to keep Cameron for a few more days. I ask what he tore up, and I learn that it was a rose bush. When I find that out, I want to tear some of their shit up too. I really want to ask *Are you fucking kidding me that I've spent an hour over a goddamn rose bush?* but I bite my tongue because if I said that, they would most likely throw me out of their house, and I'd be dragging Cameron with me. Cameron is getting off of the bus as I'm leaving. He's the cutest kid. His mom is Asian. His dad, we believe, is Cuban. The combination of the two give him the most exotic look. He's nine years old going on about thirty-five. His life's been rough.

"Hey you," I say, smiling at him.

He runs, dragging his book bag on the ground.

"Hey, Grace!" he yells, slamming into me and hugging me tight around the waist.

I've known Cameron for a while. This isn't his first time in Foster Care. I threw a childlike tantrum the last time he went home. I ranted and shouted about the fact that he would be back. Valerie's argument was that his mom had completed the case plan. Yeah, she had, but it wasn't going to last. I was right.

"What's up?" I ask him.

"Nothing but the sky," he says, grinning from ear to ear.

We do this all the time. The very first time I met him, that was my question to him, and that was his response to me. It cracked me up then, and it still does.

"Are you settling in okay?"

He shrugs. "I guess. They're all mad about the rose bush. I didn't mean to tear it up. I was chasing the cat, and he ran through it, and I did too."

I put my arms around his too skinny shoulders.

"Don't worry about it. Are they feeding you?" I ask, poking him playfully in the ribs.

He giggles, "Yeah. Mrs. Dawson's a good cook. I eat everything on my plate, and she even gives me seconds."

Malnourishment has always been an issue with Cameron. His mom is completely capable of taking care of him. She just won't.

"Are they being nice to you?"

"Yeah, they're cool. The other kids are pretty cool, too. I kind of like being the youngest."

I talk with him a few more minutes and finish out my day. I end up being so far behind that I can't go home and change my clothes before meeting Jess, Jake and his friend. I call Jess and tell her I may be late and find out that we're going to meet at The Globe for drinks and then off to dinner. We don't know where yet.

I sit at my desk and go over some of my files. Everything is pretty much up to date. I have court coming up on several cases. That's fine. I like being in Judge Wright's courtroom. Eric Wright is the Juvenile Court Judge, and I've known him for as long as I've worked here. I admire him greatly. He's fair, kind, and he cares about the welfare of children. I could spend a considerable amount of my time in his presence.

Valerie accuses me of having a crush on him. He's not bad looking, with his salt and pepper colored hair and his constant deep tan from playing hours of golf, but he's happily married and old enough to be my father. Regardless of what Valerie accuses me of or thinks, there's no crush. I just have tremendous respect for the man, and he feels the same about me.

I leave work and make my way to downtown Athens. I drive around several times hoping for a spot on the road. I have no such luck. I end up at the parking deck off of College Avenue. I look at my watch. Shit, I'm super late. I walk quickly over to Lumpkin Street, rushing in the bar and finding Jess, Jake and his friend on the couches right inside the door facing the road. They all smile at me as I collapse on the couch beside Jess.

"Sorry," I say to all of them.

Jake introduces me to William. He's a nice-looking guy and has the same boyish good looks as Jake. He dresses like he's from money. He's pleasant. He smiles a lot and laughs a lot too. I order what everyone else is having, which is the local beer on draft. William jumps up to get it for me. That's nice. He comes back, and we all settle in for some conversation. It's fairly crowded, even for a Monday.

"How was your day?" Jess asks me.

"Typical," I answer. All except meeting Nick Bassano, but that I don't say. "How was yours?"

"Great. I'm counting down to Spring Break."

"Ah yes. That's not far away, is it?"

"No," she says, smiling broadly.

William catches my attention. "Jake and Jess were telling me that you're a social worker."

"I am. I'm a case manager for Clarke County DFCS."

"Interesting," he says.

I notice he doesn't call me touchy feely. Thinking about that comment makes me think of Nick Bassano, his striking eyes and his dimples. Those thoughts lead to aggravation, because I don't want to think of him and the fact that he's such a sarcastic son of a bitch.

We all fall into easy conversation with one another. I learn that William's plan after law school is to join his father's firm here in Athens. He says his father is a real estate attorney, and he grew up in Oconee County. He smiles easily at me and constantly engages me in conversation. I notice that he enjoys talking about himself, a lot. That's fine. How else am I going to get to know him if he doesn't talk about himself?

Out of the corner of my eye, I notice a couple walking towards the front door. I look up at the same time as the guy turns around. *Shit*, are you kidding me? Nick Bassano catches my eye and grins. Oh my God, those dimples. His look is one of surprise to see me sitting here at the same place. And Holy Heaven, he's wearing blue jeans that hang off of his thick muscular frame. I can see how muscular his thighs are. He has on a short-sleeved, black polo shirt that just molds to his body. I see a USMC tattoo on his right forearm in Old English-style lettering. Dammit, he's sexy. It totally pisses me off that I think he's sexy.

"How's your car?" he asks, instead of, *Hey. How are you?*

I can see Jess, Jake and William have stopped their conversation, and they're looking at Nick and then at me. They look like they're all at a tennis match.

"Moving again, thank you," I say as politely as I can manage.

"Did you save the world today?" he asks, laughing a little.

Is he making fun of me again? *Yes, yes he is.* Damn him, the bastard.

"Did you?" I snap at him, not hiding my annoyance at all. His eyes are dancing. I make the decision right here that I hate him.

"Yes. You didn't notice the big S in the middle of my chest? Oh wait, it was probably covered with grease." He's laughing about it, but it's all so sarcastic.

I focus my attention on his date. Interesting, Lacey Carter from the Clarke County District Attorney's office is with him tonight. It's so strange why District Attorney Brison Scott would keep her around. I've met him several times, and not only is he a super nice guy, he's a devoted father and husband. Her behavior seems to go against everything that he morally believes in. She's a sexy woman. There's no denying her sex appeal. She works her looks to her advantage. She's a striking woman with jet black hair, dark blue-gray eyes and skin that's creamy white.

I really don't care for her at all. We've met a few times over the years, and I've not ever been impressed with her. She looks good on the surface, but I think if you were to scratch any deeper, you wouldn't like what was there. I think what she puts out there for everyone to see is fake.

I wonder if Nick knows what he's getting himself into and that she's fucked half of the police department and most likely half of the sheriff's department. I call her a holster sniffer, and that's kind. Looking at Nick with his arm around her and the way she has her arm around him, he knows exactly what he's getting into, *her pants.*

There's a feeling that shoots through me. Is that jealousy? *No way. There is no fucking way I'm jealous!*

"It was just a little grease," I mutter.

"Do you know Lacey Carter? I'm not sure how much time case workers and investigators spend together."

There it is again, sarcasm, and he's cocky. He's a cocky, sarcastic, sexy SOB. I really, really hate him.

"Yes. How are you?" I ask, standing to shake Lacey's hand.

"Good. How are you?" She could care less how I am.

"Very well. Thanks for asking." Did that sound as fake to her as it did to me? "These are my friends Jess, Jake and William," I say, introducing them.

"Hi. I'm Nick," he says, stepping forward and shaking hands with each of them. I see Jess smile tightly as she shakes his hand. She's not impressed. "Well, we have plans, don't we?" he says, looking down at Lacey.

"Yes, we do," she says to him, smiling.

Holy Heaven, I don't want to know what those plans are, but the way they're looking at each other, I can guess.

"It was nice meeting you all. Grace, see ya," he says, and they're out the door.

I get an eyeful of his backside, and my God, what a backside it is. I realize that I'm holding my breath again. I have to stop doing that. I'm going to pass out one day. Damn, my heart's beating wildly. I focus my attention on Jess. She looks unhappy.

"Grace. Who was that?" she asks me.

"The biggest guy I've ever seen," Jake answers.

Jess gives Jake a look. "Was I talking to you?"

He holds his hands up in front of him in surrender. "Sorry."

She turns her attention back to me, "Well?"

"That was Detective Nick Bassano. I was at the police department today and had car trouble. He helped me out."

"He's an ass," she says.

I laugh. *Yes he is*, and then some, but *damn*, he's attractive, and he has a nice-looking ass.

"I think that's the biggest guy I have ever seen in my life that doesn't wrestle for the WWE," Jake says. "How tall is he, and how much does he weigh? Because that dude's huge."

Why is he looking at me, asking that question?

"I have no idea," I mutter.

"I bet he has no problems with any of the offenders here in Athens. His hand swallowed mine," William says to Jake.

"What position do you think he played in football? He had to play football. There's no way a guy that big didn't play football," Jake almost sounds like he's in awe of this guy.

I would laugh, but that would be stupid.

"Linebacker, Defensive End, I mean damn. He had to play defense. I bet the other team would turn tail and run seeing him come at them," William says.

I cross my arms over my chest and sit back. They continue to debate over Nick Bassano's probable football past. I don't want to talk about Nick Bassano. I don't want to think about Nick Bassano, and I don't want to look at Nick Bassano. Okay, so maybe the last part is a little lie, but that's okay, because I'm lying to myself. I'm not going to think about that any deeper.

"Is anyone else hungry?" I pipe up. I have to get this conversation moved in a different direction.

"I am," William says. Jake and Jess agree.

We decide to walk over to College Avenue and eat at The Grill. I love going there. There's nothing better than fries and feta at The Grill. We get settled into a booth with William beside me and Jess across from me. Jake and William talk about law school and Spring Break, while Jess and I talk about her day at school. We order our food and continue to talk, keeping the conversation flowing all around us. After we finish eating, conversation begins to die down. I look at my watch. I should go over to the Salvation Army and see if Matt's there. Jake and William are back to talking all things UGA Law School.

"I saw Matt this morning," I tell Jess.

"And?"

"He looks really bad."

"He's using." She's not asking. She knows Matt well through me.

"He's always using," I sigh. "He said he went over to the police department yesterday to ask about Naomi. He didn't get anywhere and asked me to go there. That's what I was doing over there today when I met Detective Bassano."

"I understand. Did you find out anything?"

"No, but I think I'm going to head over to the Salvation Army and see if I can find him."

"Is that where he's staying?"

"That's where he said he's staying." I shrug my shoulders at her, indicating that I really don't know if he's telling me the truth or not. "Okay. I'm going." I turn to William. "It was great meeting you," I say.

"Are you leaving?" He looks a little surprised.

"Yeah. I need to go."

"It was great meeting you, too. Would you like to get together Friday night for a drink after work?"

"That sounds great," I say, smiling.

We exchange numbers, and I notice that he makes no comment about my phone.

"I can walk you to your car if you'd like," William says.

"Oh, that's okay. I'm parked right up here in the parking deck," I say, motioning towards that direction. "Stay and talk. I'll see you Friday." I hug Jess. "I'll see you later."

"Okay. I think I'm going to Jake's for a while, but I'll be home later."

"Have fun," I say. I blow a kiss to Jake and head out.

At the corner of College Avenue and Clayton Street, I see a couple of guys that I know from the streets. They stay at the Salvation Army and the homeless shelter from time to time. I've been hanging out with the homeless at various locations on Sunday for many years. Some people go to church; I hang out with the homeless. It's pretty natural for me.

"Miss Gracie," one of them calls.

"Street," I say, stopping to talk to them.

After getting to know him, I asked Street how he got his nickname, and he said it was because he's always lived on the streets. It's hard to argue with that kind of logic. The other guy I don't know as well. I've seen him only a handful of times.

"Miss Gracie. How is you this fine spring evenin'?"

"I'm great. How're you?"

"Straight. You know Pope?"

"I've seen him. Hi. I'm Grace," I say, smiling at him and holding out my hand to shake hands.

He makes no move to shake mine. He eyes me, suspiciously.

"Pope be wonderin' why a young good lookin' white girl be talkin' to him. He don't see that much. She cool, man," he says, turning to Pope.

They've both been drinking. From the looks and smell of it, they've been drinking for some time.

"You know you gentlemen can't go to the homeless shelter if you're drunk."

"Shit. We don't care. We find someplace to stay tonight. Besides, Miss Gracie, it be spring time. You know I like to be downtown in spring and summer."

I start laughing, well aware of that. "Make sure you're safe, okay?"

"Yep. You got any money, Miss Gracie?"

I give Street a look. "You know my rules, Street."

He starts laughing. "Shit. I know, Miss Gracie, but it don't hurt to axe you for some."

I may enable my brother, but dammit, I have to draw the line at some point with the enabling.

"Good night, guys. Stay safe," I say, walking away.

"Night, Miss Gracie," Street calls after me.

I get to my car and make my way to Prince Avenue and from there to Chase Street. I see several men standing outside the Salvation Army smoking and talking. I'm scanning the crowd for Matt, but I don't see him. I get out and walk to the guys. Some of them whistle and catcall me. I ignore them.

There's a tall, skinny guy that approaches me. His appearance is shocking, even by Salvation Army standards. He has short hair that stands up at the ends. It looks like he's been chopping it himself. None of it is symmetrical. I can see bald patches on his head. When I look in his face, I see his right eye veers to the right involuntarily, while his left eye is looking straight ahead. His face is sunken as well as his eyes. He has open sores all over his face and pock marks from being ravaged by acne at some point in his life. His movements are jerky, and his good eye darts all around. He's high on methamphetamine. He has to be. He's a ghostly looking man. The whistles and catcalls are still going on. This man turns around and tells them to shut up. Most of them do, except one.

"Can I help ya?" he asks me.

"Um, do you know Matt Mills?"

He looks at me confused. "Ralphie!" he yells back at the crowd.

The guy who approaches us is creepy as shit. He's the one who hasn't shut up with the whistling and saying super inappropriate things to me and about me. This is by far the ugliest man I have ever seen. He makes the hair on the back of my neck stand on end. He's short and squat. He has long oily hair and is bald on the top. Why not just shave it all? Does he think it's going to all grow back magically? His bulbous nose is too large for his face. His cheeks are sunken in, and his eyes are yellow. He has open sores on his face, just like the other guy, and they are in various stages of healing. He looks like a leper. When he smiles, I cringe inwardly. His remaining teeth- and there aren't that many- are past the point of decay.

"Hey, baby," he says, trying to sound all smooth. I believe I vomit a little in my mouth.

"I'm not your baby," I say, giving him a hard look.

"Chill, bitch," he says.

"Ralphie," the other guy says. It almost sounds like a plea.

"What?" he says to the other man. "Bitch is givin' me attitude. That shit don't fly with me," he says, turning back to me. He's still smiling, and it's a mean smile. Again, he's super creepy.

"Do you know Matt Mills?" I ask him.

"What's in it for me?"

"How about answering just for the sake of being nice?"

"Fuck that. How bout this? I'll tell you what I want from you, and if you do that for me, I'll tell you if I know- what'd you say his name was again?"

"Ralphie," the other guy says again.

"Shut the fuck up, Ray Ray. Me and the bitch is talkin'."

That's it. I've had enough. I'm about to walk away when I see another guy come out of the front door of the building. He looks at the two guys I've been talking to and points to them.

"You and you get off of this property. I've called the police, and they're on their way."

I see the guy called Ralphie give the middle finger to the man who told them to leave the property. I walk in his direction. As I get closer, I realize that he's familiar to me.

"Hey," he says smiling at me.

"Hey."

"You should be careful. Those two you were talking to, especially the long-haired one, are not nice guys at all. You look really familiar. Do I know you?"

"I think we've seen each other around different NA meeting locations."

"Oh, yeah. I'm sorry I don't remember your name. I'm Mike." He holds out his hand, and I shake it.

"I'm Grace. Do you know Matt Mills?"

"Yeah."

"Is he here?"

"Um, no. I haven't seen him in a while. How do you know Matt?"

"He's my brother."

Mike looks surprised. "Oh. You two look nothing alike."

"I know we don't. Well, thanks for coming out saving me from those two winners," I say, laughing.

"You really don't seem fazed by all of this," he says, waving his arm around him to the building and the crowd.

"I'm a case manager at DFCS. I see it and hear it daily. Does that make me sound jaded?" I ask, laughing.

Mike laughs. He has a nice laugh. He's not bad on the eyes either.

"No, not at all," he says.

"Well, I guess I should go. I'm going to head over to a meeting and see if Matt's there."

"If I see him, I'll tell him to get in touch with you. Does he know your number?" Mike asks.

"He never calls me. I could give it to you. You know, in case you see him." I hope he gets that I'm giving my number to him not only for Matt, but for him as well.

"Sure. I will absolutely give it to him." He's still smiling. He's nice. I like this guy. He leads me inside and gives me a pen and some paper. I write my name and number and put a smiley face beside my number and give it to him.

"Thanks again," I say, smiling at him.

I leave and drive down the street to one of the local NA and AA meeting rooms, where people can go to different meetings all day. I get out and ask around about Matt. I see several faces that I know. There's an open NA meeting about to start. I could stay. Anyone can go to open meetings. I come hoping to see my mom or Matt here. I never have. I also come to hear other addicts who are seeking recovery talk. Some know Matt, but they don't know where he's staying and haven't seen him.

It's getting late, and I'm tired. I decide to head home. When I get there, Jess still isn't home. I probably won't see her again for the rest of the evening. I get ready for bed, and when I fall asleep, I dream of Nick Bassano.

Chapter Three

I'm walking around Tent City on the East side. It's exactly what it's called. There are tents all around. Many of Athens homeless live here. I've been off from work for about twenty minutes, and I'm grouchy as hell. I've dreamt of Nick Bassano for the last three nights. I'm pissed about that. I've awakened three mornings all sexually frustrated. I'm pissed about that. I'm pissed that he's in my subconscious, because I'm sure as hell not actively thinking about him. Oh, that man makes me so mad. I'm pissed that he affects me.

I've been talking to people for about ten minutes, asking around about my mom and Matt. I see several people that I know and stop and talk with them and ask them about my mom and Matt. I'm hearing from several people that both of them aren't coming to this side of town much any longer. They're both staying closer to downtown Athens or some of the streets around the DFCS office. I'm talking to a guy who says he saw my mother a few days ago on Vine Street when I hear a familiar voice ask, "What're you doing here?"

I swing around, and I'm face-to-face with Nick.

"What're you doing here?" I ask right back.

"This isn't the safest place in the world, you know."

Why does he care? "You're here," I say.

"Gun," he says, tapping his hip.

"Brain," I say, tapping my head. I see the shadow of a smile.

"Seriously, Grace. What're you doing here?"

"I'm looking for my mom?"

"Your mom lives here?"

"My mom doesn't live anywhere. She stays here at times."

"Who's your mom?"

"Marsha Harrison."

"Marsha Harrison's your mom?" he asks, surprised.

"Yes. Do you know her?"

"Everybody in the police department knows your mom. Do you know how many times she's been arrested on drug, prostitution and theft charges?"

I probably can't count the number on all of my fingers and toes of her arrests.

"No. I don't keep up with her that often. Would you help me find her?" *Dammit, I hate asking him, but he might be able to help me.*

"I'm busy. My partner and I are working an Armed Robbery case. If you don't keep up with her, why're you looking for her? Are you feeling especially social worker-like today, or maybe you want to tell yourself you're a good daughter?"

That stings. And the fact that it stings really pisses me off, because I don't give a damn what he says to me or what he thinks about me. I turn without a word and walk away.

"Are you walking away from me?" he calls.

"Perceptive, aren't you?" I yell, all pissed while I keep walking. "When you see someone's back, and they're putting distance between them and you, that's usually what it means!" I keep going. "Asshole," I mutter to myself.

"Grace!" he calls. I don't stop. I'm making my way back to my car. "Grace, wait!" I hear him running. He catches up with me quickly. "Stop. I'll help you find your mom."

I turn and look up at him. "Why?"

"You asked me."

"You're busy," I snap, throwing his words back at him. I turn again and keep going. He doesn't try and stop me this time.

I speed off and don't give him another glance. It takes forever for me to get from the East side, back to the condo that's on the far west side of the county. I'm fuming the whole way there. Why does he have to be such an asshole? Why does he make me so mad? Why do I care about any of this shit? And why in the hell am I dreaming about this man?

I don't even like him. And why am I allowing him to take up space in my head? I'm still mad when I walk in the door, slamming it shut. Jess sees me as I'm storming upstairs.

"What's wrong?" she asks, concerned.

"Nick Bassano!" I yell and go in my room, slamming my bedroom door. I throw my handbag on the bed, and then I throw myself on the bed. I'm pouting. I'm actually pouting. I take a deep breath. This has got to stop. I cannot keep letting this man affect me like this. I hear Jess tapping lightly on my door.

"Can I come in?"

"Sure."

She comes in and sits on my bed. "Do you want to talk about it? Or talk about him?"

"There's nothing to talk about," I say, looking at her. She looks back at me. "Are we playing poker?"

"Yes," she says. I can tell she wants me to talk about him. I refuse. I lay back on my bed, exhausted. "You know it's okay to admit that you like someone."

I give her a *have you lost your mind* look.

"I don't like him," I say, firmly.

"Okay." She's looking at me. She wants to say something else.

"What?" I ask.

She shrugs her shoulders. "Nothing," she says.

"I'm going to take a shower. Have you eaten?" I ask her.

"No. How about I order pizza?"

"That sounds good," I say.

I get up and go in the bathroom. I strip down and stare at my reflection in the mirror. My cheeks are flushed. I'm sure that's because I'm so damn angry. Poker will be good. I can get lost in cards and being with my friends. Jess and I have two other friends that we've kept up with over the years, that we met in college. We all graduated from the University of Georgia.

Jess and I met each other our freshman year in an English class. We became instant friends. It didn't matter that she grew up wealthy, with two loving parents and stability, and I had none of those things. We clicked. Jess's parents have been fantastic to me over the years. I take great pleasure in seeing Jess with her mom and dad and how much they love one another. That's how it should be between parents and their children.

We met our other two friends, Ginger Sanders and Angie Wall, the next semester. We discovered that the four of us had a fondness for pool and poker. We also discovered that we were good at both. We four are an eclectic-looking group of women. Jess is blond and tall like me. Ginger has dark, shoulder-length, reddish brown hair and is short and petite. Angie has brown hair that she keeps in a pixie cut and is medium height. We're all good looking women. When we're out together, we all get hit on regularly.

Ginger and Angie both got married several years ago, but they still live in Athens, and the four of us try and get together as much as possible to play pool and poker. Guys have poker nights on Wednesdays. Why can't the ladies have it on Thursdays?

Ginger is the Human Resources Director at Athens Regional Medical Center, and Angie is teaching art at North Oconee High School over in Oconee County. We're a diverse group of women. Conversation is never boring.

I shower and change and pull my hair up in a tight bun. I feel better after my shower. I'm calmer. My blood pressure feels like it is back to normal. I walk downstairs and find Jess in our living area, reading a book.

"You look like you feel better," she says, smiling at me.

"I do. There's nothing like a good hot shower to wash the day away."

"The pizza and the girls should be here soon."

"Great. I'm having a beer. Do you want one?" I ask her.

"Please," she says, smiling sweetly at me.

I get up and get one for each of us. As soon as I sit, our doorbell rings.

"I've got it."

I jump up and walk back in the kitchen, where I pull the money off the counter and go to the door. Jess ordered us Papa John's tonight. Excellent choice. I give the guy his money and tip. As he's leaving, Ginger and Angie arrive.

"Hi," I call to them.

"Hi," they say together.

They come in, and it's five minutes of hugs and loud talking over one another. We get pizza and drinks and sit around the table, catching up with one another.

"Well, let me tell y'all about what's going on out at North Oconee," Angie says.

"Tell us," I say, stuffing a bite of pizza in my mouth.

"Tripp came home last night and said two of his players are being suspended for drinking at school." Tripp is Angie's husband, and he's the head baseball coach and a Social Studies teacher there.

"I didn't think things like that happened in Oconee County," I say, teasing her.

"Oh, please," she says. "I hate it. I hate it that those two boys made a poor decision. They're good kids. I had one of them in class last year. Tripp's so burning mad. They're two of his star players, and you know the season's close to being over. There aren't that many more games."

"It's so stupid to drink while underage, first, but then take it to school where the prospect of getting caught goes up significantly only adds to the stupidity," Jess says. We all agree with her.

"What did the parents say about it?" I ask.

"One set of parents said and did everything right, and the other set said it must've been the other boy's fault, because their son would *never* do anything like that."

"And we wonder why he chose to drink," I say sarcastically. The girls nod in agreement, understanding my statement.

"Does Preston own the bank yet?" Jess jokes with Ginger. Preston Sanders has been the President of the largest bank in Athens for over ten years.

"You're cute. I think he'll stay satisfied with being President. How's Jake doing in law school?" she asks.

"Very well. He likes it. He's good at it. He said he wondered why it took him so long to decide to go to law school. We're lucky this year that our Spring Breaks fall at the same time. We're going on a trip." She's all smiles as she says it. I was wondering if they would be going someplace together.

"Spring Break isn't next week but the week after, correct?" Ginger asks. Jess and Angie nod together.

Ginger looks at me. "I wish I had a Spring Break," she says.

"Me too," I agree with her.

"I'm thinking I should go back to school and become a teacher," she says.

I shrug my shoulders. "I think I'll stay at DFCS."

"You're going to run that place someday," Jess tells me.

A girl can dream. We finish eating, clear the table and get the cards out. We do more talking than playing, and the game moves slowly. We manage to deal the cards a second time after Angie wins, when the doorbell rings. Jess and I give each other an odd look. We aren't expecting anyone else tonight.

"I'll get it," I say.

I walk through the kitchen and look through the peephole. *What the fuck?* Nick Bassano's on the other side of the door. I sigh heavily and open it. He's leaning against the doorframe, all casual-like, with his arms crossed over his broad chest. It makes the muscles in his arms pop out more with him standing the way he is. My mouth goes dry. Oh, shit, he looks hot.

He's decked out in a white tee-shirt with what looks like a sports logo across his broad chest and jeans that hang off that thick, muscular frame. Damn, the man can wear a pair of blue jeans like I've never seen. He's smiling like the cat that ate the mouse. I like his tattoo on his arm. Dammit. I'm getting all pissed again. I don't want to see him, and I sure as hell don't want to appreciate *what* I'm seeing. I can feel the heat rising in my body, and I tell myself that it's out of annoyance and not attraction. *Liar.*

"Hey," he says, looking down at me.

"Hey," I say, looking up into his eyes. Now, why did I have to go looking in his eyes? "Why're you here? And how do you know where I live?"

"Whoa, slow down with the questions," he says, laughing wickedly. "You can't handle two questions at one time?"

"What can I tell ya? It's getting late." He's smiling at me, and God Almighty, those dimples do things to my body that I wish I could ignore and deny. He holds up a piece of paper, showing it to me. I have no clue what it is. "I may know where your mom is. I asked around, and came up with a few other places after you raced away." He hands the paper to me. "She's either at that address," he says, tapping the address on the paper. "Or she may be under the North Avenue Bridge. Either location it's probably best if you don't go alone."

Why does he care? "I'm good at taking care of myself."

"Those can be some dangerous locations." He's serious as he says it.

"Grace, who is it?" I hear Jess asking as she's walking to the door. She gets to us before I can answer her. "Oh. It's you," is all she says.

Nick looks over the top of my head and smiles at Jess. "Hi. How are you?"

"Fine," she says tightly. She crosses her arms, looks at Nick for a moment, then looks at me with raised eyebrows and turns and walks away.

"Are you going to invite me in?" he asks.

"We have company," I say.

"So, can I not come in? Are you maxed out at the number of people your condo can hold? You're not doing anything illegal are you?" He smiles as he says it.

"Fine, come in," I relent, but not hiding my aggravation.

Right as you step in our front door, there's a small seating area to the right. I move in that area, and Nick stands in front of me. He's still look-ing down at me. I'm trying to look everywhere else, but I settle back on his face. His scent floats to me. I breathe it in. My God, the man smells incredible. What does he wear, and can I bathe in it? With him? *What the hell am I thinking that for?* I get pissed about that, too.

"As I said, those are some rough places. You don't know what kind of people will be hanging out there."

I put my hands on my hips, completely frustrated by him. "Nick, what do you think I do all day long? Do you think I sit in my office and shuffle papers? Do you think that I see just the children and the foster parents? Where do you think those kids' biological parents are? Do you think they're all staying in the Hilton downtown, or maybe they all live here in my condo complex? I've been at DFCS longer than any other case worker. I know so many kids and teenagers and parents. I've lived in Athens my whole life. I've probably pounded streets and been in places you don't even know exist. I've been in rough places. I've talked to rough people. Hell, I know several of them. I probably know them better than you do. Do you have any idea at all what goes on at DFCS?"

He looks at me for a moment and says, "That was quite a speech." *Oh, he's being sarcastic again.* "No. I don't know what goes on at DFCS. I have a pretty good idea, but I'll keep it to myself, because you'll probably just get pissed, which seems to happen just about every time I talk to you." I go to say something, but he cuts me off and keeps talking. "You may have been places that I haven't and know people, but I seriously doubt it, since I'm a Robbery/Homicide Detective, and you're still not safer than I am because I'm the one that carries a weapon. And if you know them so much better, then how is it that I found your mom and you didn't? " He has raised his voice. *He did not just raise his voice to me!*

When I speak, I'm all but yelling. "Oh, that's nice! Throw my mom in my face. And you didn't even find her. You found two places that she may be staying. Like I said earlier, I have a brain, and that keeps me safe. I'm not a shrinking daisy. Just because you have a gun doesn't necessarily mean you're safer than I am. And what the hell is that supposed to mean, that I get all pissed when you talk to me? Maybe that happens because you're such a sarcastic son of a bitch!" My voice bounces off the walls. Okay, so I was yelling. Now, I'm breathing hard, and we're staring one another down. Well, I refuse to break eye contact.

"Your hair's prettier when it's down." His smile is wicked.

Huh? What the hell just happened? I'm feeling a little confused.

"I don't understand you at all," I say.

"Do I need to speak slower?" He's starting to laugh a little.

I hate him. No, I don't. Yes, I do. Good God, my blood pressure is going up. And, oh shit, there are those dimples again.

"You know damn well that I don't need you to speak slower."

"What're you doing Sunday?"

He's making my head spin. "Holy Heaven, Nick. I'm dizzy. Are you bi-polar?"

He laughs. "No. So I make you dizzy?"

"It's not a good dizzy. Why do you want to know what I'm doing on Sunday?"

"I don't know. I'm curious. Humor me. Answer the question."

"I hang with the homeless on Sundays."

My response cracks him up. Why, I don't know. He sees that I'm not laughing with him.

"You're not joking, are you?" he says.

"No."

"Why do you *hang* with the homeless on Sundays?"

"Why not?"

"Are you going to hug a tree after you finish with the homeless?" There he goes with the sarcasm again.

"Do you know the definition for compassion?"

"Maybe. So where do you *hang* with the homeless on Sundays?"

"Why do you want to know?"

He shrugs his massive shoulders. "Curiosity. Is there a quota that you have to fill in order to be considered a good social worker?"

"Okay, it's time for you to go. I've taken enough of your sarcasm and insults for one night. Thanks for the info on my mom."

"You think I'm insulting you again?"

"Do you not hear yourself speaking to me?"

"I thought you said you were no shrinking daisy." He's smiling a wicked smile again. He's all dancing dark blue eyes, perfect white teeth and dimples. I don't like it at all. *That's a damn lie.* I put my hands back on my hips again and regard him with a *get out of my condo* look. "Okay. I'm leaving. I meant what I said about your hair. It's too pretty to put up." He walks out the door without another word, and I get a look at his backside again. Damn. What a sight that is.

I close the door and lean against it, putting my head back and closing my eyes. Dammit, I held my breath again. I let every ounce of breath out of my lungs, take in a deep breath and let it out too.

He never did answer the question about how he knew where I lived. Well, he is a detective. I walk back in the living area, and the girls are staring at me. I sit, throw the piece of paper on the table that he handed me and pick up my glass of water, drinking it all. I put the glass down and look at them.

"What?" I ask.

"Jess said that's a detective that you met a couple of days ago," Ginger says.

"Yes. Unfortunately, my stupid car wouldn't start, and he happened to be the one driving by and saved the day." Now I'm being sarcastic. I think sarcasm's catching around here. I expel all of the air out of my lungs again. I can feel my blood pressure return to normal.

"Your face is really flushed, and that sounded intense," Angie says.

I ignore her and ask, "Are we ready to play?" I give them all a look that says *I don't want to talk about it.* I don't want to talk about *him.*

The girls look at one another and then back at me.

"Let's play," Jess says.

Chapter Four

"Let me take your hair down," he says softly. I feel his breath on my bare shoulder. He moves to take it down, and it falls all around me. He pushes it to the side, and his lips are on my neck. His kisses go from my neck to the top of my shoulder. I press into him and feel his erection pressing against my back.

"Nick," I moan.

He turns me around, looking down at me. His smile is sexy. He's running his hands down my naked body. He's still dressed, and I don't like that. He bends his head, kissing my neck, then lower to my breasts and then lower until he's running his tongue between my thighs, and then his tongue is in me.

I gasp. My eyes fly open, and I'm breathing hard. I'm staring straight up at my ceiling, and my room is pitch black. *What the fuck?* I almost had an orgasm in my sleep. Who in the hell has an orgasm in their sleep?

My body's on fire. My body's screaming for release. I was having a sex dream about Nick Bassano. I moan and roll over, pulling my pillow over my head. My dreams about him have been sexy, but this is the first dream where we're having sexual contact. This has got to stop. I can't take another night of this.

Why am I dreaming about someone that I don't like? I think he's attractive. Okay, he's sexy as shit, but he's such an ass. I hate him. I look at my clock. Dammit! It's slap in the middle of the night. I close my eyes, and visions of Nick are dancing behind my eyes. I don't want this.

I don't want him in my head. It's as if I've put up a *For Rent* sign, in my head and he's moved in. Well, he's getting evicted, starting now.

And, dammit, I'm all worked up. I'm going to have to take care of business, myself. So, that's what I do, but I'm unsatisfied. My orgasm ends up being like a firework that fizzled out. You light it and see the spark, but it dies down before the show gets started. I feel pissed and pouty about it. I need sex. *I want Nick Bassano*, and I don't want to want him. Why do I want someone that I hate?

I end up not going back to sleep. I'm on my side, staring out my window as the sun begins to rise. I'm exhausted. I get up and go downstairs, where I find Jess sitting at the table, reading the paper.

She looks up and smiles at me. "Good morning, sunshine," she says, way too damn cheery, and goes back to the newspaper.

"What's good about it?" I ask, grumpily.

I pour a cup of coffee add cream until it looks like I'm drinking coffee with my cream and sit at the table. I put my head down and close my eyes.

"You're grumpy this morning."

"I'm not sleeping well."

"I've noticed. I've noticed that you've not slept well in the last three nights and obviously now a fourth. Funny how that started after you met a certain detective."

I keep my head down. "I don't want to talk about him," I mumble.

"Okay."

I lift my head look at her. She's smiling and still reading her newspaper.

"I keep dreaming about him," I admit to her.

She looks up, smiling at me again. "You like him," she says.

I groan and put my head back on the table. "No, I don't. I hate him. He's an ass. I've never seen anyone with crazier mood swings, and he's so damn sarcastic and cocky."

"So, you're attracted to him."

"No," I say it too quickly. "I find him attractive. That's all," I admit.

"Okay, if you say so." She's smiling an innocent smile.

"I'm getting ready for work."

"Are you meeting William after work?"

Shit. I'd forgotten all about him.

"Yes," I mumble, walking out of the kitchen.

After my shower, I stand in my closet and think of what to wear. I'm not going to come home and change before meeting William. I long for the day when I can fill up this closet with clothes. My closet is enormous, but my clothes fill maybe a fourth of the space. I decide on a pair of black slacks with a slight flare, an indigo blue tank and a sheer chiffon blouse in the same color with ruffles down the front. When I'm satisfied with my appearance, I start the day.

The day drags, and I'm exhausted. I'm not in my usual cheery mood, and everyone notices it and asks me about it. That doesn't help my mood at all. I'm driving back to the office late in the day when I see a teenage girl walking her dog, going the other direction. I pass her and realize I know her. I find a place to turn around and drive back to her. I pull off onto the shoulder of the road and get out.

"Darla," I call.

I see Darla Grier freeze and then turn around. She's eyeing me suspiciously. I get a good look at her dog. She looks like she's walking a black mop instead of a dog. She was never in Foster Care, but DFCS was involved with her mom. There were serious drug issues and a boyfriend who enjoyed inflicting a lot of pain on her mom, and I would suspect Darla as well, but she would never say.

Her mom disappeared to Tennessee with the boyfriend; shortly after, Darla was placed with a family friend who agreed to care for her. The case worker that got the original intake was new, so I offered to help her out. The lady that agreed to take care of her is Belinda. I think that's her name. Belinda is part of the homeless now. I haven't seen Belinda in a long time, and the last time I saw her, she told me that Darla had run away and disappeared. That had to be a year ago. She hasn't moved from her spot.

"Who're you?" Her voice is hard for someone so young. I walk toward her. I see fear in her pretty blue eyes, and I wonder where that fear is coming from. What I don't see in her eyes is life. Her dog growls at me. "Hush Killer," she says to him, jerking his leash.

"You probably don't remember me. I'm Grace Harrison. I work at DFCS."

That doesn't relax her. She looks like a jumpy bunny, and she looks like she may bolt.

"So?"

"I heard a while back that you ran away. It's good to see you. Are you doing okay?"

She shrugs. I notice she has a pretty bad scar on her cheek. I don't remember ever seeing that before. She was cut by something that left a thin, lined scar.

"Is the welfare lady gonna come see me?"

"Do we need to?" I ask her, concerned. I take a look at the rest of her. She's skinny. She's too skinny. Her short blond hair looks unkempt and unclean, and I see track marks up and down both arms. She sees me looking at them and crosses them over her stomach. "How old are you now?"

"Seventeen, almost eighteen."

"Where're you staying?"

"Why do you wanna know?"

"Do you have someplace to stay? Are you safe?"

She laughs, but it's a bitter laugh. "Safe? Yeah. I got someplace safe to stay. I'm stayin' with this woman named Belinda."

"Oh, I'm so happy to hear that Belinda's off of the streets."

"You know her?"

"I do. I haven't seen her in a long time. I hang out with the homeless on Sundays." Darla Grier neither asks me why nor does she ask me if I'm hugging trees, like some other person. *Don't even let your mind go there.* "Darla, please be careful with the drugs. You have a lot of track marks on your arm."

"Why do you care? You gonna try and stop me?" she asks.

I would love to have that kind of power. I ignore the hostility coming off of her.

"No, but I would like to give you my card. If you ever need anything or decide to get clean and don't know where to go or how to do it, I can help." I pull my card out of my pocket and hold it out to her. She's hesitant to take it, but she finally does.

"I gotta go," she says.

"Take care," I tell her as she's walking away.

As I'm driving away, I notice that she's walking up the steps and onto a porch at a small, mustard-colored house. I go back to the office and spend some time talking with Valerie. I soak in her knowledge. We talk about work for a while and then weekend plans.

"Oh, I saw Darla Grier before I came back here," I tell her.

"Really? We never had her in Foster Care, did we?"

"No. We placed her with a lady named Belinda, and I don't remember her last name. Do you?"

Valerie looks thoughtful. "No. Names and faces start running together after several years, and I've been here only two years more than you. You're the memory bank around here for people, places, names and faces. How is she?"

I shake my head at her. "She's using. Whatever it is, she's shooting it."

"Meth?" Valerie asks, concerned.

"Probably. She looks bad. She's skinny and looks unkempt."

That throws us into a conversation about drug usage and how many cases we work with the main issue being drugs. There are so many. I realize the time, tell Valerie to have a happy weekend and make the short drive from North Avenue to Washington Street, which is located in downtown Athens.

I park in the parking deck that's attached to the Athens-Clarke County Courthouse. As I'm walking toward McCoy's Bourbon Bar, I get a text from William that he's running a little late. I walk in McCoy's, groaning when I see who's sitting at the bar. Nick looks at me and does a double take. My face flames, and I want to be any place but here.

My dream flashes through my mind. I don't want to think about my dream and especially when the star is right in front of me. How is it that I've never met this man until a few days ago, and now I can't get away from him? He's smiling at me. It's a wicked smile. Those dimples are on display, and it's sexy and I hate that I think it's sexy.

"Grace," he calls to me.

I walk toward him slowly. What kind of sarcastic remarks is he going to throw at me tonight?

"Hey," I say, forcing a smile.

I smell him, and he smells delicious. He's decked out in jeans and a dark navy blue and gray striped polo shirt. *Dammit*, he looks sexy.

"What're you doing here?" he asks.

Does the man have a lock down on the bar and allows only certain people to come and go?

"I'm on a date," I say.

He looks around me and smiles. "Is it with your imaginary friend?"

I don't know why, but it strikes me as funny. I don't want to laugh at anything he says, but I do in spite of myself.

"No. He's just running late."

"Running late? Men should never run late on dates. If they aren't going to show up on time, then don't show up at all."

"Is that from the Nick Bassano book on dating tips?"

He picks up his drink and takes a gulp and looks at me. "That's pretty good. I may have to keep that in mind."

"Are you drinking all alone tonight? Could you not find any friends to drink with you? Oh, wait, you probably don't have any friends."

"Look who's pulling out the sarcasm tonight." He's smiling devilishly when he says it. "No, I'm on a date. And no, she isn't imaginary. She's in the bathroom. Are you on a date with that guy from the other night?"

"Yes. As a matter of fact, I am."

"He's such a pussy," Nick says, laughing.

My mouth pops open. "He's not a pussy," I say, but I'm laughing a little too.

"You know most women don't like that word, but it just flies out of your mouth like you say it every day, and yes he is. You should try dating a real man. A man who shows up for a date on time."

"Oh really? Do you know any?"

"You're looking at one."

Is he offering? My heart feels like it's beating right out of my chest. The thought crosses my mind but only briefly. I still hate him; cocky, sexy, bastard.

"I think I'll take my chances with William."

"Oh, that's right. His name is William." He says it like he's testing out the name for the first time. He pats the bar chair beside him. "Sit. What would you like to drink? Some white wine or a wine cooler?"

I look at him. I'm totally confused by him.

"I'm a little scared," I say, eyeing him, suspiciously.

"Of wine?"

I'm laughing as I say, "No. I'm not scared of wine." I regard him with a look that has to say *Who are you, and what have you done with the real Nick Bassano?* "You're being sort of nice. It's throwing me off. Why would you assume that I would want a white wine or a wine cooler?"

"It sounds like something you social workers would like."

"Well, I guess I spoke too soon on the nice part," I mutter. I pull the seat over to put some distance between him and me. I don't want to sit that close to him.

"Do you think I'm going to bite you?"

"My chair was basically in your lap."

"I wasn't complaining." His smile is still wicked.

"Your date might."

"She's not my girlfriend."

I ignore that comment. "What're you drinking?" I ask, pointing to his glass.

"Jack Daniel's, straight."

"I'll have the same."

"You like whiskey?"

"Why would I ask for one if I didn't?" I snap.

I hear him chuckle as I look in my bag and pull out my wallet. I have enough cash for at least two drinks. I won't drink any more than that. Nick calls over the bartender by his first name.

"Bart. Another for me, and the same for the lady, please." He looks down at me. "What're you doing?"

Sitting here, talking, trying not to breathe your scent, trying to get my heart rate back to normal, hating you, wishing my date would come. I'm momentarily confused by his question. I realize he's looking at the money in my hand.

"I'm paying for my drink."

"No, you're not. I invited you to sit with me. What kind of a man would I be if I made you pay for your own drink?"

"You're a confusing man. I can pay for my own drink, thank you very much. I've got this."

"Bart, don't take her money. You've got my tab going." He gives me a look. His eyes have gotten even darker than they already are. Holy Heaven, it's really sexy the way he's looking at me. I hate him. Well, maybe I've moved from hate to dislike. I really want to keep hating him.

There's a lady that approaches us. Her seat's very close to Nick's. I have to bite my lip from laughing out loud. I want to ask her if she's going to work at the strip club down the street after her date. Her breasts are definitely implants, and she's obviously not wearing a bra. Her top couldn't be tighter, and the cut couldn't be lower. I wasn't even aware that jeans were made to fit that tight. They're way beyond low cut. *I hope she waxes.*

"Hey, baby," she says. "A glass of wine, please?"

"Sure," Nick says. He looks over at me.

I have my eyebrow raised at him. "Is she a social worker too?" I ask, smiling.

"No," he says, laughing. He turns back to his date and gets her attention. "Brandi, this is Grace. Grace, Brandi," he says, by way of introduction.

I'm nearly chewing on my lip to keep from exploding with laughter as she sits in her seat and has this look of total confusion on her face. She keeps looking all around her, for what, I don't know. She's definitely a keeper. I don't think her bulb is screwed in all the way.

"Hi," she says, waving at me as if I was way across the room instead of one seat away.

"Hi. It's nice to meet you," I say, smiling.

Bart brings me my drink. I see William coming in and smile at him.

"I'm so sorry I'm late," he says to me.

"It's okay. Don't worry about it."

He focuses his attention beyond me and sees Nick, and then beyond Nick, getting an eyeful of Brandi. He looks at her for several moments and then focuses his attention back to Nick.

"Oh, hey. I met you the other night," William says, holding out his hand.

They shake hands with one another. I notice Nick uses a little more force than what is really necessary. Is he going to pull his penis out next and try to compare it? Oh, why did I even think that? I push that thought straight out of my head.

"What're you drinking?" William asks me.

"Jack Daniel's," I say, holding up my glass.

The bartender comes over to William, and he orders a beer. The bar is beginning to fill with what looks like mostly a crowd that's getting off from work and ready to start the weekend. William slides into a seat beside me and starts talking about what he's been doing today. Again, I notice he asks me nothing about my day or about me.

He then attempts to regale me with tales of his day. I hear in excruciating detail what he's done from the time he woke up until he sat down at the bar. I nod a lot, and I say *right* even more. After this has gone on for several minutes, or has it been close to an hour? I've lost track. I do feel like my eyes are going to roll back in their sockets. William finally takes a breath and a drink.

Nick takes this opportunity, leaning into me and whispering in my ear, "Men should always ask their dates about their day. That's in the book, too. He *is* a pussy."

I bite my lip so I don't laugh. I can't see Nick's face because my back is slightly turned so I could give my attention to William. I see William frowning, but he goes back to talking. I'm not sure what he's saying because the next thing I know, Nick's yelling,

"So, Brandi, how has your day been?" He says it so loud that I jump in my seat, and I notice several people stop their conversations and look briefly at him, William being one of them.

I turn my attention to Brandi, and the poor girl looks lost and still confused. Now that I think about it, I actually haven't heard her put a complete sentence together. Is she capable?

"It's been good, baby. I thought we talked about that?"

"I just wanted to make sure that I knew all of the details of your day." He's not yelling, but he's talking too loud. Brandi still looks terribly confused. I doubt Nick's dating her for her wisdom.

I look at Nick, who has turned to look at me. His smile tells me he knows exactly what he's doing. He winks at me, and I grab onto my seat so I don't fall off. Shit, that was all kinds of hotness right there.

While I know what Nick's doing, it completely flies over William's head. The next thing out of his mouth is his life growing up in Oconee County. I look up while he's still talking and see Judge Wright and his wife Shirley walk in. He sees me, too, and smiles as they walk over to us.

"Hello, Grace. Good evening to you. How are you?" We shake hands.

"Wonderful, Judge. How are you?"

"I couldn't be happier that it's Friday. Have you ever met my wife, Shirley?"

Shirley Wright is a little shorter than I am. She looks like she fell out of a magazine. She's a beautiful woman with dark brown hair like mine, but it's wavy, and she looks like she may spend a small fortune on her cut. She's lean and has the build of someone who works out at the gym with a personal trainer several times a week.

"No. Hi. I'm Grace Harrison. I'm a Case Manager at DFCS. It's so nice to meet you," I say, shaking her hand.

"It's nice to meet you, too. It's nice to put a name with a face."

I blush. I had no idea that Judge Wright had ever talked about me to anyone, especially his wife.

"Grace is being far too modest. She's the best Case Manager at DFCS. She'll be Director one day." He's smiling broadly at me.

I blush furiously. "Thank you, Judge, you're too kind."

Nick takes this opportunity, and I have no idea why, to introduce himself.

"Judge Wright, I'm Nick Bassano. I'm a Detective at the police department." He holds out his hand for the Judge.

"Hello, Nick. It's great to meet you. Are you here with Grace tonight?"

"No," I say, too sharply. "This is my date," I say, directing his attention to William, who now looks like he's sulking.

When William introduces himself, Judge Wright realizes that he knows William's father. The Judge and his wife order drinks and invite us to sit with them at a table farther back in the bar. I grab my drink and look at Nick.

"Thank you for the drink," I say, walking away.

We find a table, and the only place for me to sit is with my back against the wall. I don't mind, but I have a bird's eye view of the bar and of Nick, whom I'm trying not to look at. Judge Wright and William are talking about law, William's father and golfing. *Boring.* I would punch myself in the face before being talked into playing golf.

I keep watching Nick, and at times, he turns and looks right at me. When that happens, I drop my eyes. Sometimes, I don't drop my eyes quickly enough, and I see him grinning at me, and it's sexy as shit.

"Grace," Shirley Wright says to me, getting my attention.

"Yes, ma'am."

"Do you ever get sad about all those poor children?"

I give it some thought. Not because I have to think about my answer, but because I don't want to seem like I'm answering too quickly.

"No ma'am. There are definitely situations that are sad. But, I decided a long time ago that if I'm going to be overly emotional about every situation, I wouldn't last. And I don't want to do anything else but what I'm doing right now."

"You sound dedicated."

"I would like to think that I am."

"Eric speaks very highly of you."

"I think very highly of him."

I like Shirley Wright. She smiles a lot, and she's very nice. I think for a fleeting moment what it would've been like to have parents like these two. I find myself glancing in Nick's direction far more than I should, and besides, I remind myself, I dislike him. I don't know how he knows when I'm looking at him, but he does, and he's glancing in my direction too. Sometimes he doesn't smile, but the look he's giving me is almost seductive. I find that I'm breathing a little faster.

I'm enjoying my evening with Judge Wright and his wife, but I'm not so much enjoying William. When he's not talking to Judge Wright, I try to engage him in some form of conversation, and he gives me short answers and then ignores me. So, it's going to be like that. William looks at his watch and says that he has someplace else to be. He doesn't offer to call me, and I don't ask. I don't know what his problem is, and I decide I don't care.

I'm talking with the Judge and Mrs. Wright, but I can't help but notice that it doesn't look as if Nick's date with Brandi is faring much better. She looks mad, and she looks like she's giving him an earful. Whatever he says to her doesn't calm her and makes her even angrier. I watch as she storms out.

Nick turns and looks at me. His look is seductive and dark, and it's plain sexy. I don't want to look at him. Even more, I don't want to like looking at him. He's holding my eyes with his. I have to look away; his gaze is too penetrating. I see Judge Wright looking at his watch.

"Grace, I hate to leave you here all alone, but the missus and I have dinner plans with some friends. Are you meeting anyone else?"

"No, sir. Don't worry about it. I'm fine. Enjoy your dinner and your weekend. Mrs. Wright, it was so nice to meet you."

"It was a pleasure meeting you too, Grace," she says, smiling warmly at me.

They leave, and I sit, twirling my glass in my hands thinking of what to do for the remainder of my evening.

"Can I sit?" I hear Nick ask me. I nod my head, not looking up at him. "Where did William rush off to?"

I look up and into his eyes. Dammit. His eyes are smoldering.

"He had some other place to be."

"So, the guy shows up late and then leaves before the date is over, essentially leaving you alone." He sounds almost angry about it.

"I guess that's a 'no no' in your dating book."

"You should never the leave the date early when there's a beautiful woman sitting with you." He lets that hang in the air.

Huh? Is he referring to me? Or is he talking generals here? I'm confused. Well, that's nothing new when it comes to him. His eyes are sparkling, and his smile is wicked sexy.

"Where did Brandi go?" I ask.

"I guess the same place as William." He's so sarcastic about it, but it doesn't bother me. I find it funny. "I'm going to ask you a question, but I don't want you to get all pissed about it, okay?"

Oh, Holy Heaven, what's he going to ask me? "Okay."

"Why do you hang with the homeless?"

"Because I was homeless," I say matter-of-factly. No reason to beat around the bush about it. I can see that my answer takes him by surprise. He doesn't say anything for several seconds.

"Oh," is what he says when he finally speaks.

"No snappy comeback or sarcastic remark?" I ask, smiling.

"No," he says, not smiling. "Were you homeless for a long time?"

"From fifteen until I was twenty. Life isn't much fun when you don't have much to call your own, and no one place to call your own."

"You were homeless at fifteen?" he asks incredulously.

"Yes. It's a long story."

He doesn't say anything for a moment. "Are you going to tell me the story?"

"No."

"Why not?"

"Because I don't want to."

He nods at me, understanding that I'm not going to say anything else on the matter.

"Now that you aren't homeless, why would you want to be with people and places that remind you of that time?"

"You just answered your own question. I like looking how far I've come and my accomplishments. I like being with that particular population and hoping that I might be an inspiration to maybe *one* person. I like talking to people who otherwise feel invisible. I remember that feeling all too well of feeling invisible. It was as if people looked right through me."

"You're always very passionate when you speak. It doesn't matter what you're speaking about. It's one thing that draws me to you."

Did he just say he's drawn to me? I want to ask him to repeat himself, but he probably would come back with a sarcastic remark.

"You're drawn to me, but yet you're sarcastic towards me, and you insult me?"

"It's because I like you."

I'm so confused by this man. I feel totally off balance.

"You like me, so you're going to insult me and make sarcastic asshole remarks to me. You realize that makes absolutely no sense whatsoever, right?"

"It does in my head," he says. He picks up his glass and drinks. He's looking at me the whole time he does this. My body temperature is rising under his gaze. I realize I'm holding my breath. "I don't want to like you, and I don't want you to like me."

"Well, that makes two of us," I mutter, but he hears it and smiles. I still don't understand what he's talking about.

"If I'm rude to you, then you won't want to be around me."

"You're talking like I want to be around you. That sounds a little egotistical if you ask me."

"I wasn't asking you," he says, but he's smiling about it. "I think you're attracted to me."

Well, damn, he's blunt.

"You sound pretty sure of yourself."

"Am I wrong?" he demands.

How did the conversation about me being homeless get to him wanting to know if I'm attracted to him? No, I'm not attracted to him. Yes, I am. *No, I'm not!*

"I'm not attracted to you." *Liar.* He doesn't seem to be fazed by my comment in the least. There's a slow smile that plays across his lips. We have to get off of this subject. "Where're you from?"

"New York City."

"Why did you decide to move from New York to Athens, Georgia?" I ask, intrigued.

"My parents are here. My mom had a stroke five years ago. I have an older brother, but he's married with two kids, and her parents are still there. I'm not married, so it was easy for me to pull up and move here to help my dad out."

Wow! That's sweet, and it seems out of character for him.

"Were you a detective in New York?"

"Yes. I worked Homicide there too, and that was it. I work a variety of crimes here, along with homicides."

"Such as?" I ask.

"Aggravated assault, robbery and armed robbery. If it's a violent felony crime, we get it, but not sex crimes."

"Interesting," I say. I point to his tattoo. "How long were you in the Marines?"

"Eight years."

"Did you like it?"

"No, I hated it; that's why I stayed in for so long. Do you think I would've stayed eight years if I didn't?"

Well, I see the sarcasm isn't always far away.

"I don't know how long you served. I was wondering if I was really sitting across from you because, you've not been sarcastic towards me, oh, in at least the last forty-five minutes." I'm smiling as I say it.

His answering smile dazzles me. His teeth are just so perfect and white. His olive features just enhance how white they are. And then there are those damn dimples. Oh, I don't want this. I don't want these feelings. I don't want to be attracted to him.

"It's a four-year commitment, and then I re-upped for four more years. Do you want to know why Brandi left?"

Talk about changing the subject. I really don't want to know, because I don't care.

"Not really."

He tells me anyway.

"She was mad because I kept looking at you. I like looking at beautiful women."

Did he just call me beautiful? I've been called pretty. Hell, I think *I am* pretty. I've been called good looking and fine, and I think one guy even said I was fine-assed. I could never understand if he thought I was fine or if he thought my ass was fine, or both. It's one compliment that I could've lived without, but I have not ever been called beautiful. None of my ex-boyfriends ever said that.

His smile is seductive, and his eyes are darker. My body temperature, which had returned to normal, has gone back up.

"Do you have any other plans tonight?" His voice has dropped, and it's low and sexy.

Do I want to know why he's asking?

"No, why?" I ask, hesitantly.

He leans over the table and says, "I want to take you home with me and fuck you."

I gasp. My heart skips one, two, three beats and drops in my stomach, and then everything shifts south, all the way down in between my thighs, where everything has tightened. *Shit!* No one has ever put it like that to me before. I've gotten the standard *wanting to have sex* or *wanting to make love,* but to come out and say that he wants to *fuck me*, it's so dirty and wanton the way he says it. *It's so hot.*

I am completely turned on by his words. I'm completely turned on by the thought of him fucking me. I bet he's good in bed. No, I bet he's great in bed. I'm burning. Can he see that my whole body has just been lit on fire? The idea of his naked body against my naked body, *shit!* I'm squirming in my seat as desire churns inside my thighs. My dream shoots through my mind. His mouth on my breasts, his tongue…*Stop!* This isn't going to happen.

"I don't want to be a notch on your belt, Nick," I say, holding his eyes.

"Is that what you think you'd be?"

"You can't take Brandi home, but you're going to go home with someone, and you choose someone that's second best?"

"Do you think that way about yourself?" he snaps at me.

"Do you?" I snap right back. I'm beginning to get angry. Good. Anger is good; wanting him isn't. "I have to go." I jump up and grab my handbag.

He jumps up and is right on my heels. "Are you walking away from me again?"

"Yes," I say and keep walking, offering no other explanation. I just know that I have to get out of here, and I have to get away from this man.

I'm out the door and walking as fast as I can to my car. Nick follows me the whole way there. I'm at my car, fumbling with my keys, when he grabs my arm, spins me around and bends down, and his hands are on my face, and his lips are on mine. His tongue invades my mouth. I don't fight him because I realize I don't want to fight him. It's not a soft kiss. It's raw, and I can taste the desire. I taste him, and he tastes sweeter than any candy I've had, *ever*. I give him my tongue. They're swirling around each other. He has me pinned against him and my car.

My God, the man is hard all over. I feel it as I run my hands from his chest to his neck. It's like holding onto a rock. I'm stretched up as far as I can go on my toes, and that presses me even more into him. Oh, my God, I want this man, and I feel his erection pressing against me, telling me that he wants me too. I moan into the kiss. I've been kissed well in my years. Hell, I've been kissed very well, but this is off the charts. His kiss just shoots me straight in the stratosphere.

He drags his lips from mine and looks down at me. Oh, Holy Heaven. His eyes are dark, and I see the hunger for me in them. We're both breathing heavy.

"What can I do to convince you to come home with me?" he asks, pushing a wayward curl out of my face. His voice is still low and sexy. I have to stay resolved, but I do feel it crumble some.

"You can't," I say, breathlessly.

He nods that he understands, pulls his fingers through my curls one more time and steps away from me. As I'm getting in my car, he says to me, "You're not second best," and walks away.

I realize I'm trembling as I start the car and drive away. Of course, I dream about him when I finally fall asleep.

Chapter Five

"Every time I walk by, you're staring at the same screen."

I look over and see Valerie perched on the edge of my desk. She's smiling kindly at me.

"You weren't yourself most of last week. I thought the weekend would help, but here we are mid-week, and you still aren't yourself. Is there anything wrong?"

What can I say? There's a man that I dream about every night, whom I don't like-- at least, I don't think I like him. He said he likes me, but what the hell does that really mean? And he drives me crazy, but kissed me like I've never been kissed before and wants to fuck me, and the more I've been thinking about it, that sounds pretty damn good to me.

"I'm good," I tell her.

"If you say so. You know my door's always open to you on all matters," Valerie says, smiling at me. She pats me on the shoulder and walks away.

I go back to staring at my computer screen and know that I need to get some work done here in the office while I have the time. I need to be typing. I need to be making some phone calls. There are a lot of things that I need to be doing. But the reality is, I'm thinking of *him.*

I've tried to put Nick out of my mind. I've tried hard. I stayed busy over the weekend. I cleaned the condo, even though it didn't need it. I forced Jess to go on a walk for an hour. I was going to walk longer, but she started bitching about being tired. I went to the movies with one of my co-workers. Anytime I was downtown over the weekend, I kept finding myself looking for him. I never saw him, and I was disappointed.

I'm very attracted to Nick. Way more attracted than I want to be. Mike from the Salvation Army called me late on Saturday, and we met up for dinner. He's a great guy, but I found my mind on Nick and the way he kissed me and the way his body felt against mine. *I want to take you home with me and fuck you.*

It left me frustrated on different levels. I was frustrated for thinking of him when I was trying hard not to. Plus, I had evicted him from my head, but he wouldn't stay gone. There's the sexual frustration. There's the frustration that not only do I think he's attractive, but I am attracted to him. There's just frustration.

It didn't help anything getting into a fight with Matt on Sunday after finding him under the North Avenue Bridge. He looked worse if that was possible. My mother wasn't there, but Matt said he'd seen her. I asked him where he had seen her, and he said he couldn't remember. I don't think he was lying about it. Matt was incredibly high when I saw him. We fought over Naomi. He asked me what I had found out about her, and when I told him I hadn't found anything out about her, he went off on me.

It was a drug-fueled rant, but it pissed me off when he accused me of not caring. He accused the police of not doing enough, and my reassurance to him that they had done everything that they could didn't help him. He started screaming again about Naomi being kidnapped, and I attempted to get him to reason that out with me, to no avail. I tried to convince him to let me take him to a treatment facility for detox. That was a stupid mistake on my part for bringing that up, yet again. I shouldn't have tried, but I was feeling pretty desperate. He cussed me, walked away from me and told me not to bother him.

The last couple of days here at work have been so busy that I've not been able to do much else other than work. Court was lengthy on Monday. I ran all over the county yesterday and even into other counties seeing some kids and chasing down one of the mothers on my caseload in an attempt to get her to sign a case plan that she should've signed thirty days ago. I couldn't find her and cussed all the way back to the office. It didn't make me feel any better. I've done little else other than work the last couple of days, and my mind didn't wander as much. But today is a different story. I feel I've been pretty useless. I shake my head in attempt to remove all of the thoughts that I don't want. It doesn't work. I have to get back to work. I put my hands on the keyboard when my phone rings.

"Grace Harrison."

"Grace, it's Rose DeWitt."

Rose and her husband Stan are foster parents, and they're my favorite parents. She sounds upset.

"What's wrong?"

"Misty left the house yesterday after getting upset. We thought she needed some cooling off time, but she never came back. I know we should have called y'all, but you know she's done this before, and she always comes back the next day. Stan drove around most of the night looking for her. We decided to wait for her to come back, but she's still not home. We're worried, Grace. I'm so sorry we've not called you until now. We really thought she would come back. We want to go to the police and do a Missing Persons Report, but we talked and thought we'd better call you and tell you what's happening."

"Rose, calm down," I say. "As you said, she's done this before. We've all seen it happen over and over again this past year."

"But she's always back by now."

"She knows her mom's parental rights are about to be terminated. She's probably more upset than usual. I'll meet you at the police department. Do you have a recent picture of Misty?"

"Yes. Her Spring school pictures were taken a few weeks ago. We got them last week."

"Perfect. Take a deep breath, and calm down. I'll meet you there in less than thirty minutes."

"Okay," she says.

I close my eyes and pinch the bridge of my nose. I finish up with what I was working on, which is easy, since I had basically been doing nothing. I find Valerie in her office, talking with the Social Services Administrator, Bev Watson. They're talking about shopping.

"Rose DeWitt called me. Misty Price ran away again, and she hasn't returned. Rose and Stan are worried and upset. I'm going to meet them out at the police department and file a Missing Persons Report."

"Okay. Keep me informed," Valerie says. She and Bev go back to talking about shopping.

I grab everything that I think I might need and leave. None of us are overly concerned about this. Misty runs away at least once a month, if not more. She's been in Foster Care for a little over two years. Misty's mother actually dropped her at the front of the office with a duffel bag full of clothes and left. The poor girl had to come in to the office all alone. We searched for her mother. The police searched for her mother. We found nothing. We looked for family members that Misty could live with. We found an alcoholic grandmother and decided quickly that wouldn't work.

She was placed with the DeWitts and pushed boundaries from the very beginning. The DeWitts have been foster parents for nearly fifteen years. She would push as far as she thought she could go, and they would love her even more. I started working on the process to terminate her mother's parental rights a few months back. Misty has been in a downward spiral since then. The DeWitts increased her visits to her therapist, but it's done little to help. She has so much anger, and she can't let it go.

Misty doesn't want to be with her mother, but she doesn't want her mother's rights terminated, either. She wants to be adopted but knows that can't happen unless we take that final step and terminate her mother's rights. She's struggled with so many conflicting emotions, and on top of all of that we've found no takers wanting to adopt Misty. The DeWitts have agreed to let her stay until she turns eighteen, but that's three years away. It breaks my heart that we can't find someone, anyone, that wants to call her their daughter.

I tend to get angry and vent when I think of the teens that need to be adopted. People want babies and young children. They reach their teen years, and suddenly no one is interested. I want to scream at them that they're still children and need and deserve loving homes and parents as much as the younger kids.

I pull in the police department parking lot. I wonder if Nick's here. I wonder if I could try to see him. And say what? *I thought about your offer on Friday night and want to take you up on it now?* It's laughable. I find Rose standing inside the door. She looks distraught. She hugs me tight when she sees me.

"I'm really sorry," she says.

I put my hands on her arms and pull her away from me and look at her.

"For what?"

"For not calling sooner."

"Rose, I'm not second guessing your decisions. Bev was in Valerie's office when I told them where I was going. It's okay. She's going to come back. She always does."

"It's just that it's getting later and later, and she's still not home."

"Have faith, Rose. She'll be back. Where's Stan?"

"He stayed back to stay with the other kids and to be home in case she did come home."

"Let's go file that report. I bet that once it's taken, and we leave, she's going to show up."

"I hope so. I'm very worried about her."

We walk and stand in front of the window and wait for Juliana Carson to finish her phone call.

"Can I help you?" she asks, after getting off of the phone.

"Yes ma'am. I'm Grace Harrison from DFCS, and this is Rose DeWitt. She's one of our foster parents. One of the girls on my caseload has run away, and we would like to report her missing."

"Is she under the age of eighteen?"

"Yes, ma'am."

"Have a seat. I'll call and see if there's a desk Sergeant available. If not, I'll call for an officer. It may be a few minutes before someone can meet with you if a Sergeant isn't here. All of our officers are out on calls."

"That's fine," I say and direct Rose to a chair.

I'm talking to Rose about everything that I can think of to divert her attention. I get her talking about her son. He's the DeWitts' only child, and he's graduate student at UC Berkeley in California. Once she gets going about her son, she relaxes somewhat and tells me about him living out in California and that he's met someone, and is getting serious about her. Rose says she thinks he's going to ask her to marry him, and she's excited about it.

I see a door open, and Nick walks out. My mouth goes dry. My heart begins to beat faster. He looks good. Bad choice of words; he looks hot in his dark gray dress pants and a long-sleeved, white button up shirt and a tie that pulls the whole thing together. The man can dress, and he dresses well. *I want to take you home with me and fuck you.*

His statement pulls at my body, right between my thighs, and I find that I want to be up against him again. God, it's hot in here. I want to yell at someone to turn the damn AC on.

"Mr..." He freezes when he sees me.

"I'll be right back, Rose," I say, getting up.

I want to fan myself as I walk over to him. He steps out of the door, letting it shut behind him.

"Hey," I say, walking to him and looking up in his eyes.

"Hey. What're you doing here?" His voice is softer, kinder. It's throwing me off balance, him talking to me like that. It confuses me. That's nothing new.

"There's a girl on my caseload that ran away, and we're here to file a Missing Persons Report."

"Is Juliana taking care of you?"

"Yes. Thank you."

There's a lengthy silence between us as we stand assessing one another. Holy Heaven, he smells so damn good. I could stand here and breathe it in for the rest of the day. I'm mentally undressing him with my eyes. *Stop it!* He's looking at me like he might be thinking the same thing. I'm not sure, but *damn someone turn on the AC for God's sake!*

"Grace, I wanted to call you and remembered I didn't have your number. I didn't know how you would feel about me showing up on your doorstep again. Of course, if I'd called, I'm not sure that phone of yours would've worked." He's smiling now. His eyes are more lit up. I find myself staring in them. "I wanted to tell you that I'm sorry for the way I kissed you on Friday night."

"I'm not," I say quickly.

I can see that my response surprises him. His smile gets bigger, and Holy Heaven, there go the dimples. I want to go on to say that I'd like a rewind of Friday night, and I would most definitely give my answer some thought.

"What would you say to a date this Friday? I'll show up on time and not leave early." His eyes are dancing now.

I don't know why I'm even thinking about my answer, because I'm going to say yes. I'm so damn attracted to this man, there's no way I'm going to say no.

"Sounds fun," I say, smiling back at him.

"Are you going to get mad and walk away from me?"

"Depends," I say.

We stand here, smiling at one another.

"You look beautiful, by the way. That color looks great against your skin."

Wow! He called me beautiful again. I like how it rolls off his tongue. He really knows how to throw a curveball at me. He says things so unexpectedly, and it comes out sweet. I think maybe he is bi-polar and has never been diagnosed. I'm wearing the same thing that I had on Friday night.

"Thank you," I say, when I find my voice.

"Do you have a picture of the girl on your caseload?"

"Oh, sure. Rose brought one with her."

He walks beside me back to Rose. She smiles when she looks up at him.

"Is this the officer that's going to take the report?" she asks.

"Oh. No, Rose. This is Detective Bassano. He works in Robbery/Homicide." I see her eyes go wide, and I realize how that sounded to her. I hold my hands out to her like I'm waving at her. "Sorry, Rose. I'm so sorry. I know Nick. I was telling him why we're here. He wanted to see Misty's picture."

She relaxes and pulls out the picture that she brought, handing it to Nick. He takes it and looks at it.

"She's pretty. What's her name?" he asks, handing it back to Rose.

"Misty Price. I hope she's okay," Rose says, looking at the picture.

"She is, Rose." I look up at Nick. "She's run away before. She's usually home by now, but I told Rose that I think Misty is more upset than usual. I'm starting the process for her mother's rights to be terminated. She's been having a hard time with that."

He looks down at Rose. "Grace is probably right. Try not to worry too much." He looks at me. "I've got to interview someone," he says, pointing at a man that has been waiting quietly.

"Okay," I say, looking up at him.

"I'll call you later, and we'll figure Friday out. I would text you, but that might kill your phone," he says, laughing. I laugh too. I don't care that he's poking fun at me. He turns to walk to the guy that has been waiting for him.

"Nick," I say, smiling.

"Yeah."

"How are you going to call if you don't have my number?"

"I was going to get it from the phone fairy." His smile is wicked. He pulls his phone out of its holder that is clipped to his belt, close to his badge.

"That looks like it could launch missiles," I say, grinning up at him, teasing him about his iPhone.

"You know I've been wondering what that sound is in the sky when I'm calling someone." We're laughing together as he's punching my number in. He gives me his number, too. "I'll call you later," he says, looking in my eyes.

He takes the guy and walks to the door to lead them into the belly of the police department. His turns around and winks at me. Dammit. I almost fall out of my seat. I take a deep breath and look over at Rose.

"That's a very big man," she says.

"Yes, he is," I agree, smiling.

"He's handsome," she says.

"He's something else," I say, letting out a long, slow breath. *Wow!*

I see Officer Blake Scott come through the door. He pulls his sunglasses off and smiles when he sees me. Blake's the District Attorney's younger brother. I like him. Like Brison, he's a family man. He's a new father for the second time.

"Hi, Grace," he says, hugging me.

"Hey, Blake. How's that sweet new baby boy?"

"Hungry all the time. I don't know how Brooke keeps up with his appetite, but she does. Do you have a missing kid?"

"Yes. Misty Price is in Foster Care. She ran away last night and hasn't returned. This is Rose, her foster mother. We wanted to report her missing."

"Sure. Let's go back and sit, and I'll get all of her information."

We go with Blake behind the locked doors. I scan quickly for Nick, but I don't see him. We sit with Blake, and Rose and I give him all of the information necessary, as well as all of Misty's background information and what's been happening to her recently. Rose gives him Misty's picture. He explains that a BOLO will be put out for her.

"Ms. DeWitt, we see this all the time with teenagers. They may stay gone one, two maybe three days. They eventually return when they see how tough it is to survive on their own." Rose is nodding that she understands. "And like Grace said, if Misty's having a hard time with what's about to happen to her, she may just need some cooling off and thinking time. She sounds like a pretty resourceful girl."

"She is that," Rose agrees, smiling.

We finish with what we need to do and thank Blake. As I'm leaving, I look for Nick again, but I don't see him. I walk Rose to her car.

"I'll call you if I hear anything. Try to relax. I'm going to drive around to some of the places where she's run to before."

"Okay. I'll call you when she comes home. I have to say when. I can't say if."

I hug her and drive away. I go to several locations, but I don't find her at any of them. The people that I talk to haven't seen her. It doesn't concern me. Misty goes from being an absolute loner to hanging with all different kinds of people back to being a loner. I call Valerie on my way home and let her know that the police report has been filed and that I attempted to find Misty as well. Valerie is satisfied, and I tell her that I'll call her if I hear any news. I eventually make my way home. It takes forever. Traffic is insane. I walk in the door, and Jess is calling my name.

"Grace."

"What?" I yell.

"I'm hungry," she says, looking at me from where she's sitting on the couch.

"Me too," I say. "I'm going to change. What sounds good?"

"Anything. You pick tonight."

"I'll think about it while I'm changing."

I change quickly and suggest Waffle House just down the road on Epps Bridge Parkway in the Kroger Shopping Center. Jess agrees. She drives separately, since she's going straight to Jake's after we eat. We sit in a booth and order.

"Did you have a good day, today?" Jess asks, sipping on her drink.

"I did, and I saw Nick today," I tell her.

"And?"

"He asked me out."

"And?"

"I said yes."

"Okay," she says. She's not smiling.

"You don't approve."

"My first impression of him isn't good, but I know you're attracted to him, and I trust your judgment."

"Yes. I'm attracted to him," I say, grudgingly.

"Well, it's about damn time you admitted it," she says, laughing. "William said you couldn't keep your eyes off of him and that Nick couldn't keep his eyes off of you."

I thought I was being subtle about looking at Nick. Apparently, I was not. Jess and I haven't talked about my unsuccessful date with William. I think she has avoided it since it would drag Nick into it, and I've tried to steer clear of anything to do with him. Not any longer. My resolve is definitely crumbling further.

"Nick couldn't keep his hands off of me, either."

She raises her eyebrows at me. "Excuse me?"

"He kissed me Friday night."

"And how was that?"

I expel all of the air out of my lungs and say, "Wow."

"That good?"

I nod my head and say,"Yeah, that good."

"At least you know he's a good kisser," Jess says, laughing. I laugh with her.

I look at her, grinning. "He wanted to take me home with him."

Her eyes pop, and her jaw all but hits the table. "I'm guessing you said no."

"You guess right." I lean into the table, and Jess does the same. "I'm kind of kicking myself in the ass about it now." I lean back and start fanning myself. Jess laughs at me. "Okay. We have to change the subject." I continue to fan myself.

I tell her about Misty and everything that surrounds that situation. She tells me that she and Jake are leaving Saturday for the beach and will be gone all of Spring Break. I'm insanely jealous and tell her as much.

"Will you bottle some sea water, some sand and seashells and bring them to me?" I ask her.

"Of course. You only have to make it until June, and then we'll be at the beach together."

"And, I can't wait," I say, smiling at her.

My very first trip to the beach was a gift from Jess's parents to me, several years ago. Max and Susan Rider were shocked to learn that it was my very first trip anywhere. They knew that I had little family. What they didn't know was the details of my past. I shared some of it with Jess's mom. From then on, I go to the beach with them every summer, and I ski with them every winter.

We've never skied the same place twice. I've been to Colorado, Wyoming, North Carolina and Tennessee. They're wonderful to me. They pay for my trips that I take with them. I was uncomfortable at first, and Susan explained to me that she always wanted another daughter. She loves Jess's younger twin brothers, but she did want another girl. She said she felt like she had found that in me and to not argue about them taking me on trips. I was incredibly touched by that, so I stopped the arguing. We talk about going to the beach in June and what beach we are going to this year. I hope we go back to someplace in the Caribbean. That's the most beautiful body of water I've ever seen. It really doesn't matter, though, I'm just lucky that I get to go anywhere.

Jess heads to Jake's after we finish eating, and I head home. I consider briefly calling some friends and going downtown tonight, but I'm exhausted and have to work tomorrow. I watch a comedy and laugh like a crazy person. I decide that taking a hot shower and going to bed sounds better than anything else, and that's exactly what I do.

Chapter Six

There it is again. I cannot understand why a constant nagging bell keeps going through my head. It's annoying the shit out of me. I roll over and open my eyes and realize the bell in my head is the doorbell. I look at the clock. *Who in the hell is ringing the bell this late or this early?* I get up and stagger downstairs. I look in the peephole. *Shit.* It's Nick. I open the door, and he looks like death warmed over.

"Do you have any clue what time it is?" I ask, my voice full of sleep. He says nothing to me and pushes past me. "Come right in," I mutter, shutting the door.

He doesn't look as if he's slept at all. He's nicely dressed in jeans and a dress shirt, but it appears he's had it on for several hours. He's not smiling at all. His face is tight.

"Is your friend Jess here?" he asks me. His voice is low and serious, with no trace of humor, no sarcasm.

My heart begins to pound, and I'm feeling panicky. "No. Nick, has something happened to Jess or Jake?"

"No. I asked because I have something to tell you, and I don't want you to be alone after I leave."

That doesn't help the panicky feeling.

"Well, she's not here. Just tell me, Nick."

He takes a deep breath. "I've been out on a scene for several hours. Misty Price's body was found last night."

My brain feels disconnected from the rest of my body. It's not possible. I must still be asleep. This is a nightmare. Yes, it is, but I'm awake, and it's completely real. I've never been through the death of a foster child. No one in Clarke County has. It happens. There are procedures and policies in place for when it happens. It's just never happened in my county to any of our children in care. I can't believe it has happened to Misty.

"Oh, God," I whisper. I'm trying my hardest to process this information, and I can't. She cannot possibly be gone. I look up at Nick and in his eyes. It's the eyes of someone who has seen something horrible. "Are you sure?" I ask, hoping. He nods his head that he's sure. "You may be wrong." I'm still holding out hope.

"I'm not wrong. I knew immediately when I saw her. It's her, Grace."

I'm processing, but at the same time I'm not. *No, no, no!*

"What happened to her?" I can't make my voice any stronger than a whisper. He shakes his head at me. I translate it into *I don't want to tell you.* "Nick," I plea, "Tell me what happened to her." My composure's slipping rapidly. I hold onto it with everything I have in me.

"You don't want that in your head."

"I'm going to find out anyway. I don't want to hear it from anyone else."

I look up in his eyes, searching them. His eyebrows are drawn. He looks like he's searching something in my eyes. What is it that he's looking for?

He takes another deep breath. "She was beaten, shot in the head and suffered some pretty substantial sexual trauma." I feel like I've been punched in the stomach. I feel dizzy. I must look it too, because Nick reaches out and puts a hand on my upper arm. "Grace?"

I hold my hands out to him, waving him off.

"I'm fine," I whisper.

"No, you aren't."

I have so many questions. I don't even know where to start.

"I want to see her. Will you take me? Where is she?"

"She's at the morgue right now. She should've been transported straight to the Crime Lab from the scene. It's a long story why that didn't happen, and no, I'm not taking you to see her." He's firm about it.

I'm still looking up in his eyes. "Please," I whisper, "I need to see her."

"No, Grace, you don't need to see her like that." His brows are drawn, and his voice is anguished.

I nod my head and step a little closer to him. I'm still looking up at him. "I need to see her."

I don't know what convinces him. He closes his eyes briefly and looks down at me.

"Go change."

I run upstairs and change. I realize the tears are streaming down my face. I have to call Valerie. Has Nick called her? What's he done? Do the DeWitts know? I throw on some jeans and a tee-shirt. I look in the mirror and gather myself together. I grab what I need and run back downstairs. I'm trying to look composed, but the look in Nick's eyes tells me I'm not fooling him a bit. I pull my car keys out of my handbag and realize my hands are shaking.

"You're not driving," he says. "You're in no shape."

I don't argue. He's right. He ushers me out the door and into his car. We pull out of the complex. I'm still trying to get my thoughts together.

"Does anyone else at DFCS know?" I ask.

"No. When I was able to leave the scene, I drove straight to your place. I didn't want you to hear it from anyone else."

That touches me.

"Thank you," I say, looking over at him. He simply nods and keeps his eyes on the road. My brain is clicking slowly. I take a deep breath. "The DeWitts don't know, do they?"

"No. Just you." I see his jaw clenching.

I realize I have to call Valerie. I find her name in my contacts, and with a shaky finger, I push the call button. She answers on the third ring.

"It must be bad if you're calling at this hour," she says groggily.

"It is." My voice is thick. "Misty has been murdered."

"Oh, my God!" she yells, fully awake. I can hear her husband in the background, asking what's wrong. "Oh, my God. Oh, shit." I can hear her begin to cry and that starts my tears again. It takes several moments before she can speak. I'm wiping my face with the hem of my shirt. "Okay. Where are you? Who told you? What happened? Shit!" she yells.

I tell her, "I'm with Detective Nick Bassano. I'm on the way to see her body."

There's nothing but silence on Valerie's end. I would swear that she hung up on me, but I can hear her breathing.

"That's a bad idea," she finally says.

"I have to do this, Valerie. I have to see her."

There's another lengthy silence. I don't know if it's because I've been at DFCS for so long or because of the gravity of the situation or because she just doesn't want to argue about with me, but she agrees.

"How was she murdered?"

"She was beaten, shot, and Nick said she suffered substantial sexual trauma."

"Oh, my God," she moans. "Okay, I'll call Bev, and I'll call Mack." She's referring to the DFCS Director Mack Wright who is Judge Wright's brother. "He'll call the Special Investigations Unit, will let them know and get them going on whatever they need. Do the DeWitts know?"

"No, and I want to be the one to tell them. Please, Valerie. They need to hear this from me."

"Okay. Your case file's in your cabinet above your desk?"

"Yes. Everything's up to date."

"I had no doubts that it is. Get to the office as soon as you can, okay? We'll all be there."

"Okay."

"How much information is Detective Bassano going to share with us? Or are we going to have to stand on our heads and play hardball?"

"I haven't had that discussion with him yet." I say, glancing over at Nick. He glances at me. His eyes are grave, and his jaw is still clenched.

"Are you up for that discussion?"

"Yes."

"I don't like the idea of you going to see her," Valerie says, firmly.

"I know, but I have to."

"Get to the office as soon as you can. I have calls to make."

I hang up and direct my attention to Nick. I look at his profile, and his demeanor is unchanged.

"Grace, would the DeWitts-"

"No," I say, firmly, cutting him off. I know what he's going to ask. "They wouldn't harm her or any other child."

"I have to ask," he says gravely.

"Well, you have. You asked me, and I said no."

"You know I have to interview them."

"I know," I say quietly. "Who found her?"

"There was a guy walking his dog last night. He said his dog kept whining and pulling him farther off of the road. He followed what his dog was after and found her and called 911. My partner, Chris Taylor, and I have been there all night into this morning. I hate murders, obviously, but dammit, I hate when a child's murdered, and it was brutal. Are you sure you want to do this?"

No I'm not. "I have to do this."

"Okay."

"Where was she found?"

"In a wooded area off of Arnoldsville Road."

"Any suspects?"

"None. When I was finally able to leave, I came straight to you. I'm hoping you and the DeWitts can give me something."

"I'll do whatever I can," I say, choking up.

"I know you will."

We pull into Athens Regional Medical Center and into the parking lot at the ER. Nick walks me in the hospital and then down to the basement to the morgue. I've never been here, and I hope I never have to come back. I honestly didn't even know that it was here. He pauses at the door with the black bold letters MORGUE. I feel sick, dizzy and sad and start second guessing my decision on this. *No. I have to do this.*

"I want you to wait here for a minute, okay?" His voice is softer. He's looking down at me, and his eyes are searching mine again. Searching for what?

"Okay." I don't ask why. I'm afraid I might not want to know.

I wait outside the door, and the letters bore into me. My heart is pounding, and it's a sick and panicky pounding. I see Nick come out of the door and hold it for me.

"You can back out," he says, giving me a chance to turn around and leave.

"No, I can't."

"Come on."

He leads the way. The Coroner is there. I have no idea what his name is. Misty is lying on a table in a body bag. The zipper is down at her neck. I walk to her, and there's nothing that could have prepared me, absolutely nothing. I was hoping against all hope that Nick was wrong, but he isn't. It's her. I stand beside her and look at her face. I thought death was supposed to make you look peaceful. She looks anything but.

Whatever happened to her was horrific. I see it in her battered features. Her skin looks waxy. There are bruises all over her face. I see the apparent gunshot wound in her left temple. I can't see the rest of her body. Her face is enough. I hear a sound. It's a wounded animal sound, and I realize *oh that's me.* I'm sobbing. I feel Nick standing close, but he doesn't touch me. That's good, because I don't think I could take it.

"Who did this to you?" I ask, crying. I look up at Nick and his eyes, oh God, his eyes. I see compassion in them. "Can I touch her?"

"No," he says. His voice is dark. "We don't want any evidence compromised."

I nod, understanding. I look back at her. Misty, for all of her problems, was feisty and lively, and now, she's...gone. I've seen enough. I leave her with this.

"We will find who did this to you." I turn and walk straight out of the door. I don't stop until I'm back at the elevator.

When I get to the elevator, I close my eyes and lean my head against the wall. It's made of cinder block, and it's cold and it feels good. I can hear Nick approaching. I hear the *click, click, click* of his shoes echoing off the floor. He says nothing to me, but he stands very close. I take a cleansing breath. When I open my eyes, I see he is holding out a tissue for me.

"Thanks," I say, taking it.

"You're welcome."

I look up at him, and he's looking down at me. His expression is grim. I'm sure mine is too.

"How was she beaten?"

"Most likely a fist."

"How can you tell?"

"You work enough homicides, you begin to notice differences in the manner in which people are beaten."

"Okay," I say, believing in what he's telling me. "I need to tell the DeWitts."

"I'll drive you. I need to talk to them."

We make our way back up to the lobby and out of the hospital. Once in the car, I tell Nick where they live, and then we drive in absolute silence. My brain is on misfire. I have nothing to say, and I have no questions at the moment. The DeWitts don't live far, and in the early hours, the traffic is almost nonexistent. We turn in their subdivision, and I point out their house to Nick. Their porch light is on, and I see a light on in the house. I can't imagine them being up, but they may be. As we approach the house, Rose opens the door. I guess she was up. Her face is hopeful, and then it changes in an instant when she sees my face and then Nick and then back to me. She understands instantly. I'm standing in front of her, and she's backing in the house.

"No, no, no!" she's screams. Then, she's crying.

I hear Stan running from upstairs. His face is one of pure panic as he sees his wife.

"What?" he yells. He's looking at me. I'm trying to form the words. I feel the tears on my lips.

"She's gone," I whisper.

If Stan hadn't been holding Rose, she would've collapsed on the floor. It's so painful to witness. They were her foster parents, but I can see at this moment, they loved her as if she were their own. Nick hasn't uttered a word. He steps forward and looks at them.

"Mr. DeWitt, I'm Detective Nick Bassano. I met your wife earlier today. I'm so sorry that this has happened to Misty and that you're now having to deal with this grief. Is there some place we could sit and talk?"

Stan looks at Nick and says, "Okay."

He pulls Rose with him and leads us to their family room. I've been here many times, with many different kids. Nick and I sit on one sofa, while Stan and Rose sit on another sofa that sits at an angle with ours.

"Do you know what happened to her?" Stan asks, looking at me. I nod at him. "Tell me."

I look at Rose.

She nods at me and says, "Go ahead." Her voice is thick with her tears. "I want to know, too."

I look at Nick. "I can't," I say quietly.

He nods at me and looks at the DeWitts. The breath that he takes seems like it would suck all of the air out of the room.

"She was beaten, shot and suffered substantial sexual trauma."

Both Stan and Rose inhale sharply at the same time.

"Where is she now?" Stan asks Nick.

"At ARMC in the morgue. She'll be transported to the GBI Crime Lab tomorrow morning. I mean later this morning."

"I want to see her," Stan says, still looking at Nick.

"No Stan you don't," I answer before Nick has a chance to.

"I want to see her," he says again, now looking at me.

I'm chewing on my lip and shaking my head at him. "I saw her," I whisper. "You don't want to."

He turns and looks at Rose.

"I'm against it," she says to him, "I want us to remember her alive and beautiful and spunky." Her voice breaks, and she begins crying again. Rose focuses her attention on me. "Stan and I were talking about a week ago, and we were considering adopting her once the TPR was filed. It was the first time we've ever felt that strongly about wanting to adopt. I wish that we would've told her that."

My tears that I was getting under control flow freely down my cheeks again. I can feel my face and eyes have that hot puffy feeling after crying for a long time.

"She knew that you both loved her."

"Where was she found?" Stan asks Nick.

"In a wooded area off of Arnoldsville Road."

"Who found her?"

"A man walking his dog."

There's a heavy silence that surrounds us all. Rose looks absolutely lost. They both look ten years older than they did when we walked in the door.

"What happens at the crime lab?" Stan asks Nick.

"They'll perform a full autopsy. They'll collect any DNA and any other evidence. I'll be there. My partner, Chris Taylor, is still out on Arnoldsville Road starting this investigation. He and I will coordinate on this the whole time. It's top priority for us. Could I ask you some questions?"

"Yes. I have a few more of my own."

"Of course. I'll answer anything that I can for you."

"How long will she be at the Crime Lab?"

"They should be prepared to release her by Monday, hopefully. I can give you more information once I get there and actually talk with someone."

"Will you tell us what they find during the autopsy?"

"Yes."

"Do you have any suspects?"

"Not one. I was hoping you, Mrs. DeWitt and Grace could help me. I want to, of course, know her better, and learn her habits and who she knew. Whatever you can tell me about her."

Rose looks at me. "What about the arrangements?" she asks.

"What do you want to do? Do you want me to take care of them?" I ask her.

"No. We'll do it. Will you help?"

"Of course I will. I'll do as much or as little as you want."

"How do we get her from the Crime Lab to the funeral home?" Rose asks, looking at Nick.

"Let me know, and I'll handle it," he says to her. He reaches in his back pocket and gives them each a card. We sit in silence again for several minutes. "Would it be okay if I asked you some questions?"

"Yes," Stan says.

"She left on Tuesday night, is that correct?"

"Yes," Stan says.

"Tell me about it. Was there anything different this time?"

Stan and Rose look at each other. It's Rose that speaks.

"She was in a bad mood. It seemed worse than usual. You know she's only fifteen." Rose stops for a moment. "I mean she was only fifteen." She starts crying again and takes a minute to collect herself. "I tried talking to her about it. She gave me her usual that I didn't understand her and I didn't understand what she was going through. Her curfew's at seven thirty on school nights. She took off out of here, and I didn't follow her. I wanted to give her some cooling off time. An hour after curfew, and she still wasn't home. I didn't think anything of it, but an hour later, she still wasn't home, and then I really started to worry. Stan started looking for her shortly after that. He couldn't find her anywhere. We felt like then she had run away. He checked with some of our neighbors. She's gone there before. Stan drove around looking for her on the streets. She's usually back by mid-morning the next day. When she wasn't, I was frantic."

"Did Misty have a boyfriend that you knew about?"

Rose and Stan look at one another again, and Rose continues.

"There were boys that she was interested in, and some that were interested in her. It wasn't hard to notice that she is, I mean, was an attractive girl. But no, she didn't have a boyfriend. Misty had a difficult, if not impossible, time forming any type of a lasting relationship with anyone. I'm sure Grace can give you much more background information about that."

Nick looks over at me, and I nod my head at him.

"Could I see her room?" he asks them. They both nod at him and take us upstairs. "You have other kids here?" Nick asks them.

"Yes, we have three other foster children." Rose points to their rooms as we walk in the hall to Misty's room. "We arranged it so Misty would have a room of her own. We felt like she needed the privacy since she's a teenager." Rose doesn't correct herself. I don't think she realizes what she said. "The other children are younger."

She opens the door to Misty's room and gestures for us to go in. I step in and take a deep breath. I've been in here many times, visiting with Misty. It's so empty without her.

"I can't come in," Rose whispers, turning away. Stan looks at us for a moment and then follows his wife back downstairs.

Nick turns on an overhead light, looks down and me and asks, "Are you okay to be in here?"

I nod and continue to walk around her room. Misty was a typical teenager in so many ways. She has a poster on her wall of Big Time Rush. I remember her telling me she liked that band. She told me they have a T.V. show on Nickelodeon. There are other posters on her wall that you would expect to see. There's makeup on her dresser and lotion and perfume. I notice there are no personal pictures of her or her friends. That's sad. She did have difficulty in forming relationships. Nick's sitting on the edge of her bed. He's found what looks like a journal and is thumbing through it. I go sit beside him.

"Did you find anything?"

He looks at me. "It's her journal." Is all he says and goes back to looking at it. He reads a few entries and then closes it with an audible *snap*. He looks over at me resting his hands on the book. "She ran away, and while she was out, someone picked her up and then murdered her."

"You think she was murdered by a stranger?"

"Yes, I do," he says, looking at me with intense, angry eyes. I don't ask him why he thinks this. I figure he's been doing this long enough; he knows what he knows. "I'm not going to find anything here," he says, putting Misty's journal back on her bedside table. He stands and looks down at me. "Are you ready?"

"Sure," I say, standing.

We make our way downstairs, where Stan and Rose are sitting. They look up when we come in the room. Nick sits, looking at them, and I sit beside him.

"Do either of you have any other questions for me right now?"

They look at one another before Stan answers.

"No."

"Okay. We're going. I'm dropping Grace back at her condo, and then I'm heading to the police department. I have my cell on me, and all of my numbers are on my card. If you have any questions, call me. If you have anything you think would be helpful, call me. If you think you're not getting information fast enough, call me."

He's very good at this. I'm impressed with him. He handles himself with the utmost professionalism, but it's apparent that he cares. It touches me. He looks at both of them and stands. Stan, Rose and I stand at the same time. I walk over to them and hug them both. I hug Rose for a long time. We're both crying again.

"I'll call you later, okay?"

"Okay. Thank you for coming with Detective Bassano and telling us. That means so much to us that you did that."

"I couldn't imagine you hearing it from anyone else."

Once we are back in the car, I notice that the sun will be rising soon. The sky isn't as dark as it was when we arrived.

"Were you asleep when you were called?" I ask Nick.

"No. I was out with a friend."

Ah, he was on a date. For some reason, that bothers me, and I don't like that it does. I shouldn't care. I tell myself that I *don't* care. I let it go. I have other things that need my focus right now. His dating life isn't one of them.

"Tell me about her mom," Nick says.

"Her name's Wanda Price. She dumped Misty at DFCS two years ago. We spent the first year looking for her and the last year figuring out what we wanted to do. Wanda disappeared. I mean, completely off the grid. We tracked her through our database. She's not even from Clarke County. She was living in DeKalb County, and they didn't even know that she had moved. We searched ten different counties that we heard she might be in, but we found nothing. It's like the woman fell off the edge of the world. We've exhausted our searches for appropriate family.

There is no family. We found a grandmother in Walton County who was an alcoholic, and we weren't even sure if she was really Misty's grandmother. There was no way Misty could go live there. We could've started TPR sooner, but we didn't."

"You're speaking in code. What's TPR?"

"Oh, sorry. Termination of Parental Rights."

I see him nodding that he understands. I wish now that we had filed it sooner. The DeWitts could've adopted her, and even if the end result was the same, she would've died someone's daughter and not in foster care. It weighs heavily on my heart.

"What about her dad?" Nick asks me.

"There isn't one listed on her birth certificate. Her mother had little to no friends. They truly lived like hermits. And it isn't that we can't find family; it's that there *is* no family. Misty had no one, and she knew it. She had a mother, and her mother didn't want her. It was an awful situation. Nick, there's child killer on the streets here."

"Yes. I know," he says. He says nothing else about it.

We drive with silence between us. I need to ask him if he's going to share his investigation with me, or I should say, with DFCS. Valerie's going to want an answer.

"Nick, when I was talking to Valerie, she wanted to know how forthcoming you're going to be?"

"As far as what?"

"As far as the murder investigation. I think she wants to know if you're going to keep us in the loop."

"As much as I can. There may be things that I can't share with you. I won't do anything to compromise this investigation."

"I wasn't asking you to do that," I snap at him. I'm looking at him, and I see a shadow of a smile across his lips. It's the most relaxed I've seen him since showing up at my door.

"If the car wasn't moving, you'd probably walk away from me," he says. He's trying to lighten the mood. I look out the passenger side window and shake my head, but I'm smiling a little too. He pulls into my complex and stops beside my car. "I'll call you later, okay?" he says, turning to look at me. I have the car door open and one foot out when I turn to him.

"Thank you for coming and telling me yourself." I get out without saying anything else and immediately get in my car.

Chapter Seven

I feel absolutely numb as I drive to the office. My eyes are burning, and blinking them rapidly isn't helping. I drive in the parking lot and rush from the car into the building and up the stairs. I look in Valerie's office first and don't find her. I immediately go to Mack's office, and she's there with Bev, and Mack's on the phone talking to someone. Valerie looks at me.

"You look a mess," she says quietly.

"I feel a mess," I say to her, not insulted at all at her remark.

I sit beside her, and she takes my hand, squeezing it. I can see she and Bev both have been crying recently. I hear the gist of Mack's conversation, and it sounds like it may be someone from the news calling. How'd they find out so fast? He hangs up the phone, rubs his face and sets his attention on me.

"Well, that was the media. Word is out."

"How'd they find out so fast? Was that local or out of Atlanta?" My voice sounds surprised, even to me.

"Atlanta," he says. "They had to find out from the police department." He's regarding me with a very serious look. I don't like it. "Grace, they're going to second guess you. They're going to talk about you and if you did anything wrong." He must see that I've gone pale. "I know you didn't. I've started going through your case file." He points to it on his desk. "I knew when I opened it, I would find every t crossed and every i dotted. There are no policy violations, and there are no ethical violations. But you may still get dragged through the mud. It won't matter what I say. It won't matter what the police say. It won't matter what Atlanta says. A foster child has been murdered. It's an opportunity for the media to bash on DFCS."

"And me," I say quietly.

"And you," he says.

"I can handle it," I say, with more resolve than I really have.

"Can you?"

I'm insulted that he would even ask that.

"Yes," I say, firmly.

"Okay. Let's get to it. Valerie said you were telling the DeWitts. Tell me how they are."

"Devastated," I say.

"I'll call them in a few minutes. Okay, Penny Johnson is on her way from SIU."

When a child dies, regardless if they are in the state's care or not, the Special Investigations Unit is called out to do a Death Investigation. They come in and investigate not only the child's death, but us as well. It would be like internal affairs going into a police department and investigating a certain officer and the police department itself. SIU was set up several years ago. Our regional office is in Gainesville, which is north of Athens. I've never been involved with SIU. I've never met Penny Johnson and wouldn't know her if she passed me on the street.

"Valerie's working on the intake referral."

I look over at Valerie, confused. "What intake referral?"

Whenever DFCS receives a call about suspected child abuse or neglect, an intake referral is generated. Then, it goes to a supervisor, who assigns a specific response time for face-to-face contact with the suspected at risk child or children. The referral is then given to one of the Child Protective Service Case Managers. I just refer to them as CPS, as does most everyone else. My mind's spinning.

"I'm doing an intake on the DeWitts," she says.

"They've just lost a girl that they were strongly considering adopting, and now on top of losing her, and not just losing her, but losing her to a brutal murder, they're now going to have to contend with an investigation on them? They didn't do anything."

"Grace, you know as well as I do that it's policy."

"Fuck policy," I say, storming out of the office.

All three of their faces are surprised. There's no one that adheres to policy like Valerie Locke. I'm right behind her with that. I've never questioned policy. I often refer to it as the DFCS Bible. I'm not prone to outbursts. Nick Bassano's seen them, but that's because he provokes them. No one at the office has seen one, because I don't react like that. I speak my mind on matters, but I don't lose my head over them. I don't drop the f-bomb in front of my boss, either.

I walk in the bathroom and look in the mirror. Valerie was right. I look a mess. My eyes are getting swollen, and my face is all splotchy. I splash some cold water on me and stare at myself. There are all different thoughts jumbled up in my head. I cannot believe I'm even thinking about Nick. But I find that I am. I shake my head and walk out. Valerie's leaning against the wall with her arms crossed.

"I'm sorry," I say.

She waves me off.

"Don't worry about it. You looked like a powder keg when you walked in. I figured you'd blow at some point over something. Come on let's go to my office and talk." I walk behind her and collapse in a chair in front of her desk. She looks at me. "I'm worried about you," she says, concerned.

"I'm fine."

The look she gives me tells me she's not buying it.

"Do you want to talk about going to see her?"

"No," I say, firmly.

"Are you just going to bury that?"

"No, I'm not burying it. I just don't want to talk about it right now."

"How badly is this affecting you?" she asks, with the same concerned tone in her voice.

"I'm still trying to process it. I don't know yet. How much is it affecting you?"

"You know I stopped smoking two years ago, right?"

"Yes," I say, remembering that awful time period well.

"Well, I bought a pack on my way here and smoked four. Does that answer your question?"

I roll my eyes at her and say, "Yes." I feel my phone buzzing in my pocket. I pull it out and see that it's Jess. "Hey," I say, answering.

"Grace. Jake and I are watching the news, and they just reported that there's a crew on the way to Athens to report on a murder of a child in DFCS custody. Grace that's not-"

"Yes," I say, cutting her off. I close my eyes and pinch the bridge of my nose with my thumb and forefinger.

"Oh, my God, Grace. Where are you?"

"I'm at the office," I say.

"When did you find out? How did you find out? What happened? Oh God, Grace, how are you? Listen to me asking all of these stupid questions. What do you need, sweetie? I'll do anything for you. You know that, right? I love you, Grace, and I just want to be here for you. I know how much you love all of those kids on your caseload."

Her words are my emotional undoing. I put my head down in my lap as far as it will go and sob. I sob harder than I have since finding out that Misty's gone. I'm sobbing harder than I did when I looked at her battered face and realized that she's really dead. Thinking of that only makes me cry harder. I can hear Jess crying on the other end. I can hear Valerie sniffling too. Jess hangs in there with me and says nothing. She lets me get all of it out. It's several minutes before I'm able to speak. I pull some tissue out of a box that Valerie has slid over to me and wipe my face.

"It was a brutal murder," I finally say. My voice is thick and hoarse. "Nick came to the condo earlier this morning and told me."

"Oh, God, Grace, you were all alone. I'm so sorry. Let me get a sub, and I'll come to you."

I smile at the phone. She's the best. I couldn't ask for a better friend. She's willing to take a day off from work to be with me.

"No. Go to work. I'm going to be here a while, I think."

"Okay. Well, Jake doesn't have to be on campus today. I'm going to send him to the condo, so whenever you leave there, you won't have to go home to an empty place."

"That's comforting, Jess. Thank you."

"I'll leave school right at two thirty today, so I'll be there too, whenever you get there."

"Thank you. I have to go, Jess."

"Okay, sweetie, I love you. I'm here for you. Call me at any time today, and I'll see you at home."

"Love you too," I manage to get out and start crying again. I take several moments to collect myself. "Jess said the news is reporting it."

"That's just freaking great," Valerie says.

"She said there's a news crew on its way from Atlanta. She didn't say what station."

"Dammit. Let me go tell Mack. He's going to want to know that."

She leaves, and I put my face in my hands, and damn, I realize I'm exhausted, and the day's only beginning.

❦

"What else do you want?" Jess asks me, sitting back on the sofa beside me handing me a glass of water.

The tissues are sitting on the coffee table, and I believe I've nearly gone through the whole box. Jake's in the recliner, flipping through the channels. He looks at me occasionally, smiles kindly at me and then turns back to the television.

"This is fine." My voice sounds hoarse and stuffy.

That would be because my nose is completely stuffed up. I drink my water, or I should say, I gulp it down. I'm dehydrated. I've been home for an hour, and when Jess began to quiz me on what I've had to eat or drink today, I realized I've had neither. When I told her that I've had nothing to drink or eat, nor did I want anything, I know she wanted to scold me, but my appearance stopped that. She made me drink water. Then, she made me drink more water. That was my third glass. I'll be floating to the bathroom later.

What a shitty day. I've never had a shittier day. Penny Johnson arrived, and I was less than impressed with her. She hit the ground running. I argued with Valerie, which I've never done. I wanted to be the one to do the initial response on the intake that had been generated about Stan and Rose. I was told no, that Penny Johnson would be doing that. I asked to at least be able to call them and let them know Penny was coming. Valerie and Bev both reminded me about policy again. I got pissed, cussed and stormed out a second time. It was worse this time, because the office was filling up, and it was witnessed by more than one of my co-workers.

79

Once I cooled off and apologized again, I asked if I could go with Penny Johnson. I got a no on that one too. I decided to hold my tongue and my temper. I gave up that battle, but I felt like the biggest traitor for not giving Rose and Stan the heads up. When I talked to them later in the day, they were both fine with it. They said they somewhat expected it and said that Penny Johnson was professional. They weren't impressed with her, either. Rose sounded sad and lost. I told her that she could call me during the night if she needed. She told me the same thing.

I have the best co-workers. Two of them told Valerie they would handle anything on my caseload today that couldn't wait for another day. Valerie agreed, and I pulled my calendar and saw that there were several things that couldn't wait another day. Julie Biel and Cassidy Michaels took my calendar and said they would handle it from there. I owe both of them my life.

Nick sent me a text, and I chuckled over it. His text was he was afraid to call because he didn't know how crazy it was for me. He was even more worried that his text would blow up my phone. That's what lightened my mood. I think that's what he was aiming for. He wanted to know how I was doing, and that touched me. He was going home to shave, shower and change and then back at it.

He had nothing new to report. He heard about the media already having the story. Misty was being transported at the time of his text. I sent him a text back that my phone did not blow up and told him I was handling everything okay. His response was asking me if he could call me later. I was going to send my yes response back in capital letters, but I thought that might look desperate? Possibly?

Mack gave a statement to the media. It was good. He was adamant that the initial review of my case file showed no violations of any sorts. He left my name out of the interview, and I was grateful for that.

I got home after the six o'clock news. Jess said that Nick gave an interview, and she was impressed with him, and it was good this time. She said he was very good with the media, and the reporters seem to like him.

I had a lengthy interview with Penny Johnson, and I would do anything to not have that happen again. It wasn't the interview. It was her. She is the driest, most personality-deficient woman I've ever met.

When I was about to pass out on Valerie's desk, she forced me home. I reminded her that she had been up and at it as long as I have. She reminded me that I've had a more emotionally exhausting day than she has. I lingered, and she finally kicked me out. She told me she wasn't staying much later herself. When I was leaving, I noticed that Valerie, Bev, Mack and I were the first ones here today and the last ones to leave.

"I think I'm going to take a shower," I say to both of them.

"You really should eat something," Jess says to me, softly.

"Maybe once I'm out of the shower. I'll think about it."

"I'll fix you anything that you want."

I squeeze her hand.

"You're the best. You both are. Thank you both for being here. I can't imagine having to be alone tonight."

"You can sleep with me if you want to," Jess says to me.

She's serious about it, but it strikes me funny. I laugh, and that action feels good to me. It reminds me that I'm still alive.

I drag myself upstairs and quickly get in the shower. I don't even stop to look at myself. I think it would scare me. I stand under the hot water for what feels like forever. I let the water wash the day away. That takes a long time. There's so much to wash off.

When I close my eyes, I see Misty on that table. I see her bruised features and how she didn't look human any longer. I start to shiver. Then, my teeth begin to chatter, and then I realize I can't stand. I sink in the floor of the shower and wrap my hands around my knees and make myself as small as possible.

Then, I really begin to think. That may be dangerous. Someone beat that poor child. She was raped. She was shot in the head and then someone dumped her like trash. That's what gets me. That after doing all what was done to her, she was discarded so carelessly, without any feeling or thought.

I'm sobbing again. I'm rocking back and forth in an attempt to comfort myself. It doesn't work. Nick would only allow her face to show. Why was that? It's starting to bother me that he wouldn't let me see all of her. Was there a reason or did he think what I would see was enough? Wasn't it? Did I need to see more? *No, her face was enough.* I must be taking more time than I thought, because I hear Jess knocking on the bathroom door.

"Grace, are you okay? You've been in there a long time."

"I'm fine," I say. I must not sound fine, because she comes in the bathroom, and I hear her sit on the closed toilet.

"Grace, it's okay that you aren't fine. You don't have to pretend with me." I hear her sigh. "Nick called, twice. Your phone's on the coffee table."

She's letting that sink in with me. He called, *twice.* I'm still crying, but now, I'm smiling. Okay. I need to get a hold of myself and finish my shower. I'm beginning to look like a prune.

"I'm not fine," I say.

"I know," she says softly.

I pull myself off the shower floor and begin to bathe. Actually, I scrub. After realizing that I may end up taking some skin off if I don't stop, I rinse. Jess is still sitting when I step out with my towel wrapped around me. She stands and hugs me.

"I'm going back downstairs so you can finish."

"Thanks," I whisper.

I get a look at myself in the mirror. I don't look too bad. I look like I've been crying for a long time, and that's exactly what I've been doing. I squeeze as much water out of my hair as possible and put it in a tight bun. I smile thinking of what Nick said about my hair being too pretty to put up. My emotions are wild. Thinking of him and smiling. Thinking of Misty and crying.

I dress and go back downstairs. I want to talk to Jess and tell her everything that I'm feeling and what it was like seeing Misty on that table, but I don't think I can handle it tonight. I need to get some rest and put some things in perspective. I know I need to talk about it with someone, and I know it will be her. She would listen to anything that I have to say. It's getting late, but I decide to call Nick back. Jess looks up at me as I pull my phone off the coffee table.

"What would you like to eat?" she asks me.

"Grapes," I say, without thinking about it.

"Grapes? You got it."

"I'm going to call Nick." I notice that Jake isn't in the recliner. "Where's Jake?"

"He went to bed. I told him I was going to stay up as long as you're up."

Again, she's the best.

"Thanks, Jess. I really appreciate you taking care of me tonight. It means a lot to me."

I see tears popping out in her eyes, and I have to look away or I'll be crying again. I can't believe that I have any tears left. I sit on the sofa and scroll to Nick's name and push the call button. He answers on the second ring.

"Hey," he says.

"Hey. You sound as tired as I feel."

I can hear him laugh softly. "You sound stuffy."

"That's because I am."

There's silence and then he asks me, "Is that because you've been crying?"

"Yeah. I've been shedding some tears. Jess said she saw you on the news. She said you did a good job."

"Thanks. Are you at home?" he asks me.

Jess sits down beside me and hands me my grapes. I mouth *thank you* to her. She answers me with a smile. She's trying to pretend that she's watching the TV, but she's listening to my conversation.

"Yeah. Are you?"

"No, but I'm leaving in a few minutes to get some sleep." I hear him yawning.

"How's it going?" He knows I'm not asking about him but about the investigation.

"Poorly. We've got nothing. I believe we'll have DNA, but that's probably not going to help us until we have a suspect, and right now, there's no one. We can hope for a hit from CODIS, but I'm not holding my breath on that. Chris interviewed the guy who was walking his dog, but he didn't see anything, and he didn't hear anything. Misty was killed someplace else and then dumped where she was found. We've interviewed neighbor after neighbor after neighbor out there. I think you get the picture on what we've done. Nothing on that, either. We've got one thing that we are working on, but I don't know if it's going to be helpful or not."

"Can you tell me about it?"

"We found some tire tracks. They looked fresh. One of the detectives in our Forensics unit poured a cast, and we have the cast of them now. We're going to work that angle. I'll let you know. I talked with the Crime Lab. They can't get to Misty's autopsy until Monday."

"Monday," I exclaim. Jess looks at me, and I shake my head at her. "Why not until Monday?"

"That's how backed up they are. I've called the DeWitts, and we talked for a long time. They obviously don't like it, but said they knew there was nothing that they could do about it."

"Are you going for the autopsy?"

"Yes. I'll be there."

There's another silence between us, but it's not uncomfortable.

"Nick. I want to tell you again how much I appreciate you coming to tell me yourself. Thanks for not letting me find out on the news or sending someone else."

"Well, like I told you last night, or whenever the hell it was, I didn't want you to hear it from someone else."

I smile, and I think he can tell I'm smiling.

"Nick Bassano, you're being nice to me."

He laughs softly again, and then says, "I hate to see women cry. Especially strong women like you."

I have no idea what to say to that. He knocks me off balance as usual. *Wow!*

"You're being nice to me, and you complimented me. Could you please put Nick Bassano on the phone because I have no idea who I'm speaking with."

We both begin to laugh. Oh, that feels good. I can feel some of the tension slipping away.

"Thanks," he says.

"For what?"

"For making me laugh. I needed that."

"Tell me about it."

"Grace, it's late. I'm going home to sleep. I hope you get some too. I wanted to see how you were doing. About tomorrow night-"

"Nick, don't worry about it," I say, cutting him off. "I understand."

"If you would let me finish my sentence. God, you're a mouthy woman." He's not being serious about it. I can tell he is smiling. "What I was going to say, is that I wanted us to do dinner and drinks, but I can't do that. So, I was thinking maybe coffee instead?"

"Coffee sounds good."

"I'll call you tomorrow and let you know what time. Is there any place in particular you would want to go?" he asks me.

"I like that Jittery Joe's on East Broad."

"The one down the hill where they converted that old building?"

"Yes, that one."

"Good. I like that place, too. I'll call you tomorrow. Try and get some sleep."

"You too," I say, hanging up. I can feel that I'm still smiling, and I see Jess looking at me.

"You have color in your cheeks," she says. "You were pale, well as pale as you can be with that beautiful tan you have, but your color has come back. So he's being nice to you?"

"For the moment. I don't know if that will hold." I laugh a little about it. "I think I'm going to bed," I say.

We tell each other good night. When I fall asleep, I don't dream of Nick, but I would take dreaming of him over my nightmare.

Chapter Eight

I'm trying to have a normal day. It's easier said than done. Thankfully, the day is nearly over, and it's Friday. I'll have the weekend to regroup and rest. My nightmare exhausted me. Misty was on that damn table in the morgue, and she was in the body bag just as I saw her. She looked exactly how I saw her, except she sat up and looked at me with dead eyes and asked, "Why did you let him do this to me?" That's when I sat up in bed and was drenched in sweat. I had to take another shower.

When I was able to let myself think of the nightmare, I started to feel guilty. I began to feel guilty that maybe there was something that I could have done. I don't know what that is, but maybe if I had taken Rose more seriously than I did, this wouldn't have happened. She was worried from the moment she called me, and I brushed her off thinking nothing was wrong. She knew it. She felt it. She has that good motherly intuition. I can't shake the nightmare, and I can't shake the guilty feelings that I'm having.

Penny Johnson is back for a second day. She's been pouring over my case file. She'll find me and ask the occasional question. I answer them, and then she leaves. I'll be happy when she's gone permanently.

I called Rose earlier, and she and Stan were doing the best that they could. She said telling the other children was hard. Those kids aren't on my caseload. Rose said she was going to increase their counseling sessions for a while. She's such a good foster mother.

I haven't talked to anyone about how I'm feeling. About seeing Misty, about how devastated I am over her loss and about this guilt that

I'm now carrying around. I pull a small stack of papers off my desk and leave the office. I drive from the office to the courthouse and go to Judge Wright's chambers. His secretary is at her desk.

"Hi, Molly," I say, walking in.

"Hi, Grace. How are you today? I heard on the news about what happened. I'm really sorry. Judge Wright pulled the file after hearing her name and saw that you're the Case Worker. I know he was going to call yesterday, but he was on the bench. He called Mack last night, and Mack filled him in on the details. He's in his office. Go on back. I know he'll be pleased to see you."

"Thanks, Molly," I say.

I've managed to not cry much today, but I don't know how much longer that's going to hold. I go to Judge Wright's office door and knock softly.

"Come in," I hear him say.

I open the door and walk in, and he smiles at me when he looks up from what he was reading and sees me standing there. He gets up and walks around his desk.

"Hello, Grace. How are you?" He hugs me, which is something he's never done. I'm sure he is offering support. It doesn't make me uncomfortable.

"I'm doing fine," I say, as convincing as I can manage. He points me to a chair in front of his desk. I sit down and put the folder on his desk. "These are some papers that were filed, and I wanted to make sure that you have them."

"Thank you. You know you're the only Case Worker to make sure I have paperwork from your office. You're always so efficient and conscientious." He smiles kindly at me. I can feel that I'm blushing. He gives me a troubled look. "Tell me how you're doing. I talked to Mack last night and heard what happened to Misty Price."

"I'm doing okay. It's hard. It's really hard for the DeWitts. Do you remember them?"

"No, I don't. How are they doing?"

"Sad. They were giving strong consideration to adopting Misty. I wish that I had done the TPR sooner."

"You sound full of guilt."

My eyes widen. This man is good. He knows me well.

"I feel full of guilt," I admit.

Judge Wright is so easy to talk to. He always has been. He smiles at me again, and I see nothing but kindness in his eyes. I can feel a lump forming in my throat. I don't want to cry. I've been doing very well today with the tears.

"Why all the guilt?" he asks me.

"I feel I should have reacted differently when Rose called me to tell me she was missing."

"My understanding of this young lady is that she ran away frequently."

"She did," I say.

He regards me with a look. It's a kind look full of compassion.

"This isn't your fault. It's the bastard that did this to her. It's his fault."

"Thank you Judge Wright. Your words mean a lot to me." I'm smiling at him and his smile back is genuine and concerned.

"Mack told me that you know the detective that's working on the Homicide. Has he told you anything?"

"No, other than they don't have any suspects."

Judge Wright shakes his head. "That's terrible. I hate it. Is that the same detective that I met Friday? Nick Bassano, right?"

"Yes."

"He seems like a smart guy. I'm sure he'll solve it. I hope he does anyway. Maybe we'll all get lucky, and he'll have to shoot that bastard and save us some tax payer money."

I give him a slight smile. "While I don't like the thought of anyone getting shot, that sounds good to me." I look at my watch. "I've taken up enough of your time. Thank you for seeing me and for your words."

"Anytime, Grace. You know you can always come and talk with me."

"I know, and that means so much to me too. Have a wonderful weekend."

"You too, Grace. Do you have plans?"

"I'm meeting Nick for coffee, and then nothing but rest this weekend. How about you?"

"Golf, golf and more golf. Have fun with Nick."

"Thanks, Judge."

I leave his office and feel my phone buzz. I pull it out of my pocket and see its Nick calling.

"Hey," I say, answering.

"Hey. Are you ready?"

"Sure. I'm at the courthouse, so I'll go straight there."

"I'll meet you there in about ten minutes."

"Does that mean you are showing up late?" I'm smiling as I say it. I hear him laughing.

"No, that means you're closer to our destination than I am. See you in ten."

After paying to park in the courthouse, I drive the short distance from Washington Street to East Broad Street to the Jittery Joe's. I love this location. It's an old tin building that's been refurbished, with a new porch. There are several people on the porch when I get there. It's crowded for a Friday after work. The inside looks like an old barn with substantial woodwork. It may have been a barn at one time. It looks out of character in the location setting, with the newer, fancier buildings across the street.

I walk inside, and I'm not waiting long when Nick comes in. *Oh, he looks good.* He's dressed down today in khaki pants and an ACCPD crested polo. His tattoo is on display, and the way he's smiling at me is making my body temperature go up. He walks over to me and stands very close. Does he see that I'm breathing heavier? He smells amazing. Holy Heaven, I've never smelled a man's cologne that I wanted to drink. I look up and in his eyes. He looks tired.

"Hey," he says.

"Hey." My voice sounds all breathy. Well, I am breathing harder. I can see that he sees that he's having an effect on me.

"You look beautiful." He's smiling a wicked smile, and it's completely turning me on.

Would I say no to him if he asked me to go home with him? My resolve is crumbling further.

"I bet you say that to all the girls," I say, kidding him.

"No, not all of them," he says softly.

What? How many? Just me?

"What're you going to have?" I ask.

I see his eyes are dancing, and he's smiling at me in a way that makes me think I am what he wants to have. That's really *hot*.

"What're you going to have?" he asks, playfully.

It feels like we're both forgetting what's happened in the last forty-eight hours and are up for a little fun, even if it's short lived.

"A simple cup of coffee with cream." But it comes out sounding like a question. What I really want to say is, *You. Here. Now.*

"Sounds good. I think I'll have the same. If you'll get us a table, I'll get the coffee." He walks to the counter, and it breaks the spell between us.

I let out a long breath and can still feel my heart's beating much too fast. Finding a table here is easy. There aren't that many of them. I think they're planning to expand further here. There's plenty of room. It's just not being used. I choose our table, and he brings our coffee.

"You look tired," I say as he sits.

He lets out a long sigh and takes a drink. "I am. You sound better today," he tells me.

I shrug my shoulders. "I'm okay."

"Is that the standard answer that you're giving everybody?" He's looking in my eyes and holding them. "You're no shrinking daisy, right?"

"How's it been today?" I ask him, ignoring his question.

I don't want to discuss it. I'm not ready, and I don't want to discuss it with him. Nick isn't the nurturing, *I want to hear all of your problems* type. He's still holding my eyes with his. His gaze is penetrating.

"We have nothing and no leads. We have no more information today than we did yesterday. Chris and I went back out to the DeWitt's place and did a more thorough interview. I didn't think either of them had any involvement last night, and I'm convinced of it today. We talked to people out in the adjacent neighborhood where her body was found, whom we couldn't talk to last night, and no one saw anything or heard anything. I'm frustrated. Chris is frustrated. There's a child killer on our streets, and we don't have a fucking clue who it could be. We've done nothing but chase our fucking tails today. I hate it. I threw more than one tantrum."

"I got a little snappish yesterday and threw a couple of tantrums, too."

"No, not you," he says, joking with me, sarcastic as usual.

We both laugh, trying to keep the mood light. I don't know how long that will last, since our main topic of conversation will be Misty. How can it not be? It's what's binding us at the moment.

"Nick, is there a reason why you would only let me look at her face?"

There's a lengthy silence, and he looks down at his coffee and then back up at me. A little fun just went south with that question.

"There was nothing else that you needed to see. I question my decision that I let you see what you did," he says it in a way that he's holding something back, something that he doesn't want me to know.

"There's something else, isn't there? Something you aren't telling me." I see a flash of frustration flicker in his eyes.

"Let it go, Grace." His voice is firm. He's not joking.

"I can't let it go, Nick. Tell me please," I say, coaxing him.

He puts his elbows on the table and puts his face in his hands, rubbing his face. He looks at me, resting his arms on the table and turning his cup around and around in his hands. He just stares at me. He looks like he's fighting some internal battle. What does he know?

"No." And he means it. There's no amount of pleading that I can do to make him change his mind.

"I had a nightmare last night," I admit, changing the subject. I'm not going to sit here and argue with him over what he knows. He's not going to tell me.

"Do you want to tell me about it?"

I discover that I do. I want to tell someone. I want to tell someone who saw what I saw, and he did.

"She was on that cold table, dead, but she sat up and wanted to know why I let him do that to her. It scared the shit out of me."

"That would've scared the shit out of me, too." He looks at me for a moment and then says, "I talked to Rose today. She said she isn't upset with you, but she feels like you didn't take it seriously enough when Misty disappeared."

Where's he going with this? Rose is right. I didn't, and I feel so horrible about it. But why is he bringing it up?

"I didn't have a reason to believe that it was any different situation than the other times that she had run away," I say, as calmly as I can manage.

"But she had always come back by mid-morning. By the time Rose called you, it was much later in the day. That didn't raise any red flags for you?"

"It didn't raise any red flags for you," I snap at him.

"My reaction was based on yours. You didn't seem concerned; therefore, I didn't feel that I or anyone else in the department should be concerned. I'm wondering if there's something else that you could've done."

He's asking the same question that I've been asking myself. Only it's coming from him, and it sounds accusatory.

"Are you implying that I did something wrong?" I'm still trying to stay calm, but it doesn't sound that way. He's tapping into all of the guilt, and I don't like it. It makes me uncomfortable. I feel bad enough as it is, and I don't need anyone else making me feel worse. And it's *him* that's making me feel worse.

"No. I'm asking a question."

"You're accusing me of either doing something or not doing something, and that led to her murder."

"I'm not accusing you of anything. I'm asking a fucking question. If I was accusing you, I would've said you *did* do something to cause her murder. There's a difference. Do you not understand the difference? Or are you going to be so damn defensive that you can't understand what I'm asking?" His eyes have gone dark and angry, along with his voice.

"I'm leaving," I say angrily, jumping up and shooting out of the door like a bullet.

Nick's right behind me. I'm acutely aware of the crowd that's still lingering on the porch, and they've stopped all conversation as I've burst outside, with him right behind me. I make it to the bottom of the porch before he catches me.

"I can't believe you're fucking walking away from me again," he says through clenched teeth. He grabs my wrist and spins me around to him. "Is this what you're always going to do when you get mad at me? You're just going to walk away?" He's angry, and he's breathing hard. Well, I'm angry too.

"There's no need for me to stay! You'll just say something else mean and sarcastic to me!" I yell.

I'm looking up at him and into his eyes. *Oh, shit*, his eyes have gone from angry to hungry, and I know that hunger's for me. He pulls me into his body, and I have to catch myself against him. My free hand is on his chest. Before I can think my next thought, his lips are on mine, and he's forcing his tongue in my mouth. He's pulled my wrist up and wrapped it around his neck. My other hand slides up his chest. God, he's so rock solid, and I wrap that arm around his neck as well. I'm kissing him, stretched up on my toes, and pressed as close as I can get to him. His hands are on my hips, holding me tight against him, and I feel all of him.

And then I remember that he's just accused me of getting Misty killed. That ignites me, but not passionately. I break the kiss and pull away from him. He's looking at me, and while it's hot, I'm pissed. I don't know what comes over me. I can't explain it. I'll still be questioning my decision for years to come, but I punch him square in the jaw. Nick stumbles back, and there's nothing but shock in his expression. Now, I don't believe it hurt him all that bad, but it stuns him. I hear gasps from the crowd behind us, and someone even says,

"Right on."

"What the fuck did you do that for?" he yells.

"You kissed me!" I yell back, stomping my foot on the ground. *Did I really just stomp my foot?*

"I kissed you last Friday, and you weren't complaining. I even apologized for it!"

"You didn't accuse me of getting a child killed last Friday!"

"I wasn't accusing you before!" he roars. "That was my apology for making you mad!" He's trying to reason with me.

"So you attack me with your mouth? How about saying you're sorry, and see what my reaction is!" I'm yelling even louder.

"Jesus Christ, Grace!" he yells.

He's about to say something else to me, or yell it rather, when we're blue lighted by an ACCPD patrol car. The guy gets out, pauses and smiles when he sees Nick standing there. He turns off his blue lights and walks to us.

"What in the *hell's* goin' on?" He's smiling as he asks Nick. "I got a call about some big guy gettin' forceful with a woman."

I feel the tears springing. *Oh, hell no,* he is *not* going to see me cry. I'm embarrassed, humiliated, and I'm trying to salvage what little dignity I have left. I can feel Nick looking at me, but I refuse to look at him.

"It's just a misunderstanding," Nick says.

I glance over at him. He's rubbing his jaw. His eyes are angry. Mine are murderous.

"Ma'am, is he botherin' you?" the officer asks me.

Would it matter if I said yes? He knows Nick very well. They're in that Law Enforcement *brotherhood.*

"No," I mutter, and walk quickly to my car.

As I'm walking, I hear the officer say to Nick, "You got more problems with women than anyone I've ever seen." I don't hear Nick's response, but I hear what the officer says back to him. "That's because you date too many at one time."

I slam my car door. I want to make some loose gravel fly getting out of the parking lot, but I would probably get stopped by that same officer and get a ticket for God knows what. My tears start.

I don't know if it's because of how exhausted I am, or if it's because Misty's gone, or if it's because of what Nick said to me, and that taps into all of the guilt that I'm having, or if it's because what the officer said to him about all of the women. It's slapped me in the face that there are many women. I knew that on some level.

It shouldn't matter to me that he dates several women at one time. What's it to me? Whatever it is, I'm sobbing by the time I reach the red light near the Arch on the University of Georgia Campus. My tears fall all the way home. I'm a snotty mess when I park my car.

I slam the condo door when I walk in, and I stomp up the stairs. Yes, I stomp. I hear Jess calling my name from the living area. I walk in my room and slam my bedroom door and fall on the bed, crying. I curl into the fetal position and continue to cry. Jess doesn't bother knocking. She sits beside me on the bed.

"I've never seen one man evoke so much emotion in you."

"How do you know it's Nick?" I ask, wiping my face on my quilt. It's not the most sanitary, but I use what I have.

"You go on a date with him and then come home slamming two doors and crying. You've slammed more doors since meeting him. I've never seen you slam a door."

"I don't want to talk about slamming doors," I say, collecting myself. I sit up and run my hands through my hair. She's looking at me like she's trying to decide what she's going to say next.

"You know you can talk to me, Grace."

I look down and pick at a loose thread on my quilt. I don't know where to start. I look at my best friend, and I see she's concerned.

"I'm devastated over Misty's death. I feel guilty, like I didn't act concerned enough when Rose called. In the back of my mind, I was wondering why we were even going through the motions of filing a Missing Persons Report, because she would be home by the time Rose got home from the police department. I keep thinking there was something that I could've done, but I don't know what that could have been. I had a nightmare about Misty, and she asked me why I let him do that to her. It feels like my fault, even though I know it isn't.

"Nick tapped into all of the guilt tonight. It felt like he was accusing me of getting her killed. He says that's not what he was doing, but dammit, it felt like it. I got mad at him and tried to leave, and he kissed me, and then I punched him."

I see the shock and surprise on Jess' face. I've never hit anyone in my life. It goes against what I believe in, and it goes back to my past and things I witnessed and was a part of, growing up. Jess knows everything about me. She knows everything that I've gone through. I keep talking.

"I like him. I admit it. I fight it, and I say I don't, but I do. He makes me crazy, and he keeps me off balance, and I like that. I think about him all the time, and I keep dreaming about him," I sigh. There's nothing else to say.

"And he kisses great," Jess says.

I laugh softly. "Yeah, he definitely kisses great." I touch my lips, thinking of the two times he's kissed me.

"And then you punch him," she smiles as she says it. "That was pretty ballsy of you. I bet that threw him."

"Yeah, he was pretty stunned." I flex my fingers and discover that my knuckles are a little sore. He has a hard face.

"Grace, it's not your fault, what happened to Misty. Don't beat yourself up about it. I know you must be devastated. You love all of those kids on your caseload. Ease up on yourself. I hate that you had that nightmare. Are you going to be okay with Jake and me gone all week? I'm really questioning this trip. I'm not feeling all that comfortable leaving you the way things are for you right now."

"Jess, no, you have to go on your trip. You can't stay here and babysit me. Go on Spring Break. Have a great time, and soak up some sun for the both of us."

"Are you sure? I can cancel, or Jake can take one of his friends. I can't imagine any of his friends passing up a paid trip to the beach."

I shake my head at her. "No, you go and have fun. I think I'm going to take a shower, and then I'll come downstairs with you and watch TV."

"Have you eaten?"

"No, I haven't," I admit, and her look is beginning to make me feel like a naughty child.

"All day?"

I start thinking about it. "I had breakfast."

"Grace, you can't keep doing this to your body. You know it's not healthy. I cooked spaghetti. I'll go warm some up for you."

"Thanks, Jess."

She leaves, and I pull my phone out of my handbag. When I look at it, I feel disappointed. I had hoped that Nick would call. I contemplate calling him. I can't do it. I cannot believe I punched him. That was out of line. I sigh and throw my phone down. I shower quickly and put my hair up.

Jess has my dinner waiting for me when I go downstairs. I pick at it, eating a few bites. I'm not hungry and give up on it. Jess is eyeing me. She's not happy with me not eating. I give her an apologetic look and shrug my shoulders.

"Can you think of anything you would like?" she asks me.

Yeah, I can think of one thing. I left him in the parking lot at Jittery Joe's.

"No," I sigh and try to watch TV. I'm not into it. I don't know what we're watching, I can't keep up with the storyline, and honestly, I can't concentrate on anything but Jake Echols snoring. I look over at Jess. "I'm going to bed." I stand, and she looks up at me.

"Are you going to be okay tonight?"

I smile down at her, but I think it may be a sad smile. "I'll be fine. Don't worry."

"Right," she snorts, "I'll get right on that."

I go upstairs and fall into my bed. I check my phone one more time. *Nothing.* Did I expect any differently? My dreams aren't pleasant when I fall asleep.

Chapter Nine

I'm standing in front of Matt, arguing with him. We've been arguing for at least ten minutes. It's exhausting me. I don't want to do this with him. I don't want my every encounter with him to be arguing. He's so unreasonable, and I know it's because of the drugs. He's high as usual, in a total drug-fueled rant, and much of what he is ranting about doesn't make sense to me. He'll sometimes say things about when we were kids, and things that we did and places we went. We never went anywhere. I don't have a clue what he's talking about. I'm listening and letting him get it out, but I don't know how much longer I'm going to be able to stand it.

Sometimes I can't hear what he's saying when the train goes by us overhead. Matt seems to not even hear it and doesn't realize that I can't hear him. He's going on and on about how I don't give a shit about anybody but myself. He's already thrown Naomi in my face, but I guess he forgot, because he's saying the exact same things again. Then, he switches gears and starts talking about what a great sister I am and that no one cares about him like I do. He's full of contradictions. It's the drugs and not Matt. He can go from making sense to not making sense in seconds. I see another guy approach us.

"What're you hollerin' about, Matt?" the other guy asks him, but he's looking at me.

"My fuckin' sister," Matt says to him.

The other guy points to me and asks, "Are you the fuckin' sister?" He's trying to be humorous about it, but I don't find it funny.

"I am," I say tightly.

The guy holds his hand out to me, and I shake it.

"I'm Billy Noble," he says.

"I'm Grace Harrison."

"Billy's sister is missin', too," Matt says to me.

I look at Billy for confirmation.

"She ran away about a month ago. She's troubled. Me and her have had a real rough life. I've tried my best to be there for her, because we sure as shit don't have parents that give a goddamn, but as you can see, I'm not the most stable person." He waves his hand around him.

I'm under the North Avenue Bridge again. Billy's sister makes me think of Misty. Where ever his sister is, I hope she's okay.

"Does your sister run away a lot?" I ask him.

"Yeah, all the time."

"What's her name?"

"Jenny Noble. She turned sixteen a few days ago. I wish she was here, so we could celebrate."

I roll her name around in my head. Her name isn't familiar to me.

"Has she ever been gone this long before?" I ask him.

"Yeah. Once or twice, she stayed gone for over a month."

"Have you filed a Missing Persons Report on her?"

"Not this time. I have before, but when she kept runnin' away, I stopped."

I'm going to ask him another question when I see someone approach us but stop when he sees me. He motions for Billy to walk to him. He walks over, and I set my attention back on Matt, but I see what is going on between the two. A dope deal. I don't like it.

"Do you and Billy use together?" I ask my brother.

"You gonna lecture me about the dangers of usin' drugs?"

"I should, but it wouldn't do me a damn bit of good. You're going to use that shit no matter what I say. Do you not see that it's killing you?"

"You're fuckin' lecturin' me. Why're you always on my back about everything?"

"I'm not on your back about everything. I'm on your back about the damn drugs. I don't want to have to bury you," I yell. I reign in my temper. "Matt," I say softly, "I love you. You're my brother, and I hate to see what this shit's doing to you. I know your childhood was a nightmare. I remember all too clearly. We lived that nightmare together. I can get you some help. I'll support you every way that I can."

Billy walks back over to where we are standing. He looks at Matt.

"You ready?" Billy asks him.

Ready for what, I wonder? Ready to use again? Ready to die? Ready for another night of begging and borrowing? I look at both of them, but I'm speaking directly to Matt.

"You know, you're so lucky that you've not overdosed. You're also lucky that you've not been arrested on drug charges, which, I can't for the life of me figure out how that's not happened. You do realize that if you're popped, it's a felony, and the D.A.'s office will prosecute you for that felony? You understand that, right?"

Matt looks at Billy and then at me and begins to laugh. "Shit. They ain't gonna touch me up there. I've got friends there."

"Whatever," I mutter, "Where're you two going, and how much dope have you got between the two of you?"

"None of your business on both," Matt says. He bends and kisses me on my cheek. "You worry about all of the wrong things. Why don't you put some of that worry and find out what's happened to Naomi."

He walks away from me without another word. I should call the police and tell them that Matt and Billy are holding. I want to so bad, but I worry about what would happen if he was in jail. Which is worse? Dying on the streets? Or being in jail? What would it do to our already tumultuous relationship?

Holy Heaven, I hate this. It's not like I don't have enough on my plate. Now, I know my brother has drugs on him. Well, actually, Billy has it on him, but Matt's with him. I sigh and decide to not make the phone call. That can be one more thing that I feel guilty about. I'm sure Nick would say something stupid if he was here with me. Well, he's not.

I talk to a few other people who make the underbelly of the bridge their home. I'm always saddened to see new people here, and more so when I find out how young they are. I hate it. I forgot to ask Matt about our mom. I ask some other people about her. None of them have seen her in several days. Someone tells me that she said she was going to stay with somebody on Odd Street, but they don't know if she did or not.

One guy asks me for another sandwich. I tell him that if I had another, I would give it to him. I always bring peanut butter and jelly sandwiches with me on Sundays. Those always go over well. I never bring enough to give more than one to everybody. I bring bottled water, too. I never feel I'm doing enough, but it's something. I could go over to Odd Street. That's where Darla was the day I saw her. I could check on her and see if she or Belinda knows my mom and know where she's staying.

As I'm making my way back to my car from the bridge, I look at my phone. I don't know why. I checked it all day yesterday, but no calls and no texts. It makes my heart sink, and I don't know why. We weren't dating. We weren't in a relationship. It's not like he was mine to lose. I throw my phone on the passenger seat and pull out of the parking lot from the building that sits in front of the bridge.

There are major plans to turn this place into a shelter. It's a great building, and it's a perfect location. The hold-up has been due to raising the money. There's a huge fundraiser coming up, and it's on my birthday this year. It's something I would like to go to but can't because of the money it costs to go. I've donated to it and would love to do more.

I head to Odd Street and look at my phone again. There are no texts from anyone. Jess was texting me every hour when they left yesterday, up until this morning. I finally sent her a text to stop and enjoy her vacation and said I would call her if I needed her.

My plan yesterday was to do nothing. I was going to veg on the couch all day with the remote and a book, but I found my mind drifting to Nick- his kisses, his body and his words. Then, I started thinking about Misty and her murder. I alternated between thinking of him and then thinking of her, and it went like that for a couple of hours until I could stand no more.

I called Ginger and Angie, and they both agreed to meet me for lunch and then a movie. They read about the murder in the paper and saw the DFCS connection, but neither of them made the connection to me. I've been fortunate with the media. The story has died down pretty quickly. I'm sad that the media hasn't taken more interest in her murder. It was front page news in our local paper for all of a day. I did everything I was supposed to do, so since there isn't the element that I breached policy in some way, then the media isn't as interested. Never mind this sweet girl has been brutally murdered. I would've taken some punches from the media if it means keeping the focus on what happened to Misty. I've taken it from Nick. Well, he took the punch from me, but his words hurt like he'd hit me.

I noticed in the paper this morning that ACCPD is asking for help from the public. I saw Nick being quoted in the paper, asking if anyone saw anything unusual or suspicious to contact him or Chris Taylor. I wonder if he's working today.

I wonder if he went out last night, and if he did, with whom? Did he take her home? Did she wake up with him this morning? Oh, how much I would like it if it could be me that woke up with him this morning. I sigh. I can't do this to myself.

I shove him out of my mind and pull into the tiny patch of yard that the house sits on. Yard isn't the right word. It's a patch of dirt. I see Belinda and Darla sitting on the porch. Is that safe? It looks like it will fall apart any minute. Darla has her dog on a leash. He's growling at me as I get out of the car.

"Hey," I say, getting out of the car. "Do you remember me?" I'm asking either one of them. Belinda looks at Darla. I don't think she remembers me.

"You're that lady from DFCS," Darla says.

"Yeah. I'm Grace." I walk to the edge of the porch. "I wanted to see how you were doing," I say to Darla. She shrugs her shoulders. I look at Belinda. "You probably don't remember me, but I used to see you when you were staying at the homeless shelter, and then I would see you around Tent City from time to time."

"Are you the lady that would bring sandwiches?" Belinda asks me.

"Yeah, I do bring sandwiches."

"Yeah, I remember you. You was always so nice to everybody. There're other charity workers that come out, but none as nice as you. You'd always stay for a long time and talk to everybody. You always seemed real comfortable with us."

Yep, I sure am. "It's great to see that you have your own place," I say to her.

"I'm on disability now. Me and Darla found each other again after she come back, and we found this place. There's this man that owns it, and he charges rent real cheap, so we can afford to stay here. We need some Food Stamps, though. How do we do that?"

I walk up on the porch and motion if I can sit. The porch feels like it'll hold. I sit next to Belinda and answer her question.

"You'll need to come to the DFCS office on North Avenue and fill out some paperwork, and then someone will meet with you. It's not hard to do."

Belinda asks a few more questions, and I find out more about how she and Darla are doing. Well, I find out about Belinda. Darla doesn't say much. It's not that she's quiet, it's that she's withdrawn from life. It worries me. She's too young for this type of behavior. I want to ask about the drug usage for both of them. Neither seem to be high at the moment, and I wonder how long that's going to last.

"Do either of you know Marsha Harrison?" I ask.

Belinda looks at me surprised. "Yeah. She's stayin' here."

My heart begins to pick up pace. I haven't seen my mother in months. I'm not so sure I'm ready to see her now.

"How do you know Marsha?" Belinda asks me.

"She's my mother." I let that hang in the air. Belinda doesn't say anything to me for several minutes.

"She told me she's got a couple of daughters. I didn't know one would be as pretty as you."

I blush. "Thank you," I say, "Is she here?"

I'm beginning to feel sweaty, and the night is cool. The fact that I'm sweating has nothing to do with the weather. It has everything to do with how nervous I feel about seeing my mom.

"No, she ain't here. She left a couple hours ago, sayin' she was gonna go meet a friend."

Right. A friend. Mom has plenty of those. As long as they'll give her money, drugs, alcohol and sex, she'll be friends with anyone. She's going to get high or have sex to get money or drugs, or possibly both. Some things never change.

"Can you tell me how's she's doing? I haven't seen her in a while."

"She's got a black eye right now. All her front teeth are gone. She's pretty bad off."

Hearing about my mother's condition shocks me. I don't know why. The black eye isn't the shocking part. She's had plenty of those, and broken bones, but the missing teeth do shock me. She must be really bad off if Belinda says that she is, because Belinda doesn't look that much better. Of course, she has most of her teeth, and she doesn't have a black eye, but she has plenty of track marks.

"Would you mind telling her that I stopped by and that I asked about her?"

"Sure. Does she got your number?"

"Yes, she has my number." I leave out the part that she's never called me. I pause and then say, "I hope both of you are being careful with the drugs, and don't tell me you aren't using. I see the track marks on both of your arms. I hope you aren't sharing needles. I gave Darla my card when I saw her last week. If either of you ever want to get clean and aren't sure what to do or where to go, I'd be happy to help you." That's what I leave them with.

I make my way home and check my phone as I'm getting out of the car. No calls and no texts. I have to stop doing this to myself. It's too early to go to bed. I haven't had anything to eat all day. Jess isn't here to chastise me about it. I think of where I would like to go. I don't want to drive back downtown. I've been there more than once today. I'm not interested in calling anyone and asking them to join me. Well, there's one person. *No, don't go there tonight.*

I decide to order pizza and have it delivered, since I don't feel like getting back out. After getting it ordered and delivered, I sit with a slice and pick at it while staring at the TV. I'm not into it, either. I'm not thinking of anything in particular. My mind's numb. That's probably a good thing.

I feel lonely here without Jess. It shouldn't be any different than if she was at Jake's, but it is. I shut off the TV and grab my book off the coffee table. I spend twenty minutes reading the same paragraph. I sigh, frustrated, and throw it back on the coffee table. There's nothing else to do but go to bed. Dammit.

Should I just call him and get it over with? I grab my phone and go to his name. My finger is on the call button, and I can't push it. This is stupid. I'm acting stupid. In fact, I bet this is how high school kids act with each other.

I go upstairs and get ready for bed. I feel sad when I lay my head down. I don't cry myself to sleep. That's ridiculous. Cry about what? Cry over a guy who isn't mine? Cry because he hasn't called me? Why would he? Cry because I punched him in the face? It's in the early morning hours before I get any sleep, and I'm exhausted.

Monday blurs into Tuesday. Valerie's constantly on my back about calling Nick to find out information about the investigation and autopsy. I put her off, but I know that isn't going to last long. I end up getting my information from Rose. We've been talking for a while. She tells me that the autopsy is done. She and Stan haven't been given any specific details about it.

They've decided to have a graveside service for Misty tomorrow. We have to have a financial talk about the cost of the burial. Valerie and I have already had the conversation. She had to guide me through on what I would have to do. It's paperwork, paperwork and more paperwork. Valerie, as always, is wonderful and has helped me through the process. Rose asks me if I will be there with them tomorrow.

"Of course, Rose. Is there anything I can do to help you get ready?"

"No. You doing all the paperwork and handling everything financially has been a huge hurdle that we've not had to deal with. We picked out her casket yesterday. We've not had to plan much. We've ordered her some pretty flowers. I thought pink roses would be good. It's girlish and innocent." Her voice breaks.

I feel tears forming in my eyes, and I blink rapidly, trying to make them go away. It doesn't work, and I feel the lump in my throat.

"Rose." My voice is thick. "Are you upset with me?"

"What? No. I'm not upset with you at all. Why would you ask that?"

"Rose. I'm sorry I asked that. This isn't about me. Forget I said anything. What do you need from me?"

"Okay," she says, but I can hear that she wants to talk about it further. I kick myself mentally for bringing that up. "All I need from you is to continue what you've been doing, and for you to be there tomorrow."

"You have both, Rose."

She pauses and then says, "Grace, I made a comment to Detective Bassano on Friday that I felt like you didn't feel as alarmed as I did when I called you about Misty. Is that why you asked if I was upset with you?"

I kick myself again.

"Yes. Rose, I'm sorry. Again, I didn't mean to turn this into something about me."

"Grace. Listen to me. Neither Stan nor I are upset with you. You've been good to us. You always have been. Nothing changes the way we view you, as a Case Worker or as a person, okay?"

I'm crying. She's so kind. She is full of grief, yet comforting me. It's too much.

"Thank you," I whisper. "Rose, I'm sorry that I didn't react the way that you did. Maybe it would've made some kind of difference."

"Grace, I've been round and round in my mind over the same thing you just said. I don't think that it would have. By the time I called you, she was most likely already gone." I hear loud voices in the background. "The other kids are home, Grace. I need to go. I'll see you tomorrow."

"Bye, Rose." I hang up and dry my eyes.

I walk in Valerie's office, where Julie and Cassidy are sitting with her, talking about various things. The expression on their faces tells me that they know I've been crying.

"I was talking to Rose," I say as an explanation.

Valerie smiles kindly at me and says, "I talked to Mack a few minutes ago, and he said he talked with Stan, and they're having a graveside service for Misty tomorrow. I was going to tell you, but it looks like you know."

"Yeah. I'm going."

"Mack, Bev and I are going as well. Mack wants to order some flowers. He wants you to have some input on what to order. He's still in his office if you want to go see him. Have you talked to Detective Bassano?"

I feel my body tense.

"Rose told me that there aren't any details on her autopsy."

She regards me with a look. "Is there a reason why you *haven't* called Detective Bassano?"

"He's been so busy, I've not gotten a chance to talk to him in detail."

Did that sound good? It's probably true. I'm sure he's very busy. Is he busy with just work? Or, is he busy with…*don't go there.* I guess the busy answer satisfies Valerie, because she nods at me.

I go and talk with Mack and give him my opinion on flowers. I suggest a mixture of flowers that are beautiful and fragrant. I also suggest a peace lily plant that Stan and Rose can keep as some kind of living memory of her. Mack likes both of my ideas and says he'll take care of it.

He wants to know how I'm handling things, and I give him my standard answer of being fine. I finish work for the day and talk to Jess on my way home. She and Jake are having a great time, and the weather is good. I keep it light on my end. I'm able to eat, able to pay attention to something on TV and finally have a decent night's sleep.

Chapter Ten

The office is buzzing when I get in. I'm running late, but I called Valerie last night and asked if I could come in a little later. I'm running on empty. She told me to take all day if I needed it. I didn't feel like sitting around my empty condo all day, then going to bury Misty and then going back to an empty condo would be healthy. I don't know what's going on, but there's a group standing around Valerie's office. Everyone is talking all at once. I walk up, and Julie turns around and looks at me.

"Have you heard?" Her voice is excited, but it's not happy excitement.

I look at her strangely. "Ah, I'm going to go with no."

"I was leaving for work this morning, and I didn't know if I was going to be able to get off my street. When I passed by the Bradberrys' house, there were police everywhere, and their entire property was roped off with crime scene tape. I told Valerie about it, and she said that Mack was on the phone with Judge Wright while driving here, and he said the Bradberrys have been murdered."

Well, I wasn't expecting to hear that. Mickey and Eleanor Bradberry are the wealthiest couple in Clarke County. They have a massive home on Hampton Court. I pass it any time I go to Julie's house. I don't know them, but I know they are highly regarded here and have political connections that go all the way to the Governor of Georgia. Jess's parents are friends with them. They're huge in charity work and are always throwing a function to raise money for something. Jess, Jake and her parents have attended several of the functions. I wonder if her parents know, and if she knows. I'll need to call her. I guess I know where

Nick is. Maybe I should reach out to him. Now, he has three murders between him and Chris Taylor. It has to be stressful.

"Does anyone know what happened to them?" I ask Julie.

"No. We haven't heard any details. They're such a nice family. They have a daughter who lives in New York."

"That's awful. Maybe they'll be able to find who did it to them, quickly," I say to Julie. I look at my watch. "We need to go," I say to everyone.

There ends up being a large group of us that attends the service. The minister does a good job of helping us say goodbye to Misty. There are many tears shed. Most of them come from Rose, Valerie and me. I say goodbye to her silently and keep my promise that her murder will be solved. I don't feel confident about it, but I hope that it happens.

After the service, Stan and Rose invite us and their other foster children to have lunch with them. Who would say no? The other kids placed with Stan and Rose are on Julie and Cassidy's caseloads. Our group makes the two-minute trip from the cemetery to Aqua Linda. Rose says it was Misty's favorite. She did have a fondness for Mexican food.

We do our best to keep the conversation light. It's hard. It's not like Misty died of sickness, and we were all able to say goodbye. She was murdered. There's a difference.

Julie and Cassidy are huddled together, and I'm sure they're talking about the Bradberrys. I give them a look that says, *Do you have to do this here?*

"Sorry," they both mutter.

My phone is on the table, and it's buzzing. I see that it's Jess calling. I excuse myself and walk outside.

"Hey," I say, answering the phone.

"Grace, have you heard?" She's upset.

"About the Bradberrys? Yes, I've heard. I'm sorry, Jess. I know your mom and dad are good friends with them."

"Momma's terribly upset. They can't get any information. Grace, could you call Nick and find out what's going on? He'd probably tell you."

I close my eyes. Call Nick. That sounds so easy.

"I don't know, Jess. He's probably running crazy. He and Chris Taylor now have three murders to solve."

"Has he told you anything about them?"

"Why would he?" I ask.

"You two haven't talked since Friday, have you?"

"No," I say, feeling all sorts of unhappy again.

"Grace," she groans. "Have you tried calling him?"

"No, and he hasn't tried calling me, either."

"Well, hell, someone has to make the first move. He may be scared of you since you punched him."

That makes me smile.

"No, I don't think he's scared of me. Jess, I don't want to talk about Nick. I'll do anything for your parents, but please don't make me call him."

"Grace, you can't just stay away from him."

"Yes, I can, and I don't want to talk about him, Jess. Please, not today. Misty was buried less than an hour ago."

"Grace. I'm so sorry. Okay, no more talk about you know who. If you hear of anything, will you call them?"

"Yes, of course I will." What would I hear? It's not like I'm in the loop. "How's Spring Break?"

"Heavenly. We'll be back late Saturday. I'll call you Friday."

"Okay. I'll let you know if I hear anything, but your mom and dad will probably know more information than I do." I hang up and don't give the Bradberrys another thought.

I'm sitting at my desk late in the day. While I've not given the Bradberrys another thought, I can't say the same for everyone else. It's big news. I hear people around me talking about it.

I went home for a few minutes, earlier in the day, to change and get some separation from all the Bradberry talk. I'd hoped that everyone would talk themselves out of this topic, but I can see that it's still the hot topic around here. I'm sick of the couple's name already. *Damn, neither one of them were God.*

I look at my watch and decide this would be a good time for me to go. I tell those around me to have a good evening. Some of my co-workers invite me out for a drink, but since the topic of their conversation will most likely be what's happened, I decline. I've talked about enough murder to last me a lifetime.

I drive the short distance from the office to Odd Street. I don't stop at the house, because it doesn't look as if anyone is home. I drive past it one more time when my phone starts buzzing. It's Ginger calling.

"Hey!" she yells at me.

I pull the phone from my ear. "Hey. Why're you yelling at me?"

"Oh, sorry. Angie and I are at the Georgia Theatre, and there's this really cool band playing. It's ladies' night tonight, so admission is free. Come join us."

"Are you going to talk anything about the Bradberry murder?"

"What?" She's still yelling.

"Never mind. Yes, I'll meet you two there."

"Okay, see you in a few minutes!" she yells, hanging up.

I drive downtown and find some parking. It's crowded around outside the Georgia Theatre and loud. It takes me forever to find Ginger and Angie. I have to send them a text for them to guide me to where they're standing. It may be ladies' night, but there are several men here, and more than one offer to buy me a drink. I say no politely. I don't ever take drinks from men I don't know. I never have, and I never will.

I have a great time and forget everything going on in my life. I have fun with my friends, and the band's good. I drink a couple of beers and chat with Ginger and Angie when we're able to hear one another. I laugh and feel the tension leave me. I take a deep breath and let all of the air out of my lungs. It feels like I've been holding my breath for days.

"Are you having fun?" Angie yells in my ear.

"Yes! I'm glad that you two suggested this!"

"We know you've been having a rough time! We thought this might help!"

I hug her.

"It does! Thanks!"

The band plays all cover songs, but they're all songs that I know, and I like them all. I sing at the top of my lungs, totally off-key, but I don't care. I feel alive again, and I don't think about *him*. Well, maybe I do, just a little. That band leaves, and another sets up quickly and begins to play. Ginger, Angie and I look at each other and shake our heads. We walk out the door, laughing with one another.

"They weren't bad," Angie says, "I didn't like the music."

"I agree," I say.

"Hello, ladies." We all turn, and I smile, seeing our friend, Simon Collins. "Y'all look lovely this evening," he says, planting a kiss on each one of our cheeks. His lips linger at my cheek. "You look especially lovely, Grace Harrison."

"Thank you." I see Ginger and Angie looking at me oddly. I know there will be questions later.

"Where's Jess Rider tonight?"

"In Destin, with Jake," I say.

"Ah, Spring Break. Why're you and Tripp here in town?" he asks Angie.

"Baseball," is Angie's explanation.

He focuses his attention back to me. "I owe you a date," he says.

"No, you don't. It was a drink after work," I say, smiling at him.

Simon's a handsome man. He's a few inches taller than me. He has light hair and light eyes and glasses. He's super smart and again one of those safe guys that I've always been attracted to. He's become a very wealthy Disability Attorney here in Athens.

His uncle is the mayor, whom I know well, and his dad is a law professor at UGA. Actually, his dad is *the* law professor. He's the most well-regarded law professor to ever hold tenure at UGA. He was the District Attorney before Brison. I know Simon's dad well, and we've had many debates over the plight of the homeless during the several years that I've known him.

Simon's uncle and dad convinced me to talk in front of a Commissioners' meeting two years ago about homelessness. That was the most nerve-racking but exhilarating experience I've ever had. I've been close with both of them since then and have gotten to know the commission members well.

Simon and Jess went to the same high school, but he's older than we are by a couple of years. We all met in college. Back then, he and I were going to save the world together. He's spent many years working with troubled teens around Athens, including teens who call the streets their home. I know as of recently, he's stepped away from that role, and I'm not sure why he's done that. He's not said why, and I've not asked.

"What are y'all doing here tonight?" he asks.

"It's ladies' night," Ginger says. "What're you doing here?"

"It's ladies' night," he says, laughing. "It looks like I don't need to look any further, since there's a lovely lady standing in front of me." He's smiling at me.

I shake my head at him, returning his smile. "I'm out with my girls tonight."

He kisses my cheek again. "Another night then, darlin'." We all hear Simon's name being called. "My friends are here. I'll call you, Grace."

After he walks away, Ginger and Angie look at me, and I can tell they want to know what that was about.

"Simon Collins could charm the pants off his grandmother," Angie says.

Ginger and I start laughing, and I blush furiously.

"It looks like he may have charmed the pants off of Grace," Ginger says.

"Oh, Grace, you didn't," Angie admonishes me like a small child.

"I was at his house a while back, not long after Cooper and I broke up, and we were reminiscing about when we were going to save the world, and I knew I shouldn't have had a fourth glass of wine, but I did. I was lonely, and my lips got loose, and then so did my panties."

Ginger and Angie burst into giggles.

Ginger asks me, "Was that one of those one-night stands that you're regretting now?"

"Yes. I never should've fallen into bed with Simon. It's blurred the lines of our friendship. I get the feeling he wants more than what I'm willing to give. He's the reason I decided not to have sex with anyone until I could find someone I'm really interested in."

And then I found him. And then I punched him. Stop! I'm shutting that down tonight. Those thoughts aren't allowed.

"Grace, we had a pact," Angie says. I look at her like she's lost her damn mind.

"Angie, we made that stupid pact over ten years ago when we were all single, and we all had a crush on Simon. I sort of felt like the pact was void, since I'm the only single girl here, and besides, I wasn't thinking of the pact that night."

"Obviously," Angie snorts and then starts laughing. "So, what was it like?"

I start groaning. "You're really asking me that question?"

"Yes. We all wanted him, and you're the one who ended up doing the dirty deed with him, so spill it."

Ginger's laughing and shaking her head at Angie. I look at Ginger with an expression that she has to see says, *Help me out here.*

"I want to know, too," Ginger says.

Holy Heaven, me and my big mouth. "Why do you think it was only a one-night stand?" I hold my thumb and index finger up, indicating the lack of size that Simon Collins is walking around with.

This results in all three of us bursting into crazy laughter, and we get some strange looks. I'm pretty sure more than one person thinks we're drunk.

"So, you took one for the team?" Angie says, laughing.

Ginger tells her that she sounds like Tripp. Angie shrugs and continues to look at me.

"I didn't think about it like that. I was looking for wild rebound sex, but yes, I took one for the team." I think I missed the boat on wild sex. *Oh, just stop it already.*

"I think Simon missed the memo on rebound sex," Ginger says.

"Simon missed more than that, and if either of you tell this to anyone other than Jess, I'll call you both dirty damn liars. Now, off this subject. I'm hungry."

"I am too," Ginger says. Angie agrees, and we discuss back and forth where we want to eat.

"How about the 5 & 10?" Angie says.

"That's too expensive," I say.

"We could go to the Last Resort," Ginger says.

"They changed their menu," Angie says.

We stand there and think about it for a few minutes, when I say, "Oh, I know. How about we go to The Grit?"

"Perfect," Ginger says. Angie agrees.

We're parked in three different directions. I walk back to my car, stopping to talk to some of the homeless that I know. I linger longer than I intend. Ginger and Angie are sitting and looking at the menu when I walk in. The Grit is my favorite restaurant in Athens. It's a vegetarian restaurant, but you would never know it when the food's in front of you. The Grit isn't downtown but on Prince Avenue. It's located in a group of old, refurbished brick buildings. I come here every chance I get.

"Sorry," I say, sitting. "I saw some people that I know and had to stop and talk."

"You know more people downtown than anybody else that I know," Angie says, laughing.

"Most of them are homeless," Ginger says. She's not being insulting about it. She's speaking the truth.

"You're right," I say.

I don't look at the menu. I know what I want. I order my usual Cup of Split Pea Dal and a Small Taboule Salad. I also order a glass of what I think is the best Pinot Grigio ever tasted. I've looked all over for what they serve here, and I can never find it, and no one that works here will tell me where they get it. We order and get our food and talk and drink and laugh, and I continue to forget about the rest of life.

We don't discuss Simon Collins any more tonight, and I think only a little of Nick Bassano. When I get home later and go to bed, I sleep well and don't dream for the first time in what feels like forever.

Chapter Eleven

"What do you think the mom's going to do after getting released from the hospital?" I ask.

I'm leaning against the wall outside of Valerie's office with a Case Worker who works Child Protective Service Investigations. Tessa Fields and I have staffed a case with her supervisor and Valerie about a child that was taken into custody last night. Tessa's been on call all week, and she's fairly new. Valerie called me at home last night, and since I wasn't doing anything and went home directly after work, she asked if I would assist Tessa. I told her that I would be happy to and was directed to Athens Regional. I tried not to think of my last trip there, but that was impossible. That led me to thinking of Nick, and I've been doing fairly well the last few days on the amount of time my thoughts go to him. I realize Tessa is talking, and I've not heard a word she has said.

"Tessa, I'm sorry. I tuned out for a minute. I'm with you now."

She laughs. "You're tired like I am, I would imagine."

I nod my head. Tessa and I were out until early this morning. She got a call from a nurse at Athens Regional that a woman was in labor and due to give birth any minute; they suspected she was on drugs. They tested her, and they were right. I went out with Tessa, and we arrived shortly after the baby's birth. The baby boy is in the NICU and was born drug-addicted. The mother was irrational and couldn't understand why she wouldn't be able to take her baby home. It didn't occur to her that she had no home to go to. She had no plan where to go. It sure as hell didn't make a difference that she was using.

Tessa and I went back and forth with the woman for over two hours. We finally got her to understand that she wouldn't be taking that baby with her when she left. She cussed us for several minutes before I told her we'd heard enough, and she needed to tell us someone that could care for her baby until she could get it together. She refused to do that, and I told her the other alternative would be Foster Care, and we were heading in that direction quickly.

She gave me one name, and I told her no, because I knew that woman to be a prostitute. She gave me another name, and I said no on that one as well, because I knew that woman to deal drugs. Tessa asked about relatives, and the woman said, *No fucking way would I send my son to live there.* My thought was, *Are they worse than she is?* How's that possible?

Our breaking point was when the woman told us she wasn't going to do shit to help us. I told Tessa to go call her supervisor while I called Judge Wright. When the state takes custody of any child, we have to call the Judge and get a Shelter Care Order. It's basically an emergency order placing the child temporarily in our custody for seventy-two hours until we can get in front of him to say whether we want the child to remain in custody, return home or go to another possible living arrangement.

Now, I'm not supposed to call Judge Wright before Tessa calls her supervisor to get permission to call the Judge, but what was her supervisor going to say? *No?*

I called Judge Wright on his cell. Yes, I have that kind of relationship with the man. I launched into what was going on, and he cut me off, telling me if I was calling for a Shelter Care Order, then the answer was yes. I told him he was the best, and he said the same to me. Tessa goes back to my original question.

"I think the mom's going to leave the hospital and disappear for a while."

"I think you're absolutely right," I tell her.

"I appreciate so much you coming out with me last night. You handled that woman great," Tessa says to me, smiling.

She's such a cute girl. She's in her early twenties, extremely bright with eyes that view the world in an innocent way. I hope she stays that way. She's short and a little chubby, but so angelic-looking with her honey blond hair and blue eyes. Her smile lights up her whole face. I like Tessa a lot. I like her energy more than anything.

"So did you. I think we did a great job balancing each other out." I'm about to say something else to her when I see Nick, Mack, a man I don't know and Chief Thompson walking down the hall. My mouth goes dry. My knees go weak, and my heart starts to pound.

Holy Heaven, he looks absolutely incredible. He was dressed down last Friday, but he's decked out, not only in black dress pants, a light blue button up shirt and tie but a jacket as well. Nick has to turn heads when he's out. He has to. He's so damn gorgeous, and the way he walks is full of confidence. He holds himself like no other I've ever seen.

I instantly flash to the way he kissed me, how he felt up against me, and then I think of what he said to me. *I want to take you home with me and fuck you.* My knees are getting weaker. Tessa sees the change in my expression and turns around to see what I'm staring at. The four walk by us.

"Grace," Nick says very seriously, with no trace of humor.

"Nick," I say back, just as seriously.

They walk in Valerie's office and shut the door. What *is* that about? Why's he here? What're they talking about behind closed doors? Has he found something on Misty's case and doesn't want to talk about it in front of me? Is it about me? Mack walks out and finds two chairs, dragging them in Valerie's office and closing the door again. Tessa looks at me.

"Who was that?" she asks me.

I know she's not asking about the Chief. She's probably not asking about the other man. She's asking about Nick. I ask for clarification anyway. I don't want to make assumptions.

"Which guy are you asking about?"

"The really big guy."

"Nick Bassano. He's a Robbery/Homicide Detective for Athens-Clarke County," I say.

She smiles at me. "He's gorgeous. Is he single?"

"Yes. He's definitely single."

"Are you two dating? I'm only asking because your whole demeanor changed when you saw him, and he was looking at you the whole time he was walking down the hall and it looked intense."

I blush. What can I say? *We could have been. Maybe? Except he dates everyone else, too. He's a great kisser and wants to fuck me. Well, he did. He probably doesn't want to anymore. Oh, and here's the best part, I punched him.*

"No, we aren't dating."

"Well, you two should be. The way you were both looking at each other. Whew!" She's fanning herself as she walks away from me.

I feel like I'm frozen in my spot. My brain finally tells my feet to move, and I walk back to my desk. It's getting late in the day, and I can hear everyone making plans for tonight and talking about their weekend plans.

A lot of discussion still revolves around the Bradberrys' murder. It was front page news yesterday and again today. Their murder is front page news for two days, but the murder of a child is not. It pissed me off yesterday, and it still pisses me off today. I refuse to talk about them.

I lean over my cubicle to Julie's cubicle. She's sitting at her desk, typing and talking to Cassidy, who is hanging over the other side of Julie's cubicle. I involve myself in their conversation, but I keep looking at Valerie's closed door. They've been in there for a long time. I hear Julie say that she and her husband are going to Atlanta to the Fox to see some comedian perform. Cassidy, her husband and their two kids are going to the lake for the weekend.

"What're you doing this weekend, Grace?" Cassidy asks me.

I focus my attention on her. "What?" I ask.

"What're you doing this weekend?" she asks again.

"Um. I'm not sure," I say to her, but I'm looking at Valerie's door.

Cassidy sees that I'm distracted and turns and looks at Valerie's door, too.

"What's going on, Grace?" she asks me.

Julie looks at both of us and stands.

"What am I missing?" Julie asks, looking at the both of us and then at Valerie's door. "Who's in there?" she asks, looking at me.

"Nick, Chief Thompson, a man I don't know and Mack," I say.

"Who's Nick?" Cassidy asks me.

"Oh, sorry. Nick Bassano. He's a detective with Athens-Clarke County."

Valerie's door flies open, and she sticks her head out.

"Grace," she calls, looking directly at me. She looks unhappy. Shit. What's going on?

I suddenly feel like I'm at school, and I have to walk to the front of the class and give a speech. I feel eyes on me. I want to ask one of them how I look, but that would sound ridiculous. I walk into Valerie's office, and Nick's scent is the first thing that hits me.

Oh, Holy Heaven, he smells so damn good. It's a big ball of tension in Valerie's office. No one looks happy. I'm nervous. I mean, I'm really nervous. I want to ask everyone if they can hear my heart pounding. I need some water. If I have to talk, I don't know if I'll be able. There's one empty chair, and it's beside Nick.

"Have a seat, Grace," Valerie says to me.

I sit and try to control my breathing. There are no happy campers in this room. Mack looks pissed. The Chief doesn't look much happier. The man I don't know doesn't look happy either. Valerie and Nick look like they're having a staring contest, and I'm not sure who the winner will be. Chief Thompson leans over Nick and sticks his hand out to me.

"Grace, I'm Chief Brett Thompson. And that man over there is Sergeant Riley Jenkins, and you know Nick."

Chief Thompson sounds like he gargled nails before coming here with his voice. He's a thick man who at one time was probably in great shape. He's completely bald, and I've always liked him, even though I've never personally met him.

"Hi," I say. I hope my voice doesn't sound as shaky to everyone else as it does to me.

I lean over and shake his hand. I look over at Sergeant Jenkins, who's sitting on the other side of Mack. He nods at me. I look at Nick out of the corner of my eye. He's still staring at Valerie, who's still staring at him, and they both look hotly pissed at one another. What's going on? I have a feeling I'm about to find out. By the looks of things, I'm not going to like it. And I'm right.

"Grace, we need your help," Chief Thompson says to me.

"O-okay," I stammer.

"I'm sure you've heard about the Bradberrys' murder."

"Yes." I'm completely confused. Why is he here about the Bradberrys?

"We need your help in identifying some kids."

I know my face shows nothing but confusion. I look at Valerie, and she does nothing but throw her hands up.

"Mack and I are completely out of this." She's pissed. I mean, really pissed.

I look over at Mack, and his jaw looks like it might break it's so tense. I look back at Chief Thompson, who continues.

"I need to connect you with a detective and let you work with him."

I'm still confused. I wish he would just get on with it and shine some light on the situation.

"Work with whom?" I ask.

"Me," Nick says, looking at me.

"I don't want to work with you," I snap at him.

He narrows his eyes at me. He looks pissed. Now, why in the hell did I go and say that? Haven't I been dying for him to call me? Yes. But I realize I'm still mad, and I'm hurt that he hasn't called.

"Would it be possible for Grace and me to speak alone?" he asks, not taking his eyes off of me.

My heart's still pounding. It seems to take forever before anyone moves. They all file out of Valerie's office silently and close the door. I stand up and walk to the window and look out. I feel Nick move behind me. I can tell he's standing incredibly close, and I'm intoxicated by it. I'm getting completely drunk with how close he is to me and how he smells.

"I should've called you," he begins. "I pulled your name up on my phone, I bet fifty times, and I didn't go through with it. I wanted to call. Hell, Grace, I wanted to drive to your apartment after you left and try and talk some sense into you. I wanted to see you. I wasn't accusing you of getting Misty murdered." He lets that hang in the air. "Look at me." His voice is low.

I turn and try to walk away from him. I can't do this. I can't do this with him. He puts his hand on my arm, but it's not rough.

"No, you don't." His voice is softer. It's playing with my emotions, the way he's speaking and what he's saying. "You aren't walking away from me this time."

I look up and into his eyes. I gasp. They're softer towards me and God, they're really beautiful. There's no denying that.

"Why can't you say you're sorry for what you said?" I ask him.

"Because I'm an asshole sometimes." I see the beginnings of a smile.

Oh, I don't want to smile. I want to stay mad, but I can't. I smile at him.

"Only sometimes?" I ask.

"Okay, maybe more than sometimes."

I can feel the tension begin to ease between us.

"I'm sorry I punched you," I say.

He rubs his jaw, remembering.

"You have a great right hook." He moves closer to me, and I stop breathing. He's looking down at me and holding my eyes. "I'm sorry for what I said. I'm sorry I attacked you with my mouth." He's smiling, giving my words back to me. "I'm sorry I didn't call you when I really wanted to."

We're silent for a few moments.

"Apology accepted," I say.

He gives me a small smile. "I need your help."

"Okay." I think at this moment, I'd probably agree to just about anything that he said or asked me to do. "What do you need me to do? Because your boss isn't making much sense. I'm feeling pretty lost here."

"Let's have everyone come back in, and I'll get to it pretty quickly. I need you to start helping me tonight. Can you do that?"

"Yes," I say, looking in his eyes.

I sit, and Nick has everyone come back in. Mack and Valerie still look unhappy. Valerie sits back behind her desk and looks at me.

"Are you okay?" she asks me.

"I am." And I mean it. I glance over at Nick, and he's looking at me.

"I found some evidence at the Bradberrys' house, and it's bad. It involves seven girls and possibly Misty," he says, continuing to look at me. My heart's still pounding and not in a good way. I still have no idea what he's referring to.

"Whatever your evidence is, you don't know who the girls are."

"No," he says.

"Why're you coming to me? You have a whole department at your fingertips. You have resources that are much more far-reaching than what I can give you."

Nick looks over at the Chief, who nods his head at him.

"I trust you," he says to me. That's news. He looks at Mack and Valerie and then back at me. "This is all very sensitive. What I've found only Chief Thompson, Sergeant Jenkins, my Lieutenant, Brison Scott, Chris Taylor and I know about."

I look at Valerie. She has a permanent scowl on her face.

"They won't tell us shit," she says. She's looking at Chief Thompson, Sergeant Jenkins and Nick again, and I'm wondering what in the hell went on between all of them before I came in.

Nick looks at me again and is holding my eyes. "You're being loaned out to the police department indefinitely," he says to me.

What the fuck? I start to speak and can't find the words. I stop and then try it again. I look at Valerie and then at Mack.

"That's not possible," I say. "That's never happened."

"Well, it has now," Valerie says. "I've already screamed about it and yelled about how this is an unorthodox situation, and that it isn't your job to solve cases for the police department. Mack has said the same thing, and we've been on the phone all day with Howard and Brison Scott. Brison's willing to pull out all of the big guns against us if we don't loan you out." Her voice is full of venom.

I really am all kinds of confused. I don't understand why they would be talking to Howard. Howard Shaw is the Special Assistant to the Attorney General, or more simply put, DFCS's attorney. We use the acronym SAAG when referring to him. He does all the legal work that comes with any court situation. He's with us on all court dates. He's older than dirt, but I've never met a sharper attorney in my life. It takes him a minute to get a sentence out because he speaks so slowly and with the thickest Southern drawl I've ever heard.

The Chief clears his throat and speaks.

"Nick, Sergeant Jenkins and I went two and three rounds how we wanted to work this. We don't know who these girls are. We've been trying to figure out the best way to find out without putting it on the table what we have or reaching out to other people, even within my own department. Nick suggested Grace. He said she's the most knowledgeable of the kids around here. He said she knows the streets well, and she's tough. Most of all, he trusts her more than he's trusted anyone else in a long time. We all trust Nick, and if he thinks this'll work, then we're going with it. We did go to Brison about this. I don't think he really threatened you," the Chief says, straight to Valerie.

I'm floored. I'm floored that Nick thinks that about me and that he said that about me. I look at him, and I swear I think he's blushing.

Valerie points a finger at the Chief. She looks like she wants to go smoke. "Were you not in here when we had that goddamn phone call with him? Did I not put it on speaker? It sounded like a threat to me."

I can feel Nick going tense.

"We're getting way off subject here," Nick says to her.

They're staring one another down again. The room goes deathly silent. The tension is on the way up again, if it ever even went down.

"What about Missing Persons Reports to identify them?" I ask, breaking the silence. I have no idea what his evidence is, but it seems like a good suggestion.

Nick breaks his stare with Valerie and looks at me. "I don't have names. There isn't anything for me to go on."

"How long are you thinking when you say indefinitely?"

"I don't know. It may take a day or two or a week. I won't know until I can show you what we have."

"I have cases," I say. "I have kids and foster parents and biological parents and court and case plans and appointments. I have a new kid on my caseload, a baby boy who was born last night. He doesn't even have a name yet." I want to keep up my argument, but as I look around at everyone, I realize it's been decided, and I don't have a vote. Well, so much for democracy. It doesn't exist in this room. I know when Nick looked at me the way he did, and I decided I would do whatever he asked, I didn't realize that it would be *indefinitely*. I look at Valerie. "What about my cases?"

"We'll divide them up," she says.

Apparently, it's not a democracy for her, either. She and Mack have been railroaded. I don't know what was said to them, and it's obvious that she's not going to share it with me, but it must have been big for this to happen.

"That's not fair to everyone else," I say. "There are only four of us to begin with, and Mandy's still gone." Mandy Abbott has been on maternity leave for the last several weeks.

"We'll make it work. Mandy comes back on Monday," Mack says. It's the first thing he's said since I've walked in the room.

"How?" I ask, looking at him.

"Grace," he says softly. "Don't worry about it. You go with Detective Bassano and help them out."

"So, this has all been decided?" I cross my arms over my breasts and sit back in my chair, looking at Valerie.

"Yes. We've been fighting it all day. We lost."

"But I'm just finding out about it now?"

"I didn't want to stress you further. You've had a full plate." She gives me a slight smile.

"Are we finished?" the Chief asks.

Valerie throws her hands up. "Yes, I guess we are."

"Let's go, Grace," Nick says to me.

"I would like to have a word with Grace alone, gentlemen, if you don't mind. That includes you, Mack," Valerie says to everyone.

The men file out of the room with a frustrated look. Nick all but stomps out. Valerie sighs and runs her hands roughly through her hair. It makes it look even crazier. I see some curls popping out in places. Her brown eyes are intense and angry.

"What happened, Valerie?" I ask, looking at her.

"A nasty fight between Brison Scott, Howard, Mack and me. I'm so pissed about this, Grace. Rather than Brison coming to Mack and me about it, he went straight to Howard and did his smooth talking. It was decided before we even knew about it. I like Brison. I always have, but I'm angry that those two...*men* decided this. We have no control here. They were going to involve one of the Superior Court judges if need be. There's some serious shit going on with this case for it to get this far. I don't have a damn clue what it is. The Chief and Nick Bassano really won't tell us anything. That's not really what I wanted to talk to you about. I was digressing."

She stops for a moment, staring at me.

"Grace, there's something going on between you and Nick Bassano." She sees my eyes widen, because hers do, too, and at the same time. "Don't tell me that there isn't. The way he looks at you, and the way you look at him; I can see it. I don't think you realize what's coming off the two of you, but I see it, and I feel it. I don't know Nick, but I've heard things about him. He has a reputation with women. I know you're a big girl, and a tough one, just please be careful and take care of yourself with him. If you like him, and you know what you're getting yourself into, then great. I couldn't let you walk out that door without saying something to you."

I nod my head and swallow hard. "Thanks, Valerie."

"Okay. Go." She gets up and walks around hugging me.

We walk out of her office together. The men are standing around the way men do when there's tension between alpha males. They all have their arms crossed over their chests and in a stance that says, *My dick is bigger than yours*. I see that Julie and Cassidy haven't left, and I can tell by their expressions that they're dying to know what's going on.

Nick steps over to my side. "Do you want to get your things?"

I look up at him. "Um, sure." I walk to my desk.

"Grace, are you in trouble?" Julie asks me.

Yes I am, but not the kind of trouble she's referring to. I smile at her and at Cassidy, who's standing right beside her wants to know as well.

"No. Nick just needs me to help him with something."

Mack calls for Julie and Cassidy.

"You didn't get fired, did you?" Cassidy asks.

"No, I haven't been fired." I grab my handbag and my phone off my desk and look at them. Julie and Cassidy could almost pass for sisters. They both have dark hair and dark eyes and are about the same height. They both look concerned. "I'm fine," I say, smiling at both of them. They look at me and walk towards Valerie's office. I sigh. I will owe them more than my life after this is over.

Nick tells me he wants me to follow him, because I'll be parking where he parks and going in the police department from the back. I guess I'm official now. My mind is spinning. What's going on? What does he have that so few people are involved? And what about the Bradberrys and unidentified girls, and possibly Misty? I don't understand.

Chapter Twelve

When we get to the police department, I park beside Nick and follow him and the Chief in the back door, up a hallway and straight into a conference room. At the table sits a nice-looking blond guy, and my guess is that he's Chris Taylor. Nick motions for me to take a seat at the table, and he sits across from me. Chief Thompson says something to Sergeant Jenkins and then leaves. Sergeant Jenkins takes a seat at the head of the table and says nothing.

"Grace, this is Detective Chris Taylor," Nick says.

Chris looks as if he' a few inches taller than I am. He's got a head full of blond hair and blue eyes. He looks like he could be a surfer. He's very handsome. He's big and muscular, too, but not like Nick. He smiles at me and holds out his hand.

"Hi Grace. It's nice to meet you. You're as beautiful as Nick said you are."

Seriously? I look over at Nick, who looks like he's been caught with his pants around his ankles and no underwear. I glance down at the end of the table, and Sergeant Jenkins looks unhappy. I realize that I've not heard him speak. I look back at Chris Taylor.

"It's nice to meet you too," I say.

"Are you done with her?" Nick snaps at Chris.

Chris smiles at Nick unabashed and then smiles at me again with the same expression. I see that I'm not the only one who gets snapped at by Nick.

"Let's get started," Nick says, looking at me. "You're probably wondering what in the hell's going on."

"Yeah, it's passed through my mind."

"The Bradberry call went out to 911 as a possible Burglary in progress. Patrol got on scene and found two of our local idiots in their house. The dumbasses thought they had disarmed the security system by pushing some buttons, but what they really did was send out a signal that someone was in the home. It's actually a good thing that they were there, or else we might not have discovered the Bradberrys for a few days. By all accounts, they were in Europe and were going to be there for a couple of weeks. One of the officers did a sweep of the house and found them in their bedroom."

He's looking at me, wanting to make sure I'm with him. I nod that I am.

"They were beaten to death. Chris and I were called, and once we were out there, we started searching the house. We first thought it was a Robbery gone bad. We all know how wealthy the Bradberrys were. When we started searching, we couldn't find that anything appeared to be missing. We searched deeper, and then I found those." He points to the end of the table, and there are stacks of pictures. They're all faced down. Oh, I don't think I'm going to like those pictures, but I have a sinking feeling I'm going to have to look at them. Nick keeps talking. "After I found them, I wanted to quit my job and shoot myself in the head."

"We wouldn't let him do either," Chris says.

"They're really bad," I say. My voice is barely above a whisper.

"Grace, Mickey Bradberry was in some sadistic, sick shit. He wasn't alone. We're working under secrecy here because of who he was, who he knew and what he was into, and there are two other men involved and a woman, in addition to someone who took all of those damn pictures. We have no idea who anyone is. We can't identify the girls, and we can't identify the other men or the woman. Mickey Bradberry knew a lot of people. He has ties that go all the way to the Governor. We don't know who's involved, and we don't know who to trust. But I do trust you. I think you can help us figure out who these girls are and maybe help us figure out where these girls are. We've got to start there."

"Okay." I'm holding his eyes.

He gives me a smile, but it doesn't go all the way to his eyes. "No shrinking daisy, right?"

"Right." But it doesn't come out sounding confident. "Could I have something to drink?"

Chris jumps up from the table. "I'll get you something. I've been tied to this room since Nick, Sergeant Jenkins and Chief Thompson left. I need to stretch my legs. What do you want, Grace?"

I break my gaze away from Nick and look at him. "Water is fine."

"You got it. I'll be back in a minute."

Sergeant Jenkins looks at Nick and me. "Are we good here?"

Nick keeps his eyes on me and says, "Yeah, we're good."

"Okay, let me know if you need anything, and let me know if she's able to identify anybody. I'd like to give the Chief an update in a few hours."

"Yes, sir. I'll let you know." And then we are alone. Nick continues to hold my eyes. "Can you do this?"

"Yes," I say, with a little more determination than what I feel. He stands and walks to the end of the table, picks up a few pictures that have been placed away from the larger stacks and brings them back, setting them in front of him on the table. "How many pictures are there?" I ask.

"Almost five hundred pictures." His voice is tight.

Oh, my God. I don't know what to say, so I say nothing for a moment.

"You said there are seven girls?"

"Yes."

"That's so many," I whisper.

"Yes." His voice is barely above a whisper. "They're going to be hard to look at. I tried to pick the most innocuous ones I could find, but there simply aren't any."

Chris has returned with a bottle of water. I grab it, take a long drink and look at Nick.

"Let me have them." I reach my hand out, and he puts the pictures in my hand, still face down.

I pull them to me, take a deep breath and then turn them over. It's not like I had anything going on in my imagination of what I would see, but even if I did, nothing would have prepared me. I've seen some sick shit in my days. I've seen kids beaten and burned and starved. I've seen kids who have the physical as well as mental scars of being restrained, and I've dealt with child molestation, but this is sick and twisted on a whole new level.

The first picture is a punch in the gut. It's Darla Grier. I can feel the goose pimples breaking out all over me. She's being posed, and she looks drugged, and she is being made to look at the camera while there's not just one sick bastard using her but three. Her behaviors all make sense to me now. Even her drug usage makes sense. She's probably living in a nightmare that's never ending.

I take a shaky breath and go to the next picture. I don't know this girl, but it's still just as shocking and sick. She's a cute blonde, and she looks drugged, too. It doesn't matter that I don't know her. Someone does. There has to be somebody out there that knows her. Is she at home like Darla and living with what was done to her?

The third picture is of a girl that I don't know very well, but I know her name. Tonya. I can't think of her last name right at the moment. She, too, has blond hair. The pictures don't get any less shocking. It's all disgusting, and Mickey Bradberry got exactly what he deserved. I feel sorry for Eleanor being married to this piece of shit and having to pay for his sins with her life.

The fourth picture is of a girl that I know from the streets. I've seen her countless times. She's one that I've never been able to get close to. I don't know her name and realize that I've not seen her in several months. She's got brown hair, and I know she's a teenager. All of the girls I've seen are young teen girls.

I flip to the fifth picture and completely freeze. My entire world falls from beneath me. I would swear that if I wasn't sitting, I would be falling. I go numb and then I begin to get cold as I stare at the girl in the picture. I can see that my hands are shaking. The bile begins to rise in my throat. I'm going to be sick.

I stand up and think that I'm moving fast, but I feel like everything's happening in slow motion. I'm absently aware that I've knocked my chair over. I can hear Nick saying my name, but it sounds incredibly far away. I stagger out of the door, and I'm confused as to where I'm going. I just know that I have to get out of here, and I have to get out of here *right now*. There are a few people here, and they're all looking at me like they've seen someone crazy.

I find a door, push it harder than what I need to, and I'm standing outside. I walk over to where there are some bushes and put my hands on my legs, doubled over. I'm as close to the ground as I can get without falling to my knees. That may be next. I'm breathing deep trying to calm my stomach. *Don't vomit, don't vomit, don't vomit.* I'm trying to slow my racing heart, and I see my tears are falling on the ground. That's how Nick finds me.

"Grace," he says softly. He puts his hand on my back. It is a gentle touch, and it feels warm through my shirt against my cold, clammy skin. "I know they're hard to look at. I'm really sorry."

I'm still doubled over when I finally speak.

"They are hard to look at." I go back to deep breathing again and trying to get the sick feeling to leave me. When I think that I won't vomit, I'm able to stand and wipe my running nose with the back of my hand. It's gross, but right now, I don't give a shit. "Nick, one of those girls is my sister."

Nick has the same expression on his face as he did last Friday when I punched him. He looks like he wants to say something, but he doesn't know what to say.

"Your sister," he says, completely astonished.

I nod my head. "Her name's Naomi Harding. She's been missing for almost a year."

"Oh, God, Grace." His voice trails off. He's looking at me and runs a hand through his hair, but it's so short it stays in the same place. "I didn't know you had a sister."

"I know. We've not had many, *Let's get to know each other* conversations."

He takes a deep breath, and he's still holding my eyes with his. "Maybe that needs to change," he says. "Can you go back in there and keep going?"

I feel sick knowing that my sister is a victim in this. Waves of guilt over doing so little for her rush me, but I have a job to do. Nick has asked me to do something, and if I can help my sister by doing this, then that's what I need to do.

I'll need to deal with what has happened to her and more than anything *where she is right now?* I want to know that. I have to help Nick however I can, so he can find her. I have to box what I'm feeling for later and get this done.

"Yes. I can do this." I'm assertive in saying it. Not only can I do this, *I want to do this.*

He moves closer to me and is standing right in front of me. He pulls his fingers through one of my curls.

"You're one strong woman." His voice is low when he says it.

How is it that he can draw me to him even at this moment? Maybe it's because of this moment. I'm in a mini personal crisis standing here, and he's being kind.

"Right now, looking at that shit, I don't feel strong," I say, still holding his eyes.

He bends down, and we are almost nose to nose. *Whoa.* He's really close.

"You're very strong." He stands back up, looking down at me. "Ready?"

I take a deep breath. "Yeah, I'm ready."

We walk back in together, and I notice that the people who were at their desks when I ran out are gone. It looks pretty empty around here. I look at my watch and see that it's getting late. *Shit*, Jess. I bet she's been calling me. I walk back in the room, with Nick behind me. Chris looks at me.

"Is everything okay?" he asks, looking concerned.

"Yes," I say, finding my handbag on the floor. Someone set my chair back where it belongs. I find my phone and look at it. "Shit." Jess has called four times. I look at both guys. "I have to make a phone call."

"Sure," Nick says. "Do we need to leave? Are you calling your boyfriend?" He's trying so hard to lighten things. It works. I give him a small grin.

"No. I'm calling Jess. She and Jake have been in Florida on Spring Break all week. They're coming home tomorrow. She said she would call this evening."

She answers on the first ring. "Where are you?" she demands. "I've been worried sick about you."

"I'm sorry. I'm out, and my phone was in my bag, and I forgot that you said you would call. I didn't mean to make you worry about me."

"What're you doing?"

"I'm with Nick." I see him raise an eyebrow at me.

"Oh, are you on a date?" I can tell she's smiling.

"Yeah, I'm on a date. Jess, can I call you later?"

"Yes. Have a great night. I can't wait to hear about it."

I hang up and sigh. She does not want to hear about this. Oh Lord, what're her parents going to think when they find out what kind of man Mickey Bradberry was?

"A date?" Nick asks, smiling at me.

"What did you want me to say? I'm here with Nick, talking about how disgusting your parents' friend has turned out to be."

"What?" Nick asks sharply, his smile gone.

I raise my hand to stop him from any other comment. "I would never say anything about what's going on here, okay?" That seems to relax him somewhat. I sit down and pull the pictures back to me and look at Chris. "One of the girls is my sister, Naomi," I say. He's shocked by that piece of information too. "Let me finish looking, and then I'll tell the both of you who I know and what I know."

They both nod, and I go back to the pictures. I keep waiting for the shock to wear off, but it doesn't. The sixth girl is Hailey West. She's a pretty, dark-haired girl. They are all pretty. I don't know her well, but again, I know her name.

The last girl is dark-haired, too, and I don't know her at all. I've never seen her and can't tell Nick or Chris anything about her. There's something nagging at me. It's not just the pictures or the girls, but it's something in the pictures. I flip through them again quickly. It's in the back of my mind, and then it's gone.

"Grace, what is it?" Nick asks.

I look up at him. "I don't know. There's something bothering me."

"Looking at those, I would hope so," he says, his voice full of disgust.

I shake my head. He's missing my point, but I'm not being very clear. I put the pictures down. Whatever I was trying to think about is completely gone. I lay all seven pictures out, side-by-side, so they are upside down to me. I take another deep breath and remind myself that I have to do this. I have to help my sister by doing whatever I can.

"That's my sister, Naomi Harding," I say, pointing to the first picture. Naomi looks a lot like my mother, with her dirty blond hair and green eyes. She's a pretty girl, and I remember my mother being pretty when I was a little girl. "She's been missing for almost a year. My brother filed a Missing Persons Report about a week after she went missing." I see Chris writing on a legal pad. "This is Darla Grier. Our office had some involvement with her. Not only that, I know where she is," I say, looking at both of them. Nick and Chris look at one another.

"Man, you're one fucking brilliant guy for thinking of Grace," Chris says, looking between Nick and me.

"This is Tonya," I say, pointing to the next picture. "I'm trying to remember her last name. It'll come to me. This is Hailey West," I say, pointing to her picture. "This girl I know, but I don't know her name. I remember seeing her on the streets. She's part of the homeless population. I know some people who could probably tell us who she is. I haven't seen her in several months." I pull the other two pictures and tap them. "I don't know these two girls. I've never seen them. Does any of that help?" I ask, looking at them. Nick is about to say something, when I exclaim, "Overby. Tonya Overby." I see Chris writing this down.

"It does help," Nick says. He looks at Chris. "Do you want to stay here and be the gatekeeper of the pictures, and see if there are any Missing Persons Reports on some of these girls?"

"Yeah. I can do that, and I'll let Sergeant Jenkins know what we've learned. What're you going to do?"

Nick looks at me. "I think I'll let Grace introduce me to Darla Grier." I tell him that I'll take him so he can talk with her.

I look at Chris. "My brother filed a Missing Persons Report on Naomi, but I guess that doesn't matter, since you know who she is, and you know who her family is, and I've told you that already, haven't I?"

Chris smiles at me. "That's okay. It's late." He stands up and looks at Nick. "I'll call you and let you know what I find out."

Nick and I sit, looking at one another.

"You said Misty could be involved with this. Are there pictures of her that you don't want to show me?"

"No. There aren't any pictures of her."

"Why do you think she's one of the victims of this?"

"Something in my gut is telling me that she is. Chris feels it, too." That's good enough for me.

"If you think Misty's part of this, and she's dead, do you think the other girls are dead? Do you think my sister is dead? And, if so, how is it that Darla's walking around?"

"I don't know. Grace. I'm asking those same questions, too. I plan on finding out and answering a shitload of questions," he says, holding my eyes for a moment. Then, he stands, going to the stack of pictures.

"Nick, isn't this a Sex Crimes case?" I ask, motioning to the pictures.

"In any other normal situation, yes. This isn't a normal situation, which is why we're hanging onto it." He's quiet for a moment, looking down at the pictures and then back up at me. "I don't know how those guys do it over in Sex Crimes. I could never work in that unit. There's no way I could deal with shit like this regularly. I hate dealing with anything to do with rape cases. Those bastards should be strung straight up by their balls. Men should never harm women like that. It's deplorable, and I can easily get on my soap box about it." He's getting angry discussing it. My breath is caught in my throat listening to him, how he feels about rapists and that men shouldn't harm women. "What?" he asks me.

I shake my head at him. "Nothing. I completely agree with you. What're you doing?" I ask him.

"I'm going to put them in seven separate stacks. I should've done this earlier."

I stand and move to the end of the table. I'm standing so close to him that our arms are brushing against each other.

"I'll help you," I say, looking up at him. He looks in my eyes, and I have to catch my breath. He's looking at me differently. His eyes are softer towards me.

"No. Those pictures were as good as I could come up with. They get much worse."

"I'll help you," I say again, full of determination.

He bends, and his face is hovering over mine. I stop breathing, but my heart is pounding. I feel his breath on me when he speaks.

"You'll come across more pictures of your sister. I know they're disgusting to look at, and you'll see those images of her. You realize that, right?"

"Yes. I know. I can do this." My voice should be stronger, but I can't make it.

"No shrinking daisy." He smiles at me.

"No," I whisper.

Between the two of us, we make quick work of getting the pictures into seven different stacks. I try not to pay too much attention, but I have to look. I cringe, a lot. Each picture of my sister is a punch in the gut. There are so many punches, since there are so many pictures. I breathe a sigh of relief after it's over.

"Well, that was unpleasant," I say, looking up at Nick. "Have you ever worked a case like this?"

"No, and I hope to hell I never do again. I can look at a dead body or bodies, but this is the sickest shit I've ever seen. Like I said, I couldn't do this all of the time."

"I agree with it being sick. I've seen sick shit in my days, but nothing like this."

"The Bradberry homicide shouldn't even be our case. We weren't supposed to be the lead on this," he says. I look at him, confused. "We're the lead detectives on Misty's case. We have hers. There're two other Detectives in this unit. They're in a two-week trial involving the murder of those two college girls two years ago. Do you remember that?"

"Who doesn't?"

"We got called out as lead on the Bradberry case because of the trial, and now that we think it relates to Misty, we get to keep it, and we're not pulling in any additional help at the moment because of all of this." He's motioning to the pictures.

Nick picks up the stack of pictures that has Darla in them, flipping through them. He chooses several pictures and puts the rest back on the table.

"What're you doing?" I ask him.

"I need to take these with us."

"Why?" I ask.

"I may need to go through them with her."

"What?" I ask, horrified. "Nick, you can't make her look at those pictures."

I can see that he's getting fired up. "What do you want me to do, draw some fucking pictures for her?"

I put my hands on my hips and look at him. I see he's back.

"That poor girl's been traumatized, and you're going to waltz in there with those pictures?"

"I'll be gentle."

I snort, "Right. Nick, please don't show her those pictures." I'm pleading with him.

"No promises on the pictures," he says, "and I don't waltz anywhere." He gives me a wicked grin.

I shake my head at him. I feel unbalanced with him as usual, and I realize I wouldn't have it any other way.

I follow him out of the room to a desk, and I see that it is his desk. He's opening and closing several drawers, looking for something. He has all kinds of things taped to his wall. He has sports memorabilia lined up on a top shelf that serves as a hutch over his desk. It's filled with UGA football pictures and a small UGA football signed by the Head Coach. There's a New York Yankees ball cap, and I see several signatures.

There's a picture of a much younger him in a Marines uniform. He looks so serious in the picture. There's a woman on one side and a man on the other. They're both smiling. It has to be his parents. He looks like his father. Nick and his dad are the same size in height and bulk. Nick looks handsome in his uniform. I smile at the picture. I focus my attention back on him and see him sliding the pictures in a small manila envelope. He looks at me.

"What're you smiling about?" he asks.

"I like your picture," I say pointing at it. "You're handsome." I'm blushing as I say it.

"You think I'm handsome?"

"Yes." *And gorgeous, super sexy, hot body, dimples that call to me, beautiful eyes and I would love for you to kiss me again and more.* I keep all of that to myself.

"You're making me blush, Grace Harrison," he says. His eyes are dancing.

I start laughing. "Stop," I say, smacking him on his hard chest.

He rubs it like I hurt him. "You're abusive. I kind of like it." He's leering at me, and then we start laughing together.

"I can't believe we're laughing in the midst of this hell," I say.

"It feels good, though, doesn't it? Sometimes, you just have to stop and laugh. Even at inappropriate times. Come on, let's get this over with."

Chapter Thirteen

I follow Nick outside, and after I tell him what street she's on and what house it is, he asks me about my brother.

"Tell me about him," he says.

"His name's Matt Mills. He's my big brother, a drug addict, homeless, and I love him dearly."

"I noticed that you and your sister don't look alike. Do you and your brother look alike?"

"No. Naomi looks like my mom. Matt has white blond hair and blue eyes that are the color of the sky. We're the product of three different dads."

"You had a rough childhood." He's not asking a question. He's making a statement of fact. I answer anyway.

"Yeah, you could say that."

"Do you not want to talk about it?"

"It's okay. I'll talk about it if I'm asked. I don't offer it up in everyday conversation."

We're on Odd Street, and I point to the house. It's dark out at this point, but we see lights on in the house. We get out and walk up the porch.

"Is this porch safe?" he asks as we walk up.

"I was wondering that, too. I was here the other night, and it held up under me."

"Yeah, but I've got a hundred plus pounds on you," Nick says, walking carefully behind me.

I see Belinda come to the screen door. She smiles when she sees me.

"You're Grace, right?"

"Yes."

"Your mom's here tonight."

I freeze, and Nick runs into me.

"Dammit, Grace," he says, so low that only I can hear.

"My mom's here?" I ask, making sure I heard correctly. Belinda nods. I let out a deep breath and prepare myself. "Could we come in?" I ask.

"Sure." She looks at Nick, and her eyes go wide. "You're a big guy," she says to him. "Who're you?"

"I'm Detective Nick Bassano. Grace and I are here to see Darla. Is she here?"

"You ain't gonna arrest her, are you?" Belinda asks, suspiciously.

"No. Grace and I need to talk to her," he says to her.

"Well, come in. She's in her room. I'll go get her."

We walk in the house, and there's my mother on the couch, watching TV. I can see her black eye from where I'm standing. She hasn't looked away from what she is watching.

"Mom," I say sharply.

She turns and looks at me. She's high or drunk or both. She sits up, swaying all over the place.

"Grace?" I want to ask her who else she thinks it is. She stands up and staggers over to me. "You look good." But it's all slurred together. I can smell her as she gets closer. She's definitely drunk.

"How much have you been drinking, Mom?" I know my voice is tight and angry. Nick's standing beside me, looking at my mother.

"Not enough," she slurs, smiling. I cringe. Yes, she has no front teeth now.

"Who hit you, Mom?"

"I wasn't hit. I ran into somethin'."

"Right," I mutter. It's the same stupid story every time with her.

"You've lost weight," she says, looking me up and down.

"I haven't noticed."

"You got any money?"

I clench my jaw tight from saying what I really want to say, which falls along the lines of, *You must be fucking kidding me that I've not seen you in how long and one of the first things you want from me is money?*

"No, Mom. No money," I say tightly.

She looks like she might want to argue with me about it, and I hope to God she doesn't. I don't want to battle my mother here with an audience, especially with Nick here. That's something I really don't want him to witness.

"I think I'll go get back on the couch," she says instead.

"You do that," I mutter.

I turn my attention to Nick. His expression is unreadable. I see Darla come up the hall, freezing when she sees us standing here.

"Hey," I say to her.

"What're you doin' here?" she asks me, suspiciously.

"This is Detective Nick Bassano. We'd like to talk to you."

"Why?" she asks.

I see a small round table, and I point to it.

"Could we sit?"

"Whatever. I don't care," she says, crossing her arms over her chest.

I look up at Nick, and he nods to me. We sit at the table and look at Darla, who's leaning against a loveseat. She's looking everywhere but at us. Belinda is standing and looks helpless. No one speaks for several minutes. All I hear are the low voices on the TV.

"Would you mind sitting with us?" I ask her softly.

Darla sighs and shoves herself away from the couch. She sits at the table and continues to eye us suspiciously. Belinda sits too. I look at Nick, fully expecting him to take this over. This is his interview, not mine. He catches my eyes.

"Go on," he murmurs to me.

Seriously? I look back at Darla and decide, *I can do this.*

"I know what you're living with. I don't know how you do it day in and day out. I don't know if you have nightmares, and if you do, I cannot imagine how bad they are. Have you ever talked to anyone about what you went through?"

"I don't know what you're talkin' about," she says, but I can see that her tough exterior is slipping.

"I know you were raped." I hear Belinda gasp. I keep talking. "I know you were raped by more than one man, and it happened more than once. Would you be willing to talk about it with us?"

We're all deathly silent, and Darla is frozen in her seat. I can still hear the faint voices coming from the TV, along with my mom's breathing as she remains on the couch, but I think she's passed out. Typical. Nick's sitting like a statue. I look at Belinda, and she's looking at Darla.

"No one would believe me if I say anything," Darla finally says.

"I'll believe you. Detective Bassano will believe you. Belinda will believe you."

She shakes her head. "No. No one's gonna believe me."

I wonder how many times she's told herself that. It's probably more times than I can count.

I take a deep breath, and decide to take a chance with her. "Darla, I understand where you're coming from. When I got raped, no one believed me, either."

I hear Nick gasp and feel him go completely tense. I know his eyes are on me. I don't break eye contact with Darla.

"You got raped?" she asks me. Her voice is so small.

"Yes," I say.

"You ain't just sayin' that to get me to talk."

"No, Darla. I would never say something like that if it wasn't true."

"You didn't get raped." I hear my mother say from the couch.

I close my eyes and reign in all of my anger. I would love to jump up and punch my mother in the face. I thought she was passed out. I look over at her.

"Mom, shut up," I say.

"You've been tellin' that same story since you were..."

"Since I was fourteen, mom. Would you shut the hell up," I say it more forcefully and look at Darla.

My mom's still mumbling some stupid bullshit. She's mumbling about me being ungrateful for the life that she gave me. She says that all the time and has always said it. I ignore her.

"Your mom don't believe you?" Darla asks me.

"No. She didn't then, and she still doesn't, but it happened, and it took me a long time to tell somebody I felt like I could trust. When I finally did tell someone who believed me, it felt so good to get that out. Darla, you don't have to hold on to it. You can tell me. You can tell all three of us. We're all going to believe you."

Darla puts her face down on her arms that are resting on the table, and she begins to sob. Her whole body shakes. I touch her arm, and she tenses but then she finds my hand and grabs hold of it, holding it tightly. I look at Belinda.

"Do you have any tissue?" I ask her, quietly. She nods and gets up.

I look up at Nick, and his jaw is rigid, and his expression is angry.

We sit patiently and let Darla cry and work through whatever she needs to work through. When she raises her face, she looks at me.

"I'm sorry," she says.

I bite my lip. I want to cry, too. She's sad, lost, has had so much taken from her, and she's apologizing.

"There's nothing to be sorry for," I tell her.

When she speaks, it's like a floodgate opens, and everything spills out of her. It's hard to listen to. It's hard to believe that what happened to her really did happen. I believe every word she tells us. She was kidnapped off of the street late one night a year ago. She was attacked from behind and knocked unconscious.

When she woke up, she was handcuffed to a bed. There was a woman who gave her drugs all of the time. She was always drugged. The same woman that gave her the drugs also took all of the pictures. Nick and I hate to stop her, but we have to from time to time to get clarification. We ask if that's also the same woman that used her. We find out that it was a different woman.

We look at each other. I think we're thinking the same thing. I was thinking Nick would be looking for another man, but he isn't. There was another woman involved. I have a sick, sinking feeling I know who that woman might be.

Darla says that she had never had sex before. She says that everything was always painful, and they were cruel, and one man loved to see her cry, and it excited him when she screamed and cried. She says that the man would slap her, and she points to the scar on her cheek, telling us that it came from his ring cutting her cheek. They called her all kinds of names. They were always calling her a whore. They thought that's what she was. She says she started to feel like one.

Listening to what was done to her is almost more than I can stand. She says there were times when all three guys were having sex with her at one time. We don't make her go into detail. We get it. There are also pictures to prove it. We ask her if any of them used any of the other's names. She says no. She tells us that if she could have killed herself, she would've. She thought they were going to kill her, and she wished for it.

She says that one night or one day, she doesn't know, because time stopped meaning anything to her, she was made to do something to one of the guys and got choked. Again, we don't ask for details. We get it. She says she passed out, and when she woke up, she was lying in a wooded area not far from here. She was naked, with a filthy blanket tossed over her like they were trying to hide her but not trying too hard. She says she thinks they thought she died and dumped her, trying to get rid of her.

She went to a house that she used to hang out at and found some people that she knew. When they asked what happened to her, she made up a story that she had been to a party, and it had gotten out of control. After that, her life spiraled down. She sold herself for drugs. She would find herself in places and didn't know how she got there and would go for days without eating or bathing. Things got a little better when she found Belinda again.

"I didn't use drugs, ever, until that happened. I started to use to forget. I used because that bitch got me hooked. I'm scared all the time. I never feel safe. I never go nowhere at night."

"She don't," Belinda says to me.

"Do you feel safe?" Darla asks me.

"Yes. But it took a long time. It took a long time for me to trust people."

"How'd you do it?" she asks me.

"What? To feel safe, or to trust people?"

"All of it. Feelin' safe, the trust, bein' able to live and not feelin' like you're trapped all the time. Do you ever stop lookin' over your shoulder?"

"I went through a lot of therapy and got lucky to have a best friend who loves me, and I can share anything and everything with her. I got to a point where I decided that I wasn't going to live in fear. But here's the thing Darla. It was bad what happened to me. Rape is rape, but it was also a one-time thing. I wasn't kidnapped, drugged and used by multiple people multiple times. What happened to you is very traumatic. You're still traumatized by it. I know it may not seem like it right now, but it does help to talk about it."

Darla nods at me, and I even see a slight smile.

"It does help. I've kept it in for a long time. I've been scared to say anything. I'm scared they'll find out I'm really alive and come back and kill me."

"I understand that feeling. I would feel the same way." I look at her and smile. "Do you realize how courageous you are?"

"I don't have no courage," she whispers.

I can feel a tear roll down my cheek. I brush it away. She doesn't need to see me cry. It won't help her.

"Yes, you are courageous. You told us, all three of us, at one time. That took enormous courage." I can hear Nick's phone buzzing in his pocket.

"It's Chris," he says, looking at his phone and then at me. He jumps up and walks out on the porch. I can hear Nick talking, but I don't know what he's saying.

"He's real big," Darla says to me.

"Yes, he is," I agree, smiling.

"He looks mean."

"His bark's worse than his bite."

That makes her smile a little. Nick walks back in, and he looks even more unhappy than when he walked outside.

"I'm sorry," he says, sitting. "Darla, you told us that one of the women would inject you with drugs. Do you have any idea or any thoughts on what they were drugging you with?"

"Yes," she says, "Morphine. Don't ask me if I'm sure, because I am. I saw the bottle more than once, and I heard one of them talkin' about it. I tried gettin' it once I was back on the streets, and I found out that you can only get it from a doctor."

"Did any of them ever take their masks off?" Nick asks her.

"No. How'd you find out about me? How'd you know what happened to me and that they all wore masks?"

"I found the pictures," Nick tells her.

"Where?" Darla asks him.

"At a murder scene."

"Who was murdered?"

Nick takes a deep breath. He looks up and over at my mother, who is still on the couch.

"Don't worry about her," I tell him. "She won't even remember I was here by morning."

He looks at Darla. "There was a couple murdered in their home on Tuesday night. While searching their home, I found the pictures. I have more questions than answers at the moment. I want to tell you everything, but I don't have much to share. After I put all of the pieces of this puzzle together, I'll tell you everything."

"Okay. Are them the pictures?" she asks, pointing to the envelope lying on the table in front of Nick.

"Some of them."

"I want to see'em." Darla says, firmly.

Nick looks at me. *Is he looking for my permission?* He looks at Darla and hands her the envelope. I hear her dog clicking his paws up the hall. He comes around to all of us, sniffing and growling. He sits beside Darla and looks up at her.

"He needs to go to the bathroom. I'll take 'em in the yard and come back." She walks to her room and comes back with a leash and attaches it to Killer's collar. She pauses at the door and then walks out.

"Is she okay by herself?" I ask Belinda.

"Yeah. She does okay in the yard. All that happened to her?" she asks me.

"Yes."

"Oh, my God, that poor child. She was so different after we found each other again. She never wanted to go nowhere or do nothin'. I wish I'd knowed. I would've tried to get her some help. I know we're both dopin' and we don't got much, and it's not the best life, but I do love her."

I can tell Belinda does love her and wants to help her. She's very motherly towards Darla, and it warms my heart.

"I'll give you some names and numbers of some people that I trust, and maybe she can learn to trust them, too."

Darla walks back in and sits at the table. She goes through the pictures. She cries while looking at them, remembering. She's not able to give Nick many other details that he doesn't already know. She tells him that the man with the ring also has an odd-shaped birthmark on his hip. She thinks it's his right hip. Nick asks if she remembers anything about where she was kept and how long she thinks she was there. She says it was a room with a bed, and that was it. Darla knows she was there for two weeks. She had to ask someone the date after waking up naked and alone. Nick asks her if there were ever any other girls there. There weren't, she says. It was just her.

"I know you couldn't see their faces, but is there anything that you can remember about their voices?" Nick asks her.

She looks thoughtful and says, "They all sounded smart. They talked real good, like they were all smart. They didn't talk like me."

Nick smiles at her. "I think you're a pretty smart girl."

She gives him a shy smile, and it melts my heart.

"They used big words. Words I don't know."

Nick goes back and forth with her on the voices, and Darla basically tells him in not so many words that they are all well-educated. I don't know if it will help him and Chris, but something is better than nothing in my book. He pulls out two cards and gives one to Darla and one to Belinda. He tells them to call him with any questions. He tells Darla that if she thinks of something she feels is important, to call. I take Darla's card and flip it over. I ask Nick for his pen, and I write some names and numbers down for her.

"These are people that helped me years ago. They're still working in the same place doing the same job. If you don't want to go alone, I'll go with you."

"Thank you," she says, taking the card.

"You don't have to live in the darkness. I promise there's light at the end," I say, smiling at her.

Nick and I stand and tell them both good night.

"Mom," I say.

My mother opens her eyes and looks at me. "What're you doin' here?" she asks me.

I sigh and look up at Nick. "What did I tell you," I say.

He looks angry. I don't know where his sudden anger has come from, but he approaches my mother and stands right in front of her. *Uh oh*, this doesn't look good. I'm absolutely surprised at what he says.

"Marsha," he snaps at her. She focuses her eyes on him. "You're a poor excuse for a mother. She tells you that she was raped, and you do nothing. You don't protect her, and you don't even believe her. Did you think she just made it up? Do you know that Grace looks for you out on the streets? She even asked me to help her one day. When was the last time you even saw her? Not the last time she saw you. And what do you ask her for? Money? If I could arrest you right now for what you did to her, you'd be sitting in jail, and I would do everything to make sure you sit for a long time."

My mother looks at him and the only thing she asks is, "Who're you?"

"Someone who gives a damn about her," he growls.

I'm frozen in my spot. I'm looking at him, and I have to tell myself to close my mouth, which is hanging wide open. He looks down at me.

"Are you ready?" he asks me.

"Yes," I can manage no more than a whisper.

We walk out the door. When we reach the front of his car, he swings around and faces me.

"I owe you so many apologies. I don't even know where to start," he says, looking in my eyes. There's a street lamp casting an amber glow all over the yard. His eyes look even darker than they are.

"No, you don't," I say.

"If I had known what happened to you, I wouldn't have said what I said to you that Friday after William and Brandi left. I-"

I hold my hand up to him. I want to put it on his chest, but I don't.

"Nick, stop." I take a deep breath. "I wasn't offended by what you said to me. I didn't tell Darla what happened to me to shock you or to make you feel bad or make you feel bad for me. I wasn't trying to get any apology from you. I dealt with what happened to me a *long* time ago. It's all in the past. I don't dwell on what happened and what my mom did or didn't do. She's sick. You saw that. She's always been that way, Nick. Matt and I took care of her when we were growing up. We were the parents. It sucked. It really did, but that's the hand I was dealt.

I don't feel sorry for myself, and I don't want anyone else to feel sorry for me, either."

There's silence between us. I can hear the crickets chirping. What's he thinking?

"I've never met anyone like you. Besides showing incredible strength, you got in there with Darla and got her to open up to you. If I had gone in there the way I was planning to, we would've gotten nowhere. I do owe you an apology for being an asshole about everything. I could've put it differently to you about taking you home with me."

I move closer to him, so close that my breasts are nearly brushing against him. His breathing is picking up. I hold his eyes with mine.

"I was turned on when you told me that you wanted to take me home with you and fuck me," I say quietly, hoping it sounded as seductive as I intended it to.

He inhales sharply. I see the change in his eyes. *Oh, yeah, he still wants to.* There's a current running between us. It screams of pent-up sexual tension, need and desire. I also want to get lost in this guy, even if it's brief, and forget about what we're doing here and what I've seen and heard. I want to forget all of it, other than how I feel when he's near me. My breathing is picking up.

I want him to kiss me. I want him. I want him bad. I want him to take me. Hell, I wouldn't mind if he laid me on the hood of his car and fucked me right here. I can hear Nick's phone buzzing. He backs away from me.

"Shit," he says, grabbing for it. "Yeah…Okay…Where?" He nods. "We'll see you there." He shoves his phone back in his pocket. "Chris has some additional information. That was him that called earlier, which I told you that, didn't I? We'll fill you in on everything. He wants us to meet him at The Grill. I'm starving. Are you?"

When I begin to think about it, yeah, I'm hungry.

"Yes, I think I could go for some food." I look at my watch. Shit, it's after midnight. I see Nick looking at his watch, too.

He takes a step in my direction and looks down at me. "Our conversation isn't over." His voice is low when he says it. Holy Heaven, it's sexy.

Oh, I hope it's not over. "Okay," I say softly, smiling at him.

Chapter Fourteen

We drive quickly from Odd Street into downtown. We drive too fast, I think, but I don't say anything. We're quiet on the drive. I keep yawning.

"Are you tired?"

"I'm fine," I say, looking over at him. He glances at me and then back to the road.

We find a place to park, and I want to question if we can even park here, and then I remember we're in his work car. No one would dare tow it. Nick pulls off his tie and unbuttons his shirt a couple of buttons. He rolls his sleeves up a little. Damn, that's hot. He sighs in relief.

"That feels better. I think I can make it a few more hours."

"Why are you in a suit today?"

"I was being official," he says, smiling at me. "I knew I was going to see you. I wanted to dress nice." *Is he joking or being serious?* I can't tell. "I thought if I dressed nice and then said something that pissed you off, you might think twice about punching me if I could wow you with the way I looked." He's trying hard not to laugh, but he's not succeeding at it.

"You were trying to *wow* me?"

"Yes, I was trying to *wow* you." His laugh is wicked.

"You are something else. You know that?" I say, laughing.

"You like it. Admit it; you do." His smile is wicked and sexy with those dimples, and then he winks at me. *Holy Heaven, he's really hot when he winks.*

"Let's go see Chris," I say ignoring his comment, but not ignoring the heat that's risen in my body over his smile, dimples and winking.

We walk the short distance from his car to The Grill. Chris is in a booth all the way at the back, as far as he can get. The problem is there are so many people in here, and I wonder if this is the best place to talk. I voice that to Nick.

He looks around and says, "We're fine."

He slides in beside Chris. They both have their backs to the wall so they can see out the windows and door. I think that's a cop thing. I notice they all do that.

"Hey, Grace," Chris says to me when I sit.

"Hey."

The server takes our drink orders, and we all say, "Coffee," at the same time. I don't need to look at the menu and tell the server that I know what I want. Nick and Chris say the same. I notice that Nick orders exactly the same thing that I do. When she walks away, I look at him.

"That's my favorite here," I tell him about the Hot Pastrami Sandwich with a side of Fries and of course the Feta. You have to have the Feta here if you have Fries. I think it's a written rule somewhere.

"Mine too." He smiles back at me.

"Should I leave?" Chris asks.

Nick keeps smiling at me and doesn't break from my eyes. "Maybe later," he tells him.

I blush. I'm blushing, not out of embarrassment, but the way he's looking at me and it's really freaking hot! He sees that I'm blushing. His expression tells me that he likes it.

"I feel like a third wheel, here," Chris mutters.

Nick rolls his eyes, but I laugh. We get our coffee and then get down to business. We lean into each other, and I know we must look conspiratorial.

"Tell Grace what you found out," Nick says to Chris.

"I looked for Missing Persons Reports on the girls that you could identify by name. I couldn't find any."

I shrug my shoulders. "I'm not that surprised by that. If I remember correctly, Tonya and Hailey have a lot of delinquent behavior. I think truancy and unruly behavior. They probably have run away and come back and then run away again, and this went on so much their parents decided not to file Missing Persons' Reports."

"Was DFCS involved with them?" Chris asks me.

"No. We haven't had any involvement with them. It wasn't a DFCS matter; it was a DJJ matter."

"How do you know about them then, if those girls went through the Department of Juvenile Justice?" Chris asks me.

"You spend seven years in Judge Wright's courtroom, you see people. I'm good at remembering people."

"Cool. Sorry, I'm getting off subject here. When I couldn't find anything on those two, it peaked my interest, so I looked for your sister's Missing Persons Report. There isn't one."

That *does* surprise me.

"That's not possible," I say, looking at both Nick and Chris.

"Are you sure that Matt filed one?" Nick says to me.

"Yeah. He showed me the card that the officer gave him with the case number."

Nick and Chris look at each other.

"What does this mean?" I ask them.

"A pain in the Chief's ass," Nick says. He's not being funny about it.

"I looked it up by name. I looked it by Naomi's name. If we had a case number, we could search it that way." Chris looks at me. "You don't happen to have the card with the case number on it, do you?"

"No, but I know that Detective Hall or Detective Rice got it."

I see Nick and Chris exchange confused looks with one another.

"Who told you that?" Nick asks me.

"Matt told me."

"Who told him?" Nick asks.

"I don't know. He said he kept bugging someone at the police department and was told that it would be picked up by one of those two detectives."

Nick and Chris look at one another again with continued confused expressions.

Nick looks at me and says, "Have you ever met Hall or Rice?"

"No. Why would I?"

"There are four of us in Robbery/Homicide. Hall and Rice are the other two."

Now, I'm as confused as they look. "What the hell does that mean?"

"I don't know. You're sure Matt told you Hall or Rice."

"Yes. I'm positive." I pause for a moment and then say, "Wait a minute. Would your unit get kidnapping cases?"

Nick and Chris look at one another again, and Nick says, "Yes. You thought Naomi was kidnapped?"

I sigh, "Matt did. He thought it from the beginning, but he never could come up with anything to back that up. It was always a feeling that he had. I brushed him off from the beginning. I think the police department did, too. He goes on a lot of rants about many things. It's the drugs." I think now that Matt knew what he was saying. He felt it, and I didn't believe him. Dammit. I see Nick pull his phone out. "What're you doing?" I ask him.

"I'm calling Hall, and then, I'm calling Rice."

"Nick, it's almost one in the morning."

"I can tell time, Grace," he mutters, scrolling through names.

I'm about to say something else, when he looks up and puts his phone down at the same time he tells me to not say anything. I want to say something flippant, but he gives me a look, and I feel someone approach us.

"Hey, Nick. Hey, Chris."

I look up, and Lacey Carter is standing at our table.

"Hey, Lacey," Nick says.

"I haven't heard from you in over a week, Nick." She flips part of her hair behind her and is looking quite sultry standing there in tight jeans and a fitted top.

"You know how murders are, Lacey."

"Yes, I remember being in Chris's shoes. We sure did work well together, didn't we, Nick?" She's smiling, and I see the steam rise from how hot she thinks she is.

Well, well, well so they were partners at work and after hours. I'm looking at Nick, and he looks uncomfortable. What's that about?

"We did solve a few murders," he admits.

"We did more than that," she says. I want to tell her to just come out and say it, because Chris and I know what you're talking about. "How's the Bradberry case going? Brison isn't saying much about it, but I know it's all you two are working on."

Has she totally forgotten that a child has been murdered? Does she even give a shit?

"We can't really talk about that, here," Nick says to her.

Lacey looks at me like she's just realized that I'm sitting here.

"I guess you can't talk about it in front of Grace, here."

What the fuck? I don't like this woman. I never have, and the feeling is obviously mutual.

"Um, Lacey," Chris begins, but stops.

She looks over at him and shrugs her shoulders. I take the shoulder shrugging as her way of saying that she doesn't give a shit about what she says and what I think about it. *That's a two way street, bitch.*

"Well, see you later, guys. Nick, call me when you can, okay?"

"Okay," he says to her, but he's looking at me. "What?" he asks me after she walks away.

"Did I say anything?" I'm smiling, mostly because he looks so uncomfortable, and I can't figure out why.

"You're giving me a look," he says. He looks a little pouty, and that makes it funnier.

"I have no idea what you're talking about," I say, laughing.

"Can we get back to important matters here?" he asks, scowling.

"Please," I smirk at him.

Our food arrives while Nick's on the phone. Based on what I hear on his side, neither Hall nor Rice ever got anything on Naomi, and they don't know who she is. They never heard anything about suspicions of her being kidnapped. Nick confirms this to both Chris and me when he gets off the phone.

We take a few silent minutes to eat. I wonder what all of this means. I don't understand how her Missing Persons Report is...well, missing. Why would someone at the police department tell Matt that it was going to Robbery/Homicide? Who told him that? It doesn't make any sense to me. Nick tells me that I need to talk to my brother, and he wants to be there when I do. I agree. I want to get to the bottom of this. I want to know where my sister is and where the other girls are.

Nick tells Chris about Darla being drugged with morphine. They decide that Chris is going to look into Mickey's friends who are in the medical community, and that includes doctors, pharmacists and possibly people who work for pharmaceutical companies. They both agree that the list is most likely going to be lengthy. They decide to start with doctors.

"I think it's going to be a local doctor," Chris says.

"I agree. I feel it, don't you?"

"Yes," Chris says.

Nick brings up that they need to find the families of the girls that I've identified and confirm whether or not they have filed Missing Persons Reports, and once the families are found, how they are going to go about talking with them about their missing daughters without tipping their hands at what they've found.

"Let me do it," I tell them. They both look at me. "I have connections at DJJ. I'll call some people that I know. I can find out who their families are and where their families are, and I'll go talk to them."

"And say what to them when you get there?" Nick asks.

"I'll tell them that I have some kids on my caseload that are friends with their daughter, and it was mentioned to me that they've not been seen in a while. Since I'm in the area, I thought I would stop by and find out how they're doing. I think that will be my in, and then I'll see what I can find out."

Chris points at me and is smiling. "You're good."

Nick is nodding his head in agreement and looking at me like he's impressed. He shares that there is another woman involved. I see surprise on Chris's face at this revelation. They bounce it back and forth between each other as to who the woman might be. Nick says he has a possible idea, but isn't sure.

"I think I may have an idea," I blurt out.

They both look at me again.

"We're listening," Nick says.

I look around me and see the place is fairly empty. *Geez,* I feel so paranoid all of a sudden. I lean into them.

"Eleanor Bradberry." I let that sink in with them.

"I like it, and that was my idea too, but I want to know why you think that? Talk to me," Nick says.

"She was murdered with Mickey." I hold my finger up to Nick. "Let me finish. We know there's another woman involved. There's one woman who is abusing these girls. We've all seen her body. She's not Eleanor's age, right? Do we agree on that?" They both nod in agreement, and I keep going. "The other woman gives the drugs and takes the pictures but isn't ever on camera. Eleanor's killed with Mickey. If she was innocent, why not wait until Mickey is alone and just kill him? Why kill her? The whole murder sounds like a revenge kill to me. Not only that, a beating sounds personal to me. Don't ask me who killed them, because I don't know. That's what you guys do."

There's nothing but silence at our table when I stop talking. Shit. What did I say? Did that sound stupid to them? Chris's face breaks into a wide grin.

"You're in the wrong damn job. You need to come over to the police department and work with us permanently."

"I think I'll stay where I am. Your job requires carrying a gun," I cringe.

"You don't like guns?" Nick asks.

"No."

"Have you ever shot one?" he asks.

"No."

He sits back in the booth and gives me a look. "We're going to have to change that."

Good luck with that. I don't stay on the gun topic.

"There's one thing that I don't understand. Well, there're a lot of things I don't understand, but how did one person beat two people? Did he incapacitate one in some way before the beating?"

"Two killers," Nick says. "Sorry. I forgot to mention that earlier."

"That makes better sense. How do you know there're two killers?"

"Someone swung to the right, while the other person swung left. It's the way the blood splatter is. I'll hook you up with someone from Forensics, and they can give you a detailed lesson on the whole thing."

"That's okay," I say. "It's not necessary. I couldn't figure out how it could be one person or how you could tell it was more than one person. You cleared that up for me."

"I'm going home and having sex with my wife," Chris says suddenly, taking me by surprise. I start laughing and think to myself *TMI.* Nick's shaking his head. "Sorry, you just feel like one of us now," Chris says to me. "You're just one of the guys."

"I don't know if that was a compliment or an insult," I say to him.

"That was definitely a compliment," Chris says to me and then looks at Nick. "You need to stop dating all other women and just start dating Grace. Don't do anything else to piss her off, and she punches you again and then you moan and groan about how you want to call her and then don't. She's smart and beautiful. What else are you looking for? If you can get a gun in her hand, you're set, man. Let me out. I'm going home to get laid. What time do we want to get started again?"

Nick slides out of the booth to let Chris out. I can see that he's giving Chris a look that I translate into, *Would you shut your fucking mouth.* They're both standing with their hands on their hips at their guns. It's funny to watch. They have the same stance.

"Seven," Nick tells him.

Chris looks at his watch. "Dammit. That means by the time I get home and wake Brit up and do my thing and then sleep, I'll be running on three hours."

"Go for a quickie, man," Nick says.

"Shit. She'll put my ass on the couch, and I won't get anything. I'll be cold, lonely and horny." Chris looks like he's contemplating hard on what he's going to do once he's home. I sit and watch them, saying nothing. Chris looks down at me. "Yes, this is how we talk to each other. When you've spent the last four years with the same person, you get pretty close."

"Where're the pictures?" Nick asks, changing the subject on him.

"In evidence under the fake case name. That was pretty brilliant on your part. Good night, y'all. Or, good morning, or whatever the hell it is. I'll see y'all at seven."

"Bye, Chris," I say.

I see Nick snatch Chris's bill from his hand. He grabs mine too, before I can get it.

"My treat." His smile is wicked, and there are those dimples. I don't argue. He puts a tip on the table, and I wait for him while he pays.

I know I should be tired, but I feel pretty keyed up. I'm sure it has everything to do with what we've been discussing. This case is such a mess and such a tangled web. I don't know how Nick does this. It also probably doesn't help that I've had three cups of coffee. We walk out, and the night is cool. It feels good to get some air after being cooped up in The Grill discussing what we've been discussing. I hear someone call my name.

"Miss Gracie."

I turn around and see Street walking towards me. He sees Nick standing beside me and stops. He sees his gun and his badge, and Nick just looks like a cop even if he didn't have the telltale signs hanging from his belt.

"Hey, Street," I say, walking toward him. Nick falls into step beside me. When we get to where he's standing, he has this look on his face that maybe he should run. "This is Detective Nick Bassano. He's cool," I assure him. "Nick, this is my friend, Street."

"Hey, Street," Nick says, holding out his hand.

"Detective," Street says, shaking his hand, still not sure if he should stay or go. He looks at me and seems to relax a little. "I seen your brother a few minutes ago. He be crazy, Miss Gracie. He be talkin' crazy."

"That's because he's high, Street."

"No, this be different. He be sayin' that he fucked up. Sorry, Miss Gracie, screwed up real good this time, and he gon' be in real big trouble."

I shake my head at Street, looking confused. "Do you know what he was talking about?"

"No. Me and some other people tried to get him to talk and make some sense. That other guy he be with kept tellin' him to shut the fuck up."

I shrug my shoulders. "I have no idea, Street. I'm as lost as you are. I haven't seen Matt in several days. Do you know which way he and the other guy went?"

Street points in several different directions and then looks at me, shrugging his shoulders. "No, Miss Gracie. I don't remember. I'm sorry."

"Don't worry about it. Take care of yourself, Street. Thanks for letting me know that you saw Matt."

Street tells us good night and shuffles on with some of his friends to another location. I look up at Nick.

"Do you want to look for him?" Nick asks me.

"No. Even if we find him, he'll be so high, he won't make any sense. Let's go."

We're walking back to Nick's car when he says, "So you think I'm cool."

No, I think you're fucking hot. "Don't let that go to your head." I look up at him, grinning. His grin back is wicked, and it's especially hot with those dimples.

He doesn't say anything. We get in, and Nick pulls away, and it doesn't take us long to get from downtown to Lexington Road and then the police department. The traffic is light at this hour. We see plenty of ACCPD patrol cars. We pull in the parking lot, and Nick stops beside my car.

"I'll be back by seven," I say, opening the door at the same time I turn to look at him.

His face is in the shadow of the dome light. It's dark and intense the way he's looking at me. There's that current flowing between us again that was there earlier when we stood outside of Darla's house. I don't want this night with him to end, and I don't want to go home, alone.

Chapter Fifteen

"Come home with me," he says, as he continues to look at me.

It takes me about two seconds to respond, "Okay." There's no reason for me to be coy about it. I want him. He wants me. We've been dancing around each other for over two weeks now. My resolve sits in a pile at my feet. I've been denying myself. I've been denying myself *him*, and I've already decided that I don't want to be alone tonght. "I'll follow you."

"No. Close the door, and I'll bring you back later."

"I can follow you."

He leans over to me, and we are all but nose to nose. I see the change in his eyes. They're hungry and sexy as shit.

"Do not argue with me, and close the damn door. If you don't, I'm going to fuck you in this parking lot and then have to explain it to the Chief later. Do you want that?"

I gulp, shake my head and close the door. He smiles at me, and I feel that smile down deep. It connects with me right between my thighs. I have butterflies in my stomach, but it's not nerves. I'm excited, turned on, and I'm squirming in my seat at the thought of what he's going to do to me when he gets me at his house. Where does he live? Lord, I hope it's not far. I can feel my body temperature on the rise.

Nick flips the radio on, and *Holy shit.* 50 Cent's *Just a Lil Bit* is on the Athens station that plays dance music, and maybe because of the time of the night, the station isn't censoring the song at all. The beat's sexy. The music's sexy, and the words. Holy Heaven, what 50's singing about is what I want Nick to do to me. He glances over at me, smiling, and I can tell he's listening to the lyrics too. I can feel the sweat forming between my breasts when the song goes off. *Are we close? How much longer?* I want to ask. *Are we almost there?* Does that scream of desperation?

We pull off of Milledge Avenue onto Whitehall Road. Less than a mile and a half off of Whitehall Road over the Oconee County Line, Nick turns onto a long, winding driveway. It begins as a gravel drive that turns into a paved driveway. We come into an opening, and I see his house. It looks like a log cabin. It's not a big house, but he doesn't need a big house, since it's just him. He pulls the car in a garage, and I'm not sure how he can get another vehicle in here because he drives a black Ford F-350 that's huge and sits up really high. It has the darkest tinted windows that I think I've ever seen. He shuts the car off and looks at me.

"Ready?"

Yes, yes I am. "Are you?" I ask him.

He takes my hand, and it feels like he's shocked me the way his skin feels against mine. He slides it to his zipper and places it there. I feel his erection. I gasp and look in his eyes.

"Does that answer your question?" His voice is low and raw.

"Yes," I say breathlessly.

We get out, and he takes my hand, holding tight to it. I like the way my hand feels in his. His is so big, and it completely wraps around mine. His skin is warm. It almost feels feverish. I like it. He opens his door off the garage and pulls me inside through the kitchen that I pay absolutely no attention to. He walks me through a hall into a living area, turning on a lamp. I spin around the room, slowly taking things in. I love his house immediately. It is a log cabin. It's rustic and a perfect bachelor pad for him.

His furniture is nice, with an enormous brown leather sofa and matching love seat. There's a recliner that's also in the same brown leather. He has a huge flat screen TV that most men like. The room is neat, clean, and I like it. I'm looking around, and I see pictures on the fireplace mantle. There are various family pictures and a picture of Nick in a football uniform. Again, he looks so serious.

I bet the girls chased him in high school. He was a good-looking teenager and big even then. I move on and see more pictures and awards hanging on his wall. There's one picture that looks like it might be when he graduated from the Police Academy up in New York. One award is for graduating at the top of his class in the academy.

I turn to him. He's leaning against his doorframe with his arms crossed over his chest looking at me. He's not smiling, and his eyes look predatory. My heart begins to beat faster. He moves towards me and takes my hand.

"Come," he says.

Oh, yes, I plan to.

We walk down another short hall and then to his bedroom. He has a king sized bed, and his room is just as neat and clean as the rest of his house. He leaves me standing in front of his bed and turns on a lamp that sits on a bedside table. It provides a low light, and I like the way he looks in it.

He's watching me, holding my eyes as he takes his gun, badge, phone and handcuffs from his belt and puts everything on the table along with all of the stuff in his pockets. He bends over and removes a gun from his ankle. How many guns does the man have on him? He walks back to me, wraps his arms around my waist and pulls me to him. I go willingly. I put my hands on his chest and marvel again at how solid he is. I can't wait to see what he looks like beneath his clothes.

"Do you know what I'm going to do to you?" he asks me.

No, but I hope I'm about to find out. "No."

He bends down and moves my hair to one side and whispers in my ear, "I'm going to fuck you so good, you won't want anyone else."

Shit! That's so damn hot! I gasp and shiver all the way down. His lips are on my neck, and I moan, closing my eyes it feels so good. He finds my pulse, and it's racing. His lips linger there. He drags his lips from my neck to my jaw and then to my lips. He pushes his tongue in my mouth. I like the way he tastes. My hands slide up his chest and around his neck. I'm on my toes again, pressed hard against him. His hands move from my waist down to my hips and then around, digging his fingers in my backside. I gasp in his kiss as he pushes me harder into him. I break the kiss, but hold his eyes with mine. His eyes are dark, and there's nothing but raw hunger for me in them.

I move my hands to the buttons on his shirt and undo them slowly, one by one. I push his shirt off and let it drop to the floor. I grab his t-shirt and pull it from his pants. He lifts his arms, and he has to help me get it off, because I can't stretch that high. *God Almighty, he is beautiful.* His skin is smooth and tan, and his muscles are perfect. He's beautifully sculpted, but again, it looks natural and athletic.

He has a tattoo that runs in a vertical line of four Chinese characters on the front of his left ribcage, right under his breast bone. It only adds to how sexy I already think he is. I can see that he has tattoos on his right and left shoulders. I can't tell what they are with him standing right in front of me.

He kicks his shoes off as I'm working on his belt and pants. I make quick work of his belt and pants, notice his sexy boxer briefs and then he's naked, and *Oh, my God*, everything about him is *big!* He's impressive from head to toe. He wants me-- that I can definitely see.

"Let's get you out of these clothes," he says. His voice is oozing with seduction. He unbuttons my shirt, and I let it fall to the floor in the pile that's there. I say a silent prayer of thanks that I'm wearing one of my sexier bras. He takes that off too, and I see his eyes go even darker. "You're beautiful."

He slides my pants off and takes my panties with them. I kick out of my flats, and my clothes pile on top of them. Then we're naked together. He pulls me back to him, and feeling his naked body against mine is incredible. He lifts me, and I wrap my legs around him. He moves us to the bed, laying me down, and stretches out beside me. We're kissing, touching and enjoying the exploration of each other's bodies with our hands.

He moves, hovering over me. I have my arms wrapped around his neck, holding his lips to mine, and I kiss him greedily. He gives to me. He's running one hand down my body, finds my breast and rolls my nipple in his fingers. I moan and arch my back, letting him know I like it, and he can keep doing it. He breaks away from my mouth and dips his head, and then my nipple is in his mouth. I arch my back even more and put my hands in his hair, pushing his mouth even further.

He stops and looks up at me. "Stop squirming."

"I can't." I'm breathless.

He grins at me, going back to my breast, and his tongue is licking and then swirling, and then he closes his whole mouth over it, and I can feel his teeth graze my nipple. I'm breathing faster, and I feel my body building.

He feels it too and doesn't stop. He pulls me to the edge, then I'm falling as my orgasm takes my body, and I scream his name while relishing in the way he makes me feel. I open my eyes while my breathing returns to normal and find him grinning at me again.

"How was that?" he asks, as if he didn't know.

Please, sir, can I have another? "I think you know." I mirror his grin.

"You have beautiful skin and beautiful breasts." He's touching them again. I like it. "I like that you wax. I'm surprised about that." He's smiling, and it looks devilish.

"Why are you surprised?"

"I figured with you being so liberal, you'd have a full bush down there." He tries not to laugh, but he can't help himself.

I smack him in his chest.

"I can't believe you said that. Should I get dressed and leave?"

He hovers over me and pushes himself between my legs. I feel his erection pressing against me, nearly in me, and it makes me gasp.

"Oh, no," he says in a low, sexy voice. "I'm not done with you yet." He puts his lips to mine, pressing harder against me. I'm not at all surprised how good of a lover Nick is, but I am surprised at how attentive he is. I figured he'd be the, *I'll get my pleasure, and whatever you get is what you get.* But he's nothing like that. He kisses me until I'm breathless. "Are you protected?"

"Yes," It comes out as a sigh.

He looks in my eyes. "I've never not worn a condom. I don't want to with you, because I want to be inside you with nothing between us."

What was that? Was that a declaration? And if so what does it mean? I don't care. I want him, and I feel the same way. I want him in me with nothing but him. I have never not made a man wear a condom. I never felt this kind of wild abandon. I just want him and want to feel him inside of me with just him. He enters me, and I moan, closing my eyes. He braces himself on his elbows, with his hands on either side of my face.I wrap my legs around him, and he begins to move. I raise my hips up to meet him. He drags his lips from mine to my ear.

"You feel so good," he growls in my ear.

We're both breathing heavy. He moves slowly and then picks up only to slow again. It's sweet agony the way he's sliding in and out of my body. The only sounds in the room are sighs and moans. He's kissing me, taking my tongue and giving me his. His movements become a steady rhythm, and it feels so amazing how hard he is inside of me. *Oh...That...Feels...So...Damn...Good.*

I close my eyes and tip my head back, feeling all of him as he continues the agony of his slow and steady rhythm. I feel his lips at my throat, kissing me, feeling my pulse. I open my eyes, find him staring at me, and his eyes are intense, and I see that he's enjoying my body as much as I'm enjoying his. My hands roam up and down his back, feeling his muscles beneath my fingers. I can't get over how solid this man is. He's got the hardest muscles I've ever felt.

He lowers his face, taking my lips, and our tongues are dancing with one another again. His kisses become more demanding as his movements begin to pick up, and then, he's thrusting in me, hard and fast, making my body build, and then I explode around him, screaming his name. My body pulses and pulses, and it is the best orgasm I've ever had.

I feel Nick go rigid over me, and then he explodes into me. He collapses on me and *Holy shit* is he heavy. I wrap my arms around his solid body and enjoy how his body feels against mine. I can feel his heart pounding and hear his heavy breathing in my ear. He lifts his head and is smiling down at me. God, those dimples.

"You're absolutely incredible," he says.

I run my fingers through his hair. *Oh, I like the way it feels.* I've wanted to do that since the first day I met him.

"You aren't so bad yourself," I say softly.

He pulls out of me and lies beside me on his stomach, wrapping his arms around his pillow. He's facing me, and he hasn't taken his eyes off of me. I can't take mine off of him. I can look at him and appreciate how his muscles look, especially the way they look with his arms wrapped around his pillow. I trail my fingers over the tattoo on his left shoulder.

"Will you tell me about them?" I ask.

Now that he's on his stomach, I see for the first time that he has Semper Fi in big, beautiful scripted letters across his broad back up close to his shoulders. He's truly gorgeous and sexy. I like a man with tattoos.

"I'll tell you about mine if you'll tell me about yours," he says, moving to put his lips at my upper back right below my shoulder on my tattoo. "What does the date mean?"

I have 4-28-1997 in similar scripted letters tattooed on my upper back.

"It's the date my life began. Don't worry, it's not the day I was born."

"That's good," he says, laughing. "I was about to run out of here screaming that I swear you looked older than fifteen. I had a flash of me serving time in prison and some guy named Leroy trying to make me his bitch."

I laugh with him. "Nick, as big as you are, I think Leroy would be the scared one."

"Explain the date to me," he says, still laughing.

"Remember the night at McCoy's when I told you I was homeless from fifteen to twenty?"

He grins at me, nodding, and it tells me he's remembering more than that.

"I was emancipated from my mother on my fifteenth birthday. I had this idea that if I was on my own in the eyes of the court, that life would be better. It wasn't, but..." I don't want to say really how bad it was that first year I was on my own. "We always lived pillar to post, but I was truly homeless and on my own when I got emancipated."

"And here you are today. It's impressive."

I smile at him. "Yes. Here I am."

"You're about to turn thirty?"

"Yes. You look surprised."

"You don't look a day over twenty-five, but you act forty," he says, smiling.

I shove him, but it doesn't do me any good. It's like pushing a boulder.

"That was a compliment," he says, leaning into me and kissing me. "I like the tattoo. It's meaningful."

I run my fingers over the two Chinese symbols, side by side, on his left shoulder. One of the symbols looks like a straight line. "What does this one mean?"

"Unity."

"I like it. Is that for when you were in the Marines?"

"Yes."

"What about the symbols running down your ribcage?"

I can barely see them. I run my finger down what I can see. I can see the change in Nick's eyes. He likes my hands on him. I like putting them on him.

"It stands for brotherhood."

"I would never take you for sentimental," I say.

"I loved my time in the Marines. I'll be one forever."

"Can I see your other shoulder?"

He rolls over with his back to me. I can really see the Semper Fi tattoo now. It's a beautiful piece of work. It's spread out across his broad back. I look at his right shoulder. It's two more symbols, side by side.

"It's Chinese for police or cop or officer. You choose," he says.

"I like them all," I tell him.

I cozy up to his back and wrap my arms around him. I press my breasts up against him, and I feel him breathe in sharply. I put my lips to his back, letting them linger there. My hand runs from his chest down his stomach and then lower. I find what I'm looking for and stroke him. He's hard and ready again.

"You're greedy." His voice is low and sexy.

"What can I say, you turn me on," I murmur.

He rolls me beneath him and shows me, again, that he's not done with me yet.

Chapter Sixteen

My eyes fly open, and I have to think for a moment to remember where I am. Nick's bed. I can hear him sleeping deeply next to me. I was sleeping very well, but there's something nagging at me. It's in those pictures. There's something there. Something that I know, and I can't grasp ahold of what it is. It's in the back of my mind.

I don't have a clue what time it is. It has to be just a little before dawn. I sit up and look down at him. He's still on his stomach. I sit and stare at him for a moment. The sheet is down around his hips, and the sight of him lying there and knowing that he's completely naked is nice to look at.

"Nick," I whisper.

He doesn't move. I whisper his name again and still nothing. I shake him, and he raises his head and looks at me. He is the cutest thing ever just waking up, looking like a little boy who's in desperate need of a shave. I start giggling.

"What in the hell are you doing?" he growls. His voice is full of sleep. He looks over at his clock. "Dammit, Grace. We've been asleep for two hours. Why are you awake?"

"We need to go."

"No, we don't. Go back to sleep." He lays his head back down, closing his eyes.

"Nick, I need to see those pictures again."

He groans, puts his head under his pillow and wraps his arms around his head. "Why?" It comes out muffled.

"There's something bothering me."

He removes the pillow and looks at me. "You said that last night. What is it?"

"There's something in those pictures that's familiar to me. I don't know what it is. It's nagging at me. There's something in the back of my mind, but every time I think I know what it is, *poof*, it's gone."

He's looking at me strangely. "Why in the hell would something be familiar to you in those pictures?"

"I don't know. I can't explain it. It's a feeling that I have, and it will not go away. I need to look at those pictures again."

He's shoved his head under his pillow again, and he's moaning again. "Fuck me." It comes out as aggravation. I'm about to say, *Sure, I'd be happy to,* but I realize that's not what he's referring to. He raises his head back up, looking at me again. "You aren't going to let this go, are you?"

"No."

"Shit," he grumbles, staring hard at me. "Can we at least have a shower and some coffee?"

"Both sound good." I say smiling, trying not to laugh at how irritable he is.

I scoot out of the bed on one side while Nick is getting out on the other. I follow him, since I have no idea where his bathroom is. Damn, he's got a fabulous backside. I want to reach out and squeeze it. He looks down at me at the bathroom door.

"You know, if we shower together, it's going to take us that much longer to get out of here, because I'm telling you right now that once I have you in there, I'm going to fuck you again."

His words melt me. They do. I should be a puddle on the floor. I'm torn. I need to see those pictures, but the thought of him having me in the shower is tempting. My libido screams at me to get in the damn shower, while the responsible part of my brain is screaming for me to get dressed and take him up on his offer later. *Oh, hell, my brain is just too responsible sometimes.*

I launch myself at him. He catches me, pinning me up against his wall with his hips, and we're kissing each other like we're hungry. I think we are, for each other. He feels amazing. He's unyielding at my front, while the wall is unyielding at my back. I'm trapped, and I love it. His hands are running from my waist up to my breasts, and he's not gentle with them, and the way he's touching them is directly connected to between my thighs. I can feel him hard and ready. I've got my arms around his back, and I can feel his hard muscles beneath my fingers.

"Forget the shower," he says, breathing hard, and he enters me.

He pulls my legs up around him, and I wrap them around him, holding him to me as tightly as I can. He's thrusting in and out so hard that it's making the wall rattle and everything that's on it. I like this. I like how hard he's fucking me up against this wall. I can barely form into a coherent thought what it feels like him being inside of me like this, and what he's doing to my body. With each thrust, my body responds to it. God, he's good. I knew he'd be great in bed. He's great with me up against this wall, too. I've been with men who are experienced in the bedroom, but Nick could teach a damn class on how to pleasure a woman. Our eyes lock, and I can feel my body racing fast to the end. He feels it too.

"Scream for me, baby," he growls.

I don't need him to say anything else. That's it for me, and I do scream. I scream his name and explode around him again. He's not finished and keeps going, and then I feel him go still for a moment, and he's pouring into me again. I lean my head against the wall with my eyes closed and steady my breathing while my heart returns to normal. *Okay, he's the best lover I've ever had.* I think I'll keep that to myself for the time being. I feel his lips on my neck, and he lets them linger. I can feel him breathing.

"You taste sweet," he murmurs.

I open my eyes and look at him. He's smiling at me. I unwrap my legs from around him and slide down his body. The sudden urgency to get out of this house and back to the police department is gone. I mentally slow myself down and think that the pictures aren't going anywhere, and it doesn't matter if we get there in five minutes or the next thirty.

"Do you want to shower first?"

"No, you go ahead," I say. "I think I'll get dressed and shower later. Do you want me to make some coffee while you're showering?"

"Sure. Do you remember where the kitchen is?" I tell him that I don't. "Come on. I'll show you where it is." He takes my hand and leads me into the kitchen. He shows me where everything is. His coffee maker is beside his kitchen sink, and there's a window looking out into his back yard. He stands behind me and points out the window. "Do you see that house up the hill?" I look where he's pointing.

"Yes."

"That's where my parents live. Their driveway connects with mine."

"Their house looks similar to yours."

"It is. Theirs is bigger. They built enough space for when my brother and his family come down to visit. You're the first woman I've had at my house and the first to see where my parents live." He kisses my hair and walks out.

What was that? Now, that was a declaration! I don't know what to make of it. So, where does he take all of the other women? I feel totally unbalanced as usual. I shake my head and get busy making coffee. While it's brewing, I go back to his bedroom and find my clothes and dress. I'm drinking a cup of coffee, leaning against the counter, when he wanders back in the kitchen. He's in jeans, a T-shirt and running shoes. He's freshly shaven and smells fantastic.

"Do you see something that you like?" His smile is wicked sexy, and I want to climb back in his arms, and his bed or the kitchen floor is fine with me.

"Don't let it go to your head." I keep drinking my coffee, but I don't take my eyes off of him.

"Are you hungry?" he asks me.

"No. I'm good."

"I'm starving. You're wearing me out, woman. I like it," he says, playfully.

I laugh. "Are you going to eat here?"

"No. I'm a terrible cook. I'll get something when we leave, and you seemed awfully desperate to get back to the police department."

I shrug my shoulders. "You took some of that restless energy out of me up against the wall." We grin at one another, and he winks at me, and I nearly collapse on the floor spilling hot coffee all over me. I take a deep breath, calming my pounding heart. "I can cook. I'm quite good at it, actually. Do you have anything worth cooking here?"

"You want to cook something for me? Really?" He's so surprised by it.

"Sure. Do you mind if I look in your fridge and see what you have?"

Nick takes a seat at his table. "Be my guest."

I can feel his eyes on me as I dig around in his fridge, scouting for something to cook. I find bologna, cheese, butter and eggs that are out of date, but when I open the lid, I find they're fine to cook. I would love to have some peppers. I doubt he'll have that. I ask him anyway.

"Yeah. Let me go out and grab a few from my garden." His response is sarcastic, but he's laughing, and I find that it doesn't bother me.

"Do you have bread?"

"Yes. It's in that big brown box labeled BREAD." He's still laughing.

"Do you want me to search your kitchen for a pan, salt and pepper, or do you want to get up and get it yourself?"

"You go ahead. I like seeing you move around in my kitchen like you are. It's strange seeing a woman here in my space, but I like it." He goes back to his coffee.

I find what I'm looking for and set out to make him an omelet. I'm comfortable here with him in his house, with his things and can still feel his eyes on me. I make his breakfast quickly. I find a plate and utensils and take it to him.

"Here you go. Do you want more coffee?" I'm surprised when he pulls me in his lap and kisses me. I can't speak when he's done. His kisses light me up.

"Thank you for making me breakfast. No one other than my mother and sister-in-law has cooked for me before."

Okay, what's going on here? He's giving me a lot of information, but I have no idea what he's trying to say. I don't know what to say to what he's telling me so I go with, "You're welcome. More coffee?"

"Please."

I get up to the get the coffee pot, and he digs into his food.

"Damn, woman. You're a good cook."

I pour another cup for him and one for me. I sit and watch him eat. He inhales everything on his plate. I take it when he's finished along with both of our cups.

"Leave those in the sink. I'll take care of them later," he says.

"That's okay. It won't take me long to do these."

I wash, rinse and dry quickly and put everything I used away. I think that will be better for when he comes back. There's no telling when he'll be back here, and he won't have dishes to do. He gets his gun, both of them, badge and everything else that he needs for the day, locks up and we get in his car.

I forgot that I didn't take my handbag with me. I dig for my phone and am grateful that Jess has sent me one text telling me she hoped I was having a fun time and that my silence was telling her that I was busy. My responding text was that I had a very busy night and will have an equally busy day. I tell her I may not be home when she gets there and to not worry. I'll let her interpret my text how she wants. Whatever it is that she thinks I'm out doing. She's only partially right.

When we get back to the police department, Nick comments that Chris is here. I look at my watch, and it's later than what I thought. We walk in together, and Chris is nowhere to be found. I go to the conference room we were in last night and put my handbag on the floor, while Nick goes in search of Chris. I can hear their voices from somewhere in the hallway. Whatever Chris says has Nick cracking up. I don't think I've heard him laugh like that. Nick walks in the room, wiping his eyes, with Chris trailing behind him.

"Good morning, Grace," he says, cheerfully.

"Good morning, Chris. I hope you got everything you wanted when you got home last night."

Nick starts laughing again. "Don't get him started on what happened to him when he got home. That's why he's here so early."

"Things didn't exactly go my way," he says. "Did you and Nick work all night? Because I noticed that your car was still here when I got here." He's smiling, while I'm blushing. "At least last night went Nick's way," he says, walking out of the room.

My mouth flies open, and I look at Nick, who doesn't say anything. He only smiles at me and winks. I almost fall out of my chair when he does that. Chris comes back in a few minutes with a small box that has seven manila envelopes in it. He puts it on the table and slides it over to me.

"Nick said you wanted these."

"Yes. Thanks. There's something bothering me." And that's all the information that I give. I see Chris looking at Nick, who shrugs his shoulders.

"She says there's something familiar to her. I don't know."

They both sit and talk about what they want to accomplish today. I tune them out as I pull one of the envelopes out of the box. I open it, take a deep breath and begin to go through a small stack rather than taking them all out. They are no less shocking than they were when I first looked at them several hours ago. I look up at them.

"Do you have any idea who Mickey Bradberry is in these pictures?"

Nick stops talking to Chris and says to me, "Yes. He's the one with the stupid Superman tattoo on his ass. I swear that motherfucker has ruined Superman for me. I won't ever be able to watch that cartoon again." I raise an eyebrow at him. "Not like I've been watching them," he says a little too quickly.

I go back to the pictures, while they continue to talk, but they are now talking about who is better, Superman or Batman? They begin to argue about it, and I have to tune them out again. I hate going through these pictures slowly, but I have to. I don't concentrate on the girls. I especially don't concentrate on my sister.

I decide to bypass any pictures of her altogether. It's not about them. It's something else. There's nothing jumping out at me in the first stack. I put them on the table and pull a few more out. I don't find it there, either. On the third stack, it hits me what has looked so familiar to me. Nick sees the change in my expression.

"Did you find it?"

I hold the picture up and point. "I've seen this ring before."

Nick and Chris look at each other, and then they look at me, all excited.

"On whom, Grace?" Nick asks me.

I think hard. The ring is out of focus because the focus of the camera is on the sex act, but I stare at that ring. I look at the hand that it's on. It's there. I know who that it is. *Dammit! Who is that? Who are you? I know who you are, you son of a bitch.* The problem is, I can't remember who I have seen wearing it. I've crossed paths with so many people. I know a lot of people.

I can't decide do I see the man all the time, and he doesn't wear the ring often, or is it that I see the man occasionally and only see the ring when I see him. I look at both of them. It's so frustrating because I do know who it is, and I'm so good at remembering people, but there's this mental block that I can't remove. I quickly run down the list of higher ups that I know, and I can't come up with it.

"The ring's out of focus. Could we try to find any other pictures where it's more in focus? I don't know if that will help me, but we could try."

Nick and Chris jump up and scramble through the pictures. They flip through them quickly and come up with a few other pictures that I look at. I stare at that ring. The harder I think of who it is, the worse it gets. Staring at it doesn't help me.

"I can't remember. I'm sorry," I whisper.

I can see the changes in their expressions go from excitement to extreme disappointment. I feel like I've let them both down. I feel like I've let all of those girls down, my sister included. I feel upset about it.

I stand and walk silently out of the room. I'm going to cry about this, and I don't want them to see me. I find a women's bathroom, slide down on the floor, and let the tears flow. After I let it all out, I make the decision that I'm not helping anyone by sitting on this cold, hard floor and feeling sorry for myself. I stand, clean up and walk out. Nick's leaning against the other wall opposite of the bathroom.

"I needed a moment."

"Better?"

"I feel like a failure," I admit.

He continues to lean against the wall and folds his arms across his chest. He's looking at me as if he's trying to decide what to say.

"Is that pity party working for you?" he asks, firmly. I know there's sudden anger that flashes in my eyes. "There we go. That's better," he says softly. He takes a deep breath and pinches the bridge of his nose. "Grace, you aren't a failure. Of the seven girls, you identified four by name, and you believe that you can find out who the fifth is. You theorized about Eleanor Bradberry, and Chris and I both think you're probably right about that. You've figured out a way to find the families of the girls that you do know and thought of a pretty clever way to try and get some information from them. Yes, it would be great if you could tell us who's wearing that ring. I'm not going to lie that you popped our bubbles in there, but I firmly believe you'll figure it out."

"Thanks. I needed that." I take a deep breath and say, "I think my sister's dead. When Naomi came in Foster Care, and I found out who she was, I made Valerie swear that she wouldn't tell anyone that Naomi was my sister. That was really shitty of me, and I still can't explain why I did that. I could've had my sister live with me. I could've helped her more and could've played a bigger role in her life. Hell, I could've done anything more than what I did, which was shit. I didn't want to be tied to my mother like that. My bitterness towards my mother and my childhood, prevented me from caring for my own sister, and now that I may be facing the possibility that she's gone, I decide to give a damn."

"Did you wake up perfect this morning?"

"No," I snap at him. I can see a smile starting on his lips. He doesn't say anything. He simply stands there and smiles at me. "What?"

"I was just waiting to see if you were going to walk away from me."

I sigh and then I smile at him.

"No, I'm not walking away," I mutter, still smiling.

"Good. I was wondering," he says, smiling still. He sighs and says, "Grace, Naomi isn't your responsibility. She's your mother's responsibility. You've had a lot to deal with. You've essentially been on your own your whole life. You were homeless. You managed to find a place to live and go to college and have a career that you obviously love, and you're very good at it. Sure, it would've been great if you'd done more to help her out. It would be great if I did more to help my mother out because she still struggles from having that stroke years ago, but she knows I have my own life. So do you. You aren't Naomi's mom. You don't know if she's dead."

"Then where is she? Where are those other girls? They thought Darla was dead and dumped her. They aren't holding on to these girls, Nick." I can see by the expression on his face he's considered this and hasn't said anything. "I'm going to go home and take a shower and change." I don't want to talk about this for a little while. I want some space from this. I think Nick senses this and respects it. He doesn't continue to discuss it.

"Okay. When you get back, let's see if we can find out about the girl that you know but you don't know her name."

"We can try to find Matt, too," I say, running my fingers through my hair.

"Yeah, we can do that. Are you going to call someone from DJJ?"

"Yes. I'll work on that as well," I say.

He pushes himself off the wall. "Come on. I'll walk you out."

We walk back in the conference room so I can get my handbag.

"Everything okay?" Chris asks.

"Yes. I was having a moment. It's passed now. Dr. Bassano over there counseled me." I'm smiling as I say it. "I'm sure he'll send me his bill."

"I'll definitely be collecting from you later one way or another," Nick says to me.

It's so suggestive and sexy the way he says it. I know I will let him collect if he wants to. I grab my bag, and Chris wants to know where I'm going.

"Home to take a shower and change. I've been in these clothes for over twenty-four hours now. It's time to retire this sad outfit."

"I'm going to walk her out, and then I'll be back."

"Take your time," Chris says, smiling at both of us.

We walk outside, and when we reach my car, he grabs me around the waist and pulls me into him. "I'll see you when you get back." He puts his lips to mine and kisses me to the point my whole body is on fire.

I sort of stumble as I turn around and feel pretty dazed. I can hear him chuckle behind me.

I drive to my condo, and it feels like ages since I've been here. I straighten up some, even though it's spotless. I would like to take a nap. I'm exhausted. I sit on my bed and text Jess, letting her know that I may not be home tonight, and I hope to see her tomorrow so we can catch up. Her response is that I shouldn't let Nick wear me out too much. She has no idea.

Chapter Seventeen

I linger in the shower, and I think about Nick. Is this the start of a relationship with him? Or, is this just sex? He's never had a woman at his house, but he took me there. No other woman besides his mom and sister-in-law has cooked for him, until me. We've been thrown together because of what's happening, and it appears that we will be spending a great deal of time together. Is it even possible for us to start a relationship like this? *Anything's possible.* Does he want to? Do I want to? I like him. I most definitely like having sex with him.

Good God, there's so much running through my mind. I've got to juggle him, working with him, identifying the girls I don't know, finding someone who knows the girls that I can identify, in order to get more information. I want to know where my sister is, and who killed Misty Price? Is she really connected to all of this?

I can't allow myself to think that my sister's dead, but it creeps in my mind anyway. And then, there's that damn ring. I need to figure out who that ring belongs to. If I could do that, he and Chris might be able to break this case wide open. It doesn't have to rest on my shoulders. They have other avenues to explore. *Like what?* They have the morphine. My focus is the girls. That's all I have to do. Everything else is them. Valerie was right. It's not my job to solve this case for them.

I finish my shower and get ready. I choose jeans, a t-shirt and running shoes. Since Nick and I both have running shoes, I hope this isn't an omen that we are going to be chasing anyone later. I like to walk, but I hate running. When I'm walking out the door, I call Nick.

"Feel better?" he asks when he answers.

"Yes. Thank you. There's nothing like a hot shower and a change of clothes to make you feel like a new woman."

"And a good fucking."

I pause and then burst into laughter. "Oh, my God, I can't believe you said that. Oh, wait, yes I can. Are you alone?"

I can hear him laughing, too.

"No, the whole department's here, and I have you on speaker phone. Of course, I'm alone." He's still laughing.

"I was calling to see if you and Chris would like some coffee?"

He lowers his voice and says, "We'd love some. Will you stop and get the good stuff?"

I start laughing again. "You make it sound like you want something illegal."

"I'm seriously considering hooking it up as an IV and take it that way. Will you stop at Jittery Joe's?"

"I'll stop wherever you guys want."

"We want Jittery Joe's. Get us the biggest cup they have. We have plenty of cream here, so don't worry about that. Don't punch anyone in the parking lot, okay?"

I continue to laugh. "Maybe no one will kiss me."

"Now, if that happens, *I'm* going to punch someone."

Right. "Whatever," I say and hang up. He's too much, but he leaves me smiling.

It doesn't take me long to get from Timothy Road to Milledge Avenue. I smile, thinking if I took a right instead of a left, I would be headed back towards Nick's house. I like the memory of being at his house. I stop at the Jittery Joe's in Five Points and get two coffees for each of them and one for me. I get the coffee situated in such a spot that I don't think it's going to turn over. I pull back out on the road and head toward Lexington Road. My phone's buzzing. It's Nick.

"Yes," I say.

"We're hungry. Will you get us food as well?"

"Nick, you had breakfast less than three hours ago."

"I'm a growing boy, and a certain beautiful lady depleted all of my energy, leaving me starving."

"You're going to grow out of your pants."

"Baby, thinking of you naked, I *will* be growing out of my pants."
Holy Heaven! I nearly drive off of the road. *Shit, that was hot.*
"I'm driving."

"I can't think of you naked while you drive?"

I laugh and say, "You can't say things like that to me while I'm driving."

"You can't drive and talk on the phone at the same time?" He's laughing. He knows exactly what I'm saying.

"What do you and Chris want?"

"Hotcakes, Sausage and Hash Browns from McDonald's. Oh, Chris asked if you would get him some Orange Juice."

"Should I just hook McDonald's to my car and drag it back with me?"

"That sounds perfect. We would be set at least until lunch. Do you have enough money? Don't worry. I'll pay you back when you get here."

"I've got you covered. What size OJ does he want?"

I hear him ask Chris what he wants. "Large. Thanks, Grace. Call me when you get here, and I'll help you get everything in."

I hang up, thinking he wasn't alone on that last conversation. I may never be able to look Chris Taylor in the eyes again. I get over to the McDonald's on Prince Avenue, get their food ordered and make it back to the police department. I call Nick, and he comes out to help me.

I'm on the passenger side, opening the door, when he turns me around, and his lips are on mine before I can ask him what he's doing. For a moment, I forget where we are, that Chris is waiting for us and why the three of us are here on this Saturday morning. I stretch up, wrapping my arms around his neck and give him what he wants. His tongue finds mine, and I lose myself in his kiss. I'm lit up when it's over, and my body wants more. He still has his arms around my waist, looking down at me and smiling a wicked smile. *Shit, those dimples are too much.*

"I hit that door and saw you in those jeans and that t-shirt, and I thought I was going to have to explain things to the Chief after all."

"It's jeans and a t-shirt," I say.

"Did you not look at yourself in the mirror?"

"No, I dressed in the dark."

"You're such a smart ass," he says, lingering at my lips again.

"You're rubbing off on me," I say breathlessly.

"Oh, I definitely plan on doing that later." He puts his lips to mine again.

I melt into him. I'm into his kiss and have totally forgotten where we are when we get yelled at.

"Hey! I'm hungry1 I'm tired, and I didn't get any last night! If y'all don't break it up, I'm finding a hose, and don't think that I won't do it!" Chris is walking towards us, trying not to laugh, but he can't help it.

I quickly turn from Nick, pulling the food bags out and hand them to him. Chris takes the coffee from me. I don't know why I'm so embarrassed. It's not like he doesn't know. There's just something about being caught. We get inside, and they pull their food out.

"You didn't get anything?" Nick asks me.

"No."

"Have you eaten?"

"No. I'm fine. I'll eat later."

"You need to eat."

I look at him. "Nick, I already have Jess on me all the time about not eating. I don't need you on my back about it too. I'll eat lunch. I can live with or without breakfast. I choose to live without it this morning. Trust me. I'll make up for it later."

He puts his hands up in surrender.

"Okay. How much money do I need to give you?"

"Don't worry about it. You can treat me to lunch later."

I think he's going to argue with me about it and then doesn't. I drink my coffee and watch them eat. They both eat like they've been starved for days.

"Can you call whomever it is that you know at DJJ?" Nick asks between bites.

"Sure. I'll do that now."

I end up making a couple of calls. When I can't get one person, I call another. I have to leave messages for both of them.

"I guess we play the waiting game," Nick says. "Do you think it's too early to hit the streets and see if we can get that girl identified?"

"We can try," I tell him.

"What would you think about taking the other pictures and ask about those girls, too?"

I know I look confused. "What do you mean take the pictures? You can't show those pictures around."

"Sorry," Chris says. "We were discussing how to go about flashing a picture around when all we've got to show is that smut, and your guy over here came up with something that might work."

I ignore the, *your guy* comment and ask them what they're thinking. Nick walks to the pictures and pulls one out.

"I was thinking since these are the closest shots of her face, we could somehow black out the fact that she's being forced to perform oral sex." He's looking at me, wanting to know what I think.

How am I going to put this? I don't beat around the bush on what I think of it.

"No."

"Do you have a better idea?" He's frowning at me.

"As a matter of fact, I do. I'm assuming that there's a color copier around here."

"Yes."

I walk to the pictures and pull one that I think will probably work.

"It's not close enough to her face," Nick says.

"I know. You two take me to the copier, and I'll show you what I have in mind."

I follow Nick, with Chris trailing me. We walk down a hall I'm not familiar with and into a small copy room. I look at the copier for a moment and orient myself to it. I make a few black and white copies of what I'm thinking. When I get the magnification how I want it, I show it to both of them. They look at each other and smile, approving what I've done.

"We'd be sitting around with our thumbs up our asses without her," Chris says.

"Don't you guys sometimes have to enlarge pictures of suspects or something?"

"Yes, but we can do that at our computers and print them at our desk. Since all of our suspects typically have prior arrests, we print out past booking photos. We don't mess with the copier that way. I hit the start button and hope it makes a copy. If I have to do anything more advanced I find somebody," Chris says.

Nick's nodding his head in agreement. I find the button to make a color copy and make one and show it to them. They both like it. We decide to make one of each of the other two girls. When we're satisfied, I hand the three pictures to Nick, and we go back to the conference room. I see that I missed a call from one of the girls I called at DJJ.

"Shit. I missed DJJ's call."

"Put that damn thing in your pocket like everyone else does so you don't miss any other calls," Nick says, aggravated. I ignore him and call the number back. She doesn't answer again, and I leave another message. "If you'd had it on you, there wouldn't be this game of phone tag going on," he says, frowning at me.

I make a point of shoving my phone in my back pocket so he sees it and put my hands on my hips and stare at him, displeased.

"Is there anything else you'd like to bitch at me about?" I snap at him.

"Maybe if you would get something to eat, you wouldn't be so crabby." He's smiling as he says it.

"Okay, truce! You two kiss and make up, because I know that's what you really want to do," Chris says to the both of us. "She's a firecracker. Now I know why you like her so much," he says to Nick.

"You need to remember that my weapon's always drawn before yours, and I'm a better shot," Nick says to him.

"I'm not scared," Chris says back to him. "I think Grace would be on my side, and she's already proven that she can kick your ass."

"Can we go?" I ask.

This train is off the track and moving quickly the wrong way. I'm never going to live down that I punched him. I grab my bag while Nick and Chris talk again about what Chris is going to do while we are gone. He's going to work on finding out about the morphine. We walk outside and get in Nick's car.

"Where should we go first?" he asks me.

I look at my watch and try to decide where a lot of people would be at this hour. I think back to the locations where I saw that girl the most. She was usually under the North Avenue Bridge, and I saw her in Tent City occasionally as well.

"Let's go to Tent City first."

Nick nods and heads in that direction. "Why don't you like guns?" he asks me.

I take a deep breath and look at him. "I saw my father shoot and kill three people."

He glances over at me, but I can't see his eyes behind his sunglasses, and he can't see mine either behind my sunglasses.

"That's some shit," he says. "Will you tell me about it, or should I change the subject to something less heavy?"

"I can talk about it. I've talked about it so much over the years that I think I sound detached about it. Maybe I am. My mother has prostituted herself my whole life. The man that I called my father may or may not really be my biological father. I look like him in that I have dark hair, tan skin and brown eyes. His name's Miguel Costa. He's serving life at Jackson State Prison.

"My mom would bring guys to where we were staying, at the time, and have sex with them there. She might have sex in her room or in the living room or wherever. I was exposed to way too much as a child. Matt did the best he could to protect me from all the shit that came with living with my mom and my dad.

"When I was five, she decided that it would be a great idea to bring three guys home. In her mind, more guys meant more money, and more money meant more drugs and alcohol. It got out of hand quickly. They didn't want to give her the money once they were done. My mom was a fighter. She gave as good as she got.

"She thought she could take on all three at the same time. She was going to get her money because she sure as hell was going to get her dope. My mom always had a knife on her, and she wasn't afraid to use it. She pulled it on one and threatened him. She forgot about the other two. They beat her up pretty badly.

"My dad came in as they were finishing and pulled a gun on them. They weren't afraid of my mom's knife, but they were very afraid of my dad's gun. They told him they would give her the money that they owed her plus some extra since they beat her up. My dad wasn't satisfied with that and shot and killed all three of them in our living room while I sat on the floor playing. My dad called his younger sister, or his cousin, I'm not sure which, and she came and got me and took me to her house.

"I wasn't there when the police got there, but the police discovered that not only was I in the house, but I witnessed the shooting. My dad's attorney and the District Attorney both tried to get him to plead guilty so I wouldn't have to testify. He refused, so when I was seven, I took the stand as a State's witness and testified against my dad. I've never been more afraid in my whole life. I was so scared that my dad would come after me and shoot me because of what I was saying about him. He obviously was found guilty and was sentenced to life in prison with no parole. The day I got off the stand was the last day I ever saw him."

There's silence between us. I don't know what Nick's thinking. I look over at him, and I see his jaw's clenched.

"Is there anything that you haven't been through?" His voice is raw.

"I've never used drugs. I've never sold my body. I've never killed anyone, and I've never been arrested. Don't get me wrong, I thought about selling my body more than once while I was homeless. When you're cold, hungry and all alone, the thought of making quick and easy money that way and having the company of someone else, even for a short amount of time, starts sounding damn good. But I didn't do it."

"What stopped you?"

"I didn't want to be my mother. There was something telling me that there was more to life than what I was experiencing at that moment. I felt like my life could be better and that it was going to be better if I could just hang in there and roll with the punches."

"Where was the first place that you were able to call your own?"

"When Jess and I moved in together in our first apartment. I had saved enough money working here, there and everywhere that I could afford paying half the rent and bills. You would've thought Jess and I moved into a mansion the way I felt about that apartment."

I smile remembering that crappy little apartment off the UGA campus. But it was ours, and I was partially paying for it. I felt on top of the world that day we moved in. Jess could've moved into a luxury apartment that Max and Susan would've gladly paid for, but I couldn't afford more than what we found. Jess being the loyal and devoted friend that she is said we were moving wherever I wanted.

"So you and Jess have always lived together?"

"Yes. For ten years. We moved one other time and then to the condo that Jess's parents bought for her a few years back. They've been gracious to me with everything."

We pull into Tent City, and Nick turns the car off and looks at me.

"Was DFCS ever involved in your life?"

"Yeah, but remember this was the eighties. Things were different then. My mom would hide me, or she'd say a friend was taking care of Matt and me. Parents could get away with more back then, and few questions were asked." I shrug my shoulders. "It was what it was. I don't blame anyone for what happened to me, other than my mother, and I've quit blaming her, too. Things were bad. Times were tough. It's not like that now."

"I don't know any other woman who's as strong as you are. You really are amazing." He smiles at me.

My heart is beating faster. He likes me, and I think it may be more than just about sex. I like him too, a lot more than what I've been thinking. I smile back at him. He's pretty amazing, too.

"Okay, Detective, let's see if we can get this girl identified."

We walk around, and I talk to a lot of people that I know. They all ask if I've brought sandwiches with me today. I tell them that I'll do my best to get back here tomorrow and have food with me then. They know my word's good. There are several people that I've seen here for years. My face is familiar to them, and theirs is familiar to me.

I introduce Nick to everyone. They're wary of him. Some of them know who he is by name, and even if they don't know him by name, they all know he is a cop since he's got his gun, badge and handcuffs on display.

Nick's holding the pictures, but we haven't shown them to anyone yet. We're making polite conversation, and I'm doing my best trying to get people to get comfortable with Nick. I'm trying to get him to be less like a cop, more like a regular person, and I decide that isn't going to happen and abandon that whole idea. Things are going fairly well, and then it all goes south.

Chapter Eighteen

"Shit," Nick says, getting angry.

I look up at him. I have no idea what's going on. We've been talking with a guy who knows my brother fairly well, and he's telling us the same story that Street was telling us last night or was that this morning? I still can't make any sense of what Matt thinks that he's done. I guess I'll try and find out when I find him, whenever that is.

"What is it?" I ask him.

He doesn't answer me. Instead he yells, "Shorty, come here dammit! Do *not* run from me because you know I'm faster than you are!" Well, Shorty doesn't listen to him and takes off like a jack rabbit with a hound on his tail. "Goddammit!" And Nick's off chasing his heels. I would think that with Nick's size, it would make him slower, but oh no, the man can move.

Shorty's running like he's not sure which direction he wants to go. His confusion lessens the distance between him and Nick. Now, I don't know how tall Nick is, but I'm guessing he's somewhere between six foot five and six foot six. He said he has a hundred plus pounds on me, and I come in at a curvy one hundred and forty-five.

Shorty is exactly his name. He looks ninety-five pounds dripping wet. When Nick tackles him, it looks just like a play you would see on a football field that would make the head coach proud. There's a hard sounding *whap* and then Shorty goes down, with Nick on top of him. I can hear Shorty crying and cussing that Nick has broken something. Nick's doing his own amount of cussing while putting his handcuffs on Shorty.

He pulls his phone out calling someone. I'm guessing he's calling for back up, but I don't know why. He's got this situation under control. I look on the ground and collect the pictures that he threw down when he took off. I see that part of my omen came true. God, I hope I don't have to chase anybody. I have no doubt in my mind that Nick was a good football player in high school. I bet all of the girls liked watching him run, because I did.

I can't think further on how much I liked watching him run and move the way he was moving because there's an irate crowd beginning to gather around Nick wanting to know why he did what he did to Shorty and why is Shorty now in handcuffs. I walk over to them and start trying to get them to move back. Nick is on his feet and has pulled Shorty on his feet as well.

"Back up!" he yells.

I'm trying to pull people away and encourage them to go back to what they were doing. He's getting angrier, and I'm desperately trying to calm the situation. It's not working. He's yelling over me while I'm still trying to talk calmly.

"Please go back to what you were doing," I say, trying to get between people.

"Back up!" Nick yells again.

Damn, we're about to have a fight on our hands. I don't want to fight. I don't want to have to punch someone else. I especially don't want to have to punch people that I'm out here with on a regular basis helping.

I think one patrol car's going to show up, but no, they send the whole cavalry, making things even more chaotic. I get caught up in a small surge of people and get knocked to the ground. Someone stomps on my ankle and it *hurts*. Nick turns Shorty over to a uniformed officer and helps me off the ground, while a couple of officers help get the crowd calmed down. That's done with threats of more arrests. Our pictures sit on the ground, trampled and dirty.

"Great," I mutter, looking down at them.

"Are you okay?" Nick asks.

I'm busy brushing my jeans off. "I'm fine." I take a step and nearly fall. Pain shoots through my ankle and halfway up my leg. "Shit," I say, making a grab for Nick. He sees that I'm about to fall and grabs me around the waist.

"What's wrong?" he asks, concerned.

"Someone stepped on my ankle, and it hurts."

"Who stepped on it?" He's scanning the crowd.

I look up at him. "I don't know. I didn't see who," I say, aggravated. Suddenly, Nick scoops me up and is carrying me to his car. "Put me down," I yell.

"Stop yelling at me. I'm going to sit you on the trunk of my car and look at your ankle." He does just that.

"I've had worse," I say as he slips my shoe and sock off and is running his hand over my ankle. The way he's touching me is getting very distracting. I like feeling his hands on me anywhere he wants to put them.

He looks up at me. "Was that when you were a kid?"

"Yes," I say, looking down at him. I wince when he squeezes a spot on my ankle.

"Is that tender?"

"Yes."

"Come on, I'll take you to the hospital to get an X-ray."

"It's not broken."

"How do you know without having an X-ray?"

"Trust me. I know. Besides, I can't afford a trip to the ER, okay?"

"I trust that you know what you're talking about, but if it's the hospital bill you're worried about, the department will pick up the bill since you're essentially working for us and this happened while working."

"No, it's not necessary. Help me off, and I'll see if I can walk around."

"At least put your sock and shoe back on."

I take it from him and put it back on. My ankle does hurt, but I don't believe it's broken. He helps me down and lets his arms linger around my waist.

"So, who's the guy that started all of this?" I ask, looking up at him. I have my arm slipped around his waist. We are standing hip to hip. Well, more like my waist to his hip.

He's smiling at me wickedly. He doesn't answer my question.

"Are you trying to cozy up to me, Grace Harrison, and using your ankle as an excuse?"

I try to push away from him, but his arm has me like a vise around my waist. I put some pressure on my foot, and it doesn't hurt as bad this time.

"No, I'm not using my ankle as an excuse," I mutter.

He's looking down at me, still smiling, sexy as shit, and I forget where we are and what we're supposed to be doing.

"I'm not complaining," he says. He bends down and whispers in my ear, "I'd like to bend you over this car."

I gasp. His words connect with me between my thighs. I feel the tingles all over. I'm sure our eyes are locked on one another, but we're still both wearing our sunglasses.

"You could very well get that chance," I whisper. Now I see him gasp.

One of the uniform officers who took Shorty walks over to us. Nick lets go of me, and I start walking around in an attempt to work some of the soreness out. I'm limping, but it isn't bad.

"Here's your handcuffs," the officer says to Nick, holding them out to him.

"Thanks," he says. He puts them back in his holder on his jeans. "There's an active warrant for his arrest for Armed Robbery of that little market on Chase Street."

"Yeah, I saw that. I'll take him and get him booked in. He said you broke his rib. I told him not to run next time, and that won't happen."

"I hit him hard," Nick says, unapologetically.

"What happened to you?" the officer asks me.

"My ankle got stepped on when I fell."

"You work at DFCS don't you? I've seen you around some locations."

Interesting. I've never seen this officer before. "Yes. I'm Grace Harrison." I hold my hand out to him. He takes it, shaking it.

"I'm Trey Bridges, and I'm single," he says, smiling at me. I look at Nick, who's not smiling.

"Well…it's nice to meet you." I don't know what else to say. What do you say to that? *I'm single too, but your co-worker over here is currently fucking me and plans to do it again.* Trey is still holding my hand.

"Okay, this is not the time for you to try and hook up," Nick says.

"It was nice to meet you, Grace," Trey says, walking away. "See you later, Nick."

After Trey leaves, taking Shorty with him, Nick looks down at me.

"I would hate to punch a fellow officer in the face," he says, walking and picking up the pictures that are still on the ground. *What? Is he jealous?* I want to laugh, but he looks so angry, I don't dare. He brushes the pictures off and holds them out to me. "I don't think they look too bad."

I look at them for a moment and decide that the girls' faces are still easily seen. They look a little mangled, but that's because they are.

"They'll work," I say. "Now, if we can find anyone who'll cooperate with us."

"I'm not apologizing for doing my job," he snaps at me.

I plant my hands on my hips and regard him with a look. "Did I say anything about that?"

"You look pretty sexy standing there with your hands on your hips like that, getting pissed at me." He's starting to grin.

I start laughing. He's far too much. He keeps me so off balance, and it makes me feel alive, and he said I look sexy.

"Can we get back to why we came here in the first place please?" We begin to walk back to the crowd when a thought hits me. "Oh, my God. I'm so damn stupid." I slap my forehead and look up at Nick.

"What is it?"

"Darla. Belinda. My mom. Well, maybe not my mom. We can take these pictures to them. They might know who these girls are."

He's looking down at me and smiling. "I didn't think of that, either." We walk back to his car. He walks. I limp. "We need to start thinking outside the box."

"Isn't that what I just did?" I say.

"It took you long enough." He's joking with me.

"You didn't think of it at all. So, shut up." I'm smiling sweetly at him.

"You better be glad I like you, or else I'd make you walk back."

I laugh, shaking my head at him and feel my phone buzzing. I pull it out and answer it. It's the girl I know from DJJ.

"Hey, Beth," I say.

"Hey, Grace. I'm sorry it took me so long to get back with you. How are you?"

"I'm good. I hate that I've had to call you on a Saturday, but I was hoping you could give me some information on a couple of girls that DJJ's been involved with."

"Sure. Is this a DFCS matter?" Beth asks me.

Shit. I wasn't planning on having her ask me any questions about why I need to know.

"It's related."

"Okay," she says, but she doesn't sound sure about it. "What do you need to know?"

"I need to know about Tonya Overby and Hailey West. Do you know where they are?"

"I don't. I didn't have either one of them. The PO that had Hailey is gone. I'd have to call Tonya's former PO and ask him. Is this something that could wait until Monday? I'd be happy to pull the file on Hailey and give you whatever it is that you need, but I don't think the file is going to tell you that."

"Would you be able to tell me where their families are?"

Beth hesitates before answering. "Sure. Once I pull the file and talk to Tonya's former PO."

"Could you call Tonya's former PO today and ask him?"

"Grace, I'm not even in town today. I'll be back tomorrow evening. I could definitely look for you on Monday."

I can tell she wants to get off the phone with me. I can't tell her the urgency of it without telling her why I need it, and I can't do that. I'm trying to come up with something good, and I can't do it.

"Thanks, Beth. I'll talk to you Monday." I get off the phone with her.

"Monday," Nick says, getting the gist of the conversation. "You can't get information from her until Monday?"

I go over my entire conversation with him, explaining to him that Beth doesn't know about either one of them, Hailey's former probation officer isn't there any longer, and Beth would have to call Tonya's. He's not happy about what I tell him.

"Shit," he says, rubbing his face with one hand while steering with the other. "Okay. We'll do what we can."

We turn into Belinda and Darla's small yard. We see them sitting outside on the porch. They both wave at us, and Darla even smiles. It's not a big smile, but I'll take anything over what I've seen.

"Hey," I say to them, walking up on the porch. I'm still limping, but it's not so bad. The pain is lessening.

"Hey. We didn't think we'd see y'all back so soon," Belinda says to us. I sit in one chair, while Nick sits in another across from me. "Why're you limpin'?"

I start laughing. "It's a long story. It involves Nick tackling someone, but it wasn't me." We all laugh at that, even Nick. "We were hoping that you two might be able to help us with something," I say to them.

"We can try," Belinda says, looking at Darla, who nods her head. "Since y'all are here, we can tell y'all what we been doin'. We didn't sleep none. After you left, I throwed your momma out." I'm sure she sees how surprised I am by that statement. "I couldn't believe that she don't believe what happened to you, and she ain't sorry about it at all. Darla and I talked all night. She told me she wants to get off the dope. I want to get off the dope too."

I look at both of them, pleased and proud.

"That's awesome. I'll do whatever I can to help you."

"I've got clean before, so I know what to do. I told Darla we need to start goin' to some meetins'. We talked about goin' to a recovery house, but we don't want to lose this place."

"I applaud both of you," I tell her.

"I want to call them people you told me about," Darla says to me.

"Do you still have Nick's card?"

"Yeah. I still got it," she says.

"Is there anything that I can do for you?"

"I don't got a way to get there when I talk to somebody."

"You do now," I say, smiling at her.

"Thanks." She sounds shy about it.

Darla tugs at my heart. I like this girl so much. I hope she realizes someday how incredibly strong she is. I hold my hand out to Nick for him to give me the pictures.

"Nick and I are hoping that you can help us identify some girls. I enlarged their faces, and most of the really bad stuff you can't see or make out what it is."

"Detective Bassano asked me last night if I was alone, and I was but there're other girls, ain't there?"

"Yes," I admit.

"How many?"

"Six, maybe seven."

"Oh, my God," Darla whispers. "Is it my fault?"

"What?" we all exclaim together.

"Why would you think it's your fault?" I ask her.

"If I'd said somethin', then there wouldn't be other girls."

"Darla," Nick says. "We don't know if you were the last girl or if there was one after you or three were taken before you. We don't know. There's nothing about this situation that you should allow to rest on your shoulders. You did nothing wrong- before, during or after." He's holding her eyes while he talks to her. "Okay?"

"Okay," she says to him. "Can I see the pictures?" she asks me. I give her the picture of the girl I've seen on the streets, but I don't know her name. Belinda leans over to look at it. "I know her," Darla says. She looks at Belinda. "Do you remember her?"

"Yes. Sherry somethin', I think. I don't remember her last name, but I'm pretty sure her first name's Sherry."

Darla looks at Nick and me. "Yeah, her name's Sherry. I'll try to remember her last name. Does that help?"

"Yes, it does," Nick says.

I give her the other two pictures. She and Belinda look at them for several minutes. They tell us they don't recognize either girl.

"Do you know anything about Sherry?" I ask both of them.

"I think she come here with a boyfriend, and the boyfriend dumped her here, and she couldn't get back home. I don't remember where home was or if she ever said," Belinda says.

I look at Nick. "Anything else?"

"Nothing I can think of right now," he says.

"Call me after you get an appointment, and I'll be happy to drive you. Belinda can go with you, too, if you want."

Darla agrees, and when we get back in the car Nick asks,

"Last night, when we were here, why did you do what you did sitting at the table? I'm only asking because I thought it was a great move, and I was just curious as to why you did it that way."

"I felt like we were hovering over her. I thought if we put some distance between us and her, and sit down while she was still standing, it would make her feel more in control. It's just something I thought of and went with it. I remember how much I wanted to feel in control after being raped. I thought Darla might want the same."

He doesn't say anything. I look over at him and see him smiling. He glances at me quickly, and then his eyes are back on the road.

"Grace, why do you search for your mom and try to see her after everything that she's done to you?"

I sigh. "It's important to Matt, and Matt's important to me. I don't think Matt has ever given up hope that our mom will love him the way he's always wanted her to. If he stays with her and keeps up with her, then maybe she'll change. I believe that's how his mind works. The other part is, I don't like who my mom is, and it would've been great if things had been different, but she's my mom, and I do want to see her from time to time to make sure she's as okay as she can be."

"You're forgiving, aren't you?"

"I don't know if it's necessarily forgiveness or acceptance. I accepted how mom is long ago, and I know that she most likely isn't going to change. If she does, that's great. I fought hard to have a happy, full life, and I don't dwell on what she did or didn't do."

He glances over at me and smiles. I smile back at him.

"You're a better person than I am. I'd be bitter and all pissed off at what I had to go through."

I shrug my shoulders. "I guess, but if I was like that, how does that help me? How would that attitude make my life better?"

I see him continue to smile, but he says nothing further on it. We decide to drive around some places where my brother could be. We hit every location on my list and we can't find him anywhere. Some people we talk to have seen him, while others haven't seen him at all. Everyone we talk to we show the pictures. We get two different names for one girl, and there isn't anyone who recognizes the other. We also show the picture of Sherry, hoping that someone, anyone, can give us a last name. We strike out on that as well. Those that have seen Matt tell us the same story; his usual ranting is worse, and he keeps saying he's done something. The last place we go, I hear that he may be at the Salvation Army. We go there next.

While we are driving there, I ask, "Who do you think killed the Bradberrys?"

"I don't know, but I know it's related to what they were involved with. I told Chris they were either killed for what they did, or because of the pictures or both."

"You feel certain of that."

"Yes. Are you doubting me?"

"Keep your pants on over there," I say. He gives me a wicked smile, and it's so sexy. "I'm not doubting you. I agree with you. I wanted to know if you and Chris reached that conclusion immediately, or did that take time?"

We're at the Salvation Army. Nick turns off the car and turns to look at me.

"I knew when I found those pictures that, that was the reason they were killed. I wasn't thinking Eleanor was involved in this, so I figured she was collateral damage. Even though I knew it had something to do with those pictures and the girls, I didn't want us to get tunnel vision. We talked to a lot of people the first couple of days. We heard the same thing. Everyone loved them. They were wonderful. They gave so much of themselves and their money. They cared about issues, and on and on and on. It was hard listening to that, knowing what I know. We looked at their finances. Did they owe money? Did someone owe them money? By all appearances, they were the most loved, the most respected and the most giving of any family ever. We know differently, don't we? Plus, what I told you last night. There was no robbery. Nothing was taken. There was plenty to take. This is all about revenge."

I nod. We get out of the car and go into the Salvation Army. Mike is here. He smiles broadly when he sees me.

"Hey, Grace." He gets up from his desk and comes over and hugs me.

"Hey, Mike. How are you?"

"I'm great. It's great to see you. I've been meaning to call you, but I've been really busy. I had a great time when we went out. I'd like to take you out again, if I could?"

I look up at Nick. He looks…unhappy, angry, uncomfortable, *jealous?* I like Mike. He's a great guy. He's funny and happy all the time. We have a lot in common. He's good-looking, too, but there isn't any chemistry. We could still go out and have a good time. Why not? Mike's a friend. I like Nick. I like him a lot, but the truth of the matter is that we've had sex; really awesome, hot sex, the best sex I've ever had, but we're not dating. Nick isn't mine, and I'm not his. I ignore the feeling in my stomach over the thought of him not being mine, and me not being his. *Okay, back to reality girl!* Mike's waiting for my answer.

"That sounds like a great idea. You still have my number?"

"Definitely. It's in my phone." He's still smiling broadly at me.

Nick looks like a total grump.

"This is Detective Nick Bassano," I say, introducing them. They shake hands, and I notice that Nick again is using too much force. Mike's flexing his hand afterwards. I give Nick a look, and he returns it with a grin. *He knows what he's doing.* "Have you seen Matt?" I ask Mike.

"No. I haven't."

"Matt never calls me, but if you do see him, would you tell him that I need to hear from him?"

"Sure. Of course. Is everything okay?" He's looking from me to Nick.

"I need to talk to him, is all," I explain.

Mike and I talk for a few minutes about various things, including some of the same people that we both know, but Nick is looking impatient and keeps looking at his watch like he has some place to be. I know what he's doing. I hug Mike again and tell him to call me.

When we are walking out, Nick asks me, "Are you really going to go out with him?"

"Maybe. What's it to you?" I'm grinning as I say it.

"You're busy. Besides, he's a pussy, too."

Is he for real? I burst into laughter as we get in the car, and I notice he pulls out a little too fast.

"Yes. I'm busy. Do you want to elaborate on what you mean, or should I guess? Mike's not a pussy. Do you say that about all men who don't tote guns for a living?"

He looks over at me and gives me a dimpled grin. "Maybe." Then, he gets all serious on me. "You're busy with life, with work and with…" He lets his voice trail off. What else was he going to say?

"And with?"

"Nothing," he says. His jaw's tight. I want to tease him about being jealous, but I don't know if that would be a good idea or not. "Are you afraid of guns?" he asks me.

Holy Heaven, he'll just bounce from one thing to the next. All I can do is try to keep up with him.

"I should be."

"Yes. I guess you should, but you aren't."

"No. I'm not scared of guns."

We give up trying to find my brother right now. We're both tired, hungry and ready for a small break. Nick calls Chris, and we agree that pizza sounds good. We talk about ordering it and taking it back to the police department, but Chris throws a fit when Nick suggests that. He says he wants a change of scenery. We decide on Mellow Mushroom on Clayton Street. Nick and I are essentially there. He finds parking, and we walk the short distance.

It's not that crowded today, since UGA has been on Spring Break. That will change tomorrow as the students make their way back to Athens. We find a table inside, and I pull my phone out, sending a text to Jess, asking her what time they left and when she thinks they'll be back. Her response is that she thinks they'll be back by six. She wants to know if I'll be home or if my plans is to not be home until tomorrow.

"How much longer do you think we'll be working today?" I ask him.

"There's not much more you can do today. You want to blow off some steam after lunch?"

I smile at him. *Is he thinking what I'm thinking?*

"I know what you're thinking. That's later." He's leering at me. *Damn, how'd he know what I was thinking?* "I want to take you to the gun range and teach you to shoot."

I stop smiling. "Nick," I groan. "I don't want to go shoot a gun, and it's not because I'm scared. Guns are dangerous. I've seen what they can do."

"Are you going to shoot me?"

I look at him like he's stupid. "Of course not."

"Are you going to shoot yourself?"

Now he's being ridiculous. "No."

"Are you going to drive here later with a gun, and open up on people?"

Did the man smoke something when I wasn't looking? I stare at him for a moment, trying to decide if I'm even responding to that stupid question.

"No," I say it in a way, that I regarded that as the dumbest question I've ever been asked.

"Then, the gun isn't dangerous.

I roll my eyes at him. I can't help it. He starts laughing at me. Shit. I forgot to text Jess back. I let her know that I may be home tonight, and if so, I can't wait to see her and hear about her trip. She responds that she has a lot to share. Chris comes in and slumps in his chair.

"I want to slit my wrists," he tells us. "But, I think I would miss because I'm cross eyed at the moment because I spent a considerable amount of what I feel like was wasted time, looking at various documents, including financial records. I decided it's stupid for me to try and run down all the doctors in the Bradberrys' life trying to find the connection to the morphine. I decided instead to try and attach the morphine to a specific doctor. I called Childers. He's a detective in Drug/Vice here," he says to me. "I asked him about morphine, and I now know more about it than I ever wanted, including but not limited to the federal regulations, which I could give two shits about.

"Anyway, I asked him if there's been any suspicious activity around morphine usage and/or distribution with local doctors, and guess what? There has been. Childers said about a year ago, an informant came to him and said a group of doctors here in Athens were unlawfully distributing morphine. There's a group of four doctors here who run a successful pain management clinic. It's called Miller and Associates Pain Management of Athens.

"Childers said they started looking into it and ran an investigation for several months. They couldn't find anything illegal, but they've always been suspicious. I looked up the doctors and called all of them. You look excited, but stop," he says, looking straight at Nick. "They're all out of town. One of the doctors who owns the practice, Greg Miller, is out of the country.

"I know you're disappointed about that, but I'm about to get you excited again." Chris smiles wickedly. I chuckle. He's a funny guy. "I talked to all the doctors, except Greg Miller. His phone must not be working down in Cabo San Lucas. I wonder if the department would financially approve a trip so I could go down there and talk with him," Chris trails off in thought.

"Chris," Nick snaps. "Excite me, man."

"Oh, sorry. I was sitting on the beach drinking a cold beer. Okay. Settle down. I gave the same story to all three of them, that their name came up as knowing the Bradberrys, and since we're investigating the Bradberry murder, I needed to speak with them. All three said the same thing. They didn't know the Bradberrys that well, other than being in the same social circles, but Greg Miller is very good friends with Mickey and Eleanor."

I look at Nick, and he does look excited.

"That's excellent. Are all of the doctors going to be back Monday? Especially Greg Miller."

"Yes, except Greg Miller will not be back until Tuesday."

"This is really good. So, an investigation was started year ago, huh?"

"Yep. Right around the time Darla Grier went missing is what you're thinking, isn't it?"

"Yes, it is." Nick looks over at me and asks, "What do you think?"

I look at both of them. "It sounds like you guys have something to work with."

"Okay, I want a break, and right now, I want some food, and I want to talk about anything else other than any of this shit that has brought us together this fine Saturday," Chris says to us.

We order two pizzas, our drinks and talk about everything else.

"I'm taking Grace to the range later," Nick tells Chris.

Chris looks over at me and smiles.

"I knew he'd get a gun in your hand," he says looking at me.

"I haven't agreed to go," I tell both of them.

"You will," Nick says. He's so sure of himself.

I look at him. "And if I don't?"

"I'll persuade you." He's smiling, sexy as shit, and his eyes have gotten darker, hungry, and I'm certain that it's for me. My body temperature just went up ten or more degrees. I don't think he's going to have to persuade me at all.

"I feel like I need to leave, and I just got here," Chris says.

I break eye contact with Nick and look at Chris.

"Chris, do you and your wife have any kids?" I need to change the subject to anything else and get my mind on something else besides Nick naked with me wherever he wants us to be naked.

"Brit and I don't have any children. We're trying, with the exception of very early this morning, which I don't want to discuss because it's still painful."

"How long have you two been married?"

"Four wonderful years. She's an ER nurse at Athens Regional, and a little over five years ago, when I was on patrol, I had to go to the ER to get stitched up after breaking up a fight. One of the guys decided it would be a smart idea to pull his knife and cut my arm. Brit was my attending nurse. I swear I fell in love with that woman that night. I asked her on a date before I left, and she agreed. The rest is history."

"That's such a sweet story," I say, smiling at him.

"I'll introduce you to her one day. You and Nick can go out with us. We can double date."

He talks like Nick and I are going to continue to see one another. Are we? I'd like to.

Chapter Nineteen

I'm off in a different world thinking of how much I would like to continue seeing Nick, when I hear a sugary sweet voice.

"Hey, guys."

I look up to see a beautiful, smiling blonde. Wow, she's gorgeous. Is she a model? She's put together very well in what looks like designer jeans and a silky top that has a halter style neckline. I catch a scent of her perfume, and it smells expensive.

"Samantha," Chris says, smiling and standing to hug her.

Nick glances at me, looks uncomfortable for a moment and then stands and smiles too.

"Hey, Sam," Nick says, hugging her.

She wraps her arms around his waist, hugging him tightly, looking up at him with more than a brief familiarity with him. *I don't even have to ask who she is. I know.* I don't like the feeling that I'm having in the pit of my stomach. Nick doesn't belong to me. He's single. He likes to date, *a lot*, and that's something that I know, but it's hard to see it staring me in the face, all blond, gorgeous and smelling great. *Stop being jealous!*

"You look good," she says. She still has her arms wrapped around him.

"So do you," he tells her. He glances over at me and then back down to Sam. He steps away from her, sitting back in his seat.

"Are y'all working today?" she asks them, continuing to stand in what I would consider to be Nick's personal space.

"Yes, we are. Sam, this is Grace," Chris says, directing her attention to me.

"Oh, hi. It's nice to meet you. I work with Chris's wife."

"It's nice to meet you, too. Chris and I were discussing how he and Brit met."

"It's very romantic isn't it? I was hoping that when they introduced me to Nick, the same thing would happen. I'm still working on him. I keep thinking maybe one day, he'll want to do something other than just the occasional date." She's smiling and looking at Nick.

Floor, open up and swallow me, please. Seriously, please, I'm waiting. Yeah, the floor does nothing. The look on Nick's face says he may want the same thing. Can anyone say uncomfortable? Even Chris isn't smiling any longer and won't look at me.

"Well, I hope that works out for you," I stumble all over that sentence trying to get it out.

Holy Heaven, what do I say? Nick's eyes lock with mine, and the look on his face says, *What the fuck are you doing?* I give him an apologetic look and shrug my shoulders.

"It was really nice meeting you," she says to me. "I have to go. I'm meeting some friends for lunch. Nick, call me so we can go out."

He breaks eye contact with me and looks up at her, saying, "I'll do my best. Chris and I are really busy right now working on these three homicides."

"Brit said that y'all were. Call me when you can." She walks away, putting some extra sway in her hips, it would appear.

Chris looks at Nick and opens his mouth to say something. Nick shakes his head at that. Chris looks at me and says, "She really wants a boyfriend." He says it in a way that tells me it was the best thing he could come up with.

"I gathered that," I say.

"Did you have to say *that*?" Nick asks me. He looks angry. What's his problem?

"I didn't know what else to say. How about, *Good luck? I'll try to make that happen for you?* Does that sound any better? Why're you angry?" My brows are furrowed.

"I'm not angry," he snaps at me. *Right, not angry.*

"I could've said that you're busy." I'm smiling at him, trying to get a smile out of him. That does get a little smile; his face and body are starting to relax.

"How about this," he says, "I'll hook Mike up with Samantha, since we are both busy, and they can go out together." His smile is wicked sexy with those dimples on full display, and his eyes are now dancing. I don't understand what's going on with him. Chris is looking at us, not understanding at all. "Grace got hit on not once, but twice today," Nick explains to him. He tells Chris about the scene out at Tent City, finding Shorty, that I got hit on by Trey Bridges and then Mike wanting to take me out on another date.

"You've got competition," Chris says, laughing.

"Shit, not if I shoot them all," Nick says.

He *does* sound jealous, and I don't know what to make of it. I can't tell if he really is jealous or if he's saying these things for my benefit. It's a mystery to me. I'm not going to sit around here and ponder over it in my head. Our pizza arrives, and we dig in. I'm starving. We end up having to order a third.

"Did you like playing football in high school? I'm guessing that was a high school picture I saw," I say to Nick, completely changing the subject.

Chris is looking at me, confused. "Where'd you see his high school football pictures?"

"At his house," I tell him.

Chris looks at Nick, shocked and starts grinning. "You took Grace to your house?"

"Yes," he says, in a way that dares Chris to say something else.

"Does she know-"

"Yes, she knows," Nick says, cutting him off. What do I know? Neither of them is going to say anything further on it. It has to be about the fact that he's not ever had a woman at his house. He looks at me. "No, Grace. I hated football. Of course I liked it."

Sarcastic son of a bitch, but I'm smiling.

"I know you played defense. You were a Linebacker, I bet."

"Very good. You like football?" Nick asks me.

"No, I hate it. I'm just good at guessing. I'm that smart." I'm trying to hide my smile, but I can't.

"I have no doubt that you're that smart," he says to me. "You're also a smart *ass.*"

"I'm hanging around you too much." We're grinning at each other, and our eyes have locked.

Oh, I want him. How much trouble would we get in if we wiped everything off the table and went for it right here. We would certainly leave people talking. My heart's starting to beat faster, and I can feel desire for him begin to pool down deep. His eyes are getting that hungry look in them again. He wants me too. I see it.

"I'm going to have them wrap my pizza up and go so you two can be alone," Chris mumbles, smiling.

"Let's get them to box the whole thing and head back. We've got a few things to do, and then I'm dragging Grace to the range if I have to."

"I'll go." *But I'm not happy about it.*

His responding smile and wink nearly sends me to the floor.

❦

I'm nodding my head that I completely understand what Nick's telling me. I want to scream at him, but I get what he's doing. We've been going over gun safety for quite a while. It's very involved. We've also gone over the mechanics of his gun, which I've learned is a Glock 22, and it uses .40 caliber ammunition. He shows me the gun that he has on his ankle. That's his backup weapon. How many weapons does one need? He informs me that it's a Smith & Wesson M&P SHIELD which also uses .40 caliber ammunition. *Okay. It's all Greek to me.*

I know he has to have weapons knowledge, but he sounds near genius about it. Maybe it's because I know nothing about guns or ammunition. He never uses the word bullet when he's giving me instruction. I learn all kinds of new words as it relates to guns. He shows me how to take the magazine out and then pop it back in. I learn how to chamber a round. He's so smooth when he does it, and I get distracted watching the muscles in his forearms when he's handling his weapon, which he's constantly referring to it as his *duty weapon.*

"Are you paying attention to what I'm doing?"

I feel like I've been caught doing something naughty.

Oh, I'm paying attention all right. "Yes."

He smiles at me. He shows me how to wrap my hands around the hand grip of the gun and stresses for me to never put my finger on the trigger unless I'm certain that I'm going to *fire the weapon*. Those are his words. He shows me how to stand. It's called the Weaver Stance. I don't know who or what Weaver is, but I'm sure he'd tell me if I asked. It's actually all kind of fascinating. He's into it, something that he clearly enjoys, and I like that he's sharing it with me. He takes all of the ammunition out of his gun, that's what I call it, *a gun*, and hands it to me. My hands suddenly feel sweaty. I've never touched a gun before in my life.

"It's not a snake, Grace," he says, sounding quite authoritative. I put my hands on my hips and give him a look. He starts laughing. "You need to stop doing that, because I find it incredibly sexy, and I can't begin to tell you how much I want you right now."

Whoa! I want him, too. I look around. We're all alone out in the middle of what seems like Nowhereville. It has possibilities. I shake my head. I can't believe I'm even considering having sex on a gun range that's used by possibly everyone in Law Enforcement in Clarke County.

What's this man doing to me? I start smiling. I remember what he did to me, and I hope it happens again. *Stop! God, Grace Harrison, are you seriously thinking of sex right now?* I shake my head slightly at myself. I'm here to learn how to shoot a gun, not have sex. I hold my hand out and take the gun. It's heavy but not as heavy as I thought.

"Show me how you chamber a round," he says, taking all the ammunition out of the magazine while watching me.

"Why're you doing that?" I ask him, getting familiar with the feel of his gun.

"Because I'm going to let you put them all back in," he says, smiling at me.

"Why?"

"So you'll get used to doing it. I want you to get comfortable with everything that involves handling a weapon. Are you going to show me or just hold it?"

"Show you what?" I ask, in my best seductive voice.

He stops what he's doing and looks at me. He puts everything in his hands on the table that we are standing next to, takes the gun from me and puts it down as well. My heart's starting to pound. I'm excited. He stands in front of me, but he doesn't touch me.

"*You* are very bad." His voice is low, sexy, and if he doesn't put his hands on me somewhere, I'm going to combust right here. He pulls me into him and hovers over my lips. My hands slide from his chest up around his neck. I'm up on my toes and pressed up against him. Our eyes are locked, and he's smiling at me. "You need to get serious about what we're doing here." He smiles as he says it. "I shouldn't kiss you because you're so bad, but you're also *very* tempting."

He kisses me, and I melt into him. He finds my tongue. I give it to him and take his. His kiss tastes of promises of later. I feel him getting aroused against me. There is no getting aroused for me. I'm there. He breaks the kiss too quickly. I'm breathing harder, and he is too.

"You're such a distraction. I like it." His voice is still low and sexy, and it turns me on even more. "Can we get back to it?"

Get back to what? Him kissing me? Thinking of later? Feeling how hard he is against me? He's referring to the gun. I feel a little disappointed.

"Okay," I finally say. He hands his gun back to me.

"Now, show me how to chamber a round," he says, motioning to the gun. I try. I have to hold it against my body to do it. It's harder than it looks. "Grace. Are you kidding me with that?" he snaps at me.

"What? It's hard. I've never done this before," I snap right back at him.

He takes it from me and shows me again what to do so quickly that I nearly miss the action and then hands it back to me. I think I do it right this time.

"No, Grace, you can't chamber a round by gliding the slide back in place the way you're doing it. It's made for you to pull it back and let it go." He demonstrates the proper way to do it again. "If you do it the way you are doing it, it could jam the weapon. You definitely don't want that to happen."

"Don't yell at me," I say, frustrated.

"I'm not yelling at you, baby. I want you to get it right."

I stop what I'm doing and look at him. Did he just call me *baby*? He did. I don't think he realizes what he said. I think about it. I like it. He said it earlier, but that was during sex. He said it when I was in my car, but it was in the context of me being naked, which again, falls along the lines of sex. The way he said it this time sounded more like an endearment. I'm smiling at him.

"What?" he asks.

"Nothing."

I go back to what I was doing, and this time I get it right. He then hands me the magazine, and I have to put all of the ammunition in it. It's not so bad putting in the first few bullets, but my fingers hurt by the time I'm finished. That was hard.

"It gets easier," Nick tells me. I hope so. I look at my fingers. I'm convinced there will be bruises on the tips later. He takes a target and walks down range and puts it up. I like watching him move. He tells me to put on my ear and eye protectors. They both look stupid. I tell him as much. "It's better than being deaf and blind by the time your birthday rolls around," he says.

He has me stand back a little and off to the side so I can see what he's doing. He fires off three shots. He makes it look so easy. He's completely comfortable with what he's doing. The sound's muffled, but the noise still makes me jump. I look at the target and see from where I'm standing that all three shots hit the target in the *center of mass*. Again, his words. It's impressive. He's really good at this. Nick motions for me to stand where he is, handing his gun off to me, and I'm suddenly extremely nervous. *Holy Heaven, I'm all kinds of nervous now.* These things kill people. I've seen it.

I hold it like he showed me, stretching my arms out, locking my elbows and standing how he stood. It's much heavier now that it's fully loaded. I raise it and line the sights up like he showed me. I squeeze the trigger, and the gun bucks in my hand. *I shot a gun.* That was pretty cool. Nerve wracking, but cool. Did I hit anything? I think I hit the dirt, but I'm not sure. My heart's beating wildly, but it's due to nerves, not excitement.

"Try again," he says. I still don't hit anything the second time. "You're jerking on the trigger. You aren't locking your elbows, and I think you're looking at the target instead of the middle sight."

I keep practicing, and he keeps instructing me on what he thinks I'm doing wrong. I empty the magazine and manage to get one shot in the target's lower leg. Hey, I feel successful about that. We stay out for another hour. He switches me back and forth between both guns. I like the Smith & Wesson. I tell him that I do. By the end, I've managed to get most of the shots on the target, and a few hit in the abdomen area.

One shot goes right between the target's legs. Nick cringes when he sees that.

"Maybe you shooting a firearm isn't the best idea," he laughs as he says it. "You did a good job. I can't believe this your first time shooting. I think you may be a natural at this."

"You're a good instructor," I say, helping him gather everything up.

"You're making me blush over here, Grace Harrison."

"Please," I snort, laughing at him.

We load everything in his car and make our way back to the police department. I'm heading home when we get back. There's nothing else for me to do. Before we came to the range, Nick, Chris and I did everything that we could do to find out who Sherry is and try to find a last name. We found nothing. I asked about searching NCIC, but Nick informed me there isn't enough information to do that. We have no idea who she is other than a picture and a first name. I'm frustrated with it, and they are too.

They had me sit down with them and look at financial records to see if anything fishy jumped out at us. Nick found withdrawal amounts of one thousand dollars at certain times. He said he wanted to look into that, but he didn't feel like it would amount to much. As I make a mental recap of the day of what Nick and I accomplished, it doesn't feel like we've done a damn thing productive. The only thing we do know is Sherry. We don't even have a last name.

There are still two girls unidentified, and we don't know if there are other Missing Persons Reports that are missing. Chris seemed to have much more success, and I hope it's something that they'll be able to work with. They both seem excited about it. I voice our lack of success to Nick.

"That's how it goes sometimes. You can work all day like you and I've done and have almost nothing to show for it."

"Doesn't that get frustrating?"

"Definitely, but it can't stop us. You have to look at what Chris did today. What he found is something that we can work with. It's a direction we can move in. We'll keep pulling on all the strings that we can until we find what we're looking for. We're bullheaded."

"No, not you two," I say, trying to sound shocked.

"It's true," he says, grinning.

Nick pulls up beside my car.

"I'm going home."

We both get out, and I find my keys.

"I'll call you when I get finished. I don't think Chris and I are going to stay much longer. I know he's itching to get out of here and home to Brit."

"Okay."

I'm unlocking my door when he asks, "Where're you going?"

I turn around and look at him, confusion written all over my face. "I said I was going home."

"You're just going to leave without saying goodbye?"

"Bye," I say, not understanding at all what he means.

He walks around his car to stand in front of me. I look up at him and there it is in his eyes, *hunger for me.*

"I was looking more for a proper goodbye from you." His voice has dropped, and it's sexy. *He's too damn hot.*

He doesn't wait for me to answer. He bends and kisses me, pinning me between him and my car. I stretch up so he doesn't have to continue to bend. He's pressed in me, kissing me until I swear I cannot breathe. We're moving from *this is only kissing* to *we're going to continue to kiss and take all of our clothes off, right here.* I run my hands in the back of his hair and pin his face tighter to me. I can tell he likes it because I feel and hear him moan into the kiss and that turns me on even more. He drags his lips from mine and is staring down in my eyes.

"Am I going to see you later?" His voice is low, sexy, *oh, shit, that's just too hot.*

"If you want to," I whisper.

"Do you?"

"Yes," I say, not denying that I want to.

He smiles at me and kisses me softly. "Then I'll see you later. I'll call you, and we'll make plans."

He kisses me again and lingers for a moment. Hell, he can linger the rest of the day at my lips if he wants.

Chapter Twenty

Once I'm in my car, I can see in my rearview mirror that he's watching me drive away. My heart's pounding over him kissing me and that we're seeing each other later. Jess calls me while I'm driving home.

"Hey. I'm on my way," I tell her.

"Great. We've been here for fifteen minutes. Where are you?"

"I'm almost to the loop coming off of Lexington."

"What're you doing on the East side?"

"Nick's working."

"I see."

I can tell she's grinning.

"I'll be there in a few minutes."

I get on the Loop 10 that makes a loop all the way around Athens. Atlanta has I-285, which is massive. We have a smaller version in Athens; one is the inner loop, and the other is the outer. Some people call it the bypass, and some people call it the Loop, like me. But really, it's just another road.

Being alone, driving and listening to music, gives me the opportunity to think. I very much like Nick. I know he told me that he likes me when we were at McCoy's, but I took it more as a sexual attraction kind of liking. What does he feel for me? What do I want from him? He's exciting. He makes me feel excited on a level that I've not felt before. I like being with him. I enjoy his company. I believe he enjoys mine. We most definitely enjoy each other naked. I'm not sure where this is going.

There are feelings I'm having for him, and that's something that I might be able to deny to everyone else, but I can't deny it to myself. I've been more than attracted to him since he pulled up to help me. The feelings I'm having are happening awfully fast. I'm getting into some deep thinking here, and deep isn't someplace I want to be at the moment. I get home and feel like I've not been here in ages. I walk in, and Jess and Jake are on the couch watching TV.

"Hey," I say, dumping my bag on the counter. She jumps up and runs to me, hugging me. I've missed her. She's tan and glowing. "Did you have a good time?" I ask, hugging her tightly.

"We had a great time." She lets go of me and stands back. Jake has joined her, and they're looking at me, smiling from ear to ear.

"What?" I ask. I can't help but to mirror her smile. She looks so happy. She holds her hand out to me, and I catch my first look at the sparkling diamond on her left hand ring finger. "Oh my God!" I scream and pull her hand closer to me. It's a beautiful ring. The center diamond is really big. I don't know anything about anything when it comes to the carat sizes of diamonds, so I'll have to ask her later. It's round, and there are two smaller diamonds on either side. It's a *past, present and future* style engagement ring, that I do know. "I can't believe you two got engaged on Spring Break. How romantic is that!" I'm squealing, and Jess and I are jumping around, hugging and laughing. I hug Jake. "I can't believe you didn't tell me you were going to do this, Jake Echols."

"You would've told her."

"I would not," I say, all insulted, but I'm still smiling.

"You would've walked around smiling just the way you are right now, and she would've asked you questions until you broke and told her."

He's probably right about that.

"I'm so happy for you two. This is so exciting. We have to go out tonight and celebrate."

They both look at me and groan.

"We've been on the road for over seven hours. We don't want to go anywhere," Jess says.

"Oh, come on. We'll go for dinner, and you two can sleep in tomorrow. I won't disturb you at all."

"Can we sit for a while?" Jess asks.

"Yes. I want to hear all about your trip. I need to shower before we go and change."

"We need to do the same," she says. We go and sit on the couch. "Can you give me any updates on Mickey and Eleanor? Momma and Daddy are beside themselves over what's happened." I should've been prepared for that question, but I'm not, and I know it shows all over my face. "What is it, Grace?" Jess asks.

"I just hate it that your parents lost their friends." I choke out the last word.

I hate lying to her. It leaves a bad taste in my mouth. I want to sit here and tell her what Nick found, what we've found out from Darla, that Naomi is involved as well as other girls and possibly Misty, and those were no friends of her parents. I can't say shit, and it bugs the hell out of me.

"Thanks. They've been really upset about it. Momma talked to Anna, and there's going to be a big service for them next week. She's had to hold off on getting arrangements ready because there are people coming in from all over."

If they all knew what was really going on, I bet those people would scatter and pretend they never knew Mickey and Eleanor.

"I can't imagine how many people will be there," I say. That's as nice as I can come up with. I'm going to move us on to another subject. "Was the beach wonderful?"

"It was heavenly. I could live in Destin all of the time. I brought gifts back for you."

"I love gifts." I'm smiling at her. "I want to hear about the proposal," I tell them.

"I couldn't have asked for anything more romantic." She leans over and kisses Jake and twirls her beautiful ring around her finger. "We got all dressed up, and Jake insisted that we go for an early dinner, because he wanted to take a walk on the beach at sunset, which I thought was really romantic. Right at sunset, he said he wanted to look at me with the sun going down, because he loved the way the light hits my eyes. He took me out on the beach, and there was a blanket and champagne in an ice bucket. In rose petals was written, "Will you marry me?" He got down on one knee and said he could never live without me and would never live without me and asked me." She's glowing.

"That's the best proposal I've ever heard. Do your parents know?"

"Jake asked Daddy before we left."

I look over at Jake. "They knew, but I didn't. Thanks, Jake. I feel so in the loop."

He's laughing at me. "I had to ask Max. Of course he was going to tell Susan."

I take Jess's hand and look at her ring again. I twirl it around her finger too. I'm so excited for my best friend. She's wanted this for a long time. I think it's even better that she wasn't expecting it. They tell me more about their trip and that they've started talking about wedding dates. They want to get married during the Christmas holidays.

"You'll be my maid of honor, won't you?" she asks me, squeezing my hands.

I feel the tears coming. "Of course." My voice is thick. "It would be an honor. I get to plan bridal showers, don't I?" I hug her and let a few happy tears fall.

"Yes. You'll get to plan many showers. Okay, tell me about Nick," she demands.

"What do you want to know?" I'm smiling at her.

"Look at that smile," Jake says. "I've never seen you smile like that."

"Me either. What has happened in a week?"

"Nothing. We hung out last night and today."

"Did he call you?" Jess asks.

"No, he came to see me at work yesterday." That part's true.

"Did you stay with him last night?"

"Yes."

"And?"

"Jess you know that's something I don't want to discuss, especially with Jake sitting here."

"Thank you," Jake says. "I was hoping you didn't want to discuss it, either."

"What did you two do today?" she asks.

"He taught me to shoot a gun."

"You shot a gun?" Jess is surprised. She knows my aversion I've had to guns.

"Yes. I shot Nick's gun that's his *duty weapon*."

"I'm amazed. Are you amazed, Jake?"

"Yes, very. How'd you do?" he asks.

"I have the target in my car. I'll go get it." I go out and pull it out and take it back in and show them. I show the three shots of Nick's. "I wish I could claim those, but no. The rest are mine."

They both laugh at the shot between the target's legs.

"Nick should be concerned about that one," Jake says.

"I think he was a little. I'm not sure if he wants to put a gun back in my hands."

"You had a good time, didn't you?" Jess says.

"Yes, I did. I didn't think I would, but Nick's a good instructor, and he taught me more than shooting. I've learned gun safety, the mechanics of the gun and how to stand, which is called a Weaver Stance if you're interested."

"I wonder if Nick would take me and let me shoot?" Jake asks.

"I'm sure he would," I say.

"How does he even have the time with three murders?" Jess asks.

"He and Chris Taylor do what they can, and when they find themselves at a stopping point, Nick takes a break." That's true. I omit that I'm part of it right now. "Where do you two want to go to dinner? I have an idea, but we'll go wherever you want. This is my treat to celebrate you."

"What do you have in mind?" Jess asks.

"Let's get a little dressed up. Not a lot. I see the look on both of your faces. We'll go to the 5 & 10."

"That's too expensive for you to pay for all three of us," Jess says.

"I don't care. I feel like splurging tonight. Come on. Why are you two even thinking about this?"

"What about Nick?" Jess asks.

"What about him?"

"Are you seeing him tonight?"

"Yes, we're going to see each other later. He said he'd call me, and we'd make plans. Come on. Say you'll go."

"Yes, we'll go," Jess says.

I clap my hands, excited. "I'm going to take a shower and get ready. Do you mind if I go searching in your closet for something to wear?"

"Of course not. Go ahead. Wear whatever you want. We're going to lounge on the couch for a little longer, and then we'll get ready," she says.

I know at some point I'm going to crash. I've been going hard for the last couple of days. It's going to be bad when it hits me. I'm too excited to be sleepy now. I'll be sleepy later.

I rummage through Jess's closet. She has more clothes than anyone I know. I love that we are pretty much the same size, and she doesn't care if I ever want to borrow something. I'm curvier in my hips than Jess, so I usually don't try and fit into her pants. My breasts are bigger, so I have to be choosy with her tops that I borrow. I don't borrow things often, but tonight, I want something different than the same outfits that I wear all of the time.

I find what I'm looking for, grab the matching shoes and take everything to my room. After I put the dress on my bed, I strip down and look at myself in the mirror. I pose, then laugh and get in the shower. I'm rinsing the soap off of me when I hear my door open.

"Jess?" I say. All of a sudden the shower curtain is pulled back with such force that I scream so loud that I'm sure people on the street can hear me. Nick's standing there, laughing and looking at me. "Nick, what in the hell are you doing?" I hurl my soap at him, which he dodges.

"I'm standing here watching you, and I like very much what I see." His grin is wicked sexy, and his eyes are roaming all over my body. I'm getting warmer under his gaze.

"How'd you get in here?"

"I scaled up the side of your condo and broke in your window."

God, he's so sarcastic. "Do I call you Spiderman, now?"

"You can call me whatever you want to, baby." He's taking his clothes off.

"What're you doing?"

"Getting in with you. I'm not passing this up. Do you know how fucking gorgeous you are wet?"

"No." I know I am *wet* and it's not from the water running down my body. He's naked and looking at me while I'm looking at him. Damn, he's a fine sight. He steps in the shower, hovering over me. "What're you doing here?"

222

"After you left, I thought about it for about two minutes and decided I wanted to see you way more than I wanted to see Chris. He's good looking and all, but..." His voice trails off, and then he adds, "Besides, why call when I know where you live. I see that I showed up at just the right time." He grins at me.

"I'm trying to get ready." But I don't sound so sure about it.

"For what?"

He's moved closer and has his hands on my waist, pulling me into him. He dips his head, grazing my jawline to my throat. I tip my head back so he can have full access to whatever he wants. *Oh, shit, that feels good, his lips brushing against my throat.*

"Jess and Jake got engaged." It comes out as a sigh.

He lifts his head and looks at me. "They did? Awesome. That still doesn't explain what you're getting ready for."

"I'm taking them out to celebrate."

"I want to go."

"Really?" I ask.

"Yeah. Where're you taking them?"

"To the 5 & 10." I'm running my hands up and down his chest. He's now all wet, slick, and I think it's hot.

"How dressed up are we getting?"

"I'm wearing a dress." He obviously wasn't paying attention to the dress on my bed.

"You in a dress? I can't wait to see that. Okay, this is going to be quick because I've got to rush home and get ready too." He rubs his face against my throat, and the tickle of his stubble makes me squeal. "But when I get you back to my house later, it's going to go so slow, you're going to beg me." His lifts his head, locking his eyes with mine. His words stir me. I feel it connect between my thighs. *Begging? There's going to be begging later? Holy Heaven, that sounds fun.* "I wanted you in the shower this morning."

"You've got me now," I say.

"Yes, I do," he bends to kiss me, and I stretch up to meet his lips. "Wrap your legs around me, baby," he says roughly. I do what he says, and he thrusts into me. It makes me scream, it feels so good. "I do like it when you scream," he growls.

My arms are locked around his neck. He's holding me at my hips, and he's thrusting in me hard. I like it. We're staring at one another. I have my legs locked tight around him. He has me pressed up against the shower wall, the water's spraying all around us, and we are slick body to slick body.

He dips his head and says roughly in my ear, "I like fucking you hard like this."

I gasp at his words and close my eyes. His words alone are such a turn on. *I like him fucking me hard like this, too.* It's hard and fast, and damn, I really like it. I've never been fucked like this before. Holy Heaven, he's a damn expert at this. He drags his lips from my ear to my mouth, and puts his lips to mine. I like his tongue. I especially like it in my mouth. This is sex in the rawest form; really raw, hot, slick sex. With each thrust, he pulls me further to the edge. It doesn't take me long to reach the peak, and I scream his name while my body pulses all around him.

"Oh, Jesus, Grace," he growls in my ear, and then he explodes in me.

I'm hanging onto him, breathing hard. He buries his face in my neck. I tilt it so he can put his face there. I can feel him breathing. I'm still holding tight to him, not really interested in letting go at the moment. He lifts his head, smiling at me. He kisses me, and it's soft and gentle, and I don't know what to make of it. It's sweet. I like it.

"That was us getting warmed up," he says, still breathing hard.

"That was quite a warm up." My breathing matches his.

"Am I going to hurt your feelings if I leave?"

"No. Go. Do you want to meet us there?"

"No. I want to come back and get you." He kisses me again and jumps out, grabbing my towel. I grab the shower curtain.

"I'm going back to my shower that was so rudely interrupted, and give my soap back to me."

He grins at me, throwing on his clothes. "You loved it." He tosses my soap back to me and is out the door.

Yes. Yes, I did.

Chapter Twenty-One

We're sitting at a table talking, laughing, and Nick and I have finally moved past our argument. We put on quite a scene. We weren't loud, but it got intense, and then the sexual tension that has been running between us since the moment he got back to the condo to get me spiked off the charts. It all started when he walked in the door, and we both froze when we saw each other. Jess and Jake were witness to it, and they left quickly, saying they would meet us there, if at all.

I've never in my life seen one man that dresses as well as Nick Bassano. His gray dress pants hang off his muscular frame in all the right places with his short-sleeved, white button up dress shirt. His tattoo is on full display. I wanted to take his clothes off right there. I moved to touch him, and he stopped me, saying he wasn't going to let me touch him, and he wasn't going to touch me, because if that happened, he was going to lay me down in the floor right where we were, and we would never make it out of the condo. I failed to see the problem with what he was saying. I still can't find the problem with it. It sounded good to me. I was ready for that.

His eyes got darker, and he told me he liked very much what I'm wearing. He told me he liked looking at my exposed skin. I explained that I had to borrow the dress from Jess because I don't own any. I hardly ever wear a dress. I find them impractical. He said he didn't care where or who I had gotten it from; he couldn't wait to take it off of me. That's when I nearly had an orgasm by his words alone. I felt pretty when I put on the brown spaghetti-strap dress. I like the way my breasts look in it.

I felt sexy standing there with Nick swallowing my whole body with his eyes in one big *gulp*.

He told me I was beautiful and had come to the conclusion that I could wear anything or nothing at all and be just as beautiful. I blushed, and my heart beat faster than it was already beating. After staring at one another for a few more silent minutes, he told me we needed to leave.

While driving downtown, he told me the Governor called the Chief and wanted to know why he and Chris hadn't found who killed the Bradberrys. The Chief told the Governor that this wasn't a one-hour television show and to be patient. I couldn't believe that he said that. Nick refused to talk about the case any more tonight. *Not a problem.*

When we got seated, I felt all sexually frustrated, because I wanted him to touch me, and I wanted to touch him. He moved his seat very close, and I could feel his body heat, smell him, and that made things worse. The actual argument started when he foolishly ordered a bottle of Cristal to celebrate Jess and Jake, and I said I could not afford that, and I didn't believe that he could, either. He said he had a handle on his finances, and he was picking up the entire tab for tonight. I said this was my treat, and I didn't need him to bust in here and take over. It went back and forth like that for minutes. I think we were both letting off steam the only proper way that we could in the setting that we're in.

He leaned into me and whispered in my ear that I didn't always have to argue with him, and if I didn't stop, I would be doing way more begging than what he originally had in mind, and then he was going to fuck me harder than he had in the shower and that I would scream louder than I had so far and that the SWAT team would probably surround his house, and he didn't care. It came out through clenched teeth. I almost fell out of my chair. The thing is, I don't think he was joking. I stopped arguing.

The sexual tension between us is still through the roof and swirling around the sky somewhere. I think the only thing that would ease how we're feeling is if we wiped everything off the table and went for it right here. Now that I think about it, *that sounds damn good.*

The champagne arrives, all two hundred and fifty dollars-worth of it. I think it's insane to spend that kind of money on something that we are going to drink, but I keep my mouth shut about it. The waiter pours a glass for each of us. I've never had anything this expensive. I begin to calculate everything I could do with two hundred and fifty dollars. *Oh, well. It's not my money.*

"Would you like to make a toast?" Nick asks me.

I look at Jess and Jake and at their happy, in love, smiling faces.

"To two of my most favorite people in the whole world. Many years of love and happiness."

"Here, here," Jake says, leaning over and planting a sweet kiss on Jess. She's smiling broadly.

We all clink our glasses together, and when I take my first drink, I get why it's two hundred and fifty dollars a bottle.

"Now, I understand what all the fuss is about," I say.

"You've never had Cristal before?" Nick asks me.

I look at him as if he's lost his mind. "Do I look like a Cristal kind of girl to you?"

He leans into me but still not touching me. *Dammit, I'm so frustrated by that.* And, he smells so damn good.

"You look like a very beautiful girl to me." His eyes sparkle.

I'm melting. Sometimes, he opens his mouth, and the sweetest things come out of it. *Whew! This man is making it easy for me to start falling for him.*

"Aww, that's so sweet," Jess says.

I put my hand on his face and stroke his smooth cheek. I don't care. I need to touch him. His eyes change as I let my hand linger there. I see the hunger for me in his eyes, but I see something else there, too. Is that affection that I'm seeing?

He smiles at me, takes my hand in his, brushing his lips softly across my knuckles. He's holding my eyes with his. I can't look away from him. My breathing has become shallow, and my heart is pounding. It feels like we're in our own bubble, but bubbles pop. Mine does.

"Well, this looks like an intimate setting."

I look up and see Lacey Carter standing at our table. *That's because it is, bitch.*

Nick doesn't let go of my hand. I'm looking between her smiling face, but it's not really a smile, and his unsmiling, almost irritated-looking face.

"What're you doing here, Lacey?" He sounds bored.

I want to ask her if she follows Nick everywhere he goes. If she said yes, it wouldn't surprise me at all.

"I'm here having dinner with a friend, and I saw you sitting with Grace. You seem to be spending an inordinate amount of time with her." It comes out as bitchy. I'm sure she meant for it to.

I glance at Jess, and her eyes are livid and her jaw is set. She's folded her arms across her chest. She's loyal to me. I love her. Jake's face is set much the same way. He's loyal, too.

"It's not any of your business, Lacey." His voice is calm, but the way he's gripping my hand tells me he's anything but.

I can't figure out what's up with this whole situation. It's as if he's uncomfortable that he has this relationship with her. I don't get it.

"You're changing, Nick. Is it her?" Her voice is hostile.

I look at Nick. *Oh, shit.* He's pissed. I see it in his eyes, his posture and the way his jaw has set, but I don't understand his anger. When he speaks, I shiver. His voice is so cold.

"I'm out with Grace tonight. *We* are celebrating her best friend's engagement. It would be best if you leave." He's still gripping my hand, and it's getting painful.

"Call me when you want to have some *real* fun." She stalks off.

Nick lets out a long breath.

"You're hurting my hand," I say quietly.

"I'm sorry." He loosens it but doesn't let it go.

"That's a bitter, nasty woman," Jess says. She looks at Nick. "If Grace gets hurt, you will answer to me. Do I make myself clear?"

"Yes," he says, without hesitation.

I want to kick her under the table over that comment, because she's talking like there's something going on between Nick and me other than what's currently going on, and then the same time, I'm grateful for her devotion to me.

Jess looks over at Jake. "You back me up on this, right?"

Jake clears his throat and looks uncomfortable. "Yes, of course."

Good answer, Jake. I look at all three of them and smile.

"She's not going to ruin this evening, okay? It's over. Let's get back to having fun. *Real fun.*" The way I say it indicates to them that the subject of Lacey Carter is closed, and I dare anyone to say otherwise.

Our waiter arrives and takes our food orders. We also order a round of drinks. Nick insists on it. This bill's going to be outrageous.

"Jess, I haven't had the chance to get a good look at your ring. Could I see it?" Nick asks smiling at her. *Good boy. What a way to move the conversation to something lighter.* Jess proudly displays her ring. "It's beautiful. Jake, you did a great job. Did you pick it out all by yourself?"

"One of my friends went with me. I knew what she wanted. She's had a couple of rings picked out, and I chose from them."

"Did you get it here in town?"

"Yes, I got it at DC Jewelers."

"Excellent choice," Nick says. "I have a friend who works Narcotics in Oconee County, and he got his fiancé's ring there, too. The man that owns it, DC, is the uncle of a Lieutenant here at the police department. Lt. Pool's name is DC as well. He gave my friend a discount. I wish I'd known you were going there, and I would've put in a word for you."

"I wish I'd known that, too," Jake says.

Our conversation bounces around the table. Jess and Jake ask Nick where he's from. Nick admits that he's lost a lot of his New York accent and that he's even used the word *y'all* a time or two. He says he can't figure out how his dad has been here for as long as he has, and it still sounds like he arrived from New York City yesterday. He thinks it has a lot to do with hanging out with Chris, who's from South Georgia, and his friend from Oconee County, named Brandon.

He says that Brandon talks very, very slowly. We all agree that Nick's friends probably have something to do with him losing his New York accent. I tease Nick that him having a Southern drawl is way better than sounding like a Yankee.

He laughs, looking at me, and says, "I've not heard you use the word *y'all.*"

I shrug my shoulders at him. "It's not in my vocabulary. I've never used it."

He grins at me with those damn dimples. "Your accent's so Southern and smooth, it sounds like it would roll off your tongue." He leans into me. "I like your accent, and the way it sounds." He winks at me, and I quit breathing and have to remind myself to stay upright in my chair. *I want him, and I want him right now!*

229

Nick directs his attention away from me and asks Jake what his plans are after law school. Jake laughs and says to pay off his student loans. Now that's funny.

"Jake, you won't have one loan to pay back. Do I have to remind you that your mom and dad are footing the bill for law school?" He has to admit that I'm right.

"Are you from here Jake?" Nick asks him.

"No. I'm from North Carolina. I grew up in a suburb outside of Charlotte called Pineville. My aunt and uncle live here in Georgia and are huge Bulldog fans. My dad and I would come to games with my uncle during the season. I decided I wanted to move here and go to college right after high school. I came here my freshman year and haven't left."

"When, where and how did you and Jess meet?" Nick asks him.

He seems that he genuinely wants to know and isn't asking just to force polite conversation. I like it. It makes me like him, even more.

Jake looks at Jess, smiling at her, and leans over, kissing her softly. She may melt at the table, too. He looks back at Nick.

"My first degree is in Education, like Jess. Four years ago, I was at this summer conference in Atlanta." He looks at Jess. "What was the conference?"

"Raising The Grade in Mathematics," she says.

"Oh yeah," he says, directing his attention back to Nick. "It ended up being the most senseless conference I've ever been to. That's why I couldn't remember what it was called; however, if I hadn't gone, I wouldn't have met Jess. We were on a break, and I saw her standing and talking and laughing with a group of people. I couldn't take my eyes off of her. I thought she was the most striking woman, ever." He looks back at Jess, who's swooning in her seat. I've heard this story countless times, but I love it still. "I had to know if she was dating, engaged or married and hoped to hell she was none of those three. Well, the dating was okay. I could probably wiggle my way into that." He grins at her again and continues, "I followed her back in the room and found that a seat close to her was empty. I looked at her left hand and saw no signs of being attached. I made the decision right then and there that neither of us were leaving until I at least talked to her."

Jess cuts in and says, "What was the first thing you said to me?"

Jake starts to laugh. "I had no idea what to say to get an *in* with her. It's probably the dumbest thing ever, but on our next break, I walked up to her and said, *This conference would be so much better next to a pool with some drinks.*"

We start laughing. I see Jake squeezing Jess's hand.

"It wasn't that bad. I had to agree. I thought it was a pretty boring conference, too," Jess says to him.

"We started talking after that and discovered that we both lived in Athens, and at the time, I was teaching up the road at Malcom Bridge Elementary in Oconee. I felt like she was interested, so I asked her out before we left."

"I was very interested," she says to Nick, smiling even bigger.

"We started dating, fell in love, and I have been wanting to marry her for the last year and a half." Jake leans over and kisses Jess again. The way they're looking at each other says they may want to wipe the table clean as well.

"Great story," Nick says to them. "Jess, are you from here?"

Jess looks at Nick. Her face is a bit flushed. I giggle softly to myself.

"I'm from Oconee County. So, yes," she says.

"That's where I live," Nick tells her. "Where do you teach?"

That launches Jess into her tale of where she's teaching and how long she's been there. That's lengthy. Jess loves being a teacher, loves her students and her dedication to them and educating them is evident. I know it about her. I always have, but I still love how her beautiful eyes light up when she talks about it. She's passionate about teaching the way I'm passionate about what I do.

It gets back to how Nick came from being in New York City to Athens, Georgia. I've heard that story, but what I've not heard is how long his parents have been here and what brought them here. I learn that he has an aunt who has lived here for the last thirty years, and when her husband died twelve years ago, his parents moved here to be closer to her.

Nick and Jake eventually get around to talking about guns. I knew Jake would get there. Nick is more than happy to discuss that. We get our food, and we take a break from the talking to enjoy our delicious meal.

I'm chewing on a bite of my mouth-watering Gulf Snapper when Jess asks Nick, "I hate to ask this question, but is there anything you can tell us about the case?"

Dammit, I forgot to warn him. I stop chewing and look over at Nick. He puts his fork down, looking at Jess. Oh God, what's he going to say?

"Chris and I are working several different leads. It's a complex case, and we don't want to rush it."

He's impressive. That was good. I'll have to tell him later how good that sounded. He didn't say anything that isn't true. I wonder if he wants to jump on the table as badly as I do and scream about how disgusting the Bradberrys really were and how they should not be celebrated in any way.

"You don't have any suspects, then?" Jess asks.

"We don't. I wish I could tell you differently."

"My mother's very distraught about all of this. Mickey and Eleanor were such wonderful people. They wouldn't have hurt anybody. Their daughter, Anna, is destroyed over losing both of them that way. I hope whoever did this is strung up."

"Jess," I say cheerfully, getting her attention, "This is a celebration. No sad talk."

She looks at me and smiles. "You're right. I'm sorry, Nick."

"Don't apologize. I would want to know, too," he says, smiling kindly at her. He leans into me and whispers, "Thanks," in my ear.

I get Jess on the subject of wedding plans. Jake looks at Nick and tells him he doesn't want to discuss wedding plans. Nick agrees, and they get back to weapons, ammunition, targets, hunting and anything guy-related, including football. I tune them out.

"When are you going to set a date?" I ask Jess.

"We're having dinner with Momma and Daddy next week. We'll set a date then."

"You'll let me know about that, right?" I'm joking with her.

"You will be the first to know after the date's set." She's smiling at me.

We get the bill after we've finished everything on our plates. It was delicious. Nick won't let me see how much damage we've done. I want to argue with him about it, but then I start thinking what he said to me earlier and that leads to thoughts of what we're going to do when we get back to his house. All that leads to thoughts of me begging, and I'm excited. I want to sprint out of here. Again, does that look desperate? Nick takes care of everything, and we're standing outside the restaurant when Jess hugs him.

"Thank you for everything. It was really sweet of you to do this for us. We really appreciate it. I didn't like you when I first met you."

We're laughing about it, including Nick.

"I don't think Grace did, either. Maybe I've changed her mind." He looks at me, grinning and winks at me. *God, I hate when he does that. No, I love it.*

Jess looks at me and says, "Yeah. I think you've definitely changed her mind." She hugs me and whispers, "Are you coming home?"

I whisper back that I don't know. Nick shakes Jake's hand, and they've agreed to go shooting with one another. Nick takes my hand while we're walking back to his truck, and I get lost in thoughts of him, even though he's right here with me.

Chapter Twenty-Two

"I like Jess and Jake," he says, as we continue to our way back to his truck.

I return from The Planet of Nick and say, "Yeah. They're great. I love them."

He smiles down at me. "They both love you. Jess is protective of you, isn't she?"

"Loyal is the word I would use."

We walk in silence for a moment. He's stroking my hand as he holds it. I like it.

"I noticed you aren't limping."

I look down at my ankle. There's a bruise forming, but it doesn't hurt to walk on it.

"It doesn't hurt now," I say, shivering.

The days are warm, but once the sun drops, it gets cool fast. It will be like this for another week, and then our nights will get warmer.

"Are you cold?" he asks me.

"It's a little cool out."

He pulls me closer and wraps his arm around my shoulder. *I like this.* I wrap my arm around his waist, and we walk that way back to his truck. He opens my door for me, and I think he's going to kiss me. He's hovering over me, staring at me. The energy between us has changed from lighthearted, back to spiking off the charts again. His eyes have changed. They're hungry-looking. I swallow hard, looking at them. I know what he wants, and I want the exact same thing.

"If I kissed you, we won't make it back to my house." He bends and whispers in my ear, "I want to take you right here."

I'm panting. My heart is pounding at the thought. He won't touch me, and I think I'm going to scream in frustration.

"Then take me here," I whisper, holding his eyes.

His breathing changes, and his eyes now look predatory. *It's really hot the way he's looking at me.* If hot could sweat, it would be dripping. He takes my hand, putting it at his zipper. He's hard and pressing at his pants. I can feel the pull deep inside. It's such a turn on to feel him like this and to know that I'm doing this to him.

"That's what you do to me." His voice is low.

I step closer to him and run my free hand up his chest to his neck, pulling him down to me, and whisper in his ear, "Why don't you run your hand up my dress, in my panties and feel what you do to me."

I hear him gasp. "Jesus Christ, Grace. Get in before I fuck you right here," he says hoarsely. I'm hot and bothered, and he is, too. He looks at me before we pull away. "We may not make it after what you said." His grin is devilish.

I may not make it, either. I may have an orgasm right here if he keeps looking at me that way. Holy Heaven, I've never had a man make my body feel this way. He turns the radio on, tunes it to a local Athens station, and I hope another song doesn't come on like it did the other night. We won't make it to his house if that happens. It's just as bad. The station is playing old eighties songs, and Chris Isaak's *Wicked Game* comes on.

"I like this song," he says.

"I like this song, too." *I definitely like thinking of what I want to do while listening to this song.*

He glances over at me and smiles. "How old were you when this song came out? Two?"

"You know I was not two. How old are you, by the way?" I'm trying not to listen to this song. *Damn, it's gotten really hot in here.*

"I'm thirty-seven. My birthday is in August."

"August what?"

"The seventeenth."

"You act fifteen sometimes," I say, grinning at him.

"I have the sexual appetite of a fifteen-year-old," he says, leering at me.

I start laughing. We're silent, and I'm listening to the song. It's such a sexy song. I would love to straddle him and let him have me while driving down the road. We'd probably wreck. *Damn, it's really, really hot in here!* I'm about to pull a Nick Bassano by changing the subject.

"Nick. Can I ask you a question?"

"Sure. What do you want to know?"

I take a deep breath. "Will you tell me what you've been holding back about Misty?"

He lets out what sounds like a frustrated or angry breath of air. "Dammit, Grace. Why're you asking me this right now? I'm over here thinking about getting you naked. You've just killed my erection."

"You'll get it back. I promise," I say softly, looking at him.

His jaw's set, and he keeps his eyes on the road. I don't think he's going to answer me. He looks like he's thinking.

"Her body was mutilated. I don't want to say anything else about it, okay?" He glances over at me, holds my eyes for a few seconds and then looks away.

"Okay," I whisper. *Be careful what you ask for, stupid.*

He reaches over and takes my hand, puts it to his lips and kisses it gently.

"I'm going to find who killed her. I'm going to find who did this to her for her, for Stan and Rose and for...you."

My feelings for him are getting stronger. The more time I spend around him, the stronger they're getting. It may bite me in the end. I know he likes me. He's told me as much. He likes a lot of other women, too. That's the problem. When I take a step back and really look at the situation, that's what it all boils down to: other women. I sigh. I'm going to keep enjoying him as long as I'm with him. Whatever happens in the end, I can deal with.

"What're you thinking about?" he asks.

You. Me. The possibility of an "us"

"I know you'll find who killed her," I say, instead. We're silent for a few minutes. I decide to go with something lighter. "I'm surprised that you live out in the country. I figure you'd want to stay in the city, since that's where you're from."

He glances at me and then back to the road. "I like it out here. I always enjoyed visiting with my mom and dad when I was down here.

The city's loud. It's much quieter here, and I like that. My parents were surprised when I said I wanted to build a house on their property. My mom was thrilled. She likes having me this close. I know she wishes that my brother and his family would move here."

"What's your brother's name?"

"Frank, and his wife's name is Danielle. We all call her Dani. My niece is seven. Her name's Claire. My nephew's five, and his name is Colin."

"Is your brother older or younger than you?"

"He's older by three years."

"What are your parents' names?"

"Sal and Iona. My mom's Irish. The deal was they would name one kid an Italian name, and one kid an Irish name. My mom named my brother, and my dad named me."

"I wondered about your mom. I didn't think that she looked Italian. She's very pretty."

"Thank you. I think so, too."

"You look exactly like your dad."

"Yes, I do. My brother's a good mix between my mom and my dad."

He turns into his driveway, pulling his truck into his garage. We get out and walk inside hand-in-hand. He left some lights on earlier, so it isn't so dark when we walk in. I realize that I've spent a solid twenty-four hours with this man. I've enjoyed every minute of it too.

"I like getting to know you," I say. It comes out sounding almost shy.

He smiles and says, "I like it, too. I like getting to know you. Would you like a drink?"

"What did you have in mind?" I ask.

He's still holding my hand and pulls me the short distance through the kitchen, into a room that I hadn't noticed. It has a pool table, and there's a nice bar. The woodwork is beautiful. It looks like it's in dark cherry finish, and it's enormous, beyond impressive.

"I like it here," I tell him. "Are you good at pool?"

"Yes. Do you like to play?"

"Yes, I do. I'm good at it."

He's standing behind the bar, looking at me. "We'll play together one night. We'll see who plays better." He's smiling, and *oh, those dimples.* "I'm going to have Jack Daniel's."

I take a seat on the high back bar chair. "Pour one for me too, Mr. Bartender. Should I tip you?"

"Yes ma'am, you can. I'll definitely be collecting a tip from you."

He's looking at me the same way as he was when he came in the condo earlier and saw me standing in my dress. I'm all for ditching the drink and getting naked. I don't think it's going to be that easy. There's going to be begging involved on my part. He's warned me. I'm aroused about it. I'm aroused wondering how much begging I'm going to have to do. He pours us both a drink, walks around the bar and stands in front of me. He's looking in my eyes again and holding them. He has a slight smile on his face. His gaze is heating my body. My heart's picking up. Desire is churning in me like a slow storm off the coast. I wish he would touch me. Damn this man for making me want him the way I do.

"If you were to go out with Mike, when would you go?"

Where's this coming from? "I don't know. I'm busy." I sound a little irritated. He chuckles softly.

"I don't want you to go out with him next Saturday."

I take a drink and feel the burn down my throat into my belly.

"O-okay," I stammer, confused. "Why?"

"Because it's your birthday, and I want to take you out and celebrate it with you. I want you to be with me."

I wasn't expecting that. What's he feeling for me? What's going on with him? I want to ask him about it, but I don't think this is the right night. It's too soon to have *that* kind of a talk. I want to be with him, too. What I really want more than anything is to be up against him. He finishes his drink at the same time that I do. He takes my glass and puts them both on the bar. He's not taken his eyes off of me. They're hungry for me.

"What do you want, Grace?" His voice has dropped. *God, that's so sexy.*

"You," I breathe.

"I'm right here." His voice remains low. I move off the bar seat and press myself up against him. Our eyes are still locked with one another. I have my arms wrapped around his neck. His hands are still at his side. "Did I tell you this was going to be slow?"

"Yes." I'm still breathless.

He smiles at me. *Touch me!*

"It's going to go so slow-- you're going to do what?"

"Beg." I can do no more than whisper.

His eyes are darker. His smile is so sexy, and I just want him to *touch me!* The anticipation of it all is incredibly arousing. I'm rubbing up against him, and he's still standing there, but I feel him. I feel that he is aroused by me. This is some heady shit here.

"What do you want me to do to you, Grace?" His voice is raw.

"Everything." I can't make my voice any stronger than a whisper.

"That's not specific enough, baby."

"Kiss me." I'm trying to pull his face to mine, and he won't budge. I might as well be pulling on a tree stump. He bends, hovering over my lips. They're so close, I can feel the heat coming off of his mouth. "Nick, please." I'm whimpering. His answering smile is dazzling. He's all teeth and dimples, and he looks like the devil smiling.

When he puts his lips to mine, I swear there are fireworks going off behind us. I melt into his kiss. He wraps his arms around my waist, holding me tight against him. He takes my bottom lip and is sucking on it. Holy Heaven, I've never had an orgasm by a kiss alone. That's all about to change the way he's kissing me.

My nipples are hard and straining against the fabric of my dress. I'm kissing him and giving him my tongue while I'm taking his. The kiss is becoming more intense. Our breathing is picking up. I'm burning, and it's not a slow burn.

He breaks the kiss and pulls away from me. *What the? What's he doing?* He kicks his shoes off, and I see that he's removing his ankle holster, which he sets on the bar. He must have it on him at all times. I move to take my shoes off as well.

"No, leave them on. I like looking at your legs in that dress with those heels."

He takes my hand and leads me to the end of the bar, where he lifts me and sets me on it. My dress rides up several inches on my thighs sitting like this. The look he gives me tells me that he likes it very much. He takes my leg, his hand roaming up and down my calf. He runs his hand up the length of my leg, inside my thigh right at my panties, and stops. I gasp, locking eyes with him. I'm wiggling, trying to get him to move his hand a little farther up and in me. He won't do it. This is agony. I'm so aroused that it's almost painful.

I'm aching for him in the worst way, but it's moving to pain, quickly. My body's screaming for him to *touch me!* He slips my shoes off and lets them drop.

"Your skin is beautiful," he murmurs, stepping closer to me. I scoot to the edge of the bar and wrap my legs around him, which hikes my dress up even more, exposing what I have on underneath. "What're you wearing underneath that dress?" His hands are on my shoulders and running down the length of my arms.

"Why don't you take a look and see." I've wrapped my arms around his neck, and I'm pulling him as close as I can to me.

He lifts my dress, looking at my panties, then at me, raising an eyebrow.

"Hot pink and lace. I can't wait to take them off," he says softly.

"Take them off," I beg.

"I will," he says.

How much more of this torture can I take? I'm damp and ready, and I can't want him any more than I do right now. He dips his head, and his lips are grazing my jawline to my throat. I throw my head back, and all of my hair falls behind me. His lips are at my pulse. He leaves them there. I can feel him smiling as he feels how fast it's racing. *Yes, that's what you do to me.*

"Your skin smells so sweet. It tastes sweet. I can't wait to taste the rest of you," he says, against my neck.

I moan at his words. How can I be more aroused? How's that possible? I can't believe what he's doing to me. I've never been this excited. His lips make a trail from my neck down to my collarbone and then lower. He stops at the swell of my breasts. My back is arched. I want him to slip my dress off and put his mouth on them. He raises his head, looking at me. His eyes have this carnal look about them. *Oh, that's hot.*

"Nick, please take my dress off." I'm begging again.

"Is that what you want me to do, baby?" His voice is so low and sexy.

"Yes," I gasp.

He eases me off the bar and has me turn around. He's pressed up against my back, and I feel him hard, urgent, wanting me. He pulls the zipper down agonizingly slow. I'm trying to stay still, and I can't.

"You need to stand still," he murmurs in my ear. *Yeah, I'll work on that.* He takes the straps and slips them down my shoulders. My dress falls in a pool around my feet. I hear Nick gasp behind me. "You're not wearing a bra, and your beautiful ass is hanging out of your panties." His voice is rough, low. I'm smiling. "Damn, baby. You're so fucking gorgeous." He puts his lips at my shoulder. His hands snake around to my front, running them up my stomach, then his hands are on my breasts. I moan and arch my back, forcing them more in his hands. "You like that?" he whispers in my ear.

"Yes," I sigh.

"You want me to keep doing it?"

"Please," I sigh.

My arms go up, behind me, around his neck. He's rubbing and rolling my nipples around. I'm breathing harder. I feel him pulling my body to the edge. I go with the feelings, and when my orgasm hits me, its mind-blowing, and I can stand only because he's holding me. He turns me around to face him. I'm still breathing heavy. He hooks his fingers in my panties, sliding them off.

He takes my hand, helping me step out of the clothes around my feet. I push them away with my foot. He puts his hands on my face and tips it up to him, and his lips are on mine, pushing his tongue in my mouth. I slide my hands up his chest and around his neck, standing up on my toes to reach him better. I love the way his hands feel on my face. He drags his lips from mine to my jaw and then lower.

He tugs at one nipple and then the other, and I'm moaning. He doesn't stop there and continues lower. He dips his tongue in and out of my belly button. He stands back up, looks in my eyes, while putting me back on the bar.

"Lie back," he whispers. I do what he says.

The wood is cool against my hot skin. He starts at my belly button and then moves lower. His lips and tongue make a trail from inside my inner thigh, almost inside of me and then back. He's tormenting me. He does this several times.

"Nick," I gasp. "Please."

Then, his tongue is in me. My mind flashes to my dream, but I never imagined it would feel like this. My back arches off the bar in almost a complete U. His tongue is probing, teasing, tasting and swirling. He's such an amazing lover. Right before I explode, he stops, running his tongue and his nose inside my thigh again. *Oh, my God, what's he doing to me?* I'm breathing hard, feeling a little cheated. I'm about to do more begging, and then his tongue goes back, and he does it all over again. My body climbs even quicker this time, and again he stops. This is absolute madness. He's making good on his promise of slow. I can't take it anymore.

"Nick," I moan. "Do that again, and don't stop."

I hear him chuckle. He's still running his tongue inside one thigh and then to the other. I'm squirming. He hesitates, and then he's swirling his tongue around and around and that's all it takes for me. He pulls me to my climax, and I scream his name, more than once. He stands, gazing down at me, smiling.

"You do taste sweet." He takes my hand and pulls me up. "That can't be comfortable on your back."

"I'm not complaining." I'm still breathless. I stand and my hands go to the buttons on his shirt. I'm ready to get him naked. I've been ready. I look up at him while I work on his buttons. He's running his hands up and down my back. "Do you know how sexy I think you are?" I ask, looking up at him.

He grins. "Tell me."

"Very sexy," I whisper.

I slide his shirt off. He takes his t-shirt off for me. I put my hands on his chest, leaving them there, feeling his heartbeat beneath my fingers. It's pounding. My hands go to his belt, and I unbutton and unzip his pants, pulling them down, along with his boxer briefs. I pull him free, and he's fully aroused.

I look in his eyes. "Like I said, very sexy," I murmur.

His lips find mine, crushing me against him. I can't get over the feeling of my skin against his. He lifts me, and I wrap my legs around him. He walks us through the house, all the while kissing me. I don't know how he makes it from that room to his bedroom without running into anything, but he does.

My hands are grasping his hair, holding his mouth tight to mine. He sits on the edge of his bed with me straddling him. His hands go from my back to my hips. I'm grinding down on him hard. I'm done with slow.

"I want you inside me now." My voice is hoarse. I take him and guide him in me.

"Jesus, baby, you're wet," he growls. Oh, my God, feeling him like this. My hands are clutched at the top of his shoulders. I feel his rigid muscles beneath my fingers. "You said I'm sexy? Baby, you are one fucking sexy lady."

Our eyes lock, and *Holy Heaven, that was too hot, those words coming out of his mouth again.* The only sound in the room is our heavy, labored breathing and sounds of complete pleasure coming from me. We're nothing but want, need and absolute hunger for one another. It's all very animalistic the way I'm moving against him. His fingers are digging in my hips as I move up and down the length of him. As I'm pounding down to him, his hips are coming up to meet me. When I reach the end, I throw my head back and scream his name as my body pulses and pulses. He goes rigid and fills me with him. I open my eyes and look at him. We're smiling at each other, breathing hard. *Damn, that was good.*

"Wrap your arms back around my neck," he says. I don't ask why. I just do it. He stands and lays us both on the bed. He stretches out beside me, and I curl up in his arms and on his chest. I can feel his heart beating. I like it. "Are you spending the night with me?"

I raise my head up and look at him. "Do you want me to?"

"Yes," he says, with no hesitation.

I lay my head back on his chest and smile. "Yes. I'll stay. I'll be yours tonight."

He strokes my back and then says, "Yes. Mine."

Chapter Twenty-Three

The work week is essentially over. My days have been busy, help-ing how I can. I didn't know what to expect from this week. We've been bombarded with information. I said to Nick that it felt like there are even more questions than answers with the information that we've gotten. He told me that everything's a piece to the puzzle, and pretty soon, the whole puzzle will be put together, and we'll know everything. When? *Be patient,* is what he told me.

Nick took me back to the range on Sunday, and we talked about the connection between the girls. There's a connection. I think it does have something to do with them being considered throw-away children, but how did Mickey, Eleanor and the other unknown people know that? Someone knew these girls were easy targets. Someone knew that the girls, essentially, call the streets their home. Nick agrees with me on everything that I've told him. He reminded me of all the charities that Mickey and Eleanor were involved in, and would've easily had knowl-edge of girls that would be considered throw-away girls.

I got the information I needed on Monday from DJJ. Before I left, Nick and Chris heard from the crime lab on Misty. She did have mor-phine in her system. The tissue taken from under her fingernails said that she fought hard and that if they could find someone quickly, that person would possibly still have signs of substantial scratches. Semen was found, but the DNA profile showed that it was from one man, and it was the same DNA under her nails. Blood was found in her mouth, and I thought, *Big deal, of course it was,* since she had been beaten, but I was quickly educated that the blood was the same DNA profile. I honestly didn't get it. I didn't know what they were talking about.

Nick said that Misty most likely bit her murderer, and it was hard enough for her to draw blood. That poor child. She fought so hard, it seems, and it did her absolutely no good. I asked Nick, if there was a group of men having sex with these girls, why was there semen from only one man? He couldn't answer it, but he said he would.

I thought Nick was going to go out with me, but he said since they now had this information, they were going to work on it, along with the information about the group of doctors. They especially wanted to get their hands on Dr. Greg Miller and talk to him. He wouldn't tell me anything else. He kissed me breathless and told me not to worry, he would lay it all out for me when it made sense.

I spent most of Monday trying to find Hailey West's parents. Tonya's parents were easier to find. They're both in jail. I made Nick go with me to see them. He was short-tempered and yelled at me over something stupid about me not being able to go to the jail by myself, and I yelled right back that he can be an asshole sometimes. Then, he made a joke, winked at me, and I nearly melted standing out front of the jail.

We learned from Tonya's mother that Tonya went missing six months ago. She did file a report but never heard anything. Ms. Overby didn't pursue it any further. She felt like Tonya would come home when she was good and ready. Her lack of concern for her daughter didn't sit right with either Nick or me. I think we both wanted to say something about it, but I felt like we would be beating a dead horse if we said anything.

We had another answer on a Missing Persons Report that's gone missing. Nick was preoccupied and said little about it when we left the jail. The only thing he asked was for me to make a timeline of when the girls started missing, based on the information that we had. I finally found Hailey's parents on my own on Wednesday. It took a long time, a trip to several addresses and talking to different people. Funny thing, I knew most of them. Hailey's dad was home and was fairly intoxicated when I talked with him. He was confused and confusing.

He said Hailey had been gone for two months, and he and his girlfriend didn't think anything of it because she had been planning on moving out with a friend of hers. He assumed that she did. I asked who the friend was, and he could only give me the name Meghan, but couldn't remember her last name. He couldn't tell me where Meghan lived, only where he thought she was living.

I asked him if Hailey had contacted him since she was gone, and she hadn't. I pressed him, asking if he didn't think that was strange, and I asked what Hailey took with her when she left. She took nothing. His explanation of her not taking anything was because he told her if she was leaving, she was leaving with the clothes on her back and nothing else.

Nice. What a piece of shit. Another parent who gives a shit less about where his daughter might be. The whole thing makes me so damn mad, I could spit, if I was a spitting kind of a woman. I asked about Hailey's mother and if Hailey could be with her. He said no, since she was dead. I left shortly after that. All of the girls were easy targets. They had little to no one who cared. It's a stab in the gut thinking of Naomi. I have to put her in that category as well.

I went looking for Matt after leaving Hailey's dad. I had the pictures with me. I hoped to find out Sherry's last name. I couldn't find Matt, and I struck out on the girls too. I went back to the police department and started on the timeline. What I had in front of me was that Darla was first, and then my sister went missing. Tonya went missing after her, and then Hailey. We have to figure out about the other girls. I looked at their ages. They're all similar, with the exception of my sister. She's the youngest at fourteen. I want to know where she is. I want to bury her if that's how it's going to end, and I think that it is.

I've talked about it with Nick every night, with the exception of the last couple of nights. My nights are filled with him. There've been a couple of nights this week where we would talk until the sun came up. We're really beginning to get to know one another. We both like to go to the movies. He's more of the action type, while I tend to go for the comedies, but we discovered that we both liked thrillers and horrors.

We talked about silly things, like favorite foods, favorite colors, the kind of jokes we like to hear. He'll eat any kind of meat. I love cake. My favorite kind is ice cream cake filled with strawberry cheesecake ice cream. His favorite color is black, while mine shifts based on my mood. Red is currently my favorite. It represents passion to me.

We both have a love for music. Our tastes are similar. I shared that music is emotional for me, that when I couldn't find the words to talk about all that happened to me, including being raped, music did that for me. He asked me about my favorite bands and songs. We're both big fans of Nickelback, Rascal Flatts and Daughtry. His two favorite bands are Five Finger Death Punch and Breaking Benjamin. My two favorites are Lifehouse and Breaking Benjamin just like him. The list got lengthy of everyone we both like. I told him about a band named Red that I discovered a few years back, and how much I love them. He said he'd never heard of them but had plans to check out their music.

He hooked up his iPhone one night, and all of his music is music that I love. I was surprised that he likes country music. He said Chris loves country music and has forced him to listen to it for the last four years, so he decided to take a listen and discovered that while he doesn't like all of it, there are certain songs that appeal to him. He said he was surprised about that I liked it, too, being as liberal as I am. *Careful*, is what I told him. I agree with him on not liking all of it, but some of it was appealing.

We both like to dance, and the man can move. I wasn't surprised by that. We dance well together. We both like dance music with a lot of bass. And the more sexual the songs, the crazier we danced. We started out dancing to Ludacris' *Money Maker* that ended up as sex on his pool table. Yes, it's such a cliché that we did that, but it was incredible as always.

I beat him at pool, but he beat me at poker. Then, we decided to play strip poker, but we didn't finish after we both started taking our clothes off. We didn't make it to the bedroom then either. I've driven him wild with my mouth, and he claimed that he'd never had his dick sucked like that before. I gave him a look that indicated I didn't believe a word he was saying and told him he had a dirty mouth. *Not as dirty as yours,* he told me.

He told me about growing up in New York City and what it has been like having an Italian father and an Irish mother. He said that family gatherings are always interesting. He said his grandmother, Isabella, didn't speak a word of English, and she taught him Italian that he doesn't know anymore. He shared many memories of his grandmother, who died two years before he moved to Georgia. When his mother's parents were still alive, they visited Ireland regularly. He hasn't been in years. Most of his mother's family lives in the states now.

I've learned more about his parents. His dad owns a successful construction business and builds mostly houses these days and built his house for him. He said his dad's a very wealthy man, but you wouldn't know the amount of money that he has by the way he lives and the kind of man he is. His mother has never fully recovered from her stroke. She stays home most of the time, and he and his dad have recently been able to get her out more and into more activities. He's close with his family. I like that.

He asked how I was able to get through high school and college while being homeless. I told him I didn't go to high school, and when I turned seventeen, I got my GED. I was working with a rape counselor named Charlene Boyd at the time, and she encouraged me to take the SAT because she felt like I was intelligent.

I took them and scored so high that she encouraged me to apply to UGA. I thought she was crazy. I had no home. I was working wherever I could find work at the time, saving every penny that I could. Charlene said to apply anyway and talk about my life history on the application, as well as what I wanted to see happen for my future. I decided I had nothing to lose, so I did and got accepted. She had me apply for several scholarships, and I did and got those. Grants covered the rest.

He told me again how astounding I am to get through all that I have and be the woman that I am today. He's funny and sweet, and then he'll be devilish and sarcastic. He loves having a good time, is playful and is incredibly fun to be around. He makes me feel so alive, and I keep falling harder for him.

I'm floored at how attentive and affectionate he is with everything. He's always holding my hand now, touching me, kissing me. In fact, when we've been in the privacy of his home, we've not been able to keep our hands off of each other. He's not seeing anyone else right now, because he's always with me.

I shared more about my childhood. Not all of the details, but more. There's so much to tell. He asked how I knew that my ankle wasn't broken. I pointed out all of the broken bones that I had as a child. There were many. I was knocked around a great deal growing up. Matt was knocked around even more because he desperately tried to protect me. Nick wanted to know if that's why I'm so devoted to my brother. *Yes.* There was no thinking of my answer.

When he took my clothes off, he kissed everywhere that I had pointed to. I don't know what came over me, but it was a very tender and emotional moment for me. No man has ever done that before, and I cried. He then kissed my tears, telling me not to cry, and it was really sweet, it made me cry even harder. Our relationship shifted in that moment. Yes, I believe that there's a relationship between us, even though neither of us has talked about it.

He has some big surprise planned for my birthday tomorrow. Jess is in on it, and neither one will tell me anything. She forced me to go dress shopping. I thought, great, we could hit Target and grab a dress there. *Oh, no,* she dragged me to a bridal shop. I threw a fit when we got there and refused to go in. I wanted to know why in the hell I needed a dress from a bridal shop? She said to trust her, and then smiled very sweetly.

I tried on several dresses and put my foot down when she brought a tenth dress to the dressing room. I ended up with a beautiful ball gown. It's a dark purple, strapless satin gown with black lace over the purple satin. The waist is fitted, and then it billows out at the hips all the way to the floor. I've never worn a dress like that. I had a heart attack when I saw the price. Jess said she was buying it for my birthday. I wanted to argue with her, but I felt like a princess in the dress, and the excitement over where Nick is taking me took over all of my reasoning, so I let her buy me the dress.

I said no to the shoes. Jess has designer black heels. I told her they would work. She said that I can't show Nick the dress, and I told her that we aren't getting married. She said Nick is right, I argue too much.

I'm back under the North Avenue Bridge again for the third time today with the pictures in hand. I look up and see Matt sitting on some boxes up the embankment. Relief floods me. I started to think I wasn't going to find him.

"Matt!" I call.

He's looking all around him. He can't figure out who's talking to him, not recognizing my voice at all. That makes me sad. I call his name again, and he finds me. He walks down to where I'm standing. I'm shocked by his appearance. I've never seen my brother look the way he does. He's high, which is usual, but it's more than that. He can't stand still. He's constantly looking around him, and it's not nervous or even him being high. He looks…scared.

He's dirtier than usual and more unkempt than what I'm used to see-ing. I think he's lost more weight. He can't keep going like this. He's about to hit rock bottom, if he hasn't already, and he can't focus on me to save his life.

"What're you doin' here?" His voice is shaky.

"I've been looking for you." My voice is soft. I'm on the verge of tears. "Matt, what's wrong? I mean, I know what's wrong, but there's something else." I move to him, putting my hand on his arm. He com-pletely freaks out on me.

"Don't touch me!" he yells, pulling away from me violently. When he does that, I'm so surprised by his reaction that I drop the pictures. He sees them float to the ground. He looks at the pictures, then at me, back to the pictures and then back to me. His eyes are huge, and when he speaks, his words all run together. "Where'd you get those pictures, where'd you get those pictures, where'd you get those pictures?" He's yelling, freaking out, falling apart in the worst way, and I don't under-stand what's going on with him.

This is more than drugs, more than being high. There's something else, and frankly, I'm scared. We both bend at the same time, and he has them in his hands before I can get to them. I can see his hands are trembling.

"Matt. Calm down. What's wrong?"

"This is Jenny," he says, pointing a shaking finger at one of the unknown girls.

"You know this girl, Matt?" I've momentarily forgotten that my brother is freaking out on me.

"This is Billy's sister."

"The one that has been missing for a month?"

"Yeah. I know this girl, too." He's pointing to Sherry. "Her name's Sherry Luke." He can't take his eyes off of the pictures.

"Matt. Look at me." My voice is firm. He looks at me, but he can't seem to stop his eyes from going between the pictures and me. "Do you know how long Sherry's been missing?"

"No. Where'd these pictures come from?"

"It doesn't matter. Do you know the third girl?"

"No. Where'd these pictures come from?"

I avoid his question. "What all have you used today?"

"I don't know. Where'd these fuckin' pictures come from?" He's screaming, and his eyes are crazy.

"Matt. Stop flipping out about the pictures. I need you to focus on something. Who told you that Naomi's case was going to be turned over to a detective in the Robbery/Homicide unit?"

"How'd you get a picture of Jenny?" he asks me. I'm not sure if he heard what I said to him.

I feel my phone buzzing in my back pocket and see that it's Nick calling when I pull it out. The last time I saw him was when we got to the police department on Wednesday. I was at the condo Wednesday night and last night for the first time in nearly a week. It felt somewhat strange not sleeping with him. I've gotten very comfortable spending a great deal of my time with him in a short amount of time. I haven't seen him today, either. Our phone conversations have been short. Something's happening, but he hasn't given me many details.

"Hey," I say.

"Hey." He sounds tired. "Where are you?"

"Trying to have a conversation with Matt." I hold my hand out to him for the pictures, and he reluctantly hands them over.

"I want you to tell me about it, but I need for you to come back. Two things are happening. There's a guy here who says a woman's been flashing pictures around, and word has reached him that someone said one of the girls is his daughter. The other thing is-- remember I told you I would lay it all out for you when it made sense?"

"Yes."

"It's making sense. Chris and I are running on this. Can you talk to this guy? His name's Don McGregor. His daughter's name's Meghan." He sounds tense as well as tired. I close my eyes and groan to myself. Oh, my God, her name is Meghan. Hailey's friend. It's got to be her.

"Grace," he snaps, impatiently.

"I'm here." I ignore his impatience. It's how he is sometimes.

"Baby, I would love to hang on the phone with you, especially since I've not seen you since Wednesday, but I've got to run. We won't be here when you get back. Go through the front. McGregor's there. I'll tell him you are on your way. Juliana knows to let you in. Don't take him in the conference room. Don't leave. We'll be back, and I'll tell you what we know." He abruptly hangs up, but again I let it go.

He immediately sends a text telling me that he's sorry and that he's an asshole sometimes. My text back is that I've gotten used to it and that he's not so much of an asshole anymore. I ask if he's losing his touch. His response is that I can tell him later if he's losing his touch. He doesn't need to go into detail what he's referring to. I've got it. I look at my brother, who still has the same expression on his face, scared.

"Matt, let me take you someplace for detox. Don't think about it. Get in my car, and I'll drive you. I'll take you…wherever we can find you a bed. Just go someplace. Please. This isn't working for you." I'm desperate at this point. I don't care if he freaks out over trying to get him some help. I'd rather him freak out on me than die on me, and it's coming.

"You're always fuckin' lecturin' me."

"No, I'm not. I want to help you. I don't want you to die. Matt, I've been hearing from people that you've been talking about being in some type of trouble."

"I don't know what you're talkin' about. I've got to go."

I look around us. "Where, Matt? Where're you going? There's nowhere to go. Come with me, and let me get you some help." I can see that I'm not getting anywhere with him. My pleas are falling on deaf ears. "Matt, who told you that Naomi's report or case would be turned over to a detective."

"Doesn't matter now," he mutters, "it's done."

I shake my head at him. "What's done? Matt, please make some sense. I don't understand what you're talking about."

I see that he's mumbling to himself. I can't hear what he's saying. My brother is so lost, and I don't know what to do to help him find his way. I'm going to lose him to this addiction. It's coming much quicker than I thought.

"When was the last time you had a meal?" I ask softly.

"I don't know. It's done, you know?"

I can feel the tears coming. "Matt, please come with me. I'll get you to a safe place, and they can help you, and they can feed you. You can get clean and have a life. You're so miserable and in pain. And what's done? I don't understand, but I would love to. Please tell me, so that it makes sense to me." I'm pleading with him. I'm pleading with him to help me save his life. I can see in him that it's not going to work.

"Got to go." He takes off, walking.

"Matt!" I take off after him. "Come with me, and at least let me give you the food I have with me. I have some snacks that I leave in my car. Come with me, and I'll give them to you."

"You'll try and get me in your car," he says, full of suspicion, and that makes me want to cry even more, that my own brother doesn't feel that he can trust me.

"No. I promise. I'll just give you the food."

He refuses to go with me. I can stay here, trying for the rest of the day to get him to go with me, and it's not going to do me any good to continue to bang my head against this brick wall that is my brother. I could get the food and leave it, but someone will take it. I don't mind that. I'd feed them all everyday if I could, but I really want Matt to have it. He needs it desperately.

I have to go. I cannot stay here any longer. I want to cry all the way back to the police department, but I have hold my tears in until after I talk to Meghan McGregor's father.

I find him sitting, waiting patiently. I introduce myself to him, and Juliana lets us back. She acts like my best friend now. I've become very familiar with the police department over the last week, in a way I thought I never would. I decide to take him to Nick's desk and borrow a chair from someone.

He sits and looks like a man who has been defeated by life. When he speaks, it sounds like it, too. He tells me about Meghan and how much he loves her and has searched for her time and time again but has found nothing.

"I miss her so much. She looks just like her mother. Her mom died when she was ten. Cancer. Ate her up. Then I was left alone to raise a girl. Look at me." He holds up his hands, putting himself on display. "I had no idea what I was doin'. I work on cars all day. I'm around cars and parts and greasy men all day. I was a shitty dad."

"No, you're not," I say softly. "You're here. You want to know where she is." I show him the picture. "Is this Meghan?"

"Yeah, that's her. Where'd you get this picture of her?"

"Detective Bassano gave it to me." *Shit, what else do I say?*

"Was that the big guy?"

"Yes, that was him."

"You don't know where this picture was taken or who took it?"

"No, I don't."

"How'd he get it?"

I start to speak, and I don't know what to say. This is the first parent that I've come across that gives a damn. I want to tell him. I want to tell him everything that I know and that his daughter probably isn't coming home. And the reality is that I can't say shit about it. Not yet.

"I'm going to have to let Detective Bassano answer that question or Detective Taylor."

"But you know."

"Yes, I know."

"I don't mean for this to be rude, but why're you here?"

I smile at him. "I ask the same question every day. I promise you that Detective Bassano or Detective Taylor will talk to you about all of this. I don't know when, so I can't tell you that, but they will. They're good guys. They want to find out about your daughter."

"They're both Robbery/Homicide detectives."

"Yes."

"Then Meghan's dead?"

"I don't know. They don't know," I say, with as much conviction as I can. He's nodding his head that he understands. He looks thoughtful, like he wants to say something else but doesn't. "Mr. McGregor, is Meghan friends with Hailey West?"

He looks surprised. "Yeah, they're friends. How'd you know Hailey?"

"From DFCS." It's out of my mouth before I even think about it.

We begin to talk about how Meghan went missing. He said she'd fallen into drugs three years ago, wouldn't go to school, would run away, and he would find her and bring her home. He was lost as to what to do about the drugs and not going to school. He went to Judge Wright to talk to him about what he could do. I smile at him hearing the Judge's name.

"That's a good man," Mr. McGregor says to me. "Someone that I work with said he met Judge Wright when his kid got in trouble at school and said I should talk to him. He said I could go through DJJ, but it sounded more like she needed help with the drug problem and losin' her mom than being in trouble. I asked him if he would talk to

Meghan. I took her up to his office one day. He was nice to her. He told her that she needed to get help for the drugs and that she needed to listen to me."

"Yes, Judge Wright's a wonderful man."

He continues, saying that she left the house one day and that she was going to meet up with a friend. She didn't come home and hasn't returned. That was eight months ago. He filed a Missing Persons Report two days after she went missing. He didn't hear anything for a while, and then a Sergeant called him about it and said that it had been picked up by her.

"A Sergeant called you and said she'd picked it up?" I can't keep the surprise out of my voice.

I'm not a genius when it comes to how things operate around here, but it seems strange to me that a Sergeant would pick up a Missing Persons Report with no evidence suggesting that Meghan was anything else other than missing.

"Yeah. She said her name was Sergeant Ross. Jillian Ross. She'd call me weekly to let me know what was going on. That went on for a couple of months, and then she called and said that she had run out of leads, but she would keep the case active and would let me know if somethin' came up."

I'm trying to keep my face impassive. I'll have to ask Nick if there's a Jillian Ross anywhere in this department. I have no idea if there is or there isn't. I'm still stuck on a Sergeant running with a Missing Persons Report. I think back when Rose and I came here about Misty, and Juliana saying something about a desk Sergeant. Could that be the case? I ask that specifically, and all Mr. McGregor says is that she called herself Sergeant Ross.

"Did she give you her phone number?"

"Yeah, she did." He stands up and pulls a bulky wallet out of his back pocket. He gives me a piece of paper with the name and a number on it. "That's my handwritin'," he explains.

"Did you ever call her number?"

"Didn't need to. She was so good about callin' me that I never felt like I needed to call her."

I scramble around Nick's desk, finding a piece of paper and a pen. I write the number down and the name. It's all very interesting, but there's something about it that feels wrong to me. I'd very much like to know who Sergeant Ross is, and if she actually exists around here.

I ask him how old Meghan was when she went missing.

"Seventeen. She'll be eighteen in a few days. I'd love for her to be here to celebrate her birthday." His voice breaks, and he's trying hard not to cry.

So am I. I'm chewing on my lip, trying to keep the tears in. I feel the lump in my throat, and my heart aches for this man and his missing daughter. We don't talk much longer. He seems like he wants to leave. I think it's so he can cry. I thank him for the information, for caring and for talking to me.

"Please find my little girl," he says.

I walk him out and then back to Nick's desk, sinking down in his chair, and cry. After I shed some tears, I go to the conference room and add to the timeline that I started. We moved it from paper to a mobile dry erase board. Nick added Misty's name to the board sometime during the week. I add to it, stand back and look at what we have. We have all the girls identified. We know when they went missing, except for Sherry Luke. We don't have her age either.

Nick or Chris may be able to find out some information about her since we have a last name. The ages are still similar, except Naomi. That hasn't changed. Nick can look for a Missing Persons Report on Meghan, but I don't think there'll be one. Was that really a Sergeant that called Mr. McGregor, and if not, *who in the hell was it?*

As I continue to study the names, I realize that I'm done. I did what Nick asked me to do. I may be able to go back to DFCS on Monday. I have mixed feelings, and that's something that I didn't expect.

I want to get back to my job, my cases, my kids, my foster parents. I want to go visit with Judge Wright. I want to tell him what I've been doing, but I'm not sure if I can do that. I don't think Nick would be happy about that. The other part of me has enjoyed being here, working with Nick and Chris.

I hate what I've had to do and what they are having to do, but having this time with Nick, watching him work, understanding how he thinks, finding out how smart of a guy he is and how much he cares not only about his job, but about these girls. He's good at his job, passionate about it. Chris is too. They complement one another. Chris is funny.

His sense of humor is sometimes a little off, and that makes it even funnier.

I hear them coming down the hall, talking in loud, excited tones. They walk in and stop when they see me. They look at each other and then at me.

Nick gives me a wide devilish grin and says,"We got the son of a bitch."

Chapter Twenty-Four

I don't think I heard him right. They're both waiting for my reaction. I'm trying to process what he's said. It was seven simple words.

"You got him?" They both nod at me, and they are still smiling. "You're sure?"

"Yes," Nick says to me. "I told you I would do it. Well, it was mostly Chris here."

"Shit. It was a combined effort," Chris says.

I stand and walk over to Nick. I haven't seen him in basically three days. He looks incredible, if not a little tired. He got Misty's killer. He did it. He and Chris. His eyes lock on mine as I move closer to him.

"You can turn around if this embarrasses you," I murmur to Chris, but I don't take my eyes off of Nick.

I slide my hands up his chest and stand on my toes and pull his face to mine. It's a quick kiss, but I drink it in like I've been in the desert, and he's the water. He feels good and tastes good, and I would love for him to take me to his house right now and show him exactly what kind of man I think he is.

When the kiss is over, he asks me, "Are you going to kiss Chris like that, too?"

"No, that's all for you."

"Good, because I sure would hate to beat his ass." He winks at me, and I hate when he does that. No, I really do love it. "Sit. I know you have information to share with us, and we have so much information to share with you." We all sit at the table, and they start laying it out for me.

They're both riding a high of catching the bad guy. I see it and feel it in them, and it's catching. It feels like my adrenaline is pumping, and it looks like theirs is too. Nick looks at Chris. "Do you want to start?"

"No, you go ahead. I think she likes to hear your voice more than mine." Chris smiles at me.

"You got this ball rolling. You can tell her."

"Oh, my God, guys, somebody tell me what happened. You're both killing me here," I exclaim to both of them.

"You aren't very patient," Nick says to me. *Would Chris arrest me if I choked him?* Probably not. Nick sees that I'm really losing my patience with him and takes pity. "Okay. Keep your pants on over there." He's smiling and throwing my words back at me that I said to him days ago. "Chris visited with the three doctors at the pain management clinic. He saw all three doctors on Monday. No big deal there. Nothing really suspicious. He was finally able to see Greg Miller late Wednesday."

Nick goes on to say the first thing Chris noticed was some visible healing scratches around Greg Miller's neck. The next thing he noticed was a bite mark on his hand. During casual conversation about the Bradberrys (because that's what he was there for) Chris asked him about it. He said that his wife caught him having an affair, and when he tried to get her to be reasonable, she bit and scratched him.

"Yeah, right," Chris says to me. "Do I look like I rolled into town on my donkey yesterday?"

I laugh at that and say, "I don't think you can roll in on a donkey." Chris looks at me while Nick rolls his eyes at me, and I say, "I'm sorry, Chris. Please continue."

He picks up right where he left off. "I knew it was bullshit as soon as it came out of his mouth. That was fine. I liked that he lied to me. He shot to the top of the suspect list right then." He says he thanked Greg Miller and asked the receptionist what kind of car the doctor drove. "Very fancy red BMW. I found it in the parking lot. It's easy to see. Cherry red motherfucker. I pulled my handy iPhone out and took a picture of the tires. I actually took several pictures and took several pictures of the car. When I got back here, we imported them to the computer, printed them and looked for a match to our tire cast. They matched. Nick decided to take the picture of the car back out to the guy that discovered the body."

I interrupt again. I don't want to, but I need to ask a question. "But he said that night that he didn't see anything or hear anything."

"You're right," Nick says. It's funny how they are bouncing back and forth between each other telling me this. "But what kind of detective would I be if I didn't make sure now that we had a car that we could identify as being *the* car."

"Okay. Sorry. I didn't mean to interrupt. Continue."

"The dog guy didn't see the car that night. However, he did see that cherry red BMW a couple of nights after her body was discovered. He thought it was odd for that kind of car to be in his location, because no one around him drives cars like that. He just thought maybe the person was lost and decided to pull on his street to figure out where he was going. He said he didn't think anything else about it. Meanwhile, Chris has located the very lovely Mrs. Miller, and she gave him an alibi."

He holds his finger up at me because I'm about to say something else.

"Hold on, beautiful. I know what you're thinking. His alibi fell to shit last night when I got a call from Mrs. Miller, who was in tears and said she lied to me. Go figure? Who lies these days? She says that the good doctor was nowhere to be found and couldn't be contacted on his reliable cell phone during the time frame that we've come up with when we think Misty went missing and when her body was found.

"We called the Sergeant, who called the Lieutenant, who called the Chief. The Chief said to call Brison. We called Brison, and he said to get our search warrant together and call a Judge. We called the Judge and laid it out for him. He said to bring it by, and he would sign it. Me, Chris, Sarg, Forensics and everybody else that we could round up, served three search warrants at the same time. Chris hit his home with some people. There was a group that hit his office. A group took his car, and I interviewed Miller. Forensics won't forgive us for this for a long time."

"Why is that?"

"We don't have but four people here in that unit. We stretched them thin as well as the equipment that they have to work with. We had to do it this way. We wanted to do all three at once. I'm going to tell you something, and I'm only telling you because of what was found in his car." Nick has lost all excitement, and he's not smiling.

"Is it about Naomi?" I know my face has gone pale. I feel slightly sick.

"No, baby. I'm sorry. I didn't realize you would take it like that. You asked me about Misty last Saturday night and what I had been holding back."

"Yeah, you said she'd been mutilated."

"Yes. Someone carved *Whore,* in her stomach, most likely shortly after she died. Crime Lab can give you all of those details, but I know you don't want any other details than that."

My stomach rolls, but I'm pretty proud of myself for handling that bit of information as well as I do.

"No, that's more than enough," I say quietly.

"While I was interviewing Miller, I got a call that I needed to come look in his trunk. Oh, I forgot to mention that I sweet-talked the doctor into coming to talk with me here. I said we needed to talk with him about the Bradberrys. When he got here, I presented him with all three search warrants. It was great. We had him here, and we had his car here." Nick says that he had someone babysit Miller, who has an enormous ego and wasn't worried about any of the searches. "He wouldn't give me his DNA, though. But here's what drove the nail in his coffin." He's looking around him and looks at Chris. "Where're the pictures?"

Chris jumps up. "Still on your desk." He walks out.

Nick looks at me and smiles. He reaches over, taking my hand in his. "I've missed you the last few nights."

My heart's starting to beat faster. "I've missed you, too. It felt weird sleeping alone."

"Tell me about it." He lets go of my hand when Chris walks back in.

"I wondered if I would walk back in here, and you two would be on top of the table. But just hand holding? That's too sweet." He throws the pictures on the table and sits, grinning at us. Nick gives him a look while he picks up the pictures, and Chris continues to grin. "What?" he asks innocently.

"Nothing," Nick says, with a complete deadpan look on his face, and then turns his attention back to me. "Would you like to know what Forensics found in his trunk?" he asks me.

"Yes," I say.

"Blood. We did a test on site to make sure, and it is indeed blood. I'm pretty sure it's Misty's blood." He puts the pictures in front of me and points to one in particular. "See that?"

"Yes." But I don't know what I'm seeing. It's blood, I guess, since he said it was, but if he'd asked me, *What's that?* I wouldn't have been able to tell him.

"What does that look like to you?" he asks.

I look up at him and shake my head. "I don't know. I know you want me to see something that's important, but I don't know what that something is."

"It looks like the partial outline of a W and H to me. Chris thinks so too, and so does everyone else that I've shown it to. Forensics took a lot of pictures at several different directions and angles. I've looked at all of them, and I still think that's what we're looking at. We found blood where her head could've been. He didn't even try to clean the trunk. The blood is faded, because she was murdered two weeks ago, but we found hair that I'm certain will match her hair. I came back in and placed him under arrest. He was surprised. After I arrested him, I took his DNA. Well, I didn't take it. I had someone from Forensics come in, but we got it. He exercised his right to remain silent at that time and said he wanted his attorney." Nick sits back, looking very pleased with himself. Chris has the same expression on his face. We sit in silence, smiling at one another.

"You guys are the best," I say, finally.

"I know you think that about Nick, but thanks for saying it about me," Chris says, laughing.

They jump back and forth, telling me about the other two searches. They're working with the Drug/Vice guys on back tracking when the morphine was purchased to see if it coincides with the dates when the girls went missing. They want to possibly match those dates with any type of distribution of the drug, who did the majority of distribution and how it was distributed. They say it's somewhat complex, time consuming and will take time to sort through. They didn't find a gun, but he could've dumped it someplace. They both find it strange that he would dump the weapon but not clean his trunk. They drift off in a conversation about that for several minutes. I listen to them, absorbed in what they're talking about. Someone found a necklace at his home with the name *Meghan* inscribed on it.

I groan when they tell me this.

"What is it?" Nick asks.

"I know who that is."

They both look at me expectantly.

"We're waiting," Nick says.

"No, finish telling me what you know, and I'll tell you what I know."

"Grace. You can't throw something like that out there and then not say anything about it." Nick's starting to look all pissed.

"Calm down. I'll tell you."

We stare at each other for several moments. I see the change in his eyes. Damn him, the way he looks at me sometimes.

"I'm sending you two out of here if you don't stop," Chris says.

Nick starts grinning at me. It's a wolfish grin. They say they didn't find much else. No bloody clothing. No note that said *I killed Misty Price*. We all agreed that if it was an hour-long show, they would've found a note of some sort. We laugh about that.

"Can I see his picture?" I ask Nick.

"Yes. Come with me, and I'll show you his booking photo. It's probably up at this point."

We walk up the hall so close that our arms are brushing against each other. We're walking like we're a couple in a relationship. I look up at him at the same time he looks down at me. We're smiling at each other.

"Have you called Rose and Stan?"

"Not yet. I wanted to tell you first. I think I'm going to go see them. I don't want it to be a phone call."

"That's really sweet, you know," I say to him, softly.

"It's the right thing to do." He's being modest. He bends down and asks, "So, you think I'm sweet?" He's grinning at me when I look up at him.

"Yes."

He whispers in my ear, "Not as sweet as you," and then sits at his desk, moving the mouse around for the computer to come on.

He goes through several screens and then the picture is there. What was I expecting? Devil horns or blood dripping from his mouth? He's an attractive man who looks very rich. There's an arrogant look about him, and he's smirking. His look says, *I'm smarter than all of you combined.*

Why'd he do it? How do you become something like that? And then to mutilate her body the way that he did is sick and twisted. It's so sadistic. I'm not a hater, but I hate this man. I hope someone beats him up while he sits in jail. I don't like thinking violent thoughts about people, but if anyone deserves it, this sicko does.

"How are you and Chris going to tie him to the other girls?" They'll be happy when I tell them about Meghan. It's something.

"We are working on it. Trust me. We'll get there." He's gazing at me.

"I trust you," I say quietly.

We walk back in the conference room and sit.

Chris has disappeared but comes back, shortly, with drinks for all of us. "I thought a little caffeine would help us; of course, I'm not sure if y'all need it."

Nick looks at him and shakes his head and then looks back at me. "What do you have to tell us?"

I open my mouth to speak and end up bursting into tears. They both look at each other, shocked, for a moment. Chris gets up to close the door, while Nick walks around the table and squats down in front of me, taking my hands in his.

"Hey," he says softly. "No shrinking daisy, remember?" He's smiling sweetly at me. It doesn't help.

I'm emotionally given out. Everything rushes me all at once. I'm going to lose my brother, and I don't want to. He's all I've got left of my family. He's all I've ever had. There's something going on with him, and I don't know what that is.

All of those girls are gone, including my sister, whether anyone wants to admit it out loud or not. I didn't do enough for her, and it gets to me. Misty being murdered and all that was done to her is too much, and it's little relief that Greg Miller is sitting in a jail cell. She's not coming back.

Hearing Darla talk about being raped, over and over again, was so awful. All of those parents who don't give a damn where their daughters are and listening to Mr. McGregor talk about missing Meghan and not wanting to cry in front of me and her being all he had left and the memory that Meghan gave him of his dead wife-- it's too much. I'm sniffling while Nick's rubbing my hands, looking at me.

"What is it, Grace?"

I finally get it together and tell them everything that I've learned. I go into great detail about my encounter with Matt. I shed more tears over that and admit to them how scared I am that I'm losing him. Nick moves to a chair beside me and holds both hands the whole time I tell them what I know. I fill in the pieces about learning Sherry's last name and that the other girl Matt knew as well. I tell them about Meghan, and I can see them smile at one another. Then, I get to Sergeant Jillian Ross. They look at each other and then at me. She doesn't exist; I can see it by the expressions on their faces.

"There's no one by that name here. We've got two female Lieutenants here, one female detective in Sex Crimes and one in Forensics. There are no female Sergeants in the department," Nick says

I knew it, and that means it's another damn piece of this puzzle. I'm ready for this whole thing to be over with. I finish telling them everything that I know. I feel better after getting all of that out. I dry up my tears and get my emotions back to something more manageable, and realize that I feel better getting all of those emotions out to them.

"You two realize that I've fulfilled my duties."

"Yes, you have," Nick says.

"We've got to figure out about these reports. We've got to figure out who impersonated a Sergeant and came across as working at this department," Chris says.

"The woman and the reports are going to be tied together," Nick says, looking at him.

"Yep. You're right. I'm going to go talk to Sarg, and then I'm going to go see Mr. McGregor. I'll take that necklace with me, see if he can identify it and talk with him for a while, then I'm going to do some other shit and then I'm going home, even if it is only for a few hours."

"I'm going to see Rose and Stan," Nick says. "I'll be back in a few hours." They agree when they'll come back here. I'm not coming back. I'm finished.

"I'll go with you to see Rose and Stan," I tell him.

Nick looks at me again and takes a deep breath. "I hate to bring this up right now, and I don't want you to feel pressured, but have you thought about that ring and who it might be?"

Chris is looking at me, expectantly. I focus my attention between the two of them. I have been thinking about it. I think about it all the time, even if it's not a conscious thought.

"I have. There's this mental block, and I know that might not make any sense. I've been trying to figure out if this is a man that I know well, and he doesn't wear the ring all the time, or if it's someone that I only see occasionally; therefore I would only see the ring occasionally. Does that make sense to you?"

"Yes, it makes sense. Just keep thinking, okay?" Nick's smiling softly at me.

"I am. I promise."

We finish with what we're doing, and Chris heads up the hall, while Nick and I walk outside.

We get to the car, and Nick asks, "After we finish with Rose and Stan, what would you say to a date, and let's forget things for a while?"

"How about a movie date with a DVD at your house, after a nap and a shower," I ask.

He moves closer to me, wraps his arms around my waist, pulling me up against him. "Is that shower going to be together?"

I stand on my toes, circling my arms around his neck. "I wouldn't have it any other way."

Chapter Twenty-Five

"Would you stop fidgeting already?" Jess says to me.

I can't help it. Why have I gotten so nervous all of a sudden? It has to be because I've never been this dressed up in my life, and I've never had a guy plan this type of birthday surprise for me. None of my former boyfriends have ever done anything like this for me. Not that Nick's my boyfriend. I'm not sure what he is. I'd like for him to be my boyfriend. It's not something we've talked about.

I have no idea what to expect from tonight. I don't know where Nick's taking me or what we're doing. All I know is that I've been subjected to getting my hair done, getting my makeup done and then getting my nails and toes done. I asked Jess why my toes, since my feet will be in closed-toed shoes. She said that it was sexy, and I wouldn't be in my dress or shoes all night.

I told Jess before we left the condo this morning that I couldn't afford all of this, and I wasn't letting her pay for anything else, because she bought me the dress. She said Nick was paying for everything and that it's all a part of my birthday surprise. I was speechless. What's he up to?

I nearly had a knock-down, drag-out fight with Jess' regular hair stylist at Salon Lux, who wanted to put my hair up. I told her I didn't want to do that. She said since I was wearing a strapless dress, it would be beautiful to have all of my hair off my back and shoulders. I told her that the guy I was doing this for likes my hair down, and that's how it was going to be.

We ended up compromising. When she mentioned a partial up-do, I told her I didn't know what the hell she was talking about. She pulled the sides and top of my hair back and put these beautiful pins in to hold it in place. She then took my curls and made them bigger. She did an awesome job with my hair. With the professionally done makeup and the hair, I didn't recognize myself at first.

Jess finishes zipping up the dress, and I stare at the girl in the mirror. *Wow! I clean up pretty good.* I love this dress. I love the feel of the satin against my skin. I think the deep purple with the black lace over it makes it somewhat original. I twirl around a couple of times, so the dress floats out and around me. I hear Jess giggling. I do too.

She goes under my dress and helps me slip on her shoes. Her heels bump me up three inches. My feet are going to hurt later if I'm on them for very long, but it's well worth it, since I'm getting the chance to wear her black, pointed-toe Manolo Blahniks. She stands back and looks at me.

"Well," I say, sounding terribly nervous, "how do I look?"

"There are no words for how you look," she says, smiling at me.

I spin around and look at myself in her full length mirror. If I don't calm down, I'm going to sweat all of this makeup off.

"I'm very nervous," I admit.

"Why?"

"I've never looked like this, and I don't know what we're doing. You know, don't you?"

"Yes. And you're going to love it." We hear the doorbell ring. I begin to follow her out. "Stop. You have to wait up here, and then I'll call you down."

I roll my eyes at her. "What? Why?"

"Because that's the way it has to be. Just do it, okay?"

"Okay," I say, flustered.

She hands me her black satin clutch. "It has your lip gloss, compact powder and phone. That's all you'll need."

She bounds down the stairs, and I hear the door open. "Look at you. Wow! Come in."

"Is she ready?" I hear him ask. Oh my, he sounds a little nervous too. That doesn't help me.

"She's ready. Are you ready to see your girl?"

What is going on with the whole " your guy, your girl" comments lately?

"I'm ready," I hear him say.

"Can I come down now?" I ask, sounding a little impatient.

I hear them both laugh.

"Yes. Now you can come down."

I want to make a sweeping entrance, but I settle for walking carefully. Nick's waiting for me right inside the door. Our eyes go wide when we see each other. *Oh, my God!* Nick Bassano has never looked as good as he does right now. He's in a beautiful black tuxedo with a gray vest and a matching tie that hangs down, disappearing in the vest. It looks like a custom-fitted tux. His jacket is unbuttoned, while the vest is fully buttoned. He's staring at me, and he's not said anything. Jess is smiling like a fool, looking from me to him. He has one hand behind his back, and he moves forward to stand closer to me.

"I would tell you that you look beautiful, but that's a poor word choice. You are absolutely breathtaking." He's smiling at me, and I see it again in his eyes what looks like affection. God, his words. He can say some of the sweetest things.

"I feel like a princess," I admit.

"You look like one."

"That's so sweet," Jess says. I want to tell her that her face is going to crack if she smiles any bigger.

"That is sweet," I say, smiling, holding his eyes with mine.

"I know you said you don't like to be given flowers, and the only time flowers are appropriate are at weddings and funerals, but I thought you might make an exception tonight." He brings his hidden hand around, holding a dozen of the most beautiful pink roses.

Jess is clapping and bouncing from one foot to the other.

"Oh, this is really romantic," she says.

"Thank you," I say softly, taking them. They smell wonderful.

"I'll take them for you and put them in a vase. Okay. Let's get some pictures." I give Jess a, *You have to be kidding me* look. "Don't look at me like that, Grace Harrison. You've never been dressed up like this before. You two look amazing. I'll get the pictures printed, and you can both frame them and put them on your desks at work."

Oh, now she's being crazy. Like either of us would do that. I look at Nick, hoping he'll bail us out of this situation. But oh no, the traitor thinks it's a great idea. After being forced to pose for several pictures, I announce that it's enough. Jess runs upstairs to get my overnight bag and hands it to Nick.

When we step outside, I stop. *What the fuck?* There's a shiny black limo waiting for us. I look at Nick and then back at Jess, who has resumed bouncing and clapping.

"Since you look like a princess," he says, by way of explanation. Jess hugs us and tells us to have a great time. Nick takes my hand, and we walk to the limo. The driver, who has been waiting patiently, opens the door. Nick puts my bag in and then helps me in. We're pulling out when he says, "Happy birthday, baby." His lips find mine, but the kiss is soft. "I would like to lay you down right here, but I don't want to ruin anything." He's holding my hand.

My heart's beating so fast. I'm more than excited to find out what we're going to do. I know how the night's going to end. He lets go of my hand, twisting around for a second and then back with a bottle of champagne and two glasses. I give him a look when I see that it's Cristal.

"Nick. Really?"

His answering grin is so wicked sexy, and those damn dimples. "It's your birthday."

I sigh and continue to stare at him. "This is all too much. Everything that you did so I could look like this and the limo and that," I say pointing to the bottle.

"You're worth every dime." He winks at me. *Dammit!* "I know you didn't go to prom because you didn't go to high school."

I groan. "Nick, we aren't going to prom, are we?"

"Yeah. We're going to bust in up at Clarke Central and go to prom. I can't believe you asked me that question." He's still smiling at me with that wicked smile.

"Sarcastic son of a bitch," I say, laughing. "I'm telling the driver to pull over, and I'm getting out."

Nick puts down the bottle, glasses and wraps his arms around me, pulling me into him.

"Oh, hell no, you're not," he growls. His lips find the pulse on my neck, where they linger. I know he feels my pulse quicken. I close my eyes, tipping my head back, enjoying the feel of his lips on my neck, enjoying feeling him against me. "Baby, you smell so good. What're you wearing tonight?"

"You," I breathe. I can feel him smile at my neck.

"Yeah, you'll definitely be wearing me later. What's that fragrance? I've not smelled that on you. I like it."

He looks in my eyes. His eyes darken, and I see desire for me in them, along with the hunger that I've gotten familiar with quickly. I'm panting just looking at them, knowing how much he wants me.

"Stella by Stella McCartney. Jess's mom gave it to me for Christmas last year. I don't wear it often, because it's so expensive. I was hoping you would like it." My hands are running up and down his jacket. "You're incredibly handsome tonight, but I can't wait to get you out of this tuxedo."

"That may happen sooner rather than later." His eyes are still dark, pooled with his hunger for me. I want him right here, in the back of this limo. I see the privacy glass that's up. "I want to fuck you so bad right now that I have half a mind to say screw the evening, but I don't want you to miss where we're going." His voice is low, sexy, *shit.*

I gasp. The way he's looking at me, and the words that he's saying connect with me right between my thighs, and I'm strongly considering to hell with it, too. My panties are getting damp.

"Well, as long as the privacy glass stays up, how about here when we're going back to your place?" I ask softly.

Now I see him gasp. He takes my hand and presses it to him. He's hard. He's hard for me. It turns me on even more. I start rubbing him softly. He closes his eyes, letting all the air out of his lungs.

"You've got to stop doing that, and we have to talk about something else," he says roughly. He pulls my hand away from him and up to his lips, brushing them across my knuckles and holding my eyes with his. He takes the champagne bottle and glasses and pours some for both of us. "Would you like to know where we're going?"

"Please." I take a drink and decide again that it is worth the money.

"I've been talking about you with my parents." His smile is sweet. I know my face looks surprised, because I am surprised. "They can't wait to meet you."

"I got all dressed up to meet your parents? I'm not complaining, but are you that embarrassed about me?"

He regards me with a look. "No and no. Hush. I was telling them your remarkable story of survival and what a tough, full-of-life woman you are. I told them that you keep me on my toes. They're impressed with you already. Anyway, my dad has a friend who's attending the Athens Area Homeless charity function that's been pulled together. I'm sure you know all about what's been going on this past year with trying to get that building at the North Avenue Bridge converted into a shelter. My dad made a call, and we have two seats at his table tonight."

I don't know what to say. He's blown me away tonight. Has he ever talked to his mom and dad about a woman that he's dating? What does he feel for me? The things that he does, and the words that he says have me falling deeper and deeper for him. Has he ever done anything like this for anyone else? The fact that this is what he came up with, knew that it would mean something to me in addition allowing me to dress up the way that I am, toys with my heart even more. We've both finished our drinks. He takes my glass and sets it with his back with the bucket and bottle.

"I wanted to go to this so bad. The tables are expensive, as you know. Jess and her parents tried to talk me into letting them buy a table for me for my birthday, and I wouldn't let them do it. I donated what I could, of course, but it didn't rise to the level for a table." I put both hands his face, stroking his cheeks, feeling his smooth, freshly shaven skin while looking in his eyes. "This is the most thoughtful and sweetest birthday present I've ever been given. No man has ever done anything like this for me. All of this, getting to wear this pretty dress and having my makeup and hair done and you in the tux and the limo and champagne and now, I get to go to a function that I've been wanting to go to since it started being planned about a year ago. Thank you." I pull his face to mine and kiss him deeply. I slip my tongue in his mouth, and I feel him moan into the kiss. The kiss goes on until the limo stops. He raises his head.

"We're here." His voice is hoarse.

I wipe the lip gloss off his lips and reapply to mine. Nick gets out first and then helps me out. He says something to the driver as he's helping me out, but I don't catch what it is.

"Are we at the Botanical Gardens?" I ask.

"Yes, we are."

"Nick, it doesn't take that long to get from the condo to here. We drove much longer, it seems."

He takes my hand, pulling me closer to him. "I told him to take a detour."

I see men in tuxedos and women in all different types of fancy dresses walking from different directions. I take a handful of my dress in one hand, while Nick helps me up the steps. I have to hand my clutch off to him, and at first, I don't think he's going to take it.

As we are walking to the entrance of the conservatory, I ask him quietly, "Were you afraid that you would look like a pussy holding my clutch?"

He looks down at me, grinning wickedly. "No. I was afraid some guy might notice it and smack me in the ass later."

I start laughing. "What if I were to smack you in the ass later?"

He squeezes my hand. "I'm more than okay with that. You've already proven that you're a little abusive." We're both laughing, possibly a little louder than we should.

I notice that we get some looks from the people milling around the fountain that's outside of the entrance. Several people are taking pictures, and I'm thankful we've done that already. We're greeted by a man, who hands Nick an invitation-style card.

The Great Room is to the right once inside the conservatory. We walk in, and I try to take everything in. I don't come here often. Julie got married here a couple of years ago, and Jess dragged me here last year, insisting on listening to a local group play classical music. I'm not knocking classical music. It's just not for me.

The Great Room is just that. It's a wide open room with high glass walls and glass ceilings, allowing nothing but natural light. The sun's beginning to set, and there's golden light that floods the area. There isn't much in the way of decorations, because none are needed. There's greenery that surrounds the room.

Nick holds the card to me, and I see that it's a casino theme. I figured as much, as I look around and see that there is a blackjack table, a roulette table, a craps table and a backgammon table. There are two other card games going on; one is obviously poker, but I'm not sure about the other. This is going to be fun.

There's a full bar and the nicest buffet table I've ever seen. There are men carving three different types of meat. I see a chocolate fondue fountain. There are a few tables set up in the room, and I see more on the terrace that is attached to the Great Room. The tables look professionally done, with the red and black table clothes and the floral centerpieces. Of course the décor is red and black. We *are* in Athens.

I hear some very slow, sexy jazz music playing, most likely outside in the gardens somewhere. It's crowded here. Everyone looks like they are having a good time. I think things have just started.

"Let's go find our table, and I would like to get you out on the dance floor, which according to our card here, is outside," he says softly in my ear. "There's my dad's friend."

We walk to a table that is situated near a corner, facing the glass wall to the outside. The man sees Nick and smiles, standing.

"Nick," he says. They shake hands. Nick hasn't let go of my hand.

"Hey, Charles. Charles, I want you to meet the beautiful Grace Harrison."

"*The* Grace Harrison? As in she's the only one?"

"That's right. There's no other like her," Nick says, looking at me and winking. I start panting at that.

"I'm Charles Hannigan," he says, laughing. "It's very nice to meet you." He shakes my hand.

"It's nice to meet you, too."

"You may just be the most beautiful woman here tonight," he says to me. It makes me blush. I look up at Nick, who's smiling at me.

"I'm not disagreeing with you Charles," Nick says. He pulls out my chair, and I sit. I'm sitting between him and Charles. "Where's everyone?"

"Gambling, smoking, drinking, dancing and who knows what else."

"Where's your lovely bride?"

"She went to the bathroom. She'll be back in a moment." Charles leans into me. "She's not really my bride. We've been married for forty years, but don't tell her I said that."

I laugh. I like this guy. His wife comes back along with some other people. Pretty soon, our table of eight is full. I meet everyone. Charles' wife's name is Margaret Jane, whom everyone calls Maggie J. She's funny, laughs loudly and drinks heavily but never seems intoxicated.

Their daughter and her husband are at the table. Their daughter looks just like Maggie J. and acts like her, too. Her name is Katie Beth, but I notice Maggie J. is always referring to her as Katie Bug. Katie Beth's husband's name is Bo. That may or may not be his real name. No one says. Katie Beth's husband is even louder and livelier.

The other couple are friends with Charles and Maggie J. They are John and Dottie Mae Bell. They both seem a little more reserved, and Dottie Mae purses her lips anytime Maggie J. lets a cuss word slip. Dottie Mae purses her lips frequently, since Maggie J. cusses frequently.

All of the women have double names, and all three women are in dresses with a lot of sequins. It's hysterical. This is going to be a fun crowd. I'm enjoying myself immensely, and the night hasn't even gotten in full swing yet. We're left alone while the men get drinks. Nick whispers that he's going to get us both whiskeys, unless I want something different. I tell him that's fine.

"Grace, what do you do?" Dottie Mae asks me.

"I'm a Social Services Case Manager at Clarke County DFCS."

"Oh, that's wonderful. Do you know Eric Wright?"

"Yes, ma'am. I've had the good fortune to be in his courtroom for the last seven years."

"He and Shirley will be here tonight."

I smile at that. "Excellent. I can't wait to see him. I haven't seen him in a couple of weeks."

Nick comes back, as do the rest of the men. When he sits down, he says, "It's Grace's birthday today." He leans in and kisses my cheek. I blush as everyone tells me happy birthday.

"I said that Grace may very well be the most beautiful woman here tonight," Charles tells the table. I blush even more.

"Thanks, Daddy," Katie Beth says, but she smiles at me. I see Charles wink at her.

Nick takes my hand and pulls it to his lips, holding my eyes with his. "You *are* the most beautiful woman here tonight," he murmurs.

It suddenly feels as if we're all alone. *Breathe, Grace, breathe.* It takes a moment for me to pull my attention away from him and back to the easy flow of the conversation around the table. The music's still floating from the outside. The band's very good.

I look at the card on the table. It shows names of those who purchased tables this evening. I see there's a silent auction down in the Gardenside Room. Nick looks over at me and smiles, taking my hand again.

"Come on. I want to spin you around on the dance floor for a while."

Who am I to say no to that? We excuse ourselves from the others. I ask the others if my black clutch will be fine left on the table. It's not like there's a ton to steal, and everyone here has more money than God. They all agree that it will be fine.

We walk hand-in-hand down the concrete winding ramp that leads downstairs. The walk itself is breathtaking, with nature's beauty on either side. There are a multitude of plants and trees on the walk as it leads to the door to go outside. I see there are several people in the Gardenside Room looking at the auction items as we get to the door and walk outside. A dance floor has been erected in an open space within the gardens straight in front of us and down three steps. The sun is beginning to slip into the horizon, and everything around us in the garden is in bloom and fragrant.

We walk out on the dance floor, and we are pressed body to body. I slide one hand up around his neck, while he slips one arm around my waist and takes the other hand in his hand. We may be the only couple out here on the dance floor or there could be twenty other people out here. I don't know. I only have eyes for the man dancing with me. His smile is sexy. His eyes are dark and full of hunger. I know it's hunger for me. I know my eyes are showing him the same thing.

He moves me around the floor. His hand is pressed firm at the small of my back, and it pushes me into him. I feel him. I smile, letting him know I feel him, and I like what I'm feeling.

"What do you think everyone would say if I were to lay you out right here on the floor?"

I start laughing softly. "We would never be invited back."

He laughs with me and then says, "Your eyes are beautiful in this light. I swear I see gold flecks in them."

Oh, my God. I'm going to melt right here on this dance floor. What a romantic evening. I couldn't have planned a better thirtieth birthday. The way Nick's looking at me is heating me up, and the saxophone along with the piano and drum intensifies it all.

"Thank you for making my birthday better than I could've ever imagined."

"Thank you for spending it with me. Has Mike called you?"

I give him a look. "*Why* are you asking me that right now?"

"I know he has."

"Nick. Don't ruin this, okay?"

He lowers his head and whispers in my ear, "You're busy next week-end, too." He lifts his head and smiles at me.

"With what?"

"I'll think of something. And, if he asks about during the week, you're busy then, too." He's looking at me with serious dark eyes.

Wow! He wants to be with me. He wants me to be with him. I could only admit this to Jess, but I'm over the moon about it.

I'm not sure what my response should be. I go with, "Okay."

The song ends and flows into another, and all I want to do is stay in this man's arms.

Chapter Twenty-Six

"I have an idea," Nick says. "Come with me."

He walks me off of the dance floor and back up the steps, leading me to the right, and we walk in no great rush, looking at all the scenery around us. I see several other couples have the same thing in mind. We go through an A-framed trellis and into a garden where there's more shrubbery, plants and other flowers. We walk on the bricks and circle around beautifully sculpted shrubs.

"Where're we going?" I ask, looking up at him.

"Up there," he says, pointing in front of us to a gazebo. We pass a few couples who have been where we're going. We all smile at one another. The men look a little drunk, and we hear their loud laughter behind us. "Sounds like they are having a good time," Nick says, looking back at them.

"No one's having more fun than I am," I smile up at him.

His answering smile is dazzling, and it makes my heart beat faster, if it has even slowed down tonight. We walk over a bridge and pause for a moment, looking at everything in bloom. We reach the gazebo, and we are all alone. Someone has wrapped small twinkling lights all around the posts of the gazebo.

The sun has slipped below the horizon, and the sky is going from bursts of orange and purple to an inky gray. I want to pinch myself to make sure I'm not dreaming, and this night is real, and Nick is real. I wasn't lying earlier when I said I feel like a princess. The music's still going, and we can hear it from where we are. Nick's standing in front of me, and he moves to close the small distance between us.

I look up at him, and everything is there in his eyes, his hunger for me, for my body, that he thinks I'm beautiful, and I still would swear that I see some sort of affection there, too. He pulls his fingers through my curls that are swaying slightly in the breeze. His hands go to my shoulders and then slide down my arms. I shiver feeling his hands on my exposed skin.

"Are you cold, baby?" His voice is that low, sexy tone.

"No," I say quietly.

The exact opposite; I've been lit on fire by him again, the way he's looking at me while running his hands lightly up my arms to my shoulders and then back down. I put my hands at his waist and then run them inside his jacket and up his back. He bends his head and puts his lips to mine. I'm gripping him at his back and feel his muscles bunch under my hands.

He's holding tight to the back of my neck and kisses me until I can feel my legs begin to tremble. He drags his lips from mine to my jaw, where they linger and then to my pulse. He finds it racing. My head is thrown back to give him full access to my neck. He lifts his head and looks at me. His dark eyes are intense, and I know he wants me right here. I feel that he does, and I can see it.

"Is it me that makes your pulse race like that?" His voice is still low and sexy.

"Yes," I sigh.

He smiles, and there are those dimples. I would love for him to take me right here. I want him right here.

"Do you want to stay here and dance?"

Can we fuck here, too? "Are you going to stay pressed against me like you are?"

"Absolutely. Do you know what I'll be thinking about?" His devilish smile and feeling him strain against his pants tells me that I have a pretty good idea. My hands go up his chest and around his neck. I am flush with his body. I can feel him straining further.

"I know what you're thinking. I feel it," I say provocatively.

His smile broadens, and his dimples go deeper. *Shit, he's so hot.* He starts dancing us around slowly. He presses into me, and our eyes lock. We very well could be kicked out of here before the night's over.

He lowers his head and whispers in my ear, "You only know half of what I'm thinking. I can't wait to run my tongue up and down your leg and then taste how sweet I know you are."

I close my eyes and moan hearing his words. I rub up against him, and I hear him gasp when I put my lips right at his jaw. His skin is smooth against my lips, and he smells delicious, as he always does.

"I'm going to explode in my pants if you keep doing that."

We both start laughing softly. We see another couple approaching, and that stops us from making out, but it does little to bring the sexual tension that's twirling around us, and then through us. We dance through two more songs and walk back inside, stopping to visit the Gardenside Room, looking at the auction items.

Nick decides he must bid on the Georgia football tickets for the upcoming season. I admit I wouldn't mind having those tickets for myself. It's for the Georgia-Florida game. That's probably the biggest game of the season. There has been a huge rivalry between the two for years. It's always in Jacksonville, Florida.

"We'll go together if I win these," he says, writing his name and his bid amount.

He's talking future here. He's talking six months away. The thought of still being with him in six months is thrilling.

"I'm sure you would rather go with Chris or one of your other friends." I'm offering him an out. He wraps his arm around my waist and pulls me into him.

"PDA with Chris may get me some strange looks." He's grinning at me, and he's all dancing dark blue eyes, teeth, and dimples. He bends and whispers in my ear, "Besides, I wouldn't want to fuck him before and after the game."

My eyes fly to his, and I'm panting. His smile is wicked sexy. After everything he said outside, and now this, I may climax right here. He's too much, and I love it. We make our way back up to the Great Room and find our table full.

"We've all been out dancing and didn't see y'all," Charles says.

"I took Grace up to the gazebo to dance with her there," Nick says to him.

Katie Beth tells Bo she wants him to take her to the gazebo to dance as well. We enjoy the food, and Nick loses two rounds of Blackjack. I see Judge Wright and his wife with a group of their friends. I drag Nick with me to speak with him, and he tells me that he heard that I'd taken some time off. He asks if I'm okay, and I tell him that I'm great and will most likely be back at work on Monday. I wondered what Valerie and Mack were going to come up with if anyone asked. Now I know. Both Judge Wright and Mrs. Wright compliment me on how pretty I look tonight.

When Nick and I walk away, he says, "That man insulted you."

I look up at him puzzled, saying, "No, he didn't."

He looks down at me and smiles. "He said you looked pretty."

I start laughing and pull his face down to me to whisper in his ear, "You're just worried that if you don't compliment me, I won't let you fuck me later."

I hear him inhale sharply. I look in his eyes, and they have that hungry look in them again. It speaks to me in all the right places.

He bends his head and whispers in my ear, "I know you'll let me fuck you later. I've seen the way you've looked at me all night."

Now, I gasp. He's right. I will definitely let him later. I'm actually good with right now.

The only downfall of the evening is when the emcee talks about how horrible it has been to lose Mickey and Eleanor. Nick and I have the same expression on our faces when we look at each other. Both of our expressions say, *Yeah, right.*

We agreed that we would discuss nothing about anything that's been happening. We both need a break and made each other promise that if one brought it up, the other would shut it down. We're going to hold tight to that promise. I made a promise to myself that I wouldn't think too deeply about Naomi's whereabouts or dwell on what's going on with Matt. I know there's something wrong, other than him using, but tonight's my night with Nick, and I'm going to continue to enjoy every minute of it.

Nick's jaw is set tight when the emcee goes on to say that he hopes the police are doing everything they can to find those responsible. I squeeze his hand, and he looks at me. I smile softly at him. His face relaxes, and he lifts my hand, brushing his lips across my knuckles.

He spins me around the dance floor until I tell him my feet can't take any more. We laugh harder than we have in days over the exchanges between Maggie J., Katie Beth and Dottie Mae. They're all close, know one another well, and it shows. My stomach hurts, I'm laughing so much. Nick asks me if I mind leaving early. Not if it means alone time with him. Everyone complains when he tells them we're going.

"Why? It's still early," Maggie J. says, protesting.

"I have something else planned for her birthday," he tells them.

He does? What? Oh, I think I know. I'm excited all over again. We all tell each other that we enjoyed meeting one another and how much fun the evening has been. I get more well wishes for my birthday, and they all hope that I've gotten everything I wanted. *I'm about to.*

Nick drags me to see how his bid's going. He cusses when he sees he's been way outbid. I tell him to let it go, and if he really wants us to go when the season starts, we'll go. When we turn around, I see Simon Collins with a very pretty blond date.

"Grace," he says, moving over to Nick and me.

Nick has his arm around my waist, and I feel it getting tighter.

"Hey, Simon."

He steps over, kissing me quickly on the cheek. Nick stiffens beside me. I look up at him, and he doesn't look happy.

"You look lovely as always," he says. I'm eye to eye with Simon in my three-inch heels.

"Thank you. Simon, this is my friend, Nick Bassano. Nick, this is Simon Collins." I'm not sure how to introduce Nick. I think he might be more than my friend, but I'm not so sure. I think the friend introduction is safe.

"Her other friend," Simon tells him, holding out his hand to shake.

Nick shakes his hand with way more force than necessary. Nick looks like he's swallowed something sour, and I'm sure he wants to pull his penis out and compare it, but I want to tell him to not bother. I've seen both, and there's no comparison. He wins by far.

"It's nice to meet you," Nick says tightly. His grip around my waist is nearing on painful.

"This is my date, Hannah Scott," Simon says to us.

We all say hi to one another, and Nick asks, "You're Brison and Blake's younger sister, aren't you?"

She smiles at him and is starting to look a little flirty. *Oh, hell no.* I grip him tighter around his waist.

"Yes. I'm the only sister. You're the detective on the Bradberry case, aren't you?"

He smiles at her. "Yes. One of them. My partner's Chris Taylor."

"Brison and Blake both talk about you. They say nothing but good things, so don't worry."

"You're also the detective that arrested Greg Miller, aren't you?" Simon asks.

"Yes, I am."

"That's such a shame. Greg and I are friends. I have a hard time believing that he's capable of this type of crime. You're sure you have the right guy?"

"Yes," Nick and I say at the same time. Nick looks down at me and smiles softly.

"I just can't imagine Greg murdering a child. She was a foster child, correct?" Simon asks.

Nick speaks before I can. "She wasn't just *a* foster child." His voice is tight. "She was on Grace's caseload, and she was deeply cared for by many people, including Grace."

Simon looks at me, surprised. "I'm so sorry about that, Grace. You didn't mention that when I saw you the other evening."

His words are kind, but they lack sincerity. Something's up with him, and I don't know what that is. There's a difference in Simon that I'm noticing for the first time. With a pounding heart, I look to his right hand, but it's shoved in his pants pocket. I think about it and look at my friend. He's not the last guy is he? I'm thinking furiously about it. Is he the one that has that ring? I don't think so.

Darla also said something about and odd shaped birthmark on the man's hip. I think quickly, and can't remember seeing one, but I wasn't paying attention to what might or might not be on his hips that night.

I'm going to have to think about this further. I question his association with Greg Miller. Hell, it's not just an association, but a friendship.

Simon Collins can't be wrapped up in this. His father is the former District Attorney, for God's sake. Simon's my old friend who was going to save the world with me at one time. He's not a man who would get involved in the rape and possible torture of young girls. It's not him, at least I don't think so, but there's something going on with him, and it leaves me with an uncomfortable feeling. I don't want to jump the gun on this. I don't want to come out and accuse Simon of something that he's not involved in. That's a strong accusation.

Do I talk about this with Nick tonight, or am I going to be selfish? *I'm going to be selfish.* I'm going to put it on a shelf for tonight and give it some thought. I can talk about this with Nick, tomorrow.

"Thank you, Simon," I say. "I didn't say anything the other night because I was out with Ginger and Angie, having a good time and trying to forget things."

Nick's still holding me tight by my waist, and he's tense, uncomfortable. I don't want this to ruin our evening. It's been magical up to this point.

"Grace, dad's here, and so is Uncle Robert. I know they would both love to see you." Simon's attempting to lighten the mood.

"We're on our way out. Please tell them both that I said hello and will try and see them soon. I would love to catch up with your dad." I'm smiling, but I don't really feel it and can still feel Nick uncomfortable at my side.

Simon looks at Nick. "Grace and I met in college. We've known one another for years. I'm sure you know my uncle. He's the mayor. My father's Brady Collins."

"The law professor at UGA?" Nick asks.

"The former District Attorney. Yes. That's him."

"You're a Disability attorney here in town, right?" Nick asks him.

"I'm *the* Disability attorney here in town," Simon says, far too arrogantly. I can't figure out his deal tonight. He's acting strange, almost like he's trying to be impressive, letting Nick know exactly who he is. There's nothing about his demeanor that's sitting right with me. Nick makes no comment to Simon's statement. "Grace, I'll call you. I know dad would love for you to come to dinner with me. He misses those talks that we all used to have."

"She's busy," Nick says quickly, answering before I can. He sounds like he's staking his claim, and he's staking his claim on me.

Simon looks at him confused. "With what?"

"With me," he pauses for a moment and then says, "Simon, it was nice to meet you. Hannah, it was nice to meet you. I'm sure I'll be seeing Brison and Blake soon." He looks down at me. "Baby, are you ready to finish celebrating your birthday?"

I want to laugh at Simon's expression. He just got told, and he got told by Nick. I don't know why I think it's so funny, but I do. I think Nick really is jealous, and it's not just for show. Nick doesn't wait for anyone to say anything and moves us out of the Gardenside Room and back up. He's expelling all the air out of his lungs as we go. We get back up, and he turns to me.

"I'm sorry I jumped in like I did and spoke for you," he says, holding my eyes.

I run my hands up his chest and hold them at his heart. "That's okay. I thought the expression on Simon's face was pretty priceless."

"That guy likes you, huh?"

"We've been friends for a long time."

"You know he's a-"

"Pussy," I say, cutting him off and laughing. "Yes, I know that's what you think."

He starts laughing. "Actually, I was going to say that he's a charlatan, but he's that too."

I shake my head and laugh with him.

"I question his loyalty to Greg Miller." I say.

"Yeah, me too."

"Okay. I don't want to talk about Simon. I want us to continue with this wonderful evening. You and me." His responding grin makes me pant again, and the encounter with Simon and Hannah is forgotten. My thoughts about Simon are shelved for later. The limo's waiting for us when we get outside. I look up at Nick. "How did he know what time to be back?"

"I told him before I got to your condo how I wanted the evening to roll." Nick helps me in the limo, and I see him hand his iPhone off to the driver. That's strange. I hear him say to the driver, "It's cued up. Will you take care of it?"

"Yes, sir," I hear the driver say.

Nick gets in, and I slide over so he has room. He eases out of his jacket and loosens his tie. He's a gorgeous sight in his crisp white shirt and vest. I hear music coming through the speakers and smile when I hear the song. *Don't You Wanna Stay* by Jason Aldean and Kelly Clarkson flows out.

"I think about you when I hear this song," he says softly.

Holy Heaven, I'm going to be a puddle on this seat by the time we get back to his house if he keeps doing and saying things like he has so far tonight. I slip my shoes off and flex my feet. They're sore but so worth it having Nick dance with me the way he did. He pulls my feet up in his lap and begins to massage them. That feels heavenly.

"Lie back and relax," he says to me, softly.

I do and prop my head up with one arm and look at him. He's watching what he's doing, while I'm studying his profile. I'm listening to the song that when he hears it, he thinks of me. *I love him.*

Chapter Twenty-Seven

The fact that I love him, hits me out of nowhere. I've been falling for him. I've completely fallen. I'm there. There's no doubt about it. My feelings for him have been running deeper and deeper. It's happened so fast, and there is nothing I can do about it. There's nothing I want to do about it. He catches me looking at him.

"What're you looking at?"

"You," I say softly.

"Like what you see?" His smile is devilish.

"Very much." I'm sure my smile mirrors his.

"Me too. Can I tell you again how gorgeous you look tonight, especially lying back the way you are right now."

His hand trails under my dress up my leg to the inside of my thigh. Our eyes lock on each other. His have gotten darker. My breathing is picking up, anticipating where his hand will go next. Simply looking at him, and the way he's looking at me, is turning me on. I'm getting wet from it. He shifts, and his body is suddenly over mine. He braces himself with one hand while the other continues to explore between my thighs. I wrap my arms around his neck and pull his face to mine.

"Do we have time for this?" I sigh.

His mouth is hovering over mine. I feel his breath when he speaks.

"I told the driver to make another detour." His voice is low and sexy. I close my eyes as his lips go to mine. I melt into him and the kiss. I slip my tongue in his mouth, and he takes and sucks on it. *Oh, I like that.* I gasp as he eases his fingers in me. He breaks the kiss and looks at me with a sexy grin. "You're so wet, baby," he growls.

"That's what you do to me," I say breathlessly.

"Then let me keep doing it," he says in that low, sexy voice. *Please do.* I pull his face back to mine as his fingers continue to expertly run in and out slowly. It's delicious torture. I grab two fistfuls of his shirt as I climax. His kiss keeps me from screaming, but I'm breathing hard in his kiss. He lifts his head, grinning at me. "Are you going to rip my shirt?"

"I may rip it off *of* you," I say breathlessly.

We continue our heavy makeout session that results in my panties being discarded on the floor, his vest and tie off with the first two shirt buttons undone, and my hand inside his zipper by the time we pull in his drive. When he lifts his head from kissing me, we are both breathing like we're a couple of long-distance Olympian sprinters. He's given me two orgasms that left me in orbit and has promised more.

He fixes himself, but pulls his tie completely off and scoops up my panties, shoving them in his jacket pocket, grinning, and then he winks at me. I nearly have a third orgasm. He grabs my shoes and bag with one hand and helps me out of the limo with the other. He tips the limo driver, and the look on the driver's face tells me he's no fool as to what was going on in the back. *Oh, well, like we're the first couple to ever make out in the back of a limo.*

We go to the bedroom, where he puts my shoes and my bag. I throw my borrowed clutch on top of my bag while he's putting his back up weapon on his nightstand. Yes, I think he must take it everywhere.

He walks to me and says, "I have something else for you."

I look up at him. "Nick. You've given me such a great present. You didn't have to get me anything else."

He closes the small space between us, pulling me up against him. "I know, but I wanted to. Can I give it to you later? Because right now, I really want to get you out of this pretty dress and make you scream my name." His voice is low. He bends his head and whispers, "Over and over and over." All of my muscles clench. "Turn around."

I turn, and he eases the zipper down and then helps me step out of my dress. I'm completely naked. He likes it and tells me as much. He walks away from me, laying my dress over my bag, and stands watching me. I love the way he looks at me. I feel like his birthday, Christmas and New Year's all rolled into one.

"Do you know how beautiful you are, Grace?" His voice is still low and sexy. His eyes are completely hungry for me. I feel so sexy standing here naked in front of him, watching him watch me.

"I know how beautiful I feel when you tell me," I say softly.

"So very beautiful," he says, closing the distance between us.

My heart is pounding, and my breathing has become shallow. I'm beyond wet and ready. I want him to take me now. This moment has been building all night, and I'm not sure how much more I'll be able to take. I want him on me, in me, and he can climb all up inside of me if he wants to. I don't care.

"I'm going to take the pins out of your hair. Can I?"

"Yes," I whisper.

It's such a sensual gesture, him taking my hair down. He runs his fingers through it.

"I like that you kept your hair down. I really enjoyed seeing your exposed skin in that dress. I liked knowing what's under that dress. Are you going to scream for me tonight?"

My eyes lock with his. "Don't I always?"

His smile is so wicked sexy, and *God Almighty, those dimples.* "Yes you do, and I always like that you scream my name when you come. The way you respond to me is such a turn on, Grace."

"You make me scream your name. That's how good you are." I finish unbuttoning his shirt where I started in the limo. I slide it off of him and take his t-shirt. "Bend down so I can take it all the way off," I say quietly. His smile is slow and sexy, and he does what I say. I make quick work of his pants, boxer briefs and stand back and look at him for a moment. Yep, I'm in love. "Nick," I say softly.

"Yes, baby."

I look up at him. "You're gorgeous. I know I'm not the only one that's told you that."

"But when you tell me, I feel it." He crushes me into him, and his lips are everywhere. He carries us both to the bed. He moves from my mouth, to my neck, to my breasts then lower, and after I climax again, he moves them back up to my mouth. I push him on his back and go on my own exploration of his body. I love doing this. I love running my hands all over him and my mouth. When I'm down between his legs, he's grinning at me. "Are you taking me all the way with your mouth like you did the other night?"

I look up at him. "I will if you want me to."

I've never been squeamish about oral sex. I've always given it because that's what guys like, but I love having Nick inside my mouth. I love tasting him and how much he wants me. I'm pretty proud of how much of him I can get in my mouth.

"No. I want to finish inside of you."

I won't complain about that. I tease him with my tongue, which I've discovered he really likes. I can hear his breathing pick up as my mouth closes around him. I go back and forth between the tongue teasing and then pulling him in my mouth several times until he grunts, "Enough." I move back up and hover over him. "You have the best mouth." His voice is low.

I slide down on him, loving the feeling of being so full of him and how hard he is inside of me. We both moan at the feelings. He grabs my hips, holding them tight. I have my hands on his chest, marveling again at how solid he is and how smooth his skin feels under my hands. I feel his heartbeat. It's beating fast for me. Yeah, I really do love him. I start to move against him. It starts off slowly, and when I begin to move faster, he holds me to him.

"Slow down." His voice is ragged, and he's breathing as hard as I am.

"Can't," I say breathlessly. "You feel too good."

"Then I'll make you slow down."

I don't know what he means by that, but then he moves without breaking body contact, and I find myself underneath him. He's over me braced up on both hands. I have my legs wrapped around him. I pull his face to mine and claim his lips. My tongue finds his, while he starts moving slowly. It drives me crazy. He eases down on his elbows, trapping my face with his hands. We are nipples to chest. I'm kissing him more urgently. I can feel my body racing to the end. I think he feels it too. He begins to thrust harder and faster. I urge him on, and he obliges going even harder.

"Nick!" I scream, when my body explodes.

My name comes out as a growl as he fills me with him, collapsing on top of me, and I welcome his heaviness.

"I always worry I'm going to suffocate you like this," he says.

"I'm tough."

He kisses me. "Yes, I know you are." He pulls out of me, and we both roll on our sides, staying connected, body to body, whispering to one another in the dark. "If you could travel anywhere in the world, where would you go?"

I give it some thought before I answer him. "I would love to see Greece."

"Why?"

"It looks beautiful; all of those old ancient buildings there on the Mediterranean. It appeals to me. Where would you go?"

"Any place tropical where I could see you in a bikini," he laughs at the look I give him.

We're silent for a few minutes. I snuggle closer to him. My left arm is tucked between us, and I have my other over his side and around his back. My hand is involuntarily moving up and down, loving the feel of his skin.

"What do you want for your future?" he whispers.

You is what immediately comes to mind. "In terms of what?"

"Career. What do you want to do for the rest of your life? Do you want to stay in Foster Care?"

"No. I would like to work my way up to Director one day. Even if it isn't in Clarke County. I could go to Madison, Barrow, Oconee, Walton, Jackson. Any of those counties would be fine. What do you want to do for the rest of your life?"

"Exactly what I'm doing right now. I've thought going out for SWAT. It's called something else at the police department, but I call it SWAT because it sounds cool." We both laugh softly. "Brandon, my friend in Oconee that I told you about, is on SWAT there and has been for years. He's been on me about it, but ultimately, I'm where I want to be. You'll be Director one day. I'm willing to put money on it; you'll be the Director of Clarke County."

His hand is slowly moving up and down my back. It goes from my back to my face, and he trails his finger over my mouth and cheek while looking in my eyes. My heart's picking up again.

The way he's touching me is soft and tender. I like it. I want him again. I just had him. How is it that I want this man this badly and this soon after? I see the change in his eyes, and they are telling me he feels the same. I can feel him getting hard against me. He starts kissing me, rolling me under him, and our conversation ceases.

It's much later before we find clothes. I'm putting some items back in my bag when he walks out of his closet.

"Damn, baby. Look at your legs in those shorts."

Jess calls them my booty shorts. I only wear them around the condo. They are tight pink gym shorts, and my butt nearly hangs out of them. I have a matching pink UGA t-shirt that I like to wear with them that's beyond fitted. It's tight, straining against my breasts. He makes a comment about the shirt, too.

"Come on, I have something for you in the kitchen." He takes my hand and leads me through his house. There's a light on over the sink, so we aren't in complete darkness. "Sit and close your eyes." He's smiling like a little kid. I'm smiling back the same way. I hear him open what sounds like the freezer. I hear cabinets open and close and then the same with the drawers. He sets something on the table in front of me. I think he got me a cake. I feel excited about this. "Okay, open your eyes."

"You got me a cake!" I squeal like a five year old.

"You said cake from Baskin-Robbins is your favorite, and before you ask, yes, it's filled with strawberry cheesecake ice cream."

I clap my hands, and I'm grinning crazily. "Thank you. I love it."

He pulls a chair to sit by me.

"I would buy you a cake every day if it meant getting to see your eyes light up like that." He's smiling at me. He holds up a three and a zero number candle, puts them on the cake and lights them. He sings "Happy Birthday" to me. "Did you make a wish?" he asks, after I blow out my candles.

"Yes, I did." I don't tell him that my wish has come true. He cuts the cake, giving me a slice that I complain is too big. I end up eating it all. After we finish with the cake, we go back to his bedroom. I crawl back in his bed and sit with my legs criss-crossed. He sets a wrapped box in front of me. "Nick," I say, smiling at him. "This is all too much."

He smiles back at me. "No, it isn't. I wanted to do this. Open it."

My excitement takes over, and when I take the paper off, there's a box that says Smith & Wesson. I open it and crack up laughing.

"You bought me a gun?" I look in his eyes, and I see he looks like he may be unsure about his gift.

"You don't like it?"

"No, I don't. I love it. It's so cool. Why's it so small?"

He smiles broadly. Oh, those dimples. "This is a Smith & Wesson Bodyguard .380. It's small because it's a .380." He takes it out of the box and hands it to me. It's really light compared to what he carries. I really do love it. It's the perfect weight for me. He shows me that it has a factory-installed laser sight. That's way too cool. "You need a gun if you're dating a cop," he says.

I look up at him. My heart's beating faster. "Is that what we're doing? I thought we were fucking." It comes out as teasing, but I'm holding my breath as to what his response will be.

"Yeah, we're doing plenty of that. Look. I'm great at dating a lot of different women. I think you've gotten that. Dating one woman all the time is new for me. I'm trying to figure this out as we go." He pulls his finger through a curl and is staring in my eyes. I have to remind myself to breathe. "I'll tell you this. I've never thought of a woman all the time like I think of you. I've never wanted to be with anyone like I want to be with you. I've never wanted to get to know anyone like I want to know you. I never wanted anyone to get to know me the way you have.

"When I think about you going out with Mike," he spits it out like a bad word, "Or anyone else, and having the knowledge that Simon likes you the way that I think he does, or watching Trey hit on you the way he did, I feel jealous, and that is something I've never felt. It hasn't mattered to me that who I'm dating may or may not be dating someone else, but it more than bothers me when I think of you with some other guy."

Oh, my God. He does feel something for me. I launch myself at him, forgetting about the gun that he's bought me and think about the other gift that he's given me- *Him.*

Chapter Twenty-Eight

I didn't think being back at work would feel as good as it does. Valerie tried talking me into taking yesterday off and coming back today. I couldn't see the logic in that and said no. I've been overwhelmed with questions from Julie and Cassidy. Mandy doesn't care and didn't ask about anything. I stumbled and fell over what to tell them. I came up with a half-truth, that it had to do something with Misty. Greg Miller's arrest was even bigger news on Sunday that it was on Saturday.

The other big news on Sunday wasn't good news at all. Nick and I were on the range, and I was getting very comfortable with my new gun, loving the built-in laser, when he got a call from Chris. Chris had gotten an irate call from an officer on patrol, who was putting something in evidence and found the evidence room unlocked, and the Bradberry evidence scattered on the floor. This officer went on to say that Nick and Chris should be more careful, and just because they were working a big case didn't mean they could be that careless.

Neither Nick nor Chris had been in the evidence room, and they hadn't scattered anything on the floor. Someone knows about the pictures, and that same someone was trying to find them. Someone associated with Law Enforcement knows about the pictures, and that person's able to gain access to the evidence room. We left immediately. Nick, Chris, Sergeant Jenkins, the unit's Lieutenant and I don't know who else had a long meeting.

I went back to the condo and spent some time with Jess and told her all about my evening. She kept asking what was wrong because

I seemed distracted and not in a good way. I told her everything was fine and showed her my gun. We laughed for a long time over it and both agreed it was the coolest present I've ever gotten. She said Nick was turning me into a gun nut. I said I was gun dumb, because I asked Nick if my gun held the same bullets as his. He said his was a .40 caliber, and mine was a .380. He tried not to laugh about it but failed miserably.

I admitted to Jess that I've fallen in love with him. She's such a romantic and thought it was the sweetest thing, had already figured that out and was wondering when I would. She gave me the pictures that she had taken, one for Nick and one for me. I looked at them and decided that we really make a great-looking couple. Jess left to have lunch with Jake and her parents, and I washed clothes and decided what to wear for my first day back to work.

Nick and Chris showed up later in the day, looking grim. Nick said they wanted to bring the pictures here. I told him he had fallen and hit his head, and that was the dumbest idea I had ever heard of in my life. We argued for well over an hour about it. I told him to take them to Brison and let him keep them at the D.A.'s office. He said no. I pressed him on why not, and all he would say was no.

I threw out that either he or Chris or anyone that knew about the pictures could keep them. He said that all of those people are Law Enforcement, and whoever is behind this is in Law Enforcement too. They were all too obvious; I'm not. He said I was the best choice because no one other than the people I had named knew what I had been doing. No one would suspect that I have them and that they're here. I looked to Chris for help, and he said after Nick explained it all to them, he admitted that it was the best idea for the situation that they're in.

They're all sick to their stomachs that one of their own is involved in this, and they don't know who. They asked me if the ring I saw was from someone I knew from the police department. After giving it serious thought, I said that didn't feel right to me, and I wasn't associating it with anyone there. I never talked with Nick about my suspicions regarding Simon, because I've not decided if I really think it's him or not. I'm struggling with trying to figure it out. I don't want to think that Simon is caught up in this.

They brought a safe and the pictures and stuck everything in my closet. I voiced my opposition again, but it was settled. I mumbled and grumbled over the stupidity of it until Nick told me to give it a rest. Chris left and said he would see Nick back at the police department later. He told him to be careful, since I was now armed. He said he already knew I was dangerous. I let Chris know that I was perfectly comfortable with my .380, and with the laser, I felt like I could shoot very well.

Nick stayed for a while, but then he had to go. He told me he wasn't sure if he would see me later, so he took me upstairs to let me know how much he would be missing me. He left me completely satisfied and breathless. He bitched about my bed being too small. I told him I couldn't help it that he was a giant, and he needed to heed what Chris told him. I showed him the pictures, and he took one with him. I don't know what he'll do with it.

I didn't see him Sunday night, and I didn't see him last night either. He took me to lunch yesterday and wouldn't give me a lot of details, because there weren't a lot of details to share. Most of it had to do with internal police business that he *couldn't* share. They still had more questions and were doing everything they could think of to get them answered.

I have the feeling that he knows something, and he's not sharing it with me. I tried to get him to talk to me about it, and he got snappy, and then I got snappy back. He apologized and said I was really sexy when I got snappy with him. I was ready to ditch my first day back at work and spend the day in the bed with him or wherever he wanted to go. It didn't really matter with me.

I pull into my complex. I was at work for an hour when the pen that I was tapping relentlessly against my desk busted and went all over my pants. I cussed like a sailor and was going to go through the rest of the day with the stain, but I want to go see Judge Wright later today, so I told Valerie I was going to go home and change.

I open my glove compartment and pull my gun out. It slips out of the holster. Oh, well. That's no big deal. I'll put it in my pocket. Nick said for me to keep it in the holster at all times when it's in my car until we can get me a carry permit, which I'm still wrestling with that idea. He said that it was to stay in my locked glove compartment in my locked car when I'm at work or out in the field at residences. He said I didn't have to have a carry permit for it to be in my car or my house.

He stressed to me that even if I go in my condo for a few minutes, to carry it with me. I asked him *why*. He simply said *safety*.

I slip it in my pocket before stepping out of my car, and as I open my door, I'm shoved from behind into my condo before I can react or even think. The door slams behind me and the other person. I whirl around and see Lacey Carter standing in front of me. I'm not only looking at her but at the wrong end of her gun. *Oh, shit.* This woman has completely gone off her rocker over Nick, and she has come after me. What she says, I never see coming.

"Where're the pictures?" Her voice is ice cold. I want to sink into the floor and lose it. *Don't panic.* I've got at least fifty thoughts running through my head at once. The first one being that I don't want to die. "Where are the fucking pictures?"

I hear her talking to me, but I'm so focused on that gun. I don't want to be shot.

"I don't know what you're talking about." It comes out much calmer than what I'm feeling inside. How does she know that I know about the pictures?

"You know exactly what I'm talking about. Don't play stupid. I want to know where those pictures are." She's waving that gun around.

I don't know what the hell I'm going to do to get myself out of this. I've got to keep this woman talking. I don't know why. It seems like that might be a good idea.

I shake my head slowly at her. "Lacey, I don't know what you're talking about."

"Bitch, I'm not asking again. Where are they?"

"I don't know. You're going to shoot me regardless of what I say."

She starts to smile, and I go cold. "You're not going to die that easily. First, I'm going to carve into you like Greg Miller and I did that little whore that was found on Arnoldsville Road. You'll tell me."

It feels like my knees are going to buckle under me. *Misty.*

"You *and* Greg Miller killed Misty." It's not a question.

Lacey Carter is the unidentified woman in the pictures. She's Jillian Ross. She was able to pass herself off as a Sergeant because she was a Detective. She had to have been the one who got into that evidence room. Who would ask questions as to why she's there? Who would suspect her?

"All those girls. Did Nick know?" *Please tell me he didn't know. Please tell me he didn't know.*

"The Boy Scout? No. Nick's a true cop. He follows all the rules to the letter. It's a bit sickening. He's a good lover, though, isn't he? I can't understand what he sees in you and why he can't leave you alone."

I care nothing of Lacey talking about Nick being a good lover. Maybe another day, yes, but staring at her gun and knowing her involvement in this, no, I don't give a shit at all.

"Lacey, why? Why all those girls?"

As I'm talking, I remember, *I have a gun.* My hand goes to my pocket. Could I? I feel sick. This woman carries a gun for a living. She has to qualify every year in order to keep carrying that gun. I've shot my gun one time. I'm comfortable with it, but I'm not *that* comfortable. I don't have any other options. I'm not going to be able to talk my way out of this. She's going to kill me, and it's going to be painful. She knows where Naomi is.

"Where's my sister?"

"You mean Naomi?" She does know my sister, but how does she know Naomi's my sister? She has to know where she is. She laughs. It sends chills all the way down my spine. "I bet you would love to know how I know little Naomi is your sister and where she is. This is so fucking fantastic."

That makes me angry. My adrenaline's flowing through me now.

"I want to know where my sister is," I say with more resolve.

"Go to hell," she snarls.

"You first."

It all happens so fast. My hand wraps around my gun, and it's out, up, and I pull the trigger before I realize I've pulled it. I hear it go off twice. I must've shot her because I hear her scream and see her go down, but not before I hear her gun go off. I feel something hot graze an area around my shoulder.

Lacey's gurgling, and then there's nothing but a roaring in my ears and the strong odor of gun powder hanging in the room. I don't know where I hit her. I don't walk over to her. I don't want to see it. I put the gun on my counter, and with trembling hands, I pick up our landline, sinking to the floor. My cell's in the car. It takes me two tries to dial Nick's number.

"Hey, ba-"

"Nick," I say, cutting him off. "I need you to come to the condo. I need you, and you need to bring people." My voice is shaky.

"Grace, what's wrong?" I can hear he's on the move.

"I've shot Lacey, and I think she's dead. I need you here."

"Grace, I'm coming. Don't hang up with me, baby. Hold on." I hear him tell someone to contact dispatch and have the closest patrol unit at my condo as well as EMS. I also hear him saying to call the GBI and then to call Brison Scott. He's giving a quick rundown of what he knows to this person. "Baby, I'm finding Chris, and we'll be there. Stay with me." Wherever he goes, he's telling Chris what's happened.

"What the fuck?" I hear Chris exclaim in the background. I hear him tell Nick to go, and that he'll find Sergeant Jenkins and will be right behind him.

I think Nick's running. It sounds like it when he starts talking to me. "Baby, I'm coming. Did she hurt you?"

"No."

"Are you still inside your condo?"

"Yes."

"Can you walk outside?"

"She's blocking the door. I don't want to walk around her, Nick." My voice sounds small.

"Stay where you are, baby. You're doing great. Where's your .380?"

"On the counter."

"I've got to get on with dispatch, but stay on the line with me."

"Okay," I say, my voice shaking.

I hear him talking with someone, giving more details. I hear sirens in the distance, and then they get closer.

"Baby, they know you're in there. They know that Lacey is lying at the door. They're going to come in with their weapons drawn, but don't be scared. They aren't aiming at you."

"Okay." My voice is still shaky. I'm losing it. I feel it. I'm starting to shake all over. Nick's talking to me in a calm voice, but it's tight.

"Grace. It's Blake Scott. I'm coming in." I hear at my door. He opens the door and has to push on it to get in. He looks down at Lacey and then at me, holstering his gun.

"Is that Blake?" Nick asks me.

"Yes."

"I'll be there in two minutes, baby. Stay on the phone with me."

Blake's hovered over Lacey, checking for a pulse with one hand while talking into the radio that's clipped at his shoulder. I see other officers coming in behind him, along with EMS. He comes over and kneels in front of me.

"Are you hurt?" he asks me.

"No."

He looks me over. "You've been shot," he says calmly. Nick's response is so loud that I jerk the phone away from my ear. "Is that Nick?"

"Yes."

"Let me talk to him." I hand the phone to him and look at my arm. I notice for the first time the tear in my blouse and the blood where my shoulder muscle ends. All I think of is that my whole outfit's going in the trash. "Calm down," Blake tells Nick. "She's okay. It nicked her at the surface of her skin. It looks more like a cross between a cut and a burn than a gunshot. It's not serious *or* life threatening. You're going to make her deaf, and I'm sure her ears are ringing already." He pulls the phone away from his ear, and all I hear is Nick ranting loudly. "I'm hanging up on you. I've got her." He's really calm. He clicks the off button while Nick's still ranting and sets the phone on the counter.

It begins to get chaotic quickly. EMS has been working over Lacey, but they determine that she's gone. Blake motions for one of them to come over to me. A really nice-looking woman comes to me, kneeling in the same fashion that Blake is. I'm still huddled against my cabinets and haven't moved. She smiles kindly at me. I must look like a frightened child. Her voice is soft when she speaks to me.

"I'm going to look at your arm." She puts on a fresh pair of gloves.

I nod my head. Nick bursts through the open door like a tornado. His face looks pale and drawn. He glances down at Lacey and takes the few short steps to me and kneels down, just like everyone else is, staring at Blake for a hard minute. Then, he focuses on me, taking my left hand, pulling it to his lips.

"No shrinking daisy." He smiles, but it doesn't reach his eyes. The tears start rolling down my cheeks. "Baby, I'm here." He looks over at the lady who's examining my arm.

"Nick. It was Lacey. She's the other woman," I whisper.

I see the expression on his face, and my heart sinks. *He knew.*

"It's going to be okay," he says softly, acting as if he didn't hear me.

"Blake's right. It grazed her," the lady says, looking at me. "You're very lucky. All you need's a bandage. Does it hurt?"

"No," I whisper.

"I'm pretty sure you're in shock right now. It's going to hurt later. It may burn as well. I'm going to clean it out really well, put some antibiotic ointment on it and get you a bandage and wrap it. I'm also going to put something on it that will keep it numb for several hours. It'll probably start to bother you late tonight. Take some Tylenol. If it starts to look infected or doesn't seem to be healing properly, get with your doctor. You may end up needing some antibiotics for it, but I think it'll be okay."

"Okay. Thank you."

The lady stands. "She's a pretty girl, Nick."

"Thanks, Becca," he says, still looking at me. "Let's get you off of this hard floor and move to the couch, okay?"

I nod. He stands and pulls me up. We move into my living area, and he wraps his arms around me. I wrap mine around his waist, burying my face in his chest. I pretend that everything's okay, that none of this has happened, that I don't know the things that I know and that I'm not suspecting things that I suspect. I want to keep that fantasy going... forever.

Chapter Twenty-Nine

Oh God, he knew. That plays in my mind, over and over, and I continue to cry while he holds me, with his face buried in my hair. I hear more people coming in. I hear more voices, including Chris's familiar voice coming closer, and I can tell that he's standing near us.

"Nick. I need you to let her go, so I can bandage her arm. I'll give her back." I hear Becca say.

Nick doesn't immediately let me go. He puts both hands on my face and looks in my eyes, finally releasing me, moving to talk with Chris, Sergeant Jenkins, Brison Scott and his Chief Assistant District Attorney, whom I don't know, but she's an attractive woman who looks to be in her fifties. There's another man with a gun and badge, but I don't know him either. They all have the same look on their faces: *Why was Lacey here in my condo with her gun out, and why is she now dead?* What're they going to think when they find out? Do they know? Am I the only fool here? I sit on the couch with Becca, who's still smiling at me.

"So, you're the girl that's gotten Nick Bassano's heart."

She's steadily working on my arm. I hear what she's saying, but right at this moment, it's not something that I want to talk about or think about, because really, do I have it? Did I ever? What's beginning to flood my mind are thoughts that I wish would stay away.

"I'm sorry," she says, "I was curious." I look at her. I've not said anything. "Whatever it is that you're doing, keep doing it. I've never seen him look happier." She finishes with what she's doing and looks at me. "Do you remember what I told you to do if it starts to hurt?"

I nod and say, "Tylenol."

"You're good to go," she says. She stands and says something to the group that has formed and leaves.

Nick's engaged in a conversation with Brison and looks at me occasionally. He knew it was her when he saw those pictures. He knew whose body he was looking at. He had to. The total relief that I felt when he burst through the door is being replaced by a nagging fear that I've been played by him in the worst way.

There's another man that walks through the door. He's about an inch or two shorter than Nick, looking like he might be in his mid-forties.

"Bill," Nick says, walking to him. The two shake hands.

"Nick," he says.

The man, Bill, stops and looks at Lacey, kneeling down beside her and does what looks like an inspection of some sort. He stands and looks briefly at my gun that still sits on the counter. There are other people that follow him. When they turn their backs to me, I see GBI displayed across the back of their jackets. They look like they might be GBI CSU, and I'm right. They get right to work. Bill stands and walks with Nick to me. I look up at the man expectantly.

"I'm Special Agent Bill Killinger with the GBI," he says, holding out his hand to me.

"I'm Grace Harrison." My voice is shaky.

He takes a seat beside me on one side, while Nick sits on the other. They have a brief discussion over Nick wanting to get me out of here, and Bill Killinger says he wants me to take him through what happened. All of the chairs at my table have been filled, along with the overstuffed chair that sits in the corner and the recliner. Everyone's here to listen to this story. They're going to get an earful, or are they?

Nick says that he needs to tell him about what's been happening, and he does that. I can see the others don't understand why he needs to tell Agent Killinger what he and Chris have been working on and how that relates to a dead DA Investigator on my kitchen floor. They're about to find out, if they don't already know. He tells the whole story, starting with Misty's murder, to the Bradberry murder, how I became involved and what I did. The look on Bill Killinger's face shows that he completely disapproves of my involvement.

Nick fills in minor details as Agent Killinger asks for them. He takes him through me identifying the girls and Naomi being one of them leading up to the break in of the evidence room, the meeting that they all had over what to do with the pictures in order to protect them and the decision made to hide the pictures here in the condo.

Agent Killinger is very vocal of his disapproval of the pictures being here and how bad of an idea that was. *Total agreement on that.* I hear my landline ringing, and I let it go unanswered. My heads snaps in the direction of the phone when I hear Valerie's worried voice wanting to know where I am.

"I'll call her," Chris says.

"Thanks," I say to him.

Agent Killinger looks at Brison. "You approved of this woman helping?"

What? This woman? I get the distinct feeling that it's not just that Agent Killinger disapproves of me but dislikes me.

"Yes. We didn't know exactly what we were dealing with, and we didn't know who all was involved. Nick came to me and said that he trusts Grace. He said he not only trusts her, but she's knowledgeable and competent. I trust Nick. She helped identify girls that we otherwise might not have known for some time. It wasn't ideal, but it's not an ideal situation. We decided we needed to be creative. Grace was that creativity. Bill, she not only identified these girls, but she has a relationship with a population and an ability to mix in with them that the detectives didn't have. I feel like she's been vital in this investigation, and I wouldn't change the way things were done." I see Brison looking at Nick, wondering where this is all going and how it's going to end.

Agent Killinger isn't satisfied with Brison's answer. He focuses his attention back to me. "Where'd you get the .380?"

"Nick gave it to me."

"When?"

"For my birthday on Saturday."

"You have a relationship with Nick?"

"Yes," Nick answers before I do.

"Don't answer my questions, Nick," he tells him. "What happened here?",

"I shot her." I sound calm. It's deceptive. I don't feel that way. I don't feel as panicked as I did, but my voice is too calm.

"I see that. How did she get into your condo?"

"I came home from work to change my pants." I point to the ink stain that's visible. "When I was walking in, she pushed me from behind and had her gun pointed at me."

"Where was your .380?"

"In my pocket."

"If you were coming home to change and leave, why did you have it in your pocket?" Agent Killinger's voice is hard.

"Nick told me to always bring it in the condo with me. He said he didn't care how long I was in here."

"So you keep it in your car?" The hardness in his voice remains. I answer his question by nodding. "Where's the holster?"

"Still in the car. I was pulling the whole thing out of my glove box, and it slipped out and I didn't think it would matter since I was going to be in and out. I stuck it in my pocket."

"She pushed you from behind?"

"Yes."

"You didn't call her to come to your condo?"

What? I shake my head, confused. "No. Why would I do that?"

"To get her out of the way."

I have no idea what he's talking about.

"I don't understand," I tell him.

"You're Nick's girlfriend. You wanted to get the other girlfriend out of the way."

"Lacey was not my girlfriend." Nick's voice is like steel.

This man thinks I shot Lacey to get her out of the way. I'm shaking my head furiously at Agent Killinger, showing that he's got it all wrong, but he's focused on Nick.

"You had a relationship with Lacey, Nick," Agent Killinger says to him.

"We dated casually. It's different."

"She was going to shoot me," I say and keep talking. "Lacey came here for the pictures. She wanted to know where they were. She helped kill Misty. There's a woman in the pictures. She was the woman." It all comes out in a rush.

I look around me, and everyone's shocked. Everyone except Nick. I can feel my world caving in around me. This is a huge revelation to everyone. The room has gone completely silent except for the voices of CSU and all that they're doing.

"Lacey Carter was involved with the kidnapping and raping of seven girls, including your sister?"

"Eight including Misty," I whisper. No one is moving a muscle

"She told you this?"

Sort of. "Yes."

"Did you tell her that the pictures were here?"

"No."

The questions continue. He has me show him how she pushed in on me. We do it in the living area, since Lacey's body is still on my kitchen floor. I show him exactly what happened. He asks the same questions over and over and then in different ways. I keep up the best that I can, but I'm giving out.

Chris eventually tells me that Valerie wanted to come here, and he told her no. He said for me to call Valerie when I can. I don't know when that will be. I don't know if I'll be able to go back to work tomorrow.

It's afternoon before Lacey's body is taken away. I've watched as CSU has looked in my ceiling, walked up my stairs and back down again, only to go back up and down several more times. I don't know what they're doing. The questions begin to wind down.

"Your .380 has to go to evidence until this is cleared up," Agent Killinger says to me.

"Take it. I don't want it."

Not many people have left. I don't think Brison, his Chief Assistant, whom I've learned is Casey Cain, and the other man who is Brison's Chief Investigator, know what to do with themselves or what to think about the information that I've given them. Surely, they don't think that I shot Lacey to get rid of her. Do they?

Agent Killinger tells me that he'll be in touch, and that at this time, he's not going to file any charges against me. *That was a possibility?* He stands, and Nick stands with him. People begin to file out, until all that remain are Nick, Chris and Agent Killinger, who's lingering in the kitchen with CSU. They look like they may be getting close to finishing. I don't know.

Nick sits beside me, taking my hand, and I pull it away.

"You knew," I say to him. "You knew it was her."

"I didn't know."

I'm not buying it. "Those times we saw her, and you were so uncomfortable with it, it was because you knew." We stare at one another, and I keep talking. "That night at The Grill, when Chris mentioned the pictures being under a different case name, it was because of her. That's why you didn't want to take them to Brison." My heart's pounding in a sick way. I swallow hard and continue to stare at him, waiting for his response.

Chris walks away from us and into the kitchen. I don't think he wants to witness this.

"I was suspicious, but I didn't know for sure," he says.

I look at him incredulously. "And you said nothing to me. You know what? That's okay, because you don't have to explain things to me, but did you tell Chris? Did you tell your partner that you were *suspicious*?" He says nothing but looks at me. I continue to speak. "Did you tell Brison, or your Sergeant, or the Chief? Did you tell anybody that needed to know, Nick?" I laugh softly, but it's full of bitterness. "On Friday, when the whole thing came up about someone impersonating a Sergeant in the department, were you still just *suspicious* of her?" I sit back and stare hard at him. "You couldn't swallow that pride, could you? That's why you chose not to say anything."

We continue to stare at one another. I don't even know what to feel. I'm not sure if I can allow myself to feel anything right now.

"I don't know what you want me to say," he says.

Well, I know what I'm going to say. "You don't have to say anything, Nick. That seems to have worked out really well for you. If you'll excuse me, I'm going to go pack some of my things and figure out where the hell I'm going to stay tonight and possibly tomorrow. I don't even know if Jess and I'll be able to come back here."

I shove my way past CSU and Chris, and stomp up my steps to my bedroom. I should walk out and forget about even taking anything, but it feels like a normal thing to do, and right now, I need something normal. I dig around my various drawers, pulling out bras, panties, socks and other things that I probably won't need, but it's mindless, and I don't have to think about it. I throw clothes on my bed, going to my closet, find my overnight bag and pull some work clothes off the hangers. I don't know if I'll need them, but it's best to be prepared. I dump everything on my bed and feel Nick walk in my bedroom.

"You know, it's not like I can call my mother up and ask if I can stay with her, or swing by my brother's place and crash on his couch."

I keep my back to him. I pull my bag off my bed, walk in my bathroom and pack all of the toiletries that I think I'll need. Nick's still standing in the same spot, watching me.

"Can you stay at Jake's with Jess?" His voice is quiet, cautious.

It hurts me that he doesn't offer for me to stay with him. It all hurts.

"It's a one bedroom apartment, you moron." I turn around and look at him. "Why did you bring those pictures here? I really want to know. It was such an asinine idea, and I haven't been able to figure out why in the world you would want them to be here. Tell me, Nick. It all had to do with *her*, didn't it?"

He looks down at me. "I've told you. We've had that conversation. I felt like this would be the best place. They would be safe here. No one outside our circle knew about you being involved in this. No one would think to look here for them. We were taking a chance with them anyplace else."

He's lying straight to my face and not blinking at all over it. *Oh my God, what did I get myself into with him? Why did I have to fall in love with him?* I pull my bag off the bed and sling it over my shoulder. I walk to him, and he moves so I can get out of my room.

"But you weren't taking a chance with my safety for them to be here with me, because my safety means nothing to you." It's not a question, and he says nothing. "Take the pictures. Take the safe. I'm done," I say, going down the stairs. I get back to the first floor and look at Agent Killinger. "Can I leave?" I think my expression is that I'm not to be trifled with right at this moment.

"Yes, you can go," he says.

"Grace," Chris says.

"No. Don't. I'm leaving," I snap, turning and walking out of the condo.

There are some passers-by that slow their cars, wondering what's going on. It's still early enough in the day that most people are probably at work. I look at my watch. Dammit. I've got to intercept Jess before she gets here. She can't come home to this. I wonder if I need to go pack her some things too. I can't go back in there. She probably has plenty of things between her parents' house and Jake's to get her through a few days. I have no idea where I'm going to stay. I have to call Jess, and then I'll worry about what to do. I throw my things in the car and pull my phone out of my handbag.

"Grace," Nick calls, walking out of my condo and straight to me.

The hurt, the rage, the fear and the betrayal by him all come out of me at once. I rush him and pound him over and over again on his chest.

"You set me up!" I scream. "How could you do that to me? You set me up, and I killed her! Did you ever give a shit about me? Did I ever matter to you, or was it all just about getting me in bed? Was it all a lie Nick? Were we a lie?" I'm breathing hard, crying and causing a scene.

Those that are still here, including Chris, Agent Killinger and the remainder of CSU, stop what they're doing and are witness to my losing it. They're all trying not to watch and trying to get back to doing something. Especially Chris. He doesn't want to see this.

"I didn't set you up."

"Why did you get me that gun? Why?"

"I wanted you to be safe."

"I *was* safe! I was *fine*! Then you dragged me into this! You used me, Nick! Don't you dare deny it! You had to know it was her the first time you saw those pictures! Don't give me the bullshit about being suspicious! You fucked her enough times; you had to know whose body you were looking at! You bought me that gun and had me take those pictures to lure her out! I'm not stupid! And here I thought it was so cool and sweet that you bought me something for my birthday, but that goddamn gun had nothing to do with my birthday! It was just part of your plan!"

"Think about what you're saying! It makes no fucking sense! I didn't buy that gun after what happened with the evidence room. Do you really think that about me?" He's yelling back at me now. "You think I would do that to you? There was no fucking plan! I got the gun for you because I wanted to give you something for your birthday, and I wanted you to be safe! I care about you so much that it scares the hell out of me!"

Oh, he's not pulling that shit about how much he cares about me with me right now.

"It's not what I think, Nick! It's what I know!" I yell, still crying.

Jess pulls up at that moment, jumping out of her car, looking terrified. "What the hell's going on?" she demands.

I turn to her, and I know I must look a mess. "The condo's a crime scene," I say to her.

She's looking at me and then to Nick and then back at me.

"What do you mean it's a crime scene? What's going on, Grace?"

"Can we please go?" I'm all but begging here. "I'll explain it. I promise. Can we go to Jake's?"

"Sweetie, you're shaking like a leaf," she says, touching me. She sees my bandaged arm. "What happened to you?"

"I was shot."

Jess's face is horrified. She doesn't know what to say. I'm losing it again, and it's worse this time, because my heart's shattering on top of everything else that has happened. The adrenaline has come and gone, and reality is hitting me hard. Jess looks at Nick.

"What did you do to her?" She demands, angrily. He says nothing to her. She's waiting for an answer. He can't give it to her, because telling the truth is that bad. She looks at me. "Yes, we'll go to Jake's. I'll drive us both. I'm not going to let you drive the way you are. Are we going to be able to come back later or what…?" her voice trails off.

Nick's the one that answers her. "Don't come back here tonight."

"Is there anything that you need?" Jess asks me.

The truth. "It's in my car." I'm all but hyperventilating.

"You go get in my car, and I'll get your things."

I nod and walk to her car.

"Grace," Nick says. It comes out as a plea.

I look at him and shake my head, crying. Jess quickly gets my things, and she's in the car with me.

"My keys," I say through my tears. Jess looks at me. "My keys are in the lock."

She nods understanding and gets out of the car and walks to our door. Nick says something to her, and she says something back to him. He pulls the keys out of the lock, handing them to her and saying something else, to which Jess nods her head. She gets back in the car and takes off down Timothy Road to the bypass towards Jake's apartment complex off of College Station Road.

"What did he say?" I ask, looking over at her.

"That none of it was a lie."

I cry harder. Lady Antebellum is singing about wanting someone more. I can't listen to it.

"Jess, will you change the station?"

"Of course." She switches it to the Athens station that plays dance music. She's got her phone out, most likely calling Jake. "Hey…No, shut up. Grace and I are on the way to your place. We're going to stay there tonight…Our condo's a crime scene…Please don't interrupt me, Jake. Grace's been shot…I said shut up…She's fine. I mean, she's not in the hospital…I don't know what happened. I haven't asked her yet." She glances over at me. "Yes…We'll be there in ten minutes." She hangs up.

All of that thinking that I've been trying not to do isn't working for me any longer. I shot someone. I killed someone. I fell in love with a man who used me. I'm such a damn fool. I'm going to be sick.

"Pull over," I moan.

Jess pulls to the shoulder of the road as quickly as she can. I jump out of the car and do nothing but dry heave. I want to sink to the ground and never, ever get up.

Chapter Thirty

Chris sits beside me on the couch. I alternate between crying and talking. I've been holed up in Jake's apartment all last night and all day. Last night was brutal, and my arm started hurting. Getting shot sucks, even if I was only grazed. I broke down and told Jess everything. I told it all. The only thing I didn't share with her is what Nick has done to me. I can't deal with that right now. I'll handle that later.

I started with Misty's death and ended with shooting and killing Lacey and every awful detail in between. There's nothing that she doesn't know now. I gave her details that she probably wishes I would've kept to myself. Jess finally stopped me, said she knew enough and wasn't sure how she was going to tell her parents. I don't think it matters at this point who knows what.

The Bradberrys are gone. Greg Miller's in jail. Lacey's dead. There's one person left, and I know who it is, but I still can't remember who wears that ring. I've been going over and over in my mind. Is it Simon? I don't think that it is, but I don't know if I think that because I really don't think it? Or is it that I'm in denial that my friend could be wrapped up in all this sickness? That can't be why he stepped away from working with troubled teens. Did he do that so he wouldn't be suspected when all of those girls disappeared? God, not Simon. I didn't discuss that with Jess, either. I can't think of it anymore. I don't care anymore. Let Nick and Chris figure it out.

I meant it when I said I was done. I'm so done. I'm done with it all, including Nick. At least, that's what I'm telling myself. My heart's telling me something different. It's physically painful when I think of him.

Chris is here, trying to talk me into letting him and Nick get the condo cleaned up so Jess and I can go back. He called me last night and said there wasn't much that needed to be done downstairs, but the floor in my bedroom has a big piece of carpet cut out where they determined that the bullet fired from Lacey's gun had lodged. Funny, I didn't notice that yesterday.

"Jess's dad, Max, and Jake went over this morning to look at it. Max is going to have a cleaning crew come in and have the floors professionally cleaned." I'm in the talking phase at the moment. I might cry again momentarily.

"What about that piece of carpet that's missing?"

I shrug my shoulders. "I'll buy a little mat and throw over it. It doesn't matter."

He's silent for a moment looking at me. "I didn't come here only for the condo."

"I didn't think that you did," I say, giving him a slight smile.

"He said he called last night and has tried calling today, and you won't answer his calls."

"That's right."

"I took him out last night because his day got much worse after you left. He got reamed. No, I'm sorry. He was chewed a new ass after the Chief got finished with him. I thought he was going to get suspended pending an internal investigation over possible misconduct. The Chief decided to do an administrative write up. That's never happened to him before, ever. Not in New York, and definitely not here. Then, he got it again from Brison. Brison doesn't yell. I've never heard of that man raising his voice at anyone. You could apparently hear him from down the hall, he was yelling so loud at Nick. He took it like a man. I don't think he cared. He's upset over what's happened to you and with you."

"They aren't happy over Lacey," I say, avoiding the last thing that Chris said.

"Unhappy is putting it mildly."

"How do you feel about it?"

Chris looks thoughtful. "Better, after he explained it to me. He said it wasn't something that he was suspicious over at first." He stops, but

I can tell he wants to keep talking about it. "Grace, I think you need to hear all this from him. He didn't set you up."

"He used me, Chris."

"No, Grace. He didn't." He pauses. "Nick's in love with you. I'm not sure if he's figured that out yet, because I don't think he's ever been in love with anyone other than himself."

I smile at that. "I feel used, Chris. And played."

"I think if you talked to him, you wouldn't feel that way. Let him explain it to you." He looks at his watch. "I've got to go. We're still working an overly active investigation. Are you good if I go?"

"Of course. It was sweet of you to come here."

"Call him, Grace."

I think about it while Jess and Jake both fuss over me. I hold my phone in my hand, my finger hovering over his name. I think about it all night and spend another restless night on Jake's couch. I think of him all night and how I've never felt more alive since he stopped to help me a month ago. How he is. Who he is. His smile, those dimples, his dancing eyes and the way he kisses me; the time that we've spent together, the things that he says, the things that he's done for me, how much fun I've had with him and how he's such a different type of man than what I've been used to, and of course the sex. *Oh, the sex.*

Dawn comes, and I'm sitting in the same spot when Jess and Jake get up that I was in when they went to bed. I'm not going to work today. Valerie told me to take the rest of the week off and the next if I need to. I told her everything, too. She was silent for nearly five minutes and then gave me the name of her therapist. Jess and Jake question leaving me alone. They were both like flies to honey yesterday with me. Jess got a sub and stayed with me all day. I kick her out the door today.

"Go," I say.

"Are you still going to be sitting there when I get back?"

"Maybe, but I will have gone out between now and then."

"What's your heart telling you, Grace?" she asks quietly.

"That I love him and that he used me."

"Are you going to call him?"

"I haven't decided." I smile at her. I know it's a sad smile.

She kisses me on the cheek, tells me that she loves me and that she and Jake are here for me no matter what. Their loyalty means everything to me. I don't see Jake until mid-morning. His advice is really simple; call Nick, and work it out. Yeah, it sounds simple, but it isn't. Max is having the condo cleaned today, but it will be later.

I stay busy with errands, including going to the grocery store to stock Jake's pitiful cabinets and fridge. It's a good thing he has Jess and they're getting married, because the man wouldn't survive feeding himself. I lose myself in the grocery store for over an hour. My mind's never far from Nick. I wonder what he's doing at work, after work, at home. I miss him. God, I miss that man. I miss being up against him. I'm finishing with my shopping when Judge Wright calls me.

"Hello, Your Honor."

"Hello, Grace. It's good to hear your voice. I heard you were attacked in your apartment."

"Yes, sir. I guess Mack told you."

"He did, and I've been very concerned about you. I'm on the bench for most of the day. Would you mind coming to see me later?"

"Of course. I've been wanting to sit down with you. I wasn't able to talk to you much on Saturday. What time would you like for me to be there?"

He tells me the time, and I agree to it. What am I going to say? No?

"I look forward to seeing you, Grace."

"Thank you, Judge Wright. I look forward to seeing you as well."

I pay for the groceries, get them back and stock Jake's place with food. Decent food. I pick at my lunch, think about Nick and think about how Lacey knew where my sister is and probably knew where all the girls are, and that leads me to thinking what I did to Lacey, and then I start to feel queasy. I dump the remainder of my food. When Jess comes in from school, and Jake returns from wherever he's been, they coax me out for dinner, talking me into eating early. Well, they eat. I push my food around and have it boxed up for Jess to take with her.

I make it to the courthouse as it's shutting down, and I spend five minutes convincing court security that I'm seeing Judge Wright, and he's expecting me. Fortunately, there's one guy that I see all the time when I'm in Juvenile Court, and I'm allowed in. The courthouse is all but deserted. When I get to Juvenile Court, even Molly has left for the day. I see Judge Wright's office door is open. I walk in and see him working at his desk.

"Grace," he says, standing and smiling. He walks around his desk and hugs me. "It's good to see you. Please sit."

"It's good to see you, too," I say, taking the offered chair.

"Thank you for coming to see me."

"Thank you for calling me and for your concern. I appreciate it."

He tells me that it's been an empty courtroom without me there. He likes Julie, Cassidy, Mandy and the other Case Workers, but I think I'm the star student with him. I needed that boost. He wants to know how I'm doing but avoids talking about what happened with Lacey. For that, I'm grateful.

I share that I hope I'm never shot again. We talk about Saturday, and he tells me again how pretty I looked. He asks if I had a good birthday. *Yes, I did and then it all went to shit*, but that I don't say. He says that I looked very happy with Nick and that he's not seen me smile that way ever. I may never smile that way again.

"I've been hearing rumors that you were gone because you were helping out the detectives in the Bradberry case. I'm curious how that came about and if that rumor is even true."

I guess there are people who are talking about it now. There's no reason that I can't talk about it. It's Judge Wright, for goodness sake. Can't I tell this man everything? Yes, I can.

"There were some girls that needed to be identified. Nick came to me and asked if I would help. Actually, it was all arranged. I'm not sure why he even asked since it was all done over my head, as well as Mack and Valerie's heads. I think they felt sand bagged by the whole thing. I was able to help, so I guess that's something."

"I don't understand how that relates to Mickey and Eleanor."

"Have you heard anything about the murder investigation?"

"Actually, I haven't. It's been very hush hush, which I've found strange. Even Brison hasn't said much about it."

"There were some pictures found at the Bradberry residence. They were bad. It involves some girls. Naomi was in those pictures." My voice has gone quieter. I've told Judge Wright about Naomi. He knows me well. I've shared so much of my past with him. He's always so easy to talk to and has always been supportive.

"Oh, Grace," he groans. "I'm sorry." He puts his elbows on his desk and steeples his hands, while regarding me.

Sometimes evil stares you right in the face, and you're too blind to see it. Looking at him with his hands up, I see it. *The ring.* The room's spinning, but I'm absolutely still. I go cold, and then I go very cold. I feel goose pimples break out all over me. I feel queasy and then all-out nauseous, but I swallow it all down. My mind goes blank, and then I think, *I have to get out of here.* I try to keep my face impassive. I must not be succeeding.

"Grace, are you okay?"

I nod my head. "Yes." That needed to come out stronger. "What time is it?"

He looks at me strangely and checks his watch. "Close to six."

"I'm so sorry. With all that's been happening, I forgot that Nick wants me to meet him at The Globe." I stand, too quickly, I believe, and I scream internally to calm down and slow down.

Judge Wright regards me with a questioning expression and then says, "Well, I'm very happy that I was able to see you. Please tell Nick that I said hello and what a great job he's doing."

"I will."

I try not to rush out of there. I don't see court security anywhere. I don't see anybody that can help me. No, not Judge Wright. *Call Nick.* This isn't happening. *Call Nick.* I keep walking, and I'm in the parking deck. I can't think. *Call Nick!* I have to do everything in steps. Put hand in pocket. Wrap hand around phone. Pull phone out of pocket. Pull up Nick's name. Hit call button.

"Grace." His voice is flooded with relief.

"Nick." My voice is fueled with anxiety and fear, and all I can manage to choke out is, "Judge Wright...The ring." Then, the world goes black.

Chapter Thirty-One

The first thing I feel is my head pounding. The second is vibration underneath me. I open my eyes, and it's dark. At first, I think I've gone blind, but feeling the vibration and hearing a humming sound, I realize that I'm in a trunk of a moving car. Judge Wright's moving car. *Oh, shit. I'm in big trouble.* I have to tell myself not to panic. I have to tell it more than once. Panic equals death. This is scarier than staring down Lacey Carter's barrel. At least, I was armed with her. I've got nothing here. Nick doesn't have a clue as to where I am. *I* don't know where the fuck I am.

All I know is when we get to where we're going, he's going to kill me. I have a decision to make. Fight or let him kill me. Nick isn't going to save me at the last minute. He's not going to ride in on his white horse and scoop me up. I'm all on my own, and it's all me. Dammit, my head hurts. I start thinking about Judge Wright and what he's done. I can't allow myself to think that right now. I have to concentrate on a plan.

I make the decision that I'm not going to willingly let him kill me. I'm not going down without a fight. I may lose in the end, but I can't think of that. I'm in total survival mode. I start feeling around for an internal trunk release. I can't see a damn thing. The harder I concentrate on what I'm doing, the worse my head hurts.

I've made the decision that if I can find the damn release, as soon as the car stops, I'm jumping and running as fast as I can. I don't care if I'm in the middle of a field with nothing in any direction. I'm making a run for it. If he catches me, well then, shit. I don't know. But I'm running.

My hand brushes over something, and I go back to it. I think this is it. I keep my hand on it and wait for an opportunity. When the car begins to slow and then stop, I yank with everything in me, and I see daylight flooding. I pop out and see very shocked faces in the car behind me as well as the car beside it. Judge Wright's car speeds away as I hit the pavement on my knees and my right elbow. Dammit, that hurt too.

I look around me and see that I'm on Atlanta Highway at the red light where New Jimmie Daniels Road runs to the south and Trade Street runs north. There are cars that are traveling from the west, and while some resume their travel when the light turns green, there are several people who have stopped and gotten out of their cars. The people in the car behind me have gotten out and have run to me. The woman's on the phone, and from the sound of it, she's on the phone with 911. There's more than one person on the phone.

"Are you okay?" the man asks me.

"Tell them to send Nick Bassano," I say, looking up at him. The man looks at me, not understanding. "Tell them to send Nick Bassano," I say again, this time to the woman.

"She says to send Nick Bassano," the woman says. The woman nods and looks at me. "Are you Grace Harrison?"

"Yes."

"She said she's Grace Harrison."

I'm still on the pavement but trying to stand. The man helps me up, and I immediately feel dizzy. My head's hurting even worse, and my knees and elbow have started to throb along with my gunshot wound. I'm a damn mess. I grab at my head. I hear sirens.

The woman is still on the phone. She answers a few more questions and then hangs up. There's a crowd forming, and traffic's getting congested as more people have stopped, and those that haven't are beginning to rubberneck. I see more than one patrol car. The man that helped me up has his hand at my left elbow, holding me.

"Grace Harrison?" the officer asks, approaching me.

"Yes," I say.

My hand's at the back of my head where most of the pain is, but I feel it in the front as well. Simply put, I hurt. I'm going to kick that son of a bitch in his balls if I ever see him again. I see one officer talking to the woman who was on the phone, and she's pointing in the direction that Judge Wright's car went. I see that officer talk into his radio.

"We've been looking for you. What happened to you? Is there something wrong with your head?"

"I think I got hit in the head from the back," I say, cringing.

I see Nick's car. It doesn't seem that he's put it all the way in park before he's out and running toward me. The man lets go of me as Nick approaches. He wraps his arms around me, saying nothing, and right now, right here in his arms is the only place I want to be.

"What happened?" he asks, looking down at me with an expression that is a mixture of fear and relief. I'm having a hard time focusing on him as I look up at him.

"I think he hit me in the head from behind."

I see other patrol cars approach and then move past us with blue lights and sirens going. Nick's hands go in my hair, gently probing. I flinch when he finds where I was hit.

"Yeah, you've got some swelling going on." He sees my elbow and that it's scratched up. "Are you hurt anywhere else?"

"I banged both knees."

He kneels down and pulls both legs of my loose cotton pants up to inspect them. Chris has found us.

"Eric Wright's car has been spotted on 316 headed west. Oconee and Barrow have been notified. They're out, alert and ready."

Nick looks up at him. "What've they been told?"

"That he's become a suspect in the kidnapping, rape and possible murder of six girls, the kidnapping and rape of another girl and the kidnapping of an ACCPD Detective's girlfriend. We've got his car description and his tag. We've given all the information out to both counties. We didn't want him to blow through and leave them with their dicks in their hands."

Nick stands and says, "I need to get Grace to the hospital. The bastard hit her in the head."

"I guess we'll be adding battery and possibly agg assault along with kidnapping. I'm going to beat him with my gun when he's found. Come on, I'll go with you. Brit's working tonight." Chris looks at me. "Thank God you're safe. I think Nick's aged twenty years in the near twenty-five minutes that we've been looking for you. You're getting the VIP treatment."

"Thanks," I say.

Nick keeps his arm wrapped around me, which is good because I stumble all over the place. I'm gripping his waist.

"Grace?" Nick says, concerned.

I'm still holding my head. "I'm really dizzy, and my head hurts."

I feel my feet leave the ground as he scoops me up. I don't complain. I put my head on his shoulder and close my eyes.

"Does that feel better, baby?" he murmurs.

"Yes," I whisper.

I feel better being with him. I'm not done with him. I still love him. There are things to work out, but right now he's here with me, and I'm safe with him. We ride in silence with one another.

I can't think of anything that's happened because there's too much pain in my head. I can't concentrate on anything else. That may not be a bad thing. I'm not so sure I can deal with everything all at once. There's so much shit to dig through. I can hear Nick talking on his phone, but I keep my eyes closed. He's talking about me, but I don't know who he's talking to.

"She's safe...Yes, it was him...He hit her in the head...On the Atlanta Highway...No, he got away...He's headed west. Oconee and Barrow have been given all the information on him as well as what he's driving...I'm taking her to Athens Regional...Okay...Yeah, we'll meet you there...Five minutes...I will...Bye."

I open my eyes and look at him. "Who was that?"

He glances over at me and smiles softly. It's the first time he's smiled since reaching me. "Jess. She and Jake will meet us there." He takes a deep breath and expels all of his air out. "I don't know what's been worse, Grace, Lacey threatening you with a weapon or Eric Wright kidnapping you. The end result was going to be the same; I was going to lose you. I could almost stomach you walking away from me again. Almost. But the thought of you dying..."

I look at his profile. He looks grim.

"I wasn't going down without a fight," I say. I see him smile at that. God Almighty, those dimples.

He glances at me. "No shrinking daisy."

"No, not today."

"I underestimated you when we first met. Since I've gotten to know you, I don't think I'll ever do that again."

We're at the hospital. He parks in a location that I wonder if he can park there, and I see it is reserved for Law Enforcement. Chris wheels in behind us. I move to get out, and Nick picks me up, carrying me in. We don't go through the front but in where EMS arrives. We bypass checking in. VIP indeed. There's a pretty, petite, strawberry blonde at a nurse's station. She's very attractive with her long hair that looks tousled. I see that it's wavy at the ends. She looks up and sees the three of us come through the sliding doors. The smile on her face and the expression that these two are familiar to her tells me this must be Brit. I'm right.

"We're ready for her," she says. She has the nicest Southern voice. Her accent sounds a lot like mine. Nick follows her, with Chris behind. She turns around as she's walking. "I'm Brit. I'm so happy to meet you. I wish it wasn't here though."

"Me too. I'm really happy to meet you too," I say, smiling. Shit, smiling like that hurts.

Nick eases me down on the hospital bed in a room.

"Chris called and said y'all were coming." She looks over at her husband, and there's nothing but love in her eyes for him. He's looking at her in the same way. I think the world of Chris, and I immediately like Brit. She starts fussing around me. She hooks me up to the blood pressure machine and slips a Pulse Oximeter on my finger. She then takes my temperature. "You're running a fever."

"How high is it?" Nick asks.

"101.4. It's not bad," she says, smiling at me.

Jess rushes in the room with Jake behind her. She takes one look at me and starts sobbing.

"Okay," Jake says softly. "You said you weren't going to do this."

"I can't help it," she says through her tears. Jess comes over to me and bends down to hug me. "When Nick called me, wanting to know where you were, and then told me that you called him, and then nothing, I didn't know what to think."

"I'll be back, Grace. I'm going to get an IV for you," Brit says.

"Thanks," I say. Chris follows her out. "It's okay, Jess. I'm fine."

She stands up and wipes her face. "No, you're not. You're in the ER after getting kidnapped, getting hit in the head and all that after being shot!"

"I'm here, and I'm going to be fine."

"What happened, Grace?" she asks, calming down.

"I'm not ready to talk about it. I don't want to deal with it right now. My head hurts too bad."

"See, you aren't fine."

Brit breezes back in the room with Chris on her heels. She hooks me up to an IV, which is possibly the most unpleasant experience of everything. God, I hate needles. I can do a tattoo but not a needle going in a vein. I hate it. I won't watch her put it in. I look at Nick instead.

"Are you okay?" he asks me.

"I can deal with anything but IV needles."

Everyone lets out some anxious laughter, but not me, because I feel certain laughing would hurt too damn bad.

"Getting shot and kidnapped's okay, but not the needles," Nick says, looking at me. I can see some life in his eyes that hasn't been there.

The IV is in, and then Brit cleans the nasty abrasion on my elbow. She changes the bandage to my gunshot wound and tells me to take it off tomorrow and leave it off. She looks at my knees, which are bruising and sore. Max and Susan Rider come in, and Susan cries too.

"I don't know what we would do if we lost you," she says, hugging me.

I've been doing great with feeling emotional. I've been pretty numb, but Susan being here and how motherly she has always been with me makes the tears start. They trickle down my cheeks at first. Then, they roll, and then I'm sobbing along with Jess and Susan. Nick, Max and Jake look at one another for a moment, not sure what to do. They move to comfort us, and we wave them off. We need to have a moment. An ER doctor walks in and sees the three of us. Susan is sitting on one side, while Jess is sitting on the other. We're still crying but trying to get it together.

"Ms. Harrison. I'm Dr. Wylie."

"Hi," I say, wiping my eyes and blowing my nose in a very un-ladylike way.

Susan stands so Dr. Wylie can get to me.

"Tell me what's going on with you?" Dr. Wylie says.

"I was hit in the back of the head."

He puts his hands in my hair and feels all over my head, not just the back. When he finds the knot, I wince.

"That's a nasty bump. Did you lose consciousness?" He continues to examine my head.

"Yes, I think I did."

"Do you know for how long?"

"No."

He moves his hand around to the front, finding another tender spot and then checks my eyes.

"What's the last thing you remember?"

"Calling Nick," I say, pointing to him.

"What do you remember after that?"

"Waking up in a trunk and realizing that I was in trouble."

He continues with the questions.

"What's your name?"

"Grace."

"I want you to give me your full name."

"Grace Adeline Harrison."

"How old are you?"

"Twenty-nine. I mean thirty. Sorry. I recently turned thirty."

"Do you know where you are?"

"Athens."

"How're you feeling?"

"I hurt. I'm dizzy, and I'm starting to feel sleepy."

He looks at my elbow, my knees and then sits on the edge of the bed where Susan was sitting. "I think you have a mild concussion. You have a knot about this big in the back of your head." He holds up his hands and makes a small circle, indicating its size. "I believe after you were hit, you fell hitting the front of your head. You're symptomatic of a mild concussion. I'm going to keep you here for a few hours and monitor you."

"What about a CT Scan?" Nick asks him.

"That's one of the reasons why I want to keep her here for a few hours. I don't think a CT Scan is needed, but if she begins to have deteriorating neurological functioning, then, yes, a CT Scan will be ordered.

She's thinking clearly. Her memory's good. Right now, I think what she needs are for the lights to be turned off and rest, and I'm going to order something for pain." Dr. Wylie looks at me. "How does that sound to you?"

I see Nick pull his phone out, look at it and then hand it off to Chris, who leaves the room with it. What's that about? I focus my attention back on Dr. Wylie.

"Fine," I say, offering a slight smile.

"Dr. Wylie, do you think she was struck in the head with something other than a fist?" Nick asks.

"Yes. I think she was struck with an object."

Chris comes back in the room and says, "GBI."

Nick nods and looks at me. "Agent Killinger needs to ask you some questions about what happened."

I groan. Dr. Wylie speaks before I can. "She needs to rest. Can she answer questions later?"

"Nick, what's he going to ask me about Lacey? I don't know what else to tell him."

"No, baby. He's coming to talk to you about Wright."

I know I look confused, because I am confused.

"The department isn't going to investigate your kidnapping, Grace," Chris says to me. He sees that doesn't clear it up for me. "You're the girlfriend of a Detective, remember?"

I put my head back and close my eyes. Am I? Is that what I am to Nick?

"Yes, she can answer questions later." Chris finally answers the doctor.

I hear the doctor walk out. I don't feel like I can open my eyes. I hear more chairs being brought in. Everyone's starting to talk. I hear Chris on the phone with Agent Killinger. Max, Susan, Jess and Jake are talking about anything and everything. I feel Brit's hands on me, but I still don't open my eyes.

"I'm going to put some medicine in your IV, Grace. It's going to make you sleepy, and it will help the pain."

"Thank you."

The lights over the bed go off. I begin to drift in and out of sleep. Sometimes, I dream, but they're flashes of dreams, and while the pictures make sense and I know who all the people are, I don't think I would be able to form it into words what I see playing out in my head. Nick's there. He's always there, but I can't figure out what he's doing. Matt's there. Naomi's there. I let my mind rest and don't think of anything that's happened in the last few days.

When I'm not in a state of dream sleep, I hear the muted voices around me. I feel Nick holding my hand, pulling his fingers through my hair. I feel his fingers tracing my nose, over my closed eyes, down to my lips. I feel his presence. I hear the buzz of the blood pressure machine and then the pressure of the cuff from time to time. I hear people shuffling in and out of the room. I hear people walking up and down the hall. Someone's phone buzzes. Someone shifts in a chair, and then I'm gone again.

Chapter Thirty-Two

I feel warm, familiar hands softly stroking my cheek. I open my eyes and see Nick looking at me with his dark eyes. The only light is flooding in from the hall. We're alone. He's still here. I can feel my heart beating faster.

"Hey," he whispers.

"Hey. How long have I been asleep?"

"Three hours."

I know I must look surprised. "That long?"

"You needed it, plus Brit pumped you full of Hydrocodone. How're you feeling?"

"Like someone punched me in the head." I'm smiling. He smiles back at me, but it doesn't reach his eyes.

"Wright's been arrested." He looks at his watch. "He's probably at our jail by now."

"Who arrested him?"

"Oconee County. Do you remember my friend, Brandon, that I told you about?"

"Yes."

"Well, he's a real badass. I'm not joking. Anyway, he lives here in Athens and was coming home and saw a car traveling at a high rate of speed in the west bound lanes of 316. The car matched the description, so he turned around, and the tag information had gone out by that time. When he hit the blue lights, Wright started running even faster, and Brandon chased him well into Barrow County. There was a foot chase, and Wright tried to fight him. Apparently, Eric Wright now has a black

333

eye and a busted lip, courtesy of him. Wright's a damn idiot. No one should ever fight Brandon Nash."

"I'm glad he's been caught."

"We got the call around the time you fell asleep. He was arrested pretty quickly, but we didn't get word until you fell asleep."

"Where is everybody?"

"Chris has gone to the police department to start working on tying Wright to everything that we've gotten. Jake and Jess have gone to get your car and take it back to the condo. Max and Susan went with them to make sure the condo's the way you two would want it."

"Don't you need to go and help Chris?"

He pulls my hand up and touches all of my fingers, interlocking my hand with his for a moment, and then puts his lips to my hand. I can feel his breath on my hand when he speaks.

"I went with him after you fell asleep. I got back about twenty minutes ago."

His lips brush across my knuckles again. He looks up at me. I see the same look in his eyes that I saw the night we went to dinner with Jess and Jake and the same look that I've been seeing over and over again lately. It looks like affection.

"There's so much I want to say to you," he says quietly. "So much I want you to hear about what's happened." He stops, taking a deep breath, still holding my eyes with his.

I have all this conflict raging inside of me. Loving him and wanting to be with him. Feeling that I was used by him and that he set me up, but he's here, and he hasn't left, and that has to mean something. There's so much to deal with.

"We'll work through this. We aren't a lie, Grace." He stops again. "Now isn't the time to say everything that I want to say. I want you to rest, but we're going to talk about it, and we're going to work through this. I don't want you to walk away from me again." His eyes are intense, looking at me.

I don't want to walk away from him again either.

Dr. Wylie walks in the room and sees that I'm awake. "How're you feeling?"

"Better since I've slept. My head isn't hurting like it was."

He feels the back of my head and looks at the front. He checks my eyes while having a conversation with me.

"You're ready to go home," Dr. Wylie announces.

"Good, because I'm ready to go."

He gives me some instructions, which includes continuing to rest, no driving at all tonight and possibly tomorrow, but he leaves that up to how I feel. He says if I feel dizzy, then don't drive. His instructions are simple. He says that I may feel sleepy easily for the next twenty-four to forty-eight hours. He offers to send me home with a prescription for pain meds, but I decline, saying that I'll stick with Tylenol. He tells Nick for me to not be alone tonight and that it would be best if someone could be with me tomorrow. Dr. Wylie is assured that I won't be left alone. Brit comes in and takes out my IV.

"The next time I see you, I hope it's when we all go out together," she says to me, smiling.

"That would be great." I thank her for taking good care of me and tell her that I think Chris is a great guy. She agrees wholeheartedly. Nick pushes me out in wheelchair that I argue about.

"Stop arguing with me," he says through clenched teeth and then smiles and it's one of those electric Nick Bassano smiles. It makes my heart pound. We go out the same way we came in. Nick calls Chris and says that after he gets me back to the condo, he'll meet him at the police department. "Bill wants to have you come in tomorrow to be interviewed."

"Great," I say sarcastically.

"I don't think he's going to ask any questions about Lacey, but if he does, don't worry about it."

"Don't worry about it?"

"I didn't mean it like that. I mean don't worry about the questions."

This is all such a nightmare. I still can't think about it. I can't think about what I've done to Lacey. I can't think about what I feel like Nick's done to me. I don't want to think about Judge Wright. That's going to take some time to really process.

"When I was in that trunk, I made the decision that I was going to run, and it didn't matter if I found myself in the middle of nowhere. All I could think about was getting away."

There's silence between us, but it's not uncomfortable.

"You're so strong, Grace. I expected a total freak out."

I laugh a little. "That's probably later. I think I'm still in shock." I put my head back against the seat and close my eyes. I'm getting sleepy again.

"Jess chewed my ass out earlier."

I smile and keep my eyes closed. "About what?"

"About you getting shot and then getting kidnapped. She blames me for everything. She feels like if I hadn't asked you for help, then none of this would have happened to you, and she's right."

"She's very loyal to me."

"She is that."

"You got your ass chewed from a few other people too, from what I hear."

"Chris told you about that, did he?"

"Yes. He said you took it like a man."

I hear Nick chuckling. "We're here."

I open my eyes, seeing my car in its usual spot. Max and Susan are still here. I get out, and when we get to the door, Nick catches me and pulls me to him. He doesn't say anything while his lips find mine. I wrap my arms around his neck, and I give to him. I love this man, but there are so many questions that he has to answer. He's right. We need to talk about this, but I need some time to think things through. I need to sort out what's happened. I need to sort out my feelings for him and what he's done to me.

I've never felt more alive than I have since Nick has walked in my life. I know exactly what I'm feeling for him, but feeling set up and used, I don't know if I can move past that. I want to move past it. I want to be with him, but I can't with this between us. If I can't let this go, then I'll end up despising him, and I don't want that. I want to love him in a way that he's never allowed or wanted a woman to love him. Am I strong enough to give him that in light of what's happened? Right now, I don't know.

I push all of that away and continue to kiss him, tasting him, loving how I feel when I'm against his body like this. He lifts his head and looks in my eyes. He pulls through one of my curls and then traces a finger down my cheek. It makes me shiver him touching me like that, gentle, and almost loving.

"We're not a lie," he says quietly, stressing it this time. "It wasn't about just getting you in bed. If you don't believe anything else about me, believe that."

"I want to, Nick. I need some time to think about things."

He sighs, "I know."

The door flies open, and Jess is standing there looking at us. "I feel like a mother who has caught her daughter being naughty with her date. Why're you two standing outside?"

I laugh at her. "Privacy," is all I say. We walk in the condo, and I see Susan standing in the kitchen at the stove. "What're you doing?"

"Cooking soup," she tells me, as if that makes all the sense in the world.

"It's late, and it's May."

"I don't care if it's the middle of August. Soup is comforting and healing. It's almost ready. You can have some tonight, and there'll be enough to eat for the next few days. I've got cornbread cooking too."

"I smell it." I walk to the couch and sit. Nick sits beside me. Jake and Max are watching ESPN. "I don't want any food," I tell Susan. She looks at me in the same way that Jess does when I tell her I don't want food. I look at Jess. "Shouldn't you be in bed? You have to be up early."

"I've called for a sub. I'm not leaving you by yourself tomorrow."

I'm simply too tired to argue with her. Nick takes my hand, and I look at him.

"I want to stay, but I need to get back and start digging deeply into Eric Wright. Bill wanted to know if you would come to the police department at three."

"Okay. Do I need to call him?"

"No. I'll let him know." He seems reluctant to leave. He leans over and brushes his lips across mine. "I'll see you tomorrow."

"Okay," I say softly. The freak out that Nick was expecting to see comes not long after he leaves. Susan, Jess and I are sitting on the couch talking about wedding plans.

"Jess, sweetheart, I really want you to consider having your attendants wearing a bright red. I was thinking the color of Poinsettias."

"I was thinking of a darker red." Jess looks at me. "What do you think, Grace?"

I hear her say my name. All of the thoughts that I've kept at bay are now rushing me at once. I can't catch my breath, and that makes things worse, the feeling that I can't breathe. I can actually hear my heart in my ears. I feel dizzy, and it doesn't have anything to do with being hit in the head. I'm sweaty and shaky. I'm having an all-out anxiety attack. I must look it as well.

"Grace?" Jess's voice is concerned.

"That man was going to kill me." It comes out strangled. Max and Jake have stopped watching the TV and have turned to look at me. "I can't breathe." I put my hand over my heart, and it's racing.

"You're having an anxiety attack," Jess says calmly.

I nod at her that I'm in agreement. I've known that man for seven years. I put him on a pedestal. I've admired him more than anyone else. I've even thought what it would have been like if I'd grown up as his child. We have deep personal knowledge of one another. He attacked me, and he was going to kill me.

Looking past what he did to me, I have to then think about what he did to all of those girls. What he did to Naomi. He raped all of those girls repeatedly. He raped my sister repeatedly. My mind goes to Darla and the scar on her cheek. She got that from him. *Enough!* I can't think.

I moan and put my head down between my legs. I hear this roaring sound in my ears. I think I may pass out. No, I'm going to be sick. I race to our downstairs bathroom. I hover over the toilet and end up doing nothing more than dry heaving that seems like it will go on forever. I'm trying to breathe deeply. Can I stay here on the floor for the remainder of my life and not deal with anything?

I do a quick assessment of everything that I have to deal with. Nick, my missing sister who's probably dead, Matt, Misty. I know a lot of sick shit. Lacey was part of this. Nick was a part of her, and she was going to kill me. I shot and killed her.

Judge Wright gave me a concussion and kidnapped me; he was going to kill me. I can sum it up in one word, *insanity*. My head's hurting again. I drag myself up off of the floor. Jess is right outside of the bathroom when I emerge.

"I want to take a shower, brush my teeth and go to bed."

"I'll come with you while you take your shower. I don't want you to be alone."

I hug her tightly. "Thank you. I don't want to be alone."

Susan stands and says that she's going to join us. They sit on my bed while I shower quickly. When I join them, I talk to Susan about Nick. I don't want to deal with anything else at the moment. He is the most important matter to me. It takes me a long time to put it all into words. Jess and Susan wait patiently while I work through it.

"It should be so simple. I love him. He says he cares for me. The things he's done for me says he cares, but it's all too coincidental for me." Before I set it up for them, I ask Susan, "How much do you know about what the Bradberrys were into?"

"I think Max and I are in denial about it."

"But you know?"

She gives me a sad smile. "Yes, we know."

"I hate it, Susan. I hate it for both of you. I know they were good friends of yours." I sigh and then continue. "He had to know who he was looking at when he saw those pictures." Jess knows what I'm talking about, but Susan doesn't. "Sorry. I need to back up even more. Nick has dated a lot of women. I've met four. Who knows how many more are out there. He's got a reputation with the ladies. He and Lacey have known one another for several years, and I don't want to think about all the things that they did together. In simple terms, he saw her naked more than once. I have a hard time believing that he didn't know it was her body. He says he was *suspicious*."

I stop and shake my head at that.

"The order of events are, the pictures are found, he comes to me for help, I fall in bed with him, and I fall in love with him. We've been out together twice, and when he saw her, he was so uncomfortable. He gives me a gun, and the evidence room is broken into and then I get the pictures. I couldn't wrap my head around why he wanted so damn bad for me to have those pictures. It didn't make any sense to me, and I thought it was a terrible idea. She comes after me, and I kill her. Problem solved."

Jess and Susan look at one another and then look at me.

"Grace, think about this. Do you really believe that he did all of this to have Lacey killed?" Jess asks me.

"No. I don't believe that. I think he used me, set me up, played me whatever you want to call it to lure her out after the evidence room was broken into. He had to know it was her that did it, and he said nothing. I thought it was the worst idea I've ever heard of when he wanted to put those pictures there." I point to my closet. "I've felt like he's been holding back something, and he was. He was holding back about Lacey. He told no one. Even if he didn't want to tell me…" My voice trails off.

We sit in silence for a few minutes.

"I killed that woman, Jess. I shot and killed that woman, and I'm sick about it." I stop talking again. I honestly can't deal with what I've done.

Not right at this moment. "He knew, Jess, and he didn't tell me, or Chris, or anybody. I'm hurt and angry and then there's so much other shit to deal with, and I love him, and I want him to love me, and I don't think that he does. Chris says that he does, but I don't know..."

We're all quiet, and then I say, "I still haven't figured out how she knew that I knew about the pictures. My role in this whole thing was so minor, and no one talked about it. Very few people knew about the pictures. It's bugging me. Hell, this whole thing bugs me. My head hurts. I need to take some Tylenol and go to bed."

"I'll get you some," Jess says. She continues to sit along with Susan. "I'm mad as hell at Nick Bassano for dragging you into this, but I have a hard time believing that he would put your life at risk. He does care about you, Grace. I got in his face at the hospital and told him what I thought about the whole deal. He stood there and took it and told me I was absolutely right. He said the last time he felt this afraid was when he thought his mom was going to die. Chris is right. He loves you."

She leans over, kissing me on the cheek.

"You've never been like this with anyone. I've been with you through one major relationship and a slew of stupid ass boyfriends that I knew weren't going to last more than a few months, but the way you look at him is in a way that I've never seen. When he's with you, from what I've seen, he has nothing but eyes for you. You two are extremely passionate about one another. There's such an intensity that flows between you two. More than anything else, I want you to be happy."

I'm trying not to cry. I want to feel hopeful. I want to make this work. I want to be with him and be happy and be in love and have him love me.

"Well, I met Nick for the first time today, and I like him," Susan says to me. "He's so big and looks like he would be the protective type and sweet to you, which is very important to me. I don't know all about this Lacey woman, but from what I've heard from you and Jess, I hope she enjoyed her first night in hell the other night."

"Well said, Momma." Jess smiles.

"He's obviously a smart man, Grace. He chose you," Susan says.

I hug her and soak in her nurturing motherly arms.

"Thank you," I say softly.

Long after Max and Susan leave, and Jess and Jake have gone to bed, I stare at nothing in the dark for several hours before sleep claims me. When it does, the images behind my eyes are terrifying.

Chapter Thirty-Three

I'm sitting in the lobby at the police department. I have my legs crossed, swinging my foot. I'm tapping my brand new phone on my leg. When I get tired of swinging that foot, I cross my legs going the other direction and start swinging the other foot. All the while, my iPhone is going *tap tap tap tap* on my leg in rapid succession. I can't even appreciate that not only do I have a new phone for the first time in six years, but I have the latest and greatest iPhone.

It didn't dawn on me until this morning that my phone's gone. I called Nick on Jess's phone, and he said that he had forgotten that as well. It wasn't with Judge Wright when they caught him. He said it was most likely lying in a ditch somewhere on 316. Jess and I went down to the local mobile phone store, and I was going to get the cheapest thing I could find.

How I got talked into getting an iPhone, I'm still not sure. Jess ran down a list of people who have them, including her, Jake, Nick, both her mom and dad, Ginger and Angie. She reminded me of all the great things I can do with it. I told Jess I don't know if I want to be that connected to the world, but I walked out with one tucked away safely in my fancy OtterBox. I look over at Jess, who has stopped reading and is staring at me.

"What?" I ask.

"Look at what you're doing."

I look, and I see that I'm tapping my phone, swinging one foot and bouncing the foot that's on the floor up and down. I roll my eyes at myself and stop moving. It's well past three, and I've not seen Agent Killinger. I've tried calling Nick, but I can't reach him. I would call Chris, but his number is with my phone, wherever it might be.

My head's down to a dull ache that's more annoying than painful. My knees look worse than anything. I have a bruise forming on my forehead, but it isn't bad. I wish Agent Killinger would come on so we can get this shit over with. He's making me wait because he doesn't like me. I'd bet on it.

"That man needs to hurry the hell up," I mutter, to no one in particular.

"Grace."

I look at Jess, and she has an eyebrow raised at me. I look down, and now both feet are bouncing. I sigh, stand up and circle the lobby, not once but twice. I start thinking of the nightmares I had. One is bad enough, but mine kept shifting, and I ended up having three different ones. The first involved my dad, and I don't want to think of that one. The second was about all seven girls. The third was the worst.

I was in my dress from my birthday, and Nick was in his tux. We were in the gazebo at the Botanical Gardens. He told me that everything had been a lie, and the only thing he ever wanted from me was sex. I told him that I loved him, and he laughed at me and said I wasn't worth loving. I shot him with the gun he had given me, and I woke up soaking wet as he was falling over the railing at the gazebo, down into the gardens. I didn't even need to analyze that dream closely to figure out what it means: *total fear of not having him or losing him.* I'm considering a third lap when the door opens, and Agent Killinger comes out. Damn, I'm nervous.

"Ms. Harrison," he says, stepping forward to shake my hand.

"Agent Killinger." I'm just as formal.

"Thank you for agreeing to meet me here."

As if I had a choice. "Of course." I turn and nod to Jess, who nods back at me. He leads me back in a room that I've never been in before. It's a formal interview room. It's stark and impersonal. "Have you seen Nick?"

He looks at me. "I have. We've both been at the D.A.'s office, meeting with Brison and Casey Cain. He wanted to come back here with me, but I told him that I didn't think you really needed him here to hold your hand." *Jerk.*

"Agent Killinger, why so much animosity towards me?"

Let's get this out and on the table and dealt with. I've got enough shit to deal with. I don't need another person adding to the growing pile.

"Is that how it feels to you?"

"Yes."

"Maybe you are being overly sensitive over what has happened. That was quite the scene you had with him in the parking lot of your condo."

Overly sensitive? Is he fucking kidding me? I'm getting pissed.

"I shot and killed someone, and then I got kidnapped by a man who I've had nothing but the highest respect for and whom I've known for seven years and poured my heart and soul out to, and you think that's overly sensitive?"

"I was referring to Nick. I couldn't help but overhear what you think he's done to you. I'm not here to talk about Nick. Let's talk about what happened."

Perfect. I don't want to talk about Nick with him either. I would really like to tell him to shove it where the sun doesn't shine and not talk about anything with him. He'd probably arrest me for some crazy law that says you can't cuss a GBI Agent.

I take him through it, starting with Judge Wright calling me asking me to come to his office and talk with him, to waking up in his trunk. It's a short interview. It feels more like he's getting my statement than an actual interview. He asks a few questions, and I notice that he asks the same questions in different ways, but they are essentially the same questions. I wonder why he does this. Does he think that I'm lying? Maybe he thinks it really wasn't me that came popping out of Judge Wright's trunk.

"I see the bruise on the front of your head. I'm going to have some-one come in and take pictures of all your injuries. Do you have any questions for me?"

"No." I would like to ask him how does it feel to be the world's big-gest asshole, but I don't.

He stands. "I'll be in touch if I need anything else, including about Lacey."

He walks out of the room, leaving me alone. I have half a mind to stick my tongue out at him. My luck would be that he would turn around and see me. Yeah, he dislikes me, and I don't know why.

There's a lady from the police department who comes in and takes pictures. She starts with a full body picture. I wish I had done something with my hair other than washing it and letting it go without doing anything with it, and I should've put on some makeup. I remind myself I'm not doing a cover shoot for a magazine.

"I'm going to look to see if I can see the bump on the back of your head." She spends considerable time trying to find it. She starts laughing. "You have the best head of hair. It's not only thick, but there is so much of it. I can't even see your scalp. I feel the swelling, but I can't see it."

She gives up and takes pictures of my elbow and my knees. She's finishing up when Nick walks in the room. He has a wild expression on his face. My heart's beating faster looking at him. He's in brown dress pants and an ACCPD crested polo that I've not seen. Absolutely handsome, as always.

"If you ever want to donate some of your hair, I'll take some," she says walking out of the room.

Nick looks at me oddly, and I wave him off.

"Is Jess here with you?" It comes out fast.

"Yes." I'm looking at him and wondering what's going on.

"Brison's here with the Chief, and we need to talk to you. I can take you home later."

"I'm not going to like this, am I?"

"Probably not, and I don't like it either. Come on, we'll explain it to you."

"I need to go tell Jess."

"I'll walk with you."

We walk up the hall and out to the lobby. Jess smiles when she sees us.

"I'm staying," I tell her.

"Why?" She's looking at Nick.

"Brison's here. We need to talk to Grace."

Jess looks at me. "Do you know what this is about?"

"Generally? Yes. Specifically? No. I'm going to find out in a minute."

Jess looks displeased. "Nick, she needs to be finished with this. I mean look at her. Look what her involvement has done to her. The last time she was this banged up was when she was a..." She stops and looks at him. I can see that she's beginning to get emotional.

"I know Jess. I agree. Nothing else is going to happen to her."

"Don't make that promise, Nick." She looks at me. "Do you want to call me, and I'll come back and get you?"

"I'll bring her," he says.

She looks at me for an acknowledgement that it's okay with me. I tell her that it is. She hugs me and leaves, unhappy with the situation.

We're walking back through the door when Nick asks me, "Did you get a new phone?" I pull it out of my pocket to show him. He starts laughing and says, "Welcome to 2012, baby."

"Shut up," I mumble, smiling.

"Are you going to put me in your favorites?"

"Am I in yours?" I ask, looking up at him.

"Your name's first."

Oh, my God. It's so silly, but it means so much. We walk in the Chief's office before I can respond to him. I wonder if the look in my eyes tells him what that means to me.

"Hey, Grace," Chief Thompson says to me, standing. Brison stands as well.

"Hi, Chief Thompson," I reply.

"Please sit," he says.

We sit, and Brison asks me, "How're you feeling?"

"Better. Thank you for asking."

Brison looks at the Chief. The Chief looks at Nick, and Nick looks at me and says, "Brison got a call earlier today from Eric Wright's attorney that he's willing to talk and answer some questions about the girls. Well, we think it will be about the girls. His attorney won't give us many details." My eyes go wide. I could have some answers about my sister. Nick continues,"But there's a catch."

"Which is what?" I ask.

"He wants you there."

"Me. Why?"

"We don't know. We know that Wright refuses to answer any questions unless you're there. I think he's fixated on you. You don't have to do this." Nick's holding my eyes with his.

"What do you have to tie Judge Wright to these girls?"

"We hit the mother-load last night or early this morning. It all starts to run together. We served search warrants on his house, office and car. During the search, we discovered that he owns property out towards Washington. We visited that property and found an old trailer there. We got a search warrant for that as well. There's DNA everywhere in this one room. There's a bed with a mattress that's a treasure box full of evidence alone. There are markings on the frame, indicating restraints were used. We found high velocity blood splatter on the walls, along with two .40 caliber fragments. Another .40 caliber fragment was dug out of the floor. It's the same caliber used on Misty and the same caliber dug out of your ceiling. We think they're from Lacey's gun. We tore the place apart, and hidden in the floor are masks that match the pictures and items that appear to have been taken from the girls."

"Oh, my God. The girls?" He knows I'm asking if they've been found.

"There's a crew out there right now using a system that looks like a metal detector, scanning the ground. Since his place is in such close proximity to where Misty's body was found, we're having some cadaver dogs brought in for that area. It's a larger area than his home, so we thought dogs would be better suited for that location. We won't know anything for either place for a while. Would you be able to identify anything belonging to Naomi?"

"Probably not." That's so sad, that I can't look at their evidence and say whether or not it belongs to my sister. What does that say about me and how I was with her? "Why do you think he's willing to talk to you? I would sit back and keep my mouth shut."

"Brison has a working theory," Nick says. I look at Brison.

"Eric Wright likes to talk. He always has. He has an ego that's bigger than his common sense. He likes power, and he likes to be in control. He views himself as far more powerful than what he really is. He thinks he's smarter than everyone around him. He knows that his house of horrors has been discovered, and he wants to explain it. I say, let him explain it."

"But he won't do it without me."

"No," Brison says.

It makes no sense why he would want me in there. But what about this has made sense? Nothing. It's been a nightmare from the start, and it doesn't look like it's going to be over any time soon. I sit quietly for a moment. I look at all of them.

"Let's see what Eric Wright has to say."

They all look at each other, slow smiles playing across their lips. It takes Brison a couple of hours to work out the scope of questioning that Nick and Chris will be allowed to do. I sit in the Chief's office. Sometimes, I'm alone. Nick wanders in and out, sitting with me, showing me different features on my phone. We avoid all talk of us. This is the wrong time to be talking about what's going on between the two of us.

"He may say some things that are hard to listen to."

I look from my phone to him. "If he gives anything about Naomi and the other girls, it'll be worth it."

He smiles at me softly. "No shrinking daisy, right?"

"No. Does Darla know anything that's going on?"

"She does. I took several of the pictures that Forensics took out at Wright's trailer, and she was able to identify that everything was familiar to her. We collected her DNA, which I have no doubt will match to some of that shit out there."

I smile slyly at him. "He's going to lose his shit when he finds out that they aren't all missing."

"I'm counting on it."

"Are you going to tell him?"

"No. I'll leave it to him and his attorney to figure out why he's being charged with six murders and not seven."

I take a deep breath. It's the first time he's said that out loud. I know he's been thinking it, because I've thought it, too.

"So you do think they've all been murdered."

His eyes find mine. "Yeah, Grace. I think they've all been murdered. I'm sorry."

He reaches over, taking my hand in his and stroking it with his thumb. I knew it. I've known it, but it doesn't make it any easier.

When the time comes, Nick reminds me that none of them know exactly what he's going to say. He asks me again if I'm ready to do this. I tell him yes, I am. He holds the door open to the now all-too familiar conference room, and I enter it.

Chris is there. Brison's there, at the head of one end of the table. Chief Thompson sits at the head on the opposite side. It's strange to see

Judge Wright sitting in an orange jumpsuit with a visible black eye and a nasty-looking cut on his lip. That was the least of what he deserves to get.

There's a man in a sharp business suit sitting beside him. I guess that it his attorney. Nick positions me between him and Chris. Nick's directly across from the Judge. I get introduced to his attorney, who is Phillip Edwards. He's the best criminal defense attorney here in Athens, from what I've heard. Why is this man allowing his client to talk?

"Hello, Grace," Judge Wright says.

He smiles at me, and the man looks absolutely crazy. I shrink back in my chair. I want to scoot it a little closer to Nick, but I refuse to give the man the satisfaction of seeing me scared. I can feel Nick's eyes on me, and he must sense it, because he positions his body closer to mine. I'm instantly comforted by it.

"You said you would talk if I was in here. I'm here." I wanted that to come out much braver than what it sounded.

Phillip Edwards speaks before his client can speak. "I'm going on the record again that I've strongly advised my client to exercise his right to remain silent."

Judge Wright's looking at me and doesn't seem to want to look anywhere else.

I hear Brison clear his throat, and he says, "Phillip, there's no record. It's not being recorded, remember?"

Phillip Edwards looks over at Brison. "I felt like I needed to say it again. I'm opposed to this. Eric said if I didn't go along, he was going to fire me. I don't want him to be here alone."

"Yes, Grace. You are here." He acts as if he's not heard a word his attorney said. He continues to smile. He's a psychopath. "You know, I've always been so fond of you. I've always known how smart you are. It would've been so nice for me, of course, if you hadn't figured me out."

Is he looking for an apology? "I'm not here to talk about me."

"No, of course you aren't." His voice is smooth and sweet. He's looking at me and talking as if we're having dinner with each other at our favorite restaurant. The whole thing gives me cold chills. He turns his attention to Nick. "You have questions, Detective. I have answers."

"How did you, Miller, the Bradberrys and Lacey all know about one another? How does that happen?"

"Eric, I'm going to advise you not to answer that question," Phillip Edwards says.

"Shut up, Phillip," he snaps. He looks at his attorney and then back at Nick. Phillip Edwards is not a happy man. "Lacey and Mickey had been having an affair for years. Eleanor would join in sometimes, or not. It was all about how she felt. Greg also had a fondness for Lacey, and he was invited in as well. When they asked me, well, who was I to say no to that? You could never say no to her either, could you, Detective?"

Nick says nothing, but I can feel his body tense.

"It was Greg's idea to bring in some younger girls. We decided to start with the girls on the streets. Who's going to miss them? Then, Greg decided he wanted more inexperienced girls. He liked that. He asked me if I would be the one to find girls who wouldn't be missed if they disappeared. I did the picking, and Greg did the taking. Lacey was in charge of getting rid of any Missing Persons Reports." He talks about it like it's no big deal. "Greg took the first one. What can I say; I discovered that I liked having sex with younger girls. Sex is sex. Who cares if we had sex with a little prostitute from the streets? Those girls are used to it. We alternated on who we took. No need to trace all the girls back to my courtroom."

I can't believe what I'm hearing. I feel dizzy and sick, and I don't want to be here. I don't want to hear this, but I don't think I could move if I tried. It feels like I've been nailed to my seat.

"You raped those girls," Nick says through his teeth. "You kidnapped them, and then raped them."

"I didn't kidnap anyone, Detective. Greg did that."

Oh, because that makes such a difference. If I could get up and punch this man in his face and then spit on him, I would. I also owe him a kick in the balls for the knot on my head.

"Lacey enjoyed it just as much as we did. She was quite the freak, but I guess you knew that. I would love to know how Grace sizes up in bed compared to all of the things that you did with Lacey."

I can feel every pair of eyes on me, except Nick's. I hate that he's bringing up private moments that Nick and I have shared, putting it out there for everyone else. I know my face has gone pale. It feels like the room is spinning. I'd like to hide under the table.

"Do *not* talk about her like that." Nick's voice is full of venom. I can almost feel him shaking.

"Ahh, I see that you've gotten very protective of Grace. Lacey hated her. She hated that Grace has gotten to you in a way that neither she nor any other woman could. I guess you don't have to worry about Lacey any longer. Grace took care of that for you, didn't she?" He's looking at me again. I don't want to think about that now. I hate this man for so much that he's done, and now he's bringing that up.

"The pictures," Nick says tightly. "Who made the decision for the pictures to be taken?"

"Eric, I'm advising you not to answer that question."

Judge Wright looks at his attorney, and it's an impatient look. "Phillip. You're going to advise me to not answer any of the questions. I'll let you know, and everyone else, if I don't want to answer questions. Got it?"

Phillip Edwards has an expression on his face like he's a kid whose rear end has been spanked. Judge Wright turns his attention back to Nick.

"That was Mickey's stupid idea. He went on and on about how wonderful it would be to look at them after we got rid of them. Greg thought it was a good idea, too. Lacey and I were against it from the beginning. We both felt like that could be our downfall, and we were right. We went along with it in the end, though. We were simply having too much fun."

I wrap my arms around myself in attempt to what? Protect myself? To try and warm up? To keep out all of what he is saying? All of the above? I'm cold. I've never felt as cold as I do right now. I glance around the room, and everyone has the same expressions: anger, disbelief, disgust. It's all there. Even Phillip Edwards looks like he wants to be anywhere else but where he's sitting.

"What do you know about Misty Price?"

"Misty Price was a total fuck up on Greg's part. It was a crime of opportunity. It was a complete coincidence that she was the one he took, and she happened to be on Grace's caseload. I wasn't even there when he killed her. In fact, I wasn't there for any of it. He was feeling a little needy."

"You weren't there, but you knew about it."

"Yes, I knew about it. Greg called me in a panic that the girl had bitten him very badly while he was trying to subdue her. He gave her the drugs and did his thing with her, but he said she was still fighting, and he lost it and beat her."

"Who shot her?"

"Lacey did that. Lacey got there, and they realized she was still alive. Well, she had a pulse. They dumped the body." He's so cold the way he talks about it. He talks like they threw trash on the side of the road. It all makes me sick.

"Who cut 'Whore' into her stomach?"

Even though I know about it, it still makes me cringe.

"Greg did that. After that happened, Mickey reached out to me and said that Greg was getting out of control, and he and Eleanor wanted to come to you with the pictures and tell you everything. We couldn't let that happen."

"So you killed them."

Judge Wright looks surprised that Nick would think that *he* killed the Bradberrys.

"No, Detective. I didn't kill them."

"But you know who did."

He smiles at Nick, and it's pure evil. "Ask me another question. I'll think about letting you in on that little secret."

Why is he not answering that question? He's told us everything else. Why stop there? It doesn't make sense to me, but none of this does. I don't know if and when I'll ever fully process what's happened.

"Did Greg Miller supply the morphine?"

Judge Wright looks at Nick, surprised. "Very good, Detective. I told Grace you're a smart guy. Yes, he supplied all of it."

"Were all the girls taken to your place out towards Washington?"

"Eric, I'm going to advise you not to answer that question."

Judge Wright completely ignores him. "Yes. We had them all there."

"Are any of them alive?"

Phillip Edwards opens his mouth to speak, and Judge Wright shakes his head at him to not speak. Judge Wright directs his attention back to me. When he answers Nick's question, he's speaking to me.

"Are any of them alive? I'm sure you would like to know that, wouldn't you Grace?" His expression is he's trying to remember whether or not any of them are alive, but what he's really doing is toying with all of us. He wants to make it as bad as he can. Why? *Because he is a sick son of a bitch.* "No, they aren't alive." He's still looking at me.

I knew Naomi wasn't, but it's still a punch in the gut. My thoughts go to Mr. McGregor. Sherry Luke may have family out there somewhere that miss her. I even think of the families of the other girls. They don't give a damn, but we all do. We will miss them. *No tears! Cry later!* I can feel all eyes on me again. They're gauging my reaction. I show nothing. When it comes to Darla, a part of me wants to jump on the table and put my finger in his face and say, *Ha! You think you know everything, but you don't!* I don't say anything.

"Who killed them? Did *you* kill them all?"

Judge Wright's assessing Nick, and his smile is sick. "Wouldn't you like to know? You're a smart guy. I'm going to leave you to figure that out."

Nick stares at him for a long moment and then asks, "Where're the girls?"

"You mean their bodies? Where *are* the girls? That's a great question." Judge Wright turns his attention to me. "I bet you would like to know where the girls are, wouldn't you, Grace? I bet you would really like to know where Naomi is."

"Yes," I whisper.

He keeps smiling at me. He says nothing. He's stringing me along and enjoying it. He's absolutely getting off on what he's doing. I'm sick. I can feel a lump in my throat. *Don't cry. Don't cry. Do not let this bastard see you cry!*

"Tell Brison not to seek the Death Penalty, and I'll tell you where they all are but one. I don't know where she is."

"That's not my decision to make." I wish my voice sounded stronger. I wish I felt stronger, but I don't.

"Sure it is. Brison's going to consider what the families want. Everyone will want to know what happened to their dear, dear daughters, or *sister*, because now they give a shit about them." His words are an echo of my thoughts. I don't like it at all. "Brison's sitting over there, thinking about his own sweet, sixteen-year-old daughter. He's thinking what if he didn't know where she was, but what if someone could tell him?

"Mickey and Eleanor are gone. Lacey's gone. That leaves Greg and me. Brison's going to try and hang us both for this. The wheels are turning in his head already, that he's going to turn this into a Death Penalty circus. It's election year, right Brison? You have an opponent this year. You don't want to lose the election, now do you? You're sitting there thinking of all these things, aren't you?" Judge Wright glances at Brison and then right back at me. I want to look at Brison, but I can't take my eyes off this man. Brison says nothing. "Do you want to hear about Naomi first?"

Oh, my God, is he going to tell us anyway? My heart's beating in the craziest way, and I feel incredibly nauseous. He's really going to tell us, regardless of what Brison decides. I feel a glimmer of hope that we're going to know where they all are. I'm going to know where Naomi is, and I can bury her and tell her goodbye and make amends to her the only way I can now. I look quickly around the room, and everyone is in rapt attention. We all want to know where these girls are.

"Yes." It comes out strangled.

"I liked her more than the others." *Oh, no, where's he going with this?* This isn't what I was expecting him to say. He leans over the table, as if he's trying to get closer to me, but it's such a wide conference table, he can't. "I liked fucking her more than the others, because it felt like I was fucking…you."

Chapter Thirty-Four

Nick erupts beside me.

"You son of a bitch," he yells, and he's up, across the table and on Judge Wright before anyone else, including me, can react.

I jump up and back while Chief Thompson tackles Nick from one side, and Chris crawls up on the table and tackles him from the other. All three men go down on the other side of the table, and Judge Wright has disappeared from view. Chris has his whole body wrapped around Nick and has pinned Nick's arms against his body.

"Nick! Calm down, man! He's not worth it!" Chris is yelling, and I swear it looks like he may try to sit on him.

The Chief is barking orders at Nick. It's complete chaos in the room. Phillip Edwards is yelling with Brison. The Chief and Chris are trying to calm Nick, but all I hear is the crazy, manic laughter coming from Judge Wright. Chris and Chief Thompson pull Nick from the floor, but they haven't let go of him.

"That was beautiful," Judge Wright says as he stands up and sits in his chair. His eyes are on me.

"Shut up, Eric," Phillip says to him and then goes back to his argument with Brison. After he finishes with Brison, he turns his attention to the Chief. "If this is what's going to happen, then we're done. I have been against this from the moment Eric told me that he wanted to talk to you. I'm absolutely opposed to this line of questioning. I will not allow your detective to hit my client." He's pointing his finger at Chief

Thompson, who still has his arms around Nick in the front, while Chris is still holding him at the back. It takes both of them.

"He didn't hit him," Chief Thompson says. He looks up at Nick. "Step out for five minutes. Take Grace with you. Both of you, get out of here, *now*."

I can't move. I can't make my brain connect with my feet. My eyes are wide, and I'm looking from one person to the other. I see Nick walk around the table, and my eyes follow him until he's standing in front of me.

"Come on," he says softly, taking my hand. I let him drag me out of the room. I walk like I'm in some trance. We step out, and Nick expels all of the air out of his lungs. I lean against the wall, not knowing what else to do. Nick tips my face up to look at him. "How are you holding up? That's a lot of shit to hear. You've been through more than any one person should have to go through. You're so strong, and you amaze me like you always do. You don't have to go back in there."

"Yes, I do. I have to know where Naomi is, and I have to know where those other girls are. He's not going to tell you without me."

"I don't think he's going to tell us, Grace. I think his whole plan was to get you in the room with him so he could twist that knife that he put in your back. I'm certain at this point he's got a sick fixation with you. He basically said that when he said...well, you know. I don't want to repeat that. He's using you."

"So did you."

I can see that my words sting.

"Grace, I didn't use you. I swear it." He takes a deep breath and blows it out. "We're going to get this solved. You and I, but we've got some other things to get through. Let's not do this right now."

"That's fine." I cross my arms over my chest. I'm looking everywhere but his eyes.

"Hey," he says softly. I look in his eyes, and my heart melts. "I never meant to hurt you. Not ever."

I can feel the tears in my eyes. I'm blinking rapidly trying to get them to go away.

"Don't," I say. "Not here. Not now." I whisper.

I need for this to be over. All of this is too much. Dealing with all of it is snowballing around me. Hearing Judge Wright say all of those things and then saying that about Naomi. I feel queasy again. And she's gone. She's just…gone.

Chief Thompson steps out of the room, and he looks pissed. Nick steps away from me. He stands in front of Nick, looking up at him.

"If you *ever* pull anything like that again, I'll suspend you for a week," the Chief growls. "You're walking a very thin line here, with me, Nick. Do you understand me?"

"Yes, sir. I apologize that I reacted that way. I was out of line, horribly unprofessional, and it won't happen again."

Chief Thompson gives Nick a sly smile. "That's officially what I wanted to say." He leans into Nick and says quietly, "Unofficially, why didn't you hit the son of a bitch when you had the chance?"

Nick grins at him. "You and Chris are just too damn quick." They look at one another again. Chief Thompson nods at me and walks back in the room, closing the door behind him. Nick looks at me. "Are you ready?"

"Yes." I look up at him.

He gives me a slight smile. "No shrinking daisy, right?"

"Right." But the word lacks confidence.

We walk back in, and I sit where I was. I look at Chris, who has nothing but concern for me in his eyes. It touches me.

"We've been talking while you two were out," Brison says. "*Mr.* Wright won't tell us where the girls are, unless I agree not to seek the Death Penalty against him. Mr. Wright's familiar enough with criminal law that I would never make that decision while there's an ongoing investigation. I've explained to him that I'm not going to be pressured into making any decisions."

There's nothing but silence as we all process what this means. We aren't going to find out where the girls are. I'm not going to walk out of here knowing where my sister is. I know she's dead. I just want to know where she is. I need to know. These other families of the other girls need to know as well. It feels like all the air has been let out of my favorite balloon as reality sets in with me that it won't be tonight that I know where she is. I can feel Judge Wright's eyes on me.

"Don't you want to know where Naomi is, Grace?"

"Yes, but I won't pressure the District Attorney for you to get what you want," I say with more resolve than what I really feel.

"You don't love your sister?"

"Yes, I love my sister."

"But not enough to want to know where she is?"

"Stop," Nick says. "That's enough. Have you not tormented her enough?" Nick's staring at him. He may shoot him. I haven't decided if he will or he won't. Judge Wright is staring back at him and smiling. "Who murdered the Bradberrys?" he asks.

Judge Wright sits back in his chair, looking at me. "It's someone that Grace knows very well. Would you like to know, Grace?"

No. "Yes."

He lets me linger. He gets off on it. It makes me sick. He's just sitting there, smiling at me in that sick way. I may go across the table next.

"Your brother and his friend, Billy."

"You're lying," I hiss at him.

"No, I'm not lying. Lacey set it up. You could ask her about it, but that's right, you can't, because you shot and killed her."

"I've heard enough." I jump up and storm out of the room. No one stops me.

I go to Nick's desk and sit. I put my face in my hands with my elbows on Nick's desk. The hits keep coming. There's no way in hell Matt and Billy murdered the Bradberrys. It's not possible. How in the hell would Matt know Lacey? He's a drug addict who lives on the streets. My brother hasn't even been to jail. I've always wondered about that.

I start thinking. That leads to deeper thinking, and pieces of memories start creeping in. I think back to the night at The Grill when I was told that someone swung left during the beating death of the Bradberrys. I have a dizzy sick feeling that has nothing to do with being hit in the head. Matt's left handed.

He told me he had friends at the D.A.'s office. How in the hell was I supposed to believe that? I moan when a new thought hits me. Matt told people that he had done something and was going to be in big trouble. When Matt saw the pictures, he flipped out on me. I thought it was a combination of him being high and seeing Jenny Noble. It wasn't. He knew about those pictures.

It has eaten at me and eaten at me-- how did Lacey know that I knew about the pictures? She knew because my brother told her. She somehow sucked him into her and her sick, sadistic web. I'm not sure if things could get any worse. This is about as bad as it gets.

I go over it in my mind again. By the time it runs through my mind a fifth time, I feel certain that Matt's involved, along with Billy. Nick said the Bradberrys were killed over the pictures and what they had done. They were right. My brother and his friend did it for revenge.

I text Jess to let her know I'm not sure when I'll be home. I continue to sit and think and stare. I have a long time to do all of that, because it's three more hours before I see anyone. I'm looking around, and my eyes zero in on a picture that's sitting beside Nick's computer. I stop what I'm doing and pick it up. He framed the picture of us and put it on his desk. I thought about doing the same thing. Mine's attached to my dresser mirror.

It's in this moment that I know I can forgive him for whatever he's done. I want to know what he has to say, but he's forgiven. I want to be with him and love him, and I have hope that he does indeed love me. We can make this work. I'm holding the picture and looking at it when Nick finds me. I move to get up.

"No, stay there," he says. He pulls a chair and sits in it. He looks worn, haunted and I wonder what all he's had to hear. "I wish we could go back to that night."

I put the picture back where I found it and look at him. "It was a great night. You made it that way."

He smiles at me. "My heart skipped a few beats when you came down your stairs in that dress. I'd never seen anyone look the way that you did." He sighs and keeps looking at me.

"You were in there a long time," I say, changing the subject.

"We asked a lot of questions. Phillip kept advising. He identified Naomi, Meghan McGregor, Hailey West, Tonya Overby and Jenny Noble. He knew those girls. They'd all come through his courtroom, which you knew."

"I didn't know about Jenny Noble."

"He couldn't identify Darla or Sherry Luke by name. He said they never asked, and what did it matter? I'm grateful that you left. He got very detailed and descriptive. It took everything in me to not go across the table at him again."

"Is there anything that you can tell me about Naomi?"

There's that haunted look again. I also see the same expression on his face when I asked him about Misty at Jittery Joe's. He doesn't want to tell me.

"It was very bad, and I would really like to protect you from at least one thing. Okay?"

I nod. Do I really need to know all of the details of what those sick people did to my sister? How's that going to help? She's gone and not coming back. I see Chris walking towards us, and his expression is exactly the same as Nick's.

"Goddamn. I need a shower after that," Chris says, standing beside Nick. "What all have you told her?"

"Not much." He keeps his dark eyes on me.

"Good. Keep most of that shit to yourself, okay?"

Nick continues to look at me with intense dark eyes. "I plan on it."

That seals it for me. I don't want to know.

"Why do you think he wanted to talk, other than what Brison said?"

"Part of it was his own sick showcasing for you. For whatever reason, I think he wanted to push my buttons, and I let the bastard do it. The other part is he knew we would find that property of his with that house, shack, pits of hell, whatever you want to call it. He's absolutely right that the only two people left to take the fall for this are him and Miller. I'm not buying that Wright did none of the kidnapping. Darla getting hit from behind, and you getting hit from behind is way too coincidental for me. I think we're about to see a lot of finger pointing between Miller and Wright.

"Plus, it's Wright's property and Wright's house. I firmly believe we'll have Greg Miller's DNA from that place, but I think in Wright's mind, whoever talks first is going to get a sweetheart of a deal. Of course, after all the shit we've heard, I think Brison would like to put the needle in himself right now. Wright could've said that Miller, Lacey or either of the Bradberrys did the actual killing. He said none of that.

"It's almost as if he wants to confess because he's so damn proud of what he's done, but he's stopping short of it because he knows what's going to happen to him if he tells us exactly what he's done. I honestly don't know who did the actual killing of these girls, but I believe that it was him. I think he killed all of those girls, and I know for damn sure he's going to go down for them in some way. Both he and Greg Miller are.

I don't know what Brison will decide to do. He'll be talking to you about it, along with everyone else. He'll do the right thing. He always has."

"He's been doing this long enough. I trust that he will," I say.

He's silent, studying me, and finally says, "We need to talk about Matt." His voice is tense. I close my eyes and hang my head for a moment. I look back up at Nick, while Chris drags a chair from his desk and joins us. "Why do you think Wright would throw it out that your brother and his friend are involved?"

When I speak, it comes out sounding strangled. "I think they are."

Nick and Chris look at one another, shocked, and then back at me. I tell them what I came up with in my mind, how long I had to think of it, and as I replayed it over and over, it made sense. I didn't want it to, but it does.

Nick rubs his hands across his face. "Dammit," he says. He looks over at Chris and then back at me. "Where would be the first place you would look for Matt? Under the North Avenue Bridge?"

It takes me a long time to answer him. "Yes," I finally say.

"Is his friend Billy Noble usually with him?"

"He wasn't the last time I saw Matt, but I have seen them together."

We all stand up at the same time, and he says to me, "I'm going to take you home, and then we are going to look for them." He looks at Chris. "We need to get patrol out looking for them as well."

"Let me go with you," I say.

"No. You are out of this."

"He's my brother, Nick."

"Exactly, who has now become a murder suspect. I'm taking you home, and you're to stay there."

I put my hands on my hips. "You can't tell me what to do, Nick Bassano. You can't make me stay home." It comes out sounding more pouty than angry.

He moves so that he's right in front of me. He's as close as he can get without touching me. I look up, and his eyes are angry.

"Dammit, Grace. For once, just once, would you not argue with me? It's getting late and it's dark. If you get out there on your own, I'll be worried about you."

Knowing that he would be worried about me takes the fight out of me.

"Okay. I'll stay home, but you will call me if you find him, right?"

"I'll call you. Even if we don't find him tonight, I'll call you." He looks at Chris. "See if Billy Noble has been arrested, and if so, let's get his picture printed and out." He looks back at me. "Do you have a picture of Matt?"

I nod that I do.

Chris looks at me before walking to his desk and says, "Grace, try not to worry about him too much. We aren't going to hurt him."

Probably not, but Matt will be scared. I saw the fear in him.

Nick drives too fast to my condo. I should be used to that now. He drives fast everywhere he goes. We don't say much on the drive. We're both deep in thought, and our thoughts are probably running on the same line. I'm just far more emotionally attached to all of this than he is.

I never had a mother. My father took himself away due to his actions. As if he were ever there in the first place. I had a sister that I never really knew, chose not to get to know or help, and she's gone. I'm going to lose the most important family member I have, because he wanted to avenge something horrible that happened to our sister. It isn't fair. I don't know how I'm going to process all of this and then deal with it and then heal from it. It's going to take a long time. I'm not sure where to start.

We get back to the condo and find Jess, Jake, Max and Susan around the table, eating soup and cornbread. Jess looks relieved to see me walk through our door. I've thought little how this has affected her. What a great friend I am. I add the guilt over that to the pile.

"Why're you all not eating out?" I ask them.

"We didn't know what time you'd be back. None of us wanted you to come home to an empty place," Jess tells me.

I can feel the tears rising. I take a shaky breath and smile at her.

"Thanks," I say.

"Grace," Nick says quietly. "Can I get that picture of Matt?"

I look up at him. This is really happening. He's going to look for my brother.

"Yes, it's upstairs in my room." He follows me upstairs. "It's from a few years ago, but he pretty much looks the same. He's skinnier and probably much dirtier."

I hand it to him. He looks at it for a moment and then puts it in his back pocket. I'm chewing on my lip because for some reason I think that I won't cry if I do that. It doesn't work.

"All we are going to do is interview him and Billy. We just want to talk to them."

"No, you aren't just going to talk to him, Nick. He's going to get arrested. That's what's going to happen."

"Being arrested might be the best thing for him, Grace. It would get him off the streets and possibly a chance to get off the drugs."

"The Bradberrys deserved it, Nick. He and Billy did this for their sisters. Matt did this for our sister."

"I know that, Grace. I get what they were thinking, but you can't murder people." He sees that doesn't help. "I'll take care of him. I'll do that for you." My tears are sliding down my cheeks. "Baby, I hate when you cry," he says softly. He pulls me in his arms. His hands go to my face, brushing my tears away with his thumbs. I have my hands on his chest, feeling the steady beat of his heart. "Look at me." His voice is quiet and soft. I look up at him. "I *will* take care of him," he asserts. I nod that I understand.

"Promise?" I choke out.

"I promise," he murmurs, brushing his lips across mine.

I close my eyes and drink him in. I think we both thought it would be a quick, soft kiss. I slide my hands up his chest and wrap my arms around his neck. His hands move from my face to around my waist, and he is holding me tight against him. I feel him hard against me. His kiss becomes urgent, needy, as his tongue finds mine. I feel him move me, and I'm up against the wall. He's pressed firmly into me, and I'm holding tight against him. I'll give him what he wants, because I want it, too. I need him right now. With everything that has happened, I need him to fill me with him.

"Take me," I whisper.

His eyes are filled with nothing but want for me.

"I can't stay here with you all night, and it feels wrong in light of what's happened with us," he whispers.

"I know you can't stay. It doesn't matter."

The want is still there in his eyes, but I see conflict in them, too. Wanting me but feeling like he may not be doing the right thing if we do have sex with what is hanging in the air between us. Right now, I simply don't care about anything else, other than I love him, and I want to be with him, and I need that connection with him right now. He moves away from me and takes both of his guns, handcuffs, phone and badge, putting them on my dresser. He comes back to me, looking down and in my eyes.

"You know I want to stay here with you all night, right?" His voice is low.

"Yes," I whisper.

He still seems hesitant. That's so different for him. There has been very little that he's been hesitant about. I think he's known from the beginning that I've wanted him, even when I didn't want to.

"Nick," I plead, "I need you."

His hands go to the hem of my shirt, and I raise my arms so he can take it off. My cotton pants are next. I kick off my flip flops and step out of my pants. He doesn't wait for me to take his clothes off. He discards them quickly. I go to take off my bra and panties.

"No. I've got it." His voice is still low, and it's sexy. I look at him, my eyes roaming over how spectacular I always think he looks. He really does have the perfect body, especially with those tattoos. My bra and panties go on the floor with the rest of our clothes. He picks me up, and I wrap my legs around him. He places me on the bed and hovers over me. "I don't know which is louder, you or your bed." His grin is devilish, and I've not seen it in several days. That's more like it. That's the man I love.

"Why don't you fuck me hard, and we'll find out." I see him gasp as I pull his mouth to mine.

He trails his lips to my cheek and then whispers in my ear, "How hard, baby?" He raises his head and locks eyes with mine.

"Surprise me," I say softly.

His smile makes my heart beat even faster, and he sinks in me. I close my eyes and tip my head back. *Oh, he feels so good.* I feel his lips at my throat as he begins to move. My arms are wrapped around his broad back, and I feel his muscles beneath my fingers. I open my eyes as he eases down on his elbows, holding my face with both hands. My arms go from his back to around his neck, pulling his face to mine. Our eyes are locked with one another, and then his lips are on mine.

His steady back and forth movements make the bad stuff go away. The sounds in the room are my sighs and his heavy breathing. He begins to pick up the pace, and his kisses are urgent again. His thrusts are becoming more urgent. His kisses and movements feel like he's apologizing for everything that he's done. I hold tight to him and feel him pulling my body to the end. I feel that he's coming with me. My orgasm takes me, and I call out for him. I feel him go rigid, and then he pours into me and then collapses on me. He tries to shift, taking some of his weight off of me.

"No," I say breathlessly, keeping him in me. I want to feel him against me.

His light kisses go from my cheek to my ear. I can hear him still breathing heavy.

"Your bed was louder."

We both start laughing softly.

"There are four people downstairs. Two of them are like parents to me."

He presses his lips against mine, softly. "You'll scream for me next time." He looks at me more serious. "Grace, I...um...I."

"I know. You need to go."

"Um, yeah. That's what I was going to say." He has a strange look on his face.

"Nick. It's okay." He kisses me again and eases out of me. We get dressed. I sit on my bed while he's inspecting himself in the mirror. "You look very handsome, if that's what you are wondering."

He turns around and is grinning at me. He's all dimples, and my heart starts beating faster again. "I like that you think that I'm handsome, but I look in the mirror to make sure my weapon and badge are where I want them. You look like you want to laugh at me about it."

"No. I'm not going to laugh about it. I think it speaks to how neat and tidy you are about everything, including your appearance. I like it." *Actually, I love it.*

He takes my hand in his as we walk downstairs. He talks for a few minutes with everyone who has moved to the living area and are now watching a movie. We walk out together.

He looks down at me while he's still holding my hand. His face is serious again. "I'll call you later, okay?"

"Okay."

I know he's gotten serious again because of what he has to do. He pulls my face up to him.

"Grace," he whispers, "I..."

"Go," I say. "I know you have to go. Stop worrying about it."

He nods, looking in my eyes. He sets his lips to mine for a moment and then walks to his car. I watch as he drives away and then go back in the condo.

"What're you all watching?"

"I don't know. Something that Jake found." Jess pulls me on the couch with her and Susan. "Did you and Nick talk things over?"

"Sort of."

"That's good."

"Can I tell you what happened at the police department?"

"Of course. Jake, turn the TV off," Jess says to him.

"Judge Wright agreed to talk."

They look surprised.

"What?" Max exclaims. "The man is being represented by Phillip Edwards."

"He agreed to talk as long as I was in the room."

Jess groans and looks at me. "Oh, no, Grace, you didn't."

"He was willing to talk, Jess. I wanted some answers about Naomi. I wanted them to have some answers about all of the girls."

"I don't want to know, do I?"

No, she doesn't, but she asks me to tell them anyway. I tell them what I know. I cry, and then Jess starts crying, and then Susan starts crying. I knew my sister was gone, but Judge Wright confirming that made my worst fears about her fate a reality. There isn't any hope for me to hold on to that she might come back. All the things that I should have said to her and never did. All of the things that I can't do for her now and will never be able to do. There's guilt, and I don't know the depth of that guilt yet. I've not even scratched the surface of it. Not knowing where she is, and him knowing and not telling us is worse. I want to bury her. When I've exhausted everything about Judge Wright, I hit them with my suspicions about Matt and Billy. They are astounded, and their faces say the same thing, disbelief.

"No, Grace, not Matt. Nick's looking for him, isn't he? That's why he left in such a hurry and didn't stay with you," Jess says.

"Yes."

"Why didn't you go with him?"

"He wouldn't let me. He said I'm out of it."

"Right," she snorts. She's disgusted. "I don't believe that. You're right in the middle of it all. I can't believe you aren't out on your own looking for Matt. Don't get me wrong, I want you here, because I think some of those places you go aren't safe."

"I thought about going after Nick dropped me off, but he told me that if I was out there, he would worry about me. I decided not to go tonight."

"You didn't say anything about not going tomorrow, did you?"

"No, I didn't."

As the night wears on, we all talk about Matt, and then I change the subject to Jess's wedding. I can only talk about it and deal with it for so long and then I need a break. Max and Susan leave late. Nick calls me at midnight.

Chapter Thirty-Five

"Hey," he says, when I answer. He sounds like he's about to drop, but still edgy as well.

"Hey."

"We can't find either of them. I even went to the Salvation Army in hopes of finding Matt."

"What now?" I ask.

"I'm going to go home for a while, try and rest for a few hours and then get back out there. I want to find him, Grace. I want it to be me that finds him."

Nick caring for my brother like that means a lot to me.

"He'll be scared, Nick."

I hear him sigh. "I know. Listen, the search out at Washington yielded nothing. I wanted to make sure you heard that quickly, and I'm sorry for that."

I take a shaky breath. "Arnoldsville Road is next?"

"Yeah, the cadaver dogs will be out there on Sunday. If nothing's found there, we don't have a clue where to look next." He's quiet for a moment and then, "Grace, I'll most likely be working on this all week-end, but I'd like to have a few hours at some point with you this week-end. I want to explain things to you. You've got to feel that it's more than just sex between us. You feel that, right?"

"Yes," I whisper, "I feel it."

Does he really love me? God, I hope that he does, because I know I love him.

"Are you going to sleep tonight?"

I sigh. "I don't know. There's too much going on in my mind right now. It's so busy up there, I'm not sure if I'll be able to sleep."

"Grace, I'll find him and take care of him."

"I trust you, Nick."

"If you sleep, will you dream of me?"

I can hear him smiling. I smile, too.

"Yes," I whisper.

We talk a few more minutes, and he says he'll text me later if he doesn't find Matt, but will call when he does find him. I feel that he's reluctant to hang up with me but finally does. Jess, Jake and I stay up and watch movies until nearly dawn Saturday morning. I get the sense that neither of them want me to be alone, and I think they both sense that I'm having a hard time sleeping.

Nick texts and says they still have nothing. Patrol will continue to look for both of them, and he'll be out there too. They're going to keep going back to the same places and keep talking to people in hopes that someone will eventually see them. I fall asleep after his text. It's mid-morning when my phone starts buzzing. I think it's Nick calling me, but looking at it, I don't recognize the number.

"Hello," I say, answering my phone.

"Grace."

I close my eyes. "Matt. Where are you?"

"I need you. Will you help me?" His voice is shaky and frightened. Matt has never called me and has never asked for my help.

"Of course. Where are you?" He gives me a location on Vine Street. I memorize the address. I've been in that location several times. I think I know what house he's referring to. "I'll be there as quick as I can."

Jess and Jake are out. They know that I probably wouldn't be here when they got back. I consider calling Nick. I need to call him. I want to talk to my brother, and then I'll call Nick. I may be able to coax my brother into going with me to the police department. That would be so much better than him being taken by patrol or Nick. I know Nick's heart is in the right place over wanting to take care of my brother, but Matt will be less scared with me. I can't imagine what my brother is going through. He's having to live with so much.

My heart's breaking for him. I drive a little too fast and find the address quickly. The house that Matt is staying at is rundown, and it doesn't look like a safe place. It's a roof over his head, and that's more than what he lives with regularly. I put my keys in my front pocket and put my phone in my back pocket. I walk up the steps and knock on the wooden screen door.

"Matt," I call.

"I'm in here."

I walk in, and while it's bright outside, it's not as bright inside as I thought it would be. Matt's standing in the middle of a bare room, and it looks like he's the only person here. His appearance has been shocking to me the last few times I've seen him, and it's just as bad today. He's high. He's incredibly high. I want to ask him what he's used, but I don't want it to turn into a fight. It takes me a few minutes to fully assess him and then I see the gun that's in his hand. My heart starts to pound in my chest.

"Matt. Why do you have a gun?"

My brother starts to cry. I haven't seen my brother cry in almost twenty years. My heart breaks further.

"I don't know what to do," he chokes out.

"Okay," I say softly, moving closer to him. "I'm here. Why don't you give me that gun, and we can talk about whatever you want to talk about."

"Do you love me, Grace?"

I start crying. "Yes, Matt. I love you so much. You're the best brother a sister could ever want to have."

"I'm such a fuck up."

"No, you aren't. Matt, we had such a shitty childhood. You took such good care of me." I hope he hears how much I love him and how much he's done for me. My brother saved my life. He gave me a life while sacrificing his.

"No, I didn't. You got raped. You got hurt all the time. Naomi got hurt. She got raped, and now she's dead. I couldn't take care of her, either."

"Matt, it wasn't your job to take care of either of us. It was mom's job. You did so much more than what you had to do. Don't you see that? Will you give me that gun?"

"No. I need to tell you what I did."

"Okay. You can tell me whatever you want to tell me. I love you so much, Matt."

"Me and Billy killed them people. We heard the police are lookin' for us. Billy's gone there to turn himself in. He thinks that we won't go to jail. I can't do that, Grace. I don't want to go to jail."

"Matt. You're going to be taken care of."

"There're bad things that happen to people in jail. I've heard my friends talk about it. I don't want to get beat up no more."

I bite my lip, and my tears keep falling. He's talking about when we were kids. While neither of us has forgotten it, Matt has dealt with it differently, if at all. It still haunts him. That I can see.

"Matt. I promise you'll be taken care of. I have a friend who's a Detective. He's the one that wants to talk to you. He's going to take care of you. He promised me, and I trust him. You can trust him too."

He doesn't seem to hear what I've said and continues to talk. "Lacey told me what they'd done to Naomi and Jenny. She said there was other girls. She said there was pictures, and that if me and Billy killed them, no one would ever know, and that it was okay because of what they did. Lacey was my friend. She said they hurt her, too, and that I would be helping her if me and Billy killed them and took those pictures. She wanted me to get the pictures, so she could get rid of them so the families wouldn't have to know what happened. Me and Billy couldn't find the pictures. I told Lacey that I thought you knew where they was. She said she was gonna to talk to you about them. I haven't heard from her, and when I started askin' around, I heard that she was dead."

So that's the story the bitch told my brother, and he fell for it hook, line and sinker.

"How did you and Lacey meet?"

"She used to work at the police department, and we met one day when I was on the streets, and I had some drugs on me. She said she liked me and didn't want to take me to jail. She would find me all the time, and we started bein' friends. We been friends since then."

I feel sick. I feel sick for my brother and that he played right into her sick hands. If I never had a reason to hate Lacey before, I do now.

"Lacey used you, Matt."

"No she didn't!" he screams. "She was my friend! She was always nice to me and made me feel special. She told me one time that she loved me and wanted me to get some help so we could be together."

I close my eyes. I feel the bile rise in my throat. That bitch twisted my brother all around her finger.

"She told me that she loved me, and if I really loved her, I would kill those people who hurt her, and that I would be helpin' Naomi and Jenny and all those other girls."

"Matt, Lacey didn't care about you. She used you."

I hear sirens coming close to us, but I don't pay them any attention. There's always something occurring here.

"Grace, I want to talk about when we was kids."

"Okay. We can talk about whatever you want to talk about, Matt. I want to hear everything you have to say."

I hear the sirens stop and cars pulling up, with doors opening and shutting.

"I want to tell you somethin'," Matt says. He opens his mouth to continue to talk but closes it when we hear my name being yelled.

"Grace!" It's Nick's voice.

I turn around, and suddenly Matt grabs me from behind. Nick and Chris come rushing in, and as soon as they see me and Matt and the gun, they have their guns out so fast that if I had blinked, I would have missed it. It becomes crazy, and everyone is screaming at one another.

"He's not going to shoot me!" I scream.

Nick's screaming for Matt to put the gun down. I'm screaming at Nick and Chris to put their guns up, and that my brother is not going to shoot me and that he's just scared. Matt's screaming, but it's becoming incoherent. I scream over and over that Matt isn't going to shoot me. We're talking over one another, and I don't think anyone is listening to me.

"Put your gun down, Matt," Nick's so forceful.

He's completely focused on Matt and where Matt has that gun pointed. He doesn't have it pointed at me. He's not going to point it at me because he's not going to shoot me.

"He's not going to shoot me. He's scared!" That's all I can think of to scream at them. "Nick." My voice is forceful in saying his name. He won't look at me. He's completely focused on Matt. "Nick. Look at me. He's not going to shoot me. He's scared. If you and Chris would put your guns away, it would solve this." He still won't look at me. He and Chris aren't budging. The tension is thick and raw. I can't get him to look at me.

"Matt, put the gun down. Do it now." Nick's voice is harder. Matt makes no moves, and I'm at a loss as to what else to say. No one is listening to me. "Matt, put the gun down, and let's talk." His voice softens but not much.

"Grace," Matt says to me, "I'm sorry. I love you." He starts crying.

I open my mouth to tell him again how much I love him at the same time I hear Nick scream, "No, Matt, don't do it," I hear the boom of a gun and see that it's Nick that pulls the trigger.

I feel Matt fall and pull me with him. I feel something warm splatter the back of my hair. Nick's on me while Chris is on Matt in an instant. I turn over and see a large spot where my brother's head had been intact, and it no longer is. There are other officers that have rushed in.

"No! No!" My eyes are wild when I look at Nick. I put my hands all over my brother. He can't be dead. No, he can't be dead. *No, he's not dead!* But he is. My hands are shaking when I feel the back of my hair. I look at them, and there's blood. My brother's blood. Nick pulls me up. "You shot him!" I scream at him. I push at him. I see that my brother's blood is now on his shirt. "You said you would take care of him! You promised me, Nick! Is that what you meant by taking care of him? I fucking trusted you!" I'm still screaming, and it's nearing on hysteria.

"He was going to shoot you." He's amazingly calm. He's too calm.

"He was not going to shoot me. He's my brother. He wouldn't do that to me. What else do you want to take from me, Nick? Do you want my life too? What else do you want to do to me?" I'm still screaming.

"He turned that gun on you. I couldn't stand there and watch you die."

"I wasn't going to die because he wasn't going to shoot me!"

Everything that Nick and I have done and been through and what he's put me through in the last month, and everything that I could forgive all goes out the window. I fell totally and hopelessly in love with him, and now my heart is shattered, sitting in a broken mess at my feet. There's nothing left of me. He's taken it all.

"I can't believe you've done this to me." My voice is barely above a whisper.

So, this is how we end, and we never really got started. I look at Matt and then I look at Nick. I should stay with my brother, but he's gone. There isn't anything holding me here. I turn to leave.

Nick grabs my arm. "Please, don't walk away from me. Please, not like this." He's begging me. I see hurt in his eyes, but I can't focus on that. I'm too focused on my hurt to deal with his.

"You did this," I say through clenched teeth, jerking my arm from his hand and stumbling out of the door. There's an officer who stops me.

"Ma'am, we need you to stay so we can get your statement."

"Let her go. We can get it later," I hear Nick say from behind.

I don't turn around to look at him and continue to my car. Tears are streaming down my face as I get in. I'm choking on the grief that's threatening to completely consume me. As I'm driving away, I know Jess and Jake will be back at the condo when I get there. I know they'll call Max and Susan to come be with me. They'll call Angie and Ginger if I need them to. I have friends. I have family in Jess, Max and Susan. I have the love that they all give to me. I know all of that, and I know that I have all of them, and others, but I've never felt so…alone.

Epilogue

One Week Later

Nick focuses on what he's staring at and then un-focuses again. It's getting harder and harder to stay focused on what's in front of him, but since he's been staring at the same thing now for, he looks at his watch, Jesus Christ, the last five hours, that's probably why he can't stay focused. He takes the deepest breath that he can and then lets it all out. It feels like someone's sitting on his chest. He rubs it, realizing that it's his heart aching.

He's got his ear buds in, the music flowing in his ears, to his mind, to his heart, and all he can think of is Grace. He's listening to Lifehouse's *From Where You Are*. Everything about the song makes him think of her, and he just misses her. He shifts around on the bench, ignoring the fact that his ass has gone numb. It would be nice if the rest of him felt like his ass, but he's not numb. He feels it all. And everything just fucking hurts. Hurts at a level that pisses him off. He's not hurt like this before because he never gave a shit before.

He's gotten really pissed over the last week and tried getting pissed at her, but the way he feels about her and what she's gone through, doesn't allow him to do that. He punched the shit out of the bag at the gym yesterday after work. Brandon told him to ease up, or he was going to break the bag, and as soon it was out of his mouth, the goddamn bag broke. He thought about punching Brandon but knew if he did, he might just kill him since he was in that kind of a rage.

He sends a text to Jess that says, *How is she?* Jess's response is immediate. *She's in her room with the door closed. Jake and I talked her into sitting with us at breakfast, but she went back up to her room quickly, and that's where she's been.* He sighs and sends a text back, telling Jess how much he's missing Grace. Her response is that she knows and says that Grace is missing him, too, she just won't admit it.

He sighs again, looking up, around him and can't believe that he was dancing with her under this gazebo two weeks ago. He closes his eyes, remembering the way she looked, the way she smelled, the way she felt up against him, and the way that she looked at him with those beautiful eyes of hers. She looked at him that night like she was in love with him. He could feel how fast her heart was beating and her breasts against him. He loved trailing his lips at her throat, feeling the racing of her pulse and finding out that it's been him all along that does that to her.

He lets out a slight groan and leans over, bracing his elbows at his knees, still keeping his eyes tightly shut, thinking about that night. He rubs his chest again at his heart. He thinks about the limo ride back to his house, the way she kept looking at him, how much pleasure he was bringing to her and the feel of her hands on him. He thinks about her telling him that he's gorgeous, and yes, he's heard it before from many other women, but to hear it come out of her sweet mouth…Jesus Christ, what a mess it all became after that night.

There's still a part of him that can't accept that she's gone, can't accept that it's over, can't accept that maybe he should just move on and let her do the same. Maybe he should just go back to what he was doing. Hell, he could go out tonight and pick up anyone. He'd see someone that he knows, or find someone new. He could fuck her senseless. The thought of it leaves him feeling empty. He doesn't want just anyone. He wants Grace. He wants her like a dying man wants his last breath. He's got to get her back, or he thinks he might die.